THE HORN AND HORN-PLAYING

al vivum delineavit et fecit
29 Juny 1735
Crvanuel Joachim Haas

Frontispiece. Franz Anton, Count Sporck, at the age of 73. Lissa, his favourite country palace, provides a backdrop for a group of mounted horn-players.

THE
HORN
AND
HORN-PLAYING

*and the Austro-Bohemian tradition
from 1680 to 1830*

HORACE FITZPATRICK

London
OXFORD UNIVERSITY PRESS
NEW YORK   TORONTO
1970

Oxford University Press, Ely House, London W.1

GLASGOW NEW YORK TORONTO MELBOURNE WELLINGTON
CAPE TOWN SALISBURY IBADAN NAIROBI LUSAKA ADDIS ABABA
BOMBAY CALCUTTA MADRAS KARACHI LAHORE DACCA
KUALA LUMPUR SINGAPORE HONG KONG TOKYO

SBN 19 318703 5

Printed in Great Britain by
W. & J. Mackay & Co Ltd, Chatham

PREFACE

IT is surprising that, in nearly one hundred years of serious research into the history of the horn, writers with only two exceptions have overlooked the basis upon which the study of the pre-valve horn must rest: the existence of a parent school of horn-players and makers in Austria and Bohemia during the century and a quarter before the invention of the valve. Since the appearance of Julius Rühlmann's article 'Das Waldhorn' in the *Neue Zeit-schrift für Musik* in 1870—which may be regarded as the first historical writing on the horn in recent times—only the late W. F. H. Blandford and Reginald Morley-Pegge have mentioned the probability of an early tradition of horn-playing in Bohemia. Blandford, in his wide-ranging article 'The French Horn in England',[1] refers to the development of the horn's low register as being one of the contributions of the 'Bohemian school of players'. He credits the Bohemians with the discovery of hand-stopping, and points out 'the greatness of the debt which music owes to the Bohemian players, to whom alone the credit for this transformation is due'. Morley-Pegge, in the section on hand-stopping in his book, *The French Horn* (London, 1960), to date the most complete and definitive work on the history of the instrument, mentions 'the luxuriant crop of virtuoso soloists, nearly all of them of Bohemian or Saxon origin, who were so much appreciated on the concert platform from about 1760 onwards'. Although the idea of an early Bohemian school of horn-players is explicit in both of these passages, neither author has expanded the concept further, either by documentary or musical evidence: nor, as we have said, have other writers.

When the present writer began the preliminary research for the study at hand in 1958 while playing professionally in Vienna neither of the above-quoted writings had come to his attention; nor were they to do so until 1961. However, the possibility of an Austrian tradition of horn-playing in the eighteenth century had been suggested to him by several archaic practices which he had observed amongst the horn-players there, notably the reten-tion of the narrow-bore F horn and the deep, conically profiled mouthpiece, long since superseded elsewhere. As more documentary, organological, and musical evidence came to hand in the course of following up this original supposition, it became increasingly evident that not only the Austrians but even more the Bohemians had established what appeared to be the first great tradition of artistic horn-playing. It was furthermore evident that although the influence of this tradition or school of playing was felt throughout

[1] *Musical Times*, August 1922.

Europe during the eighteenth century, its geographical and musical centre remained where it originated and first developed: in the Habsburg Crown lands and their neighbouring provinces, with Vienna and Prague as its dual fountainhead. The great horn-players of the eighteenth century came mainly from Bohemia, their instruments from Vienna. Though in the last decades of the century this pattern was reversed to a degree and certain virtuosi changed to the French instrument, the school as a whole continued to be fed from these first sources.

To trace the development of this school from the introduction of the cor-de-chasse into Bohemia in 1680 down to the decline of the hand-horn in Austria about 1830 is the theme and purpose of this work. It is a manifest— but often overlooked—truth that any study of the instrumental music of earlier periods is imperfect unless assessed from two perspectives: that of the contemporary instruments for which it was composed, and that of the players themselves, their technique, style, and musical ideals; and this latter is far the more difficult. In the interests of casting new light on these neglected facets of horn-playing, the instrument itself, its players, and their effects upon its music will be dealt with in detail.

Much of the evidence embodied in this account is obviously documentary in character. But contemporary instruments themselves can yield considerable information when examined, measured, and played. Often, indeed, it is impossible to obtain exact measurements of certain important features because of the construction or, what is more frequent, the condition of many instruments, which to a strictly organological study might pose a serious obstacle. But since we are dealing here rather with the stylistic aspects of the horn, sufficient dimensional statistics have been obtained to furnish a basis from which to draw historical conclusions. There is a growing tendency to attach too much importance to measurements and figures. Some persons have gone so far as to construct actual instruments from an average of measurements taken from specimens of a given period, rather than copying faithfully an original example. The fallacy of this practice is obvious. A musical instrument is an organic whole: even mass-produced instruments of identical dimensions differ noticeably from one another. In the case of hand-made instruments this individuality is much more pronounced, of course, for here human intuition, judgement, and rule of thumb combine to make each one unique. Since an average of measurements does not refer to individual instruments, it can only afford a general idea of a type of instrument in a given period or country; apart from this, such statistics are of no value either to the maker or to the performer.

Many of the conclusions relating to performance practice given here have been drawn from experiment on contemporary instruments under actual concert conditions. It is well known to any professional player that an instrument's behaviour on the concert platform will differ from that which it exhibits in the practice-room. This is especially so in the case of old instruments. An impression of an early instrument's playing characteristics may be had from trial in the collection-room or studio, to be sure; but where detailed information is sought on points of playing technique, performance conventions, aptness in a particular musical context, one is best advised to consult the instrument under the battle conditions of a public concert, where there is no time to favour its weaknesses, much less go back for dropped notes. There only do an instrument's advantages, limitations, and preferences show up fully; so do the player's.

To bridge the gap between source material and musical experiment the author has made frequent use of the workbench and lathe. The reconstruction of working models for trial has proved especially helpful in the study of historic mouthpieces and mutes. Where actual examples were not available for use, measurements were taken and copies were made. In the more frequent cases where historical specimens of the article to be studied were not known to exist, reconstructions were carried out according to contemporary illustrations, or, as with the Böck hand-horn mute, from dimensions given in contemporary sources.

An appreciable amount of underlying background material has come to the writer from persons whose family traditions or personal experiences embrace that manner of life and thought which gave such impetus to music in eighteenth-century Austria. Although space does not allow the writer to acknowledge all those to whom thanks are due, he wishes here to express his gratitude to those who have most stimulated and guided his thinking.

Especial thanks are owing to Count Eugen Waldstein of Schloss Carlslust for much general historical information, and for providing a unique glimpse into the life of those smaller courts where music was cultivated to such a high degree. Count Friederich Schönborn of Prague has kindly given much advice concerning the eighteenth-century *Jagdwesen* in Bohemia, and has pointed out sources which would otherwise have escaped the author's notice. Dr. Marie-Luise von Friedberg has shared generously her knowledge of the political and social structure of the old Danube empire, and her continued encouragement has been of great value. Dr. Ernst Paul, technical consultant to the Vienna Philharmonic and Musicological Director of the Austrian Radio, advised the author in the planning of this work and gave freely of his unique knowledge of the early instrument. The late Professor Gottfried von Freiberg, Solo Horn of the Vienna Philharmonic, was the first to confirm the suppositions which led to the present study, and to encourage the author's initial researches. To him goes the credit for the original inspiration, and it is to be regretted that his untimely death prevented his seeing this work's completion. Freiberg's brilliant musical tutelage and the example he set as a musician and a gentleman had a profound influence upon all who were privileged to be his pupils; and the present writer stands greatly in his debt. For help of a more material nature the writer is particularly indebted to Leonard Elmhirst of Dartington Hall and to the Elmgrant Trust for the financial support which made these researches possible.

It is hoped that an account of the horn and its music in this period and context will be of service not only to horn-players but to scholars and other musicians as well, and especially to conductors. If the information presented here could in a measure prevent the horn from vanishing into the mechanized degeneration which daily threatens it, the author would feel amply rewarded. To that end it is hoped in these pages to reacquaint musicians and listeners with the innate beauty of the natural horn and its appropriateness to its music. For if we were to lose this sound which so enriched the music of our forebears we should be deprived of one of the most characteristic sounds in Western music: and it is our music which sets us apart from all other cultures.

CONTENTS

PLATES

(h) The Viennese second-horn mouthpiece of *c.* 1770, shown in profile and end views. Note the narrow rim to facilitate the wide leaps characteristic of second-horn parts at this period. The wide bore enhances the low notes.

(i) Side and end views of a first-horn mouthpiece, Prague, *c.* 1790. The wider rim and narrower bore are typical of the high-horn player's mouthpiece. This example probably belonged to a soloist. It is well to remember that, then as now, there were as many individual mouthpieces as there were players.

XVI (a) Giovanni Punto at the age of 35.

(b) left to right: Side and end views of mouthpieces: (i) English, brass, 18th century, probably by Nicholas Winkings, whose initials are chased on the body. (ii) English or French, brass with silver rim, 18th century. (iii) French, silver, late 18th century, associated with a hand-horn by Courtois Neveu l'aîné. (iv) Modern English, silver-plated brass, the Aubrey Brain model. (v) Modern English silver-plated brass, showing German influence in its convex-sided cup.

Plates IX–XVI will be found between pages 138 and 139.

To the memory of
Gottfried von Freiberg

INTRODUCTION

The Beginnings:
Roman Antiquity to France in 1680

THE art of concert horn-playing came not from France, as many writers have thought, but from Austria. Yet the orchestral horn itself does, in fact, trace its ancestry to the hunting-fields of France. Although its modern form was foreshadowed in Germany at the beginning of the sixteenth century, the scanty evidence available suggests that it was in France that the horn first reached a degree of refinement sufficient to attract the notice of composers.

The idea of a hooped horn of conical tube-profile was not new. Its earliest expression was in the cornu of the Roman military band, an instrument having a cup mouthpiece and a conical tube of brass, formed into a large single hoop ending in a bell which peered forward over the player's shoulder. The three cornu players shown in relief in Trajan's Column furnish what is perhaps the best-known record of this instrument. Classical writers tell us that the cornu was sounded in battle fanfares, that it had a loud tone and that it required some skill to play.[1] This art evidently enjoyed the protection of a kind of brass-players' guild, to judge from the illustration and inscription on an altar-stone in the Catacombs which commemorates one 'M. Julius victor ex Collegio Liticinum et Cornicinum'.[2] Yet as Rome declined and things Roman were slowly forgotten in Europe, so too the technique of smelting brass and the art of bending thin metal tubes passed into oblivion, to be relearnt by trial and error in the later Middle Ages.

This skill had been recovered by the end of the fourteenth century; and it is in German illustrations of the early sixteenth that we see it again applied to the horn. The thrice-wound, open-hooped horn depicted in a woodcut illustration in the Strasbourg edition of Virgil of 1502 is indeed fanciful in

[1] Roman writers seem to choose the names of the military brass as much for the sound of the words themselves as from any considerations of accurate nomenclature. This is no doubt why the *lituus* and *cornu* are apt to be confused: both are cavalry instruments, and both are bent, the first in the form of a J, the second, like a G. Most writers keep the straight *tuba* and *buccina* clearly distinct from the curved brass, however: 'Non tuba directi, non aeris cornua flexi' (Ovid Met. I, 98.). Juvenal speaks of 'Cornicini, sive hic recto cantaverit aere' (II, 117). Vegetius, writing in the fourth century A.D., makes what well may be the first mention of the art of cornu playing: 'Cornu quod ex uris agrestibus, argento nexum, temperatum arte, et spiritu, quem canentis flatus emittit auditur' (*De Re Militarii*, Basle, 1532, iii, 5). A detailed description of the military instruments of the ancients is also to be found in Bernard de Montfaucon's *L'Antiquité Expliquée* (Paris, 1724), Supp. III, p. 189.

[2] Caspar Bartholinus, *De Tibiis Veterum* (Amsterdam, 1679), p. 390.

appearance,[1] but a comparison with Virdung's drawing of a snail-shaped Jägerhorn in his *Musica Getutscht* of 1511[2] shows that the two instruments clearly present different versions of the same idea. That the concept of a helical horn was very much in the air at the time is further borne out by Burgkmair's chimerical cornu-player shown in the Triumphal Procession of the Emperor Maximilian from the year 1517.

In Germany and the Netherlands the spirally-wound horn appears to have undergone a steady development, continuing in use as a hunting-instrument until the eighteenth century. An example differing little in its essentials from Virdung's drawing and dated 1572 was preserved in the State Museum at Dresden until the beginning of the last war. Similar instruments, though more refined, can be seen in the painting by Jan Breughel (1568–1625) entitled *Allegoria dell'Udito*, now in the Prado Museum; and in the sumptuous etching by the Bohemian-born engraver Wenzel Hollar (1607–77). (Unfortunately the latter is undated, so it is impossible to say whether Hollar drew this instrument during his German or English period.)

The spirally-wound German horn mentioned in Virdung appears to have been taken up in France and used in the hunting field alongside the native French signal horn, itself a development of the medieval oliphant. The spiral horn, known subsequently as the 'cor a plusiers tours', is undoubtedly the subject of the first mention of the horn's use in a purely musical, albeit out-door, context. This occurs in the dedication to the tenth volume of a collection of 'Battles, Hunts and Bird-Songs', published in 1545 by Tylman Susato.[3] Here Susato addresses himself to those 'Noble Musicians who

---

[1] Reproduced on Pl. I of R. Morley-Pegge, *The French Horn* (London, 1960).

[2] Sebastian Virdung, *Musica Getutscht und Ausgezogen* (Basle, 1511), D iv, verso.

[3] *Le Dixiesme Livre contenant la Bataille a Quatre de Clement Jannequin ... et deux Chasses de Lievre a Quatre Parties ... Nouvellement Imprime en Anvers par Tylman Susato ... lan MDXLV.* The text is given here in full:

Aux nobles Musichiens hanteurs de guerres, de chasses, & de volleries, Tylman Susato Salut.

A l'imitation (chiers amys) des anciens & modernes imprimeurs qui veiullantz imprimer quelque bonne oeuvre au prouffit & commodite de la Rep. la dedient aux amateurs ou exercitateurs de la chose comprise & instruite en icelle, ie me suis appense de vous dedier che dixiesme livre, contenant aulcunes chansons concernantes vostres exercices pource qu'en iceulx vous usez d'instrumentz desquels le plus souvent nous usons en lexercice de la noble & excellente art de musicque, car en la guerre vous usez de trompettes, bucines, & phistres d'allemans, a la chase de cornetz & trompes, a la vollerie de flaioletz, representantz le chant naturel des oyseletz, par quoy souvent il se trouvent de cheus, Daultre part ainsi que l'harmonie de la musicq donne recreation au cueur de l'homme, si donne le son de la trompette en la guerre courage aux chevaucheurs & chevaulx, La phistre & le tambour aux gens de pied, A la chasse le son de la trompe ou cournet aux chiens, Par quoy telles & samblables raisons (avecq che que ie m'esbatz aulcunne fois es mesmes exercises de la chase & vollerie) m'ont induict a vous dedier che present livre, vous priant le vouloir accepter d'aussi bon cueur & amour, qu'avons entre prins la despence & labeur. A dieu soyes Commandes.

frequent battles, hunts and field sports'. He goes on to explain that this particular collection of descriptive *chansons* is offered because of their aptness to the use of certain musical instruments in the exercise of the art of music: 'as the sound of the trumpet in battle encourages the cavalrymen and horses, the fife and drum the infantry, and in the hunt the sound of the *trompe* or *cornet* [animates] the hounds . . .'.

The practice of sounding verses of madrigals and motets on instruments in the sixteenth century is well documented; indeed by 1530 Attaignant had begun to publish the first instrumental transcriptions. It is to this usage that Susato is referring. In fact the bass and tenor parts of the programme-chanson *La Chasse de Lièvre* by Gombert, which Susato includes, could be played on a horn in F, the key of the piece: some notes would have to be left out, but the idiom is unmistakable. The only hunting-instrument then in current use whose tube-length would have been enough to generate the F below middle C, its fifth, third, and octave, was this cor a plusiers tours, or 'trompe' as it was variously known. The fact that Susato included a *chanson* of which the two lowermost parts at least were meant to be played on this instrument suggests that the helical horn was in use in France some years before the Susato collection was published. It is mentioned without comment, whereas had it been a novelty the fact would surely have been noted.

The helical horn's field-companion in France at this time was a small, singly-wound horn. This 'cornet de chasse' is sometimes called the Du Fouilloux horn from its first appearance in 1561 in the woodcuts illustrating Du Fouilloux's *La Venerie*,[1] a treatise on hunting decicated to Charles IX. When we recall that the stag hunt had taken more and more to horseback during the first half of the sixteenth century, it is not difficult to see how this coiled horn developed from the crescent-shaped oliphant of the late Middle Ages. Obviously the parties of a mounted hunt would be able to range farther afield than could their foot-bound forerunners. The need would then arise for a signal instrument with greater carrying power than that of the oliphant. Lengthening the instrument (the oliphant rarely exceeded fifteen inches) would enhance the fundamental and thereby increase tonal projection; and still more resonance could be had by sounding the one-note rhythmic calls of the period on a higher partial. For ease of carrying in the field, the longer tube was now bent into a little loop half-way between mouthpiece and bell. Gradually it would become apparent that the longer the tube, the greater would be the horn's penetrating power; and so as the tube became longer the loop was made proportionately larger.

At some point the distinguishing features of the cornet de chasse and the cor a plusiers tours appear to have merged to produce an instrument having the hoop of the one and the long, conical tube of the other. This fusion pre-

[1] Jacques du Fouilloux, *La Venerie* (Poitiers, 1561).

sumably took place round about the turn of the seventeenth century, for the
tapestries of *c.* 1655 preserved at Fontainebleau and in the Louvre show a
singly-wound instrument which embraces both features and clearly foretells
the form of the fully-developed cor-de-chasse.

The fact that this hybrid, which was to become the orchestral instrument
of the sixteen-nineties, escaped mention in Marin Mersenne's treatise on
musical instruments in 1636 need not surprise us. Mersenne does not
display his usual exhaustive knowledge when writing on the horn, possibly
because as a hunting instrument it lay outside his sphere of interest. His
illustration, an isolated instance in the period 1600 to 1650 during which
little pictorial evidence of the horn's development in France has been found,
shows rather the instrument of the previous century. Mersenne describes it
as the cor a plusiers tours; it is indeed the instrument of Susato's day, a
direct offspring of Virdung's snail-like creature. Mersenne mentions the
practice of playing harmonic fanfares in six or seven parts; but as this was a
comparatively recent development, it seems unlikely that these new fanfares would have been played on anything but the newer cors-de-chasse in
the hunting field, especially as the earlier helical horns appear to have been
of fragile construction.[1] Obviously Mersenne was writing more from the
point of view of theory and tradition than from first-hand experience. It is
likely that, from the first years of the seventeenth century, groups of these
new cors-de-chasse enlivened hunting-scenes in ballets with the rudimentary
four-part fanfares of which Mersenne speaks.

So far as is known the cor a plusiers tours did not survive in use beyond
Mersenne's undoubtedly retrospective mention, if indeed it was still played
then; though the cor-de-chasse's other parent, the little single-loop cornet,

[1] Mersenne, *Harmonie Universelle*, Paris 1636, Book V, Proposition 10. We can do no
better than to quote from page 318 of Roger Chapman's translation (The Hague, 1957):
'If the hunters wish to have the pleasure of performing some concerts in four or more
parts with their horns, it is rather easy, provided they know how to make their tones
exact, and they so proportioned the length and thickness of their *trompes* that they
maintain the same ratios as the organ pipes. For example if the largest horn is six feet
long, it will make the fifth below the one four feet long. And if there is added a third horn
three feet in length, it will produce the fourth against the second, so that the three
principal chords of the first mode may be had. To this it will be easy to add three or
four others to make some other chords.... I add only that they can be made of crystal,
of glass, of earth, of stone, etc., and that the makers can mix these with great skill to
make them as much admired as the other instruments.' It seems unlikely that horns
made of these fragile materials would long survive in daily use, whether indoors or in
the hunting-field.
   These simple fanfares would have contributed much in the way of colour and
atmosphere to the hunting-scenes which occur fairly frequently in the ballet of this
period. Castil-Blaze mentions a stage direction from Act I, scene 3, of the ballet *La
Cour des Miracles* performed in 1653 as saying 'Cors de chasse avaient sonné sur le
théâtre et dans l'orchestre' (J. F. H. Blaze, *L'Academie Imperiale de Musique*, Paris, 1855,
p. 343).

continued to be used as a hunting instrument in both France and Germany until late in the eighteenth century.

In spite of this early use, however, the French remained unaware of the horn's possibilities as an orchestral instrument for another hundred years.

Francesco Cavalli wrote the first surviving horn fanfare in 1639, in his opera *Le Nozze di Teti e di Peleo*.[1] This fact has led at least one author to conclude that the horn itself originated in Italy.[2] Cavalli's acquaintance with the French instrument need not surprise us, however, when we remember the close musical connections which Italy had maintained with France since the beginning of the seventeenth century. The Florentine composer Giulio Caccini and the poet-librettist Ottavio Rinuccini had travelled to Paris with Maria de' Medici following her marriage to Henry IV of France in 1600; and it was Rinuccini who brought back the *ballet de cour* to Florence in about 1605. Such was its success that no opera was thenceforth thought to be complete unless a ballet with separate music was performed between its acts. French ballet troupes continued to be engaged by the Italians during the first half of the century, and with them no doubt French horn-players when hunting scenes were to be enlivened by horn calls. This is the most reasonable explanation for Cavalli's knowledge of the horn before he had himself set foot in France.

[1] Francesco Cavalli's opera *Le Nozze di Teti e di Peleo* was first performed in Venice in 1639, and again in Paris in 1654. The *Chiamata alla Caccia*, a short fanfare in five parts, appears as a set piece in the first scene of Act I (see footnote 1, page 53). It is reproduced in modern notation in Reginald Morley-Pegge's *The French Horn* (London, 1960), p. 81. Georg Karstädt in his popular book, *Lasst Lustig die Hörner Erschallen* (Hamburg, 1964), p. 60, seems unaware that Cavalli's flourish is the earliest known appearance of the horn in opera, and states that 'As early as 1637 an Italian composer with the euphonious name of Michelangelo Rossi used a horn choir in the opera *Erminio* [sic] *sul Giordano*.' This work was first performed in the Barberini Palace at Rome in 1633; it was published at Venice in 1637. A copy is preserved in the Bodleian Library.

A 'Coro de' Cacciatori' occurs in Act IV which would point to a possible horn accompaniment were it not for the scalic character of each of the four voice parts. A 'Coro di Soldati' appears later in the score which is more triadic; but even here the seventh note of the scale is used frequently, and this note would only be available in the fourth octave of the horn, hardly a normal part of the technique of that period. The point is that no horn parts are included, nor is there any indication that any instruments apart from the normal strings should accompany. Both are present in Cavalli's score. What does strike the attention is that these two scenes in *Erminia sul Giordano* appear to have provided the material for their counterparts in *Le Nozze di Peleo*.

One cannot help wondering whether the use of corni in a battle scene might represent a revival of the Roman cavalrymen's cornu. *Le Nozze* is based on the Greek legend of Peleus' marriage to the sea-goddess Thetis. The cornu would have been known to the seventeenth-century Italians as a classical war-horn, and it seems logical that the big hooped horn would have served as a modern equivalent.

[2] Kathleen Schlesinger, 'Horn', in *Encyclopaedia Britannica*, eleventh edition (London, 1910), xiii, p. 702.

Once Cardinal Mazarin, himself a Roman, had created a thirst for Italian opera amongst the Parisians in the late 1640s, performances by Italian players came into great demand. It was on the crest of this wave that Mazarin invited a Venetian troupe to Paris in 1654 to perform *Le Nozze di Teti e di Peleo*, replete with scenic effects and horn fanfares.

Lully, also a Florentine, appears to have taken his cue from Cavalli ten years later when he set the five-part 'Air des Valets de Chiens et des Chasseurs avec des Cors de Chasse' in the ballet *Les Plaisirs de l'Isle Enchantée*, performed between the acts of Molière's play *La Princesse d'Elide*.[1] Lully would have probably met the horn while a boy in Italy in much the same way that Cavalli would have done; certainly he would have heard the occasional battery of cors-de-chasse later at Paris in the course of his duties with the *Vingt-quatre Violons du Roi*. Cavalli's *Le Nozze* was given two years after Lully had become their leader, and it is here that the use of a horn ensemble on stage appears to have been suggested to him.

Neither Cavalli's nor Lully's fanfares can lay much claim to musical merit, since they keep to the tonic and dominant triads with only the simplest of dactyls and trochees for rhythmic articulation. The point is rather that they brought the horn before the public in a new capacity which was purely musical. Particularly as a result of Lully's using it in this way, the cor-de-chasse now appeared to be worth refining and developing as a musical instrument; so that by the 1680s it had attained to a considerable degree of mechanical perfection and tonal beauty. Equally important, Lully had set the pattern for the kind of pictorial role which the horn was to fulfil in French music until the mid-1750s.[2]

From about 1660 onwards the cor-de-chasse began to be taken up more

[1] This fanfare appears in a manuscript by Philidor l'aîné in the Paris Bibliothèque Nationale. It is reproduced in Morley-Pegge, op. cit., p. 83.

[2] It must be said in fairness that the appearance of the horn in ballet music after 1700 was due as well, perhaps more, to the influence of the Marquis de Dampierre. In 1700 he attracted the attention of the Dauphin at a royal banquet, by playing a solo in a *Sinfonie guerrière* by Philidor l'aîné. From 1709 he served as Lieutenant des Chasses to the Duke of Maine, becoming Master of Harriers to Louis XV in 1727. Dampierre was the first to compose functional harmonic fanfares for the cor-de-chasse, apart from Lully's isolated example. These were imitated by such composers as Jean-Joseph Mouret and J. B. Morin, the latter's being purely recreational as opposed to those of Dampierre, which were based on the signal codes of the actual hunt. A collection of 'Tons de Chasse et Fanfares à une et deux trompes composées par Mr. de Dampierre gentilhomme des plaisirs du Roy' was published for the first time in 1734 as an appendix to Serre' de Rieux' *Les Dons des Enfants de Laton*. They had, however, been in circulation since the early years of the century. Morin had included similar fanfares in his *La Chasse du Cerf*, a ballet-opera performed at Versailles in 1708. Campra's opera *Achille et Déidamie* of 1733 contains a fanfare on Dampierre's model; this form of call was idealized by Rameau in *Hippolyte et Aricie* in 1735. Girdlestone rightly says of the de Rieux collection that 'they are the mob of the tribe of which Rameau's *air* is a chief' (*Jean-Philippe Rameau*, London, 1957, p. 174).

and more by hunting establishments and ballet troupes in other countries. It is mentioned, though not by name, in the Royal Household Accounts in England as early as 1661, and again in 1667.[1] When William Bull, as trumpet-maker to Charles II, speaks of his removal to the Haymarket, 'where any gentleman may be furnished with Trumpets, French Horns, and other articles of silver and brass', he uses a term peculiar to the English language which hints clearly at the instrument's country of origin. Defoe's *The Fortunate Mistress* contains a reference to the French horn's existence here in 1696,[2] and about this time Dr. Talbot's list of instruments gives a detailed description of it.[3] A magnificent copper horn by Bull bearing the date 1699 survives in the Horniman Museum. Its workmanship and playing qualities show the remarkable refinement which the instrument had experienced in the hands of this skilled maker. The same year finds that captious journalist, Ned Ward, accepting his 'Dame *Butterfield's* Invitation to her *Essex* Calf and Bacon, with her *Six* Brass Horns, to accomodate Sports-men with the delightful harmony of Hunting'.[4] The fact that the French horn became so popular here after its arrival in the wake of the Restoration would suggest that Charles's courtiers found its tonal qualities desirable. Obviously it had arrived at some degree of perfection in France by the 1650s.

The taste for things French was slower to catch on in Germany than in England. This, and the fact that more records perished in successive wars than here, may well account for the horn's comparative absence from the German musical scene. Only in isolated instances do we meet the cor-de-chasse there before 1680.

The hunt held near Calbe (Saxony) in 1671 in which Prince August's diary mentions that the 'trumpets and horns sounded bravely'[5] may well have used horns of the earlier German pattern. The cor-de-chasse is probably what is meant, however, for it was known in those parts at that time. One proof can be seen today in the sandstone statue of a huntsman blowing a large-hooped French horn which stands in the park at Schloss Moritzburg, some hundred miles east of Calbe. This figure dates from within a year or so

[1] H. C. de Lafontaine, *The King's Musick* (London, 1909).

[2] Daniel Defoe, *Roxana, or The Fortunate Mistress* (London, 1724). Defoe's heroine, had come over from France at the age of 10 in 1683; had married at 15; and lived with her husband four years when her father died. Three years later her profligate mate had spent the inheritance. This brings us to 1695, when one August morning the scene which she describes on page 9 occurs: '. . . . early the next Morning he gets out of Bed, goes to a Window which look'd out towards the Stables, and sounds his *French* Horn, as he call'd it, which was his usual Signal to his Men to go out a-hunting.' And later, after his final flight from wedlock: 'All that I cou'd come to the Knowledge of, about him, was, that he left his Hunting-Horn, which he called the *French* Horn, in the Stable, and his Hunting Saddle.'

[3] Christ Church MS. 1185.

[4] Ned Ward, *The London Spy* (London, 1699), vi (April), p. 13.

[5] Dresden State Archives, *Hofdiarium Augusts*, Loc. 8698.

of the palace's completion in 1670.[1] German ballet scores about this time contain the occasional scene which does imply the use of horns for outdoor effect,[2] but no music set specifically for them has as yet come to light. Nor do any horns survive from the period before 1681.

One instance of horn music in the Lullian manner occurs in 1680 in Austria, where Muffat and the Schmelzers were writing ballet music in a style which mixed both French and Italian elements. A libretto from a ballet by the elder Schmelzer performed at Linz on the Emperor Leopold's name-day, 15 November 1680, remarks that 'the Intrada was sounded apart from the main band by Violins and Hunting-Horns'.[3]

Yet this was a final echo of the French practice, so far as the horn in Austria was concerned. It was a nobleman of Leopold's Austria who was to start the horn on its career as an orchestral instrument the following winter.

[1] Wilhelm Kleefeld, 'Das Orchester der Hamburger Oper 1678–1738' in *Sammelbände der Internationalen Musikgesellschaft* (Leipzig, 1901), I, 2, p. 279.

[2] An example of a situation which implies the use of horns without actually calling for them occurs in the libretto to the ballet *Floren Frühlings-Fest*, performed before the Dowager Electress of Saxony at Dresden in 1696. The complete text to this work, whose composer is not given, is reproduced in H. von Besser, *Schrifften in Gebundener und Ungebundener Rede* (Leipzig, 1720). On page 388 we find a stage direction for 'Six little Shepherd-Boys led on by Shawms (Schalmeyen)'—this clearly means oboes, whether sounded on the stage or off. Later, on page 392, there follows a scene entitled *The Hunters and Nymphs of Diana*. 'Sylvan, God of Forests, enters together with Vertumnus, God of Seasons, Flowers and Fruits. The one praises the beauty of his Woodlands, the other his Gardens.' Sylvan sings 'Rejoice ye, O my Forests'. A setting more conducive to the woodsy sound of horns would be difficult to imagine. Yet none are called for, nor are they in similar scenes in other German ballets of this period. Perhaps horns were an optional extra if available—they do begin to appear in German ballet music after 1700.

[3] Austrian National Library, Kodex 16588:3. The German text reads 'Und ist die *Intrada* neben der Banda von Geigen mit Jägerhorn producirt worden.' An Aria per la Diana was sung, and indeed here is an instance where horns are indicated. (See preceding note.) In Austrian usage at this period the term *Horn* has the same form in both singular and plural. See also Egon Wellesz, 'Die Ballett-Suiten von Johann Heinrich und Andreas Schmeltzer' in *Sitzungsberichte der Kaiserlichen Akademie der Wissenschaften in Wien*, 176. Band, V. Abhandlung (Vienna, 1914), p. 43.

I

THE *COR-DE-CHASSE*

and its Transplantation to Bohemia

The Bohemian background

BOHEMIA in 1680 was an Austrian dominion. Following the Imperial victory at the Battle of the White Mountain in 1620, the Crown of Bohemia had passed to the House of Habsburg, marking the end of her long history as an independent kingdom. Large areas of the country which had been populated by the original Czech inhabitants were laid bare under the new laws, which exiled all Protestants, and in their place a new populace took root, Roman by persuasion and of Sudeten German or Austrian origin. The *Vernewerte Landesordnung* of 1627 abolished Czech as the official language and established the German tongue in its place. An entirely new landed aristocracy was brought in, principally German, but including Italian, Spanish and even Irish lords as well. Ferdinand's Government dispossessed those Bohemian nobles who had not fallen in the executions of 1621; vast properties were now put up for sale or presented by the Emperor to his victorious generals and court dignitaries as tokens of favour.

Within a few years after the decrees prohibiting the Protestant faith, Roman Catholicism had become fully established. The Clergy was created a fourth Estate and given precedence over the three older Estates of Nobles, Knights, and Towns: the supremacy of the Church was now absolute. Legislative power was transferred from the Assembly of the Estates to the Emperor in his capacity as King of Bohemia. Thus Prague was obliged to forfeit her former autonomy and accept a role subsidiary to Vienna's. From that time onward Bohemia followed the trends set by Vienna in matters of government and culture. Within two generations Bohemia was transformed into an integral part of the Austrian *Kulturraum*.[1]

The period immediately following the Thirty Years War was a time of burgeoning prosperity and a general resurgence of activity for Austria and her dominions. Flushed with new conquests and believing the Turkish

---

[1] For a more detailed description of the events leading up to the Battle of the White Mountain and the reforms which followed, the reader is referred to Count Franz Lützow's *Bohemia* (London, 1896), pp. 259–361; to Hugo Hantsch, *Die Nationalitätenfrage im alten Österreich* (Wiener historische Studien, i, Vienna, 1953), p. 19 ff.; and to Franz Martin Pelzel, *Geschichte der Böhmen* (Prague, 1817), pp. 792–844.

threat to be quelled for ever, she plunged into the rejuvenation of commerce and the arts which followed in the wake of the Counter-Reformation.

The triumphal re-entry of the Catholic Church into Bohemia stimulated a revival of the arts. Nobility and clergy alike poured their new wealth into an intense programme of building. Artists and craftsmen from all the dominions came to join forces with the Bohemian glaziers and stone-masons. Sumptuous palaces, monasteries, churches, and town houses arose, in whose architecture the natural exuberance of the landscape combined with the affluence and religious fervour of the times to express that spirit which was the Bohemian Baroque.

In the great country palaces a new way of life arose whose grandeur and intense luxury had seldom been equalled and were never to return. Wealth was represented not only in vast landholdings and grandiose country seats, but in rich furniture, ornamental gardens, grottoes, statuary, fountains, and follies; and above all in troops of chamber-servants and lackeys, whose livery was not to be surpassed in richness and taste by any subsequent fashion. Music was the special delight of the nobles, and from among the servants were recruited players for the orchestra upon which every palace prided itself.[1]

The Church, in her new position of power, greatly furthered the arts as well, and lent her support to the nobility in the patronage of music especially. In Bohemia the Jesuit order had gained a particularly strong footing under the Habsburg reforms, and the emphasis which music received in their monasteries, colleges, and seminaries came to be felt throughout the country. Music schools were set up in every village to train prospective novitiates, for a seminary candidate who lacked musical training and ability would not be admitted. Should a village child show particular promise on an instrument, he would be trained in the monastery and sent on to one of the palace orchestras, since acceptance there meant a betterment of social position and an opportunity to make a name in the world. Organists and *Regenschori* were sent to Vienna, Venice, and Rome to complete their musical studies, often at the expense of the local lord. Each monastery had its orchestra and choir school, and high standards of performance were exacted. Operas and instrumental concerts took place regularly in the cloisters, attended by gentry and village folk alike. Music was thus given a double impetus from both clergy and aristocracy, and was enjoyed by the entire populace.[2] It was this tradi-

[1] The social and intellectual backgrounds of the central European nobility of the late seventeenth century are to be found in detail in Otto Brunner, *Adeliges Landleben und europaeischer Geist* (Salzburg, 1949), pp. 61–138.

[2] This point is borne out by many contemporary writers. The anonymous Verfasser der Nachrichten über Polen, in his equally anonymous *Ausführliche Nachrichten über Böhmen* (Salzburg, 1794), pp. 55, 56, observes that 'Where music is concerned Bohemia is the German Italy. Old and young alike make music, most of them playing several instruments, and often showing remarkable skill. Not that the Bohemians have more

tion which was to nurture many of the most prominent composers of the eighteenth century—the Stamitz family and Gluck come immediately to mind—and which was to give Bohemia its reputation as the 'Conservatory of Europe'.[1]

Sporck and the introduction of the cor-de-chasse into Bohemia

Franz Anton, Count von Sporck, Lord of Lissa, Gradlitz, Konoged, and Heřmanměstec, Imperial Privy Counsellor and Chamberlain, and Viceroy of Bohemia, represented the ideal Austrian nobleman and Bohemian cavalier of the period. Statesman, courtier, and patron of the arts, he embodied in his life and works the cultural and political history of Bohemia under three emperors. Born in 1662 and a contemporary of Prince Eugene of Savoy, Sporck was intimately involved in the developments which led to the establishment of the Danube Empire as a major power rivalled only by France. The influence of his artistic activities was enormous. In Lissa he set up his own printing-press, not only for disseminating his own philosophical and theological writings and translations, but to encourage a host of native poets —amongst them Günther, the Silesian harbinger of Goethe. From the Tyrol, Sporck brought Matthias Braun to fill his countless commissions for statues, monuments, and fountains; and in so doing founded a major school of Baroque sculptors whose works still adorn the Bohemian countryside today.[2] Sporck's love of music was rivalled only by his passion for the hunt, however, and both took precedence over all his other interests. The first Venetian opera troop in Bohemia was introduced on the stage of his private theatre in Prague, later enlarged to become the first opera house in the land.[3]

---

natural aptitude for music than the Silesians or the Austrians: it is merely that more subjects are trained in music here!'

[1] The musical situation in eighteenth-century Bohemia is exhaustively discussed in Charles Burney, *The Present State of Music in Germany* (London, 1775), ii, pp. 1–25; and Gottfried Johann Dlabacž, *Abhandlung von den Schicksalen der Künste in Böhmen* (Prague, 1797). This latter article also appeared in the *Neuere Abhandlungen der Königliche Böhmische Gesellschaft der Wissenschaft* (Prague and Leipzig, 1788), iii.

[2] A complete list of Sporck's statuary commissions, as executed by Braun and his circle, is given in Dlabacž, *Allgemeines Historisches Künstler-Lexicon für Böhmen* (Prague, 1815), iii, pp. 142 ff. See also A(nton) Voigt, *Abbildungen der Böhmische und Mährische Gelehrten und Künstler* (Prague, 1775), ii, pp. 116 ff.; Johann Quirinus John, *Nachrichten von einigen Böhmischen alten Malern und Künstlern* (*Neue Bibliothek der schönen Wissenschaften und der freyen Künste*), 75 vols. (Leipzig, 1763), xix, 1, 320–32; xx, 1, 140–53; and Eugen Tietze-Conrat, *Österreichische Barokplastik* (Vienna, 1920), pp. 12 ff.

[3] Heinrich Benedikt, *Franz Anton Graf von Sporck* (Vienna, 1923), pp. 127–39. This is by no means the first opera in Prague. Here we must distinguish between the popular travelling opera companies from Venice proper and those performances by the Imperial operatic forces given for the Emperor when in Prague. Dlabacž, op. cit., iii, p. 23, cites the year 1704 as the date of the first opera performed in Prague. This was Sartori's *La Rete Di Vulcano* given for Leopold I; but see Alfred Lowenberg, *Annals of Opera* (London, 1943), under 1680 and 1703; and Dlabacž, op. cit., i, pp. 149, 466.

The brilliance of Sporck's house orchestra was the delight of all who visited Lissa.[1] Sporck enjoyed an international reputation as a huntsman. Like most of the great nobles he maintained a vast hunt whose splendour, together with his personal marksmanship and integrity in the field, earned him a name as the 'Premier Huntsman of Europe'.

It is in connection with the hunt that Sporck's services to music are best remembered. His *Jägerchor*, through its legendary perfection, stimulated the development of the German hunting-song epitomized in the 'Hunting Chorus' of Weber's *Der Freischütz*. Sporck's ultimate significance as a musical patron, however, lies in one act: the introduction of the cor-de-chasse and its harmonic hunting-music into Bohemia from the court of Louis XIV.

In 1679 Sporck's studies at Prague University were interrupted by the death of his father, Johann von Sporck, General of the Imperial Cavalry.[2] This famous old warrior had amassed a considerable fortune in the course of his many victories. On a number of occasions the elder Sporck had received handsome rewards in money from his Emperor, particularly for his conquests in Hungary. With these sums he had shrewdly acquired sizeable estates surrounding Lissa, which Ferdinand III had given him in 1647.[3] Clever investing had further enlarged the Sporck fortune. Thus by the time of his death at the age of 84 the old general's legacy to Franz Anton had grown to be one of the largest in the Empire. So great was the responsibility of this inheritance that no time could be lost in completing his education. Franz Anton's studies were stopped in the midst of his fourth year of reading philosophy and theology, and he set out on a two-year tour of the foremost courts in Italy, France, England, Holland, and Germany.

The high point of Sporck's tour was the Court of Louis XIV. Indeed, no German-speaking aristocrat of the day could be considered versed in the ways of Society unless he had spent some time at the French Court. 'Toute l'Allemagne y voyageoit', Frederick the Great was to write in 1750;[4] 'un

[1] The Imperial Vice-Chancellor Schönborn to Count Friederich Grossa: 'The brilliant House Orchestra here [at Lissa] played last night until eleven o'clock.' A later copy of this letter of *c.* 1720 is in the Schönborn family archives in Vienna. See also Hantsch, *Reichsvizekanzler Friederich Karl Graf von Schönborn* (Augsburg, 1929), Anhang i, p. 4.

[2] Count Johann von Sporck's black armour is preserved in the *Waffensammlung* of the Kunsthistorisches Museum in Vienna.

[3] Hofkammerarchiv, Vienna: Landtafel Nr. 149, M. 20. The deed of presentation is dated 2 December 1647. Ferdinand I had bought Lissa in 1548. The estate had been confiscated by Protestant forces during the disturbances preceding the Thirty Years War, but fell again to the Habsburg Crown following the Battle of the White Mountain.

[4] Frederick II von Brandenburg, *Memoires pour servir à l'histoire de Brandenbourg* (1750), ii, p. 771. 'Le goût des François regla nos Cuisines, nos Meubles, nos Habillements. . . .' This was certainly true of Prussia, where Frederick set the tone by aping everything French: but it is well to remember for the purposes of the present study that the Court at Vienna was still the capital of Italian culture, although some French influence was present. Louis XIV's queen after all, was a Habsburg.

jeune homme passoit pour imbécille, s'il n'avoit séjourné quelque temps à la cour de Versailles.' Sporck was no exception. The art of polite conversation, still mostly unknown in Bohemia, made a lasting impression on the young Count, as did the French manners and general life at Court.

It was the *chasse à courre*, however—*Parforcejagd* as it was later called in German-speaking countries—and its music which stirred the young cavalier so deeply, that he decided to transplant the French art of mounted hunting and the cor-de-chasse to his Bohemian home.

'In the year 1680 he set out upon a tour of foreign countries, according to the custom of the Bohemian nobility. He visited the foremost royal and princely courts, where he noted everything which struck him as beautiful, artistic, or useful; and brought them back with him for the ornament and benefit of his native land. In this connexion we must not omit mention of an incident which forms a proper part of the history of music in Bohemia.

'At Paris he heard the hunting-horn for the first time, an instrument which had been invented there a short time before. He found this instrument so agreeable that he caused two men from his retinue to be instructed in the art of playing it, which they brought shortly to the highest degree of perfection, and upon their return to Bohemia taught it to others: so that today [1790] the Bohemians surpass virtually every other nation in this kind of music; and for some considerable time if one has wanted good horn-players even in Paris, one has had to send to Bohemia for them. The names of the artists who first enriched music in Bohemia with this instrument were Wenzel Sweda and Peter Röllig, both bondsmen of Count Sporck.'[1]

The exact details of how the French hunting-horn (at this period still a single-coil instrument whose hoop was large enough to encircle the shoulders of the mounted sportsman) came to Sporck's attention are not available. Prochaska, writing in 1784,[2] tells us that Sporck was attracted by the sweetness of the horn's sound, and had two of his retainers taught to play it on the spot: 'Vix Parisiis instandi cornua venatoria inventa ars est, quum delectatus suavite cantus duo ex hominibus sibi obnoxiis ea instituendos curavit. Id principium nos artis, qua hodie Bohemi excellere putantur.' Prochaska gives the date of this event as 1680. Gerber[3] and other eighteenth-century writers

[1] The clearest summary of the event appears in Hirsching, *Historisch-Litterärisches Handbuch Berühmter und Denkwürdiger Personen* (Leipzig, 1792), xiii, p. 146.

[2] Faustinus Prochaska, *De Saecularibus Liberalium Artium in Bohemia* (Prague, 1784), pp. 400, 401.

[3] Ernst Ludwig Gerber, *Historisch-Biographisches Lexicon der Tonkünstler* (Leipzig, 1792), ii, p. 146. It is to Gerber's account of Sporck's introduction of the horn to Bohemia that most later writers are indebted for their facts concerning Sporck, and indeed the eighteenth-century horn. Such is the importance of this article to the study of the pre-valve horn that I have included it complete in the Appendix. An equally well-known and often-quoted account is that given in Dlabacž, op cit., iii, p. 142.

are not so clear as to the actual first encounter; and Sporck's contemporary biographer van der Roxas omits mention of it altogether.[1] All accounts agree, however, as to the names of the two who were to become the first Bohemian horn-players: Wenzel Sweda and Peter Rölig (or Röllig—many spellings are used), who will be discussed in a later chapter.

Although the earlier writers on Sporck are silent on the details of his actual stay in Versailles, they do give the date of his return from the *Cavalier-tour*. Van der Roxas[2] wrote in 1715: '1681. His Excellency having now returned from his travels in good health and spirits, he petitioned the Emperor for dispensation to take possession of his goods and bondsmen; for he was not yet of age. It was thus that he found himself a free owner and lord of his estates and vassals in his nineteenth year.' These dates agree with that of Franz Anton's birth, 1662. Similarly, the highly detailed memorial article on Sporck, probably written by the poet Ferdinand von Bresler, in Zedler's *Universal-Lexicon* of 1744,[3] says: 'In 1680, after completing his studies and noble exercises, he undertook travels to foreign countries, and spent two years observing the principal courts of Europe. Following his return in 1681 he took up the government of his hereditary estates. Sporck's greatest diversions were reading, and next to hunting, music, in which he possessed great ability:[4] he it was who first brought the hunting-horn or Waldhorn to Bohemia and made it known.'

[1] That Sporck would have sent his two men to Paris for instruction after his return to Bohemia, as von Riegger states, is unlikely (Johann Anton von Riegger, *Materialen zur Alten und Neuen Statistik von Böhmen*, Prague, 1798, xii, pp. 277, 288). The *Allgemeine Musikzeitung* for 9 April 1800 compounds the error by implying that these players were Frenchmen. 'Er brachte die ersten Waldhornisten aus Frankreich in seinen Vaterland' (p. 493). Both suppositions contradict all other writers except Constant von Wurzbach (*Biographisches Lexicon des Kaiserthums Österreich*, Vienna, 1863–91, xxxvi, p. 220) and Hermann Eichborn (*Die Dämpfung Beim Horn*, Leipzig, 1897, p. 15), both of whom wrote in the nineteenth century.

[2] Ferdinand van der Roxas (pseudonym for Friederich Rotscholz), *Leben Eines Herrlichen Bildes . . . Wahrer Frommigkeit . . . F. A. Reichsgrafen von Sporck* (Amsterdam, 1715), p. 20. Rotscholz published an identical edition of this work in 1720, this time under the pseudonym of Gottfried Caspar von Stillenau.

[3] Johann Heinrich Zedler (ed.), *Universal-Lexicon* (Leipzig, 1732–50), xxxix (1744), p. 363.

[4] This point is debatable. Benedikt, op. cit., p. 2, says that 'Although he had not mastered the instrument himself nor become a connoisseur of music, he could nevertheless boast of having a brilliant house orchestra in his service. . . .' Yet a thorough grounding in music was part of every nobleman's education. Furthermore, no candidates were admitted to the Jesuit colleges unless they could show proficiency on at least one instrument; and the records show that at the age of 8 Franz Anton was accepted at Kuttenberg, a monastery which was particularly well known for its music. When one considers the emulation inspired amongst the aristocracy by the musical Habsburg family (the reigning Emperor Ferdinand III was a skilled composer, and enjoyed the title of 'Musizierender Kaiser'), it seems unlikely that Sporck was without musical ability in some form. His activities in the field of operatic patronage would further con-

Besides these accounts by lexicographers and biographers of the time, there exists pictorial and poetic evidence of Sporck's close association with the hunting-horn. A copy of Sporck's last portrait has recently come into this writer's possession. A copper engraving dated 1735 and signed Emanuel Joachim Haas, 'ad vivum delineavit et fecit', it is reproduced as the frontispiece to this book.[1] Sporck, richly clad in embroidered doublet and walking-coat and wearing a peaked wig, is shown with his left hand raised toward a landscape in the background. The view is remarkable for its clarity of detail. Against a backdrop of rolling, wooded Bohemian countryside, a fine *Landschloss* appears, which may easily be recognized as Lissa. Wild duck and otter are seen in the foreground, together with sundry game traps of Sporck's design. In the centre of the scene we see a mounted stag hunt in full cry; and the lead horseman, in three-corner hat and riding-coat, is sounding a Wald-horn. It is understandable that the old cavalier should wish to be portrayed against a scene of his favourite country seat and the pastime in which he most delighted, surrounded with the trophies and keepsakes of his long and eventful life. This hunting-scene is unique amongst such contemporary portraits of Austrian nobles, and the appearance of the horn in this context at such an early date is surely relevant.

There are also two literary references by the poet Johann Christian Günther.[2] In his apostrophe to Sporck entitled *Das Ebenbild der Wahrheit und Gerechtigkeit* he says:[3]

---

firm this supposition. One is inclined to cede the point to von Bresler; but see page 16, and footnote 1.

The old Count died in September or October of 1679. Whether Franz Anton began his travels late that year or early in 1680 does not detract from the validity of the article's chronology.

[1] From *Das Christliche Jahr oder Die Episteln und Evangelien* (Prague, 1735). This edition, the last of Sporck's publications, is considered to be a masterpiece of late Baroque printing. The edition itself was printed two months before the portrait was finished, and the portrait was included as a loose leaf in the later examples. It is fitting that this last of all the many portraits of Sporck should also be the finest, both for quality of execution and for accuracy. Sporck remarked that the likeness was the best of all, and he was particularly pleased with the wig. On 4 January 1735 Sporck said in a letter to Frau von Barthold that he had decided 'to stop with the Christian Year in prose and verse, still at press'.

[2] 1695–1723. One of the first High German poets. Günther's works, even in the earliest lyrics, show a clarity and consistency of form and a freedom from foreign usages quite remarkable for the time. His innovations in metre and rhetoric later came to influence Goethe. The poems concerning Sporck are published together in Vol. IV of Wilhelm Krämer's complete edition of Günther's works in six volumes which appeared as a series in the *Bibliothek des Literarischen Vereins in Stuttgart* from 1930 onwards. The volume in question is contained in Publikation 283, 1. Jahresgang (Leipzig, 1935). 'Das Ebenbild' may be found on p. 197. See also Carl Enders, *Chronologisch-Biographische Studien zu den Gedichten Joh. Chr. Günthers* (Dortmund, 1904); and *Zeitfolge der Gedichte und Briefe Joh. Chr. Günthers* (Dortmund, 1904).

[3] *Das Ebenbild der Wahrheit und Gerechtigkeit, Vorgestellt in einem Kurtzen Entwurff*

Pan, glaub'ich, hätte selbst sein liebstes Rohr zerschmissen,
Und mit den grössten Lust dein Waldhorn hören müssen![1]

Pan truly would have smashed his fav'rite pipe,
and heard thy hunting-horn with wild delight!

In another of Günther's poems, written in 1722 and entitled, 'Auf das Kukusbad in Bohmen',[2] 'Virtue' surveys Bad Kukus, Sporck's celebrated mineral baths:

Ach! sprach sie: ist der Welt die guldne Zeit entflogen?
O nein! sie hat sich nur ins Kukusbad gezogen.
Hier hat das Waldhorn einen andern Klang.

. . . Ah! quoth she, Hath the Golden Age from Earth forever flown?
Nay, nay! it hath to Kukus-Bad for solace but withdrawn.
. . . Here sounds the hunting-horn with far more charming tone.

It is significant that this earliest mention of the Waldhorn as such in formal German literature should occur in a direct context with Sporck.

All in all, it is reasonably certain that Sporck came to know the cor-de-chasse while at Versailles, and that he brought it back to Bohemia. We may conclude that the Bohemian school of horn-playing started with Rölig and Sweda's first lesson on the hunting-horn in 1680.

The Parforcejagd and the affective connotations of the horn

The horn's entry into the orchestra in ballet and opera may be more readily understood if considered in the light of its importance as the instrument of the mounted hunt. Let us review for a moment the significance of the Parforcejagd in the social life of the time.

The Bohemian countryside was ideal for hunting on horseback. Mild in summer and bracing in winter, its wooded hills and open fields teemed with game of every kind. Now and again a palace or chapel refreshed the eye, often mirrored in the many lakes and rivers which adorned the valleys. Here the noble would find both his sporting and aesthetic inclinations amply requited. It was into this graceful landscape that Sporck introduced the mounted hunt. That the Parforcejagd should flourish in such surroundings

---

des Lebens Seiner Excellenz Herrn Frantz Antonii Grafen von Sporck (Vienna, 1721). First printed privately for Sporck by Schönwetter, this poem is perhaps more readily available to the modern reader in Sammlung von Johann Christian Günthers, aus Schlesien, Theils Noch Nie Gedruckten, Theils Schon Herausgegebenen, Deutschen und Lateinischen Gedichten (Frankfurt and Leipzig, 1726).

[1] Again the question of whether Sporck himself played the horn. Günther's line would suggest that he did.

[2] Quoted in Enders, Zeitfolge der Gedichte und Briefe Joh. Chr. Günthers (Dortmund, 1904), p. 74.

seems highly appropriate: so, too, the development of an elaborate hunting-music against this exuberant natural setting, for in the sound of the horn was embodied the essence of the out-of-doors and the noble country life.

Whether or not Sporck himself could claim to be the first to introduce the chasse à courre (as opposed to the Waldhorn itself) to the Habsburg lands is perhaps debatable, owing to the scarcity of contemporary records. But it is certain that he was its first major exponent, if only from the folk-songs and fables which surround his deeds as a marksman and rider. Sporck anticipated even the Court at Vienna in the practice of this royal sport, and it was not until some time after the Turkish siege of 1683 that we find mention of a formal mounted hunt in the Court records.[1]

As the 'premier huntsman of Europe' Sporck was in a position, aided by his elegance, wealth, and social standing, to bring his new pastime to the attention of the leading nobles of Bohemia and the neighbouring royalty. Soon the Brandenburg Court and August the Strong of Saxony boasted mounted hunts, and it remained Sporck's lifelong pride that Charles VI as Archduke sent two hunters to him for instruction in the new art of hunting. Bohemia remained the centre of the mounted hunt because of its fortunate combination of ideal landscape and noble country residences: and of all the great Bohemian hunting-estates none were so prized among huntsmen as Sporck's own Lissa and Konoged. Charles VI himself was to spend many days hunting there when returning from his coronation as King of Bohemia at Prague in 1723.[2]

[1] Staatsarchiv, Vienna: Obersthofmeisteramt, Stallbücher, 1687–1700. Also Oskar Freiherr von Mitis, *Jagd und Schützen am Hofe Karls VI* (Vienna, 1912), p. 5. Even so, the standing hunt or *Treibjagd* remained the predominant form at the Imperial Court until nearly 1720. But, as can be seen from the following passage, the Waldhorn was the standard instrument. A description of a wild-boar hunt in the early years of Charles VI's reign is given in Eduard Vehse, *Geschichte der Deutschen Höfe Seit der Reformation, II: Geschichte des Oestreichischen Hofs und Adels* (Hamburg, 1852), p. 246: 'At this time the Imperial stag and boar hunts were carried out on foot. The Emperor and his family stood under the Imperial canopy and shot at the game driven toward it by the beaters. At the end of the hunt the Master and the assembled huntsmen came forward; the horns were sounded; and the Imperial party were presented with green twigs, which the Emperor and Empress pinned to their hats. Then they removed to the banquet.' The Imperial couple were then serenaded at table with fanfares in as many as six parts. See also Ernst Paul, 'Musikalisches in der Jagd: die Jagd in der Musik', in *Wild und Weidwerk der Welt* (Vienna, 1955).

[2] loc. cit., pp. 27, 29. Also Benedikt, op. cit., pp. 104 ff. Following the coronation on 5 September 1723, the Emperor remained in residence and made daily excursions into the near-by forests to hunt. On 3 November, the Feast of St. Hubert, a ceremonial hunt was held at Bonrepos at which the entire Court was present. The Holy Roman Emperor allowed Sporck to decorate him with the Order of St. Hubert, a hunting-order which Sporck had founded in 1695. After the hunting-banquet, Sporck offered Charles the insignia of the order, a golden horn on a green ribbon, saying that, he 'as the eldest Privy Councillor to hold the office of Chamberlain since the late Leopold of most grateful memory, might myself pin this horn on your breast'. The Emperor signed his 'Carl'

The social importance of the hunt was given great significance by its adoption at the Habsburg Court. The size and splendour of a noble's hunt came to be the yardstick by which his wealth was measured. 'The most shining parts of a German Court', Burney was to write in 1775,[1] 'are usually its *military*, its *music* and its *hunt*. In this last article the expence is generally enormous.' And indeed it was, for the capital outlay necessary to purchase, equip and maintain a presentable number of horses and hounds was considerable: not to mention the weapons, instruments (a man could live for a year on the price of one Waldhorn), uniforms and the like. Trained personnel were expensive, too: and large sums were paid for bondsmen who could ride, shoot, and play the horn to perfection.[2] Indeed, many a petty prince's treasury crumbled under the burden of keeping up a good front in the hunting-field.

As the hunt itself was a measure for social standing amongst the nobles, so the horn became a status symbol within the hunt. The skill which the

---

in the order's register and said, 'Now we too are in thy hunting-order'. The register, with the signatures of Charles VI and August the Strong can be seen in the Haas portrait of Sporck (frontispiece). Charles was fond of the Waldhorn, and kept a band of eight horn-players in Vienna which was known as the *Kaiserliche Jagdmusik*. This ensemble continues today as the *Lainzer Jagdmusik* under the direction of Dr. Ernst Paul.

[1] Burney, op. cit., i, p. 104.

[2] The importance of the horn in the hunt is made clear in one of the very earliest German parforce-hunting manuals. Hanns Friederich von Fleming, in his *Der Vollkommene Teutsche Jäger* (Leipzig, 1719), i, p. 259, describes the ceremony for the signal to begin the hunt, stating expressly that no one is to take part unless equipped with a parforce-horn. 'With everything ready, and permission to charge having been given, he [the King or the Master as the case might be] had the honour to sound his horn first, followed by the Hunting-master and the others. By law every mounted member of a Parforce-hunt must wear his Parforce-horn round his neck, otherwise he will not be admitted to the field.' Heinrich Wilhelm Döbel, in setting out the requirements for the various ranks of hunting-lackeys in a similar manual, urges the need for skill in horn-playing. We read in his *Jäger Practica, oder der Wohlgeübte und Erfahrener Jäger* (Leipzig, 1746), ii, p. 90: 'The Head Huntsman ... must display particular firmness in all his skills ... but especially he must have stag-sense, play a good horn and ride well.... For a hunt to be truly well-equipped, a futher three to four huntsmen are necessary, who have a trained stag-sense, ride perfectly and blow a stout horn.' In Vehse, op. cit., iii, pp. 24, 25, is given a description of a hunt at the Court of Friederich Wilhelm I of Prussia which further bears out this point. 'For the Parforce-hunt proper, twelve huntsmen are employed who must be good hunters, good horsemen and good horn-players. ... When the stag has fallen the Master gives him the death-stab. Then he removes both front hooves and presents them to the King on a silver platter, accompanied by vigorous fanfares from the horns.' The tradition of horn-playing huntsmen continued well into the nineteenth century, and provided many court orchestras with recruits for their horn departments. In 1808 the art of horn-playing was still taught in the forestry schools undiminished: 'Prince Nicolaus von Esterhazy ... founded and endowed a forestry school at Eisenstadt a few years ago.... All the students are given instructions in playing the horn.' (*Vaterländische Blätter für den Oesterreichischen Kaiserstaat* (Vienna, 1808), xxiv, p. 199.)

I The mounted hunt at Versailles, from a series of paintings now at Fontainebleau. Dating from the early years of the eighteenth century, they show the
cor-de-chasse in the fully-evolved form of the late seventeenth. An impression
of the mounted playing position may be gained from (a), as well as a good
view of the instrument in profile. The shape of the bell and mouthpiece can be
seen in (b). (*Conservateur du Musée du Chateau, Fontainebleau*)

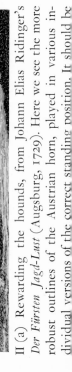

II (a) Rewarding the hounds, from Johann Elias Ridinger's *Der Fürsten Jagd-Lust* (Augsburg, 1729). Here we see the more robust outlines of the Austrian horn, played in various individual versions of the correct standing position. It should be

II (b) Mounted Huntsman with pack (the latter not shown), from Ridinger's *Jäger und Falkoniers* (1728). The wider bore of the Austrian instrument is noticeable here, and the mouthpiece is distinctly more steeply conical

mounted horn-players displayed on their instruments was as important to their lord as their prowess in the field. Soon an elaborate word-of-mouth tradition for playing the calls grew up, each hunt having its own special signals. This early code was to have far-reaching consequences upon the idiomatic use of the horn in early ballet and opera, and ultimately upon the early horn-playing style. One of the first mentions of this basic code of horn calls is found in Döbel's *Jäger Practica* of 1746.[1] 'I could well include here the notation for the various hunting-calls as they are played. These are best perceived, however, in actual practice, rather than from notes or descriptions here. For the hunting-calls are not played exactly from notes, nor in the manner of orchestral or church music; nor do Piano and Forte, Adagio and Allegro, and the like, enter into hunting-calls: on the contrary, for everything is blown with great force, mostly with double-tongued notes.' (See Ex. 1.) A good band of horn-players was a showpiece—it was a favourite

Ex. 1.

Zusammenrufen der Treiber.
Late 17th century Austrian.

Hase tot. Early 18th century Austrian.

boast of Sporck's that his Jagdmusik and Jägerchor had performed for Charles VI and August the Strong.

The hunt was not only a means of social display, but served an important purpose as a form of genuine relaxation as well. In this connection, too, the horn was an emblem of all that was pleasant in sport, music, and the out-of-doors. This has been well brought out by Hantsch when writing of the Imperial Vice-Chancellor Friederich Count Schönborn. 'In pleasant company, far from the distractions of city pleasures, he sought an ever-effective antidote against the bitter "court-pills" from which no one was spared. In the joys of the hunt, the sound of the horns, and in the enchanting music of the serenades he found a balance for the capricious moods of life at court.'[2]

In addition to these strong associations with royalty and the outdoor life of the privileged, the parforce hunt embodied certain moral and philosophical precepts which were basic to the ideals of the time. It is perhaps through these concepts that we may best perceive the strength of the horn's symbolic connotations when used in the concerted music of the period.

The introduction of the Parforcejagd to Bohemia and the Austrian

[1] Döbel, op. cit., iii, p. 105.
[2] Hugo Hantsch, *Reichsvizekanzler Friedrich Karl Graf von Schönborn* (Augsburg, 1929), p. 353.

dominions in the late seventeenth century occurred at a time when the courtly ideals of the Middle Ages were searching for new outlets which better suited the prosperity and worldliness of the late Baroque. The mounted hunt provided a perfect form for expressing these older ideals against the backdrop of sumptuous freedom which the nobility now enjoyed. The hunt stood for all that was desirable in worldly virtue,[1] representing a new embodiment of the older *ritterlich-höfisch* (chivalrous-courtly) ideals which were at the centre of aristocratic thought.[2] As the ceremonial and signal instrument of the hunt, the horn in turn became a symbol for these values. To a nobleman of the time the sound of the horn had the power to excite deep feeling, for it called forth those ideals and aspirations which lay at the very heart of the *adeliches Landleben*.

Ex. 2.   Keiser: *Octavia*

Corni de Chasse

Ex. 3.   Greeting Call. Early 18th century German.

Fanfare, Brandenburg Concerto No. 1.

Ex. 4.   Hunting-Call Figures: Quoniam, B Minor Mass.

etc.

Because of these rich associations the effect of the horn in concerted music was immediate and powerful. In its earliest appearances in opera and ballet the horn was thus a potent device for evoking outdoor atmosphere and an

[1] '*Tugend*', a fundamental concept in seventeenth-century Austrian aristocratic thought. 'Virtue' is an inexact equivalent at this period. For Günther and Sporck *Tugend* implied rather a more complex mixture of bravery, industry, honesty, and chivalry. The moral principles inherent in this concept were basic to the world of pre-Enlightenment nobility. *Tugend* occupies a prominent place in German lyrics from the time of the Minnesänger down to the early eighteenth century, when it came more to represent a continuation of medieval courtly ideals in the face of a changing system. For a fuller discussion see Brunner, *Adeliges Landleben und Europaeischer Geist* (Salzburg, 1949), pp. 75 ff.

[2] See Wolf Helmhard von Hohberg, *Georgica Curiosa oder Adelige Landleben* (Regensburg, 1687), xii; and Brunner, op. cit., for commentary.

aura of royalty. The fanfares from Keiser's *Octavia* of 1705 are good examples of this early colouristic usage; in the opening bars of the Brandenburg Concerto No. 1 of J. S. Bach, the horns sound the greeting-call of the hunt; and in the 'Quoniam' of the B Minor Mass the horn's affective connotation of worldly *Tugend* underscores the image of God marching into the world. (Exx. 2, 3, and 4.)

Sporck and the use of the horn as an orchestral instrument

The exact circumstances of how the horn came to be introduced into Sporck's house orchestra following his return to Bohemia in 1681 are not known. That the hunting-music at Lissa was soon equipped with the new instrument is evident not only from contemporary comment, but from the dates of the earliest extant horns made on this model by Haas of Nürnberg in 1682 and 1689,[1] and from the early appearance in print of hunting-songs. These tunes were based on French models which derived their melodic idiom from the horn's natural scale,[2] and were set to German texts which Sporck had commissioned. But for proof of the horn's earliest indoor use in consort with strings and woodwinds we must rely on those few documents which remain.

The first reference comes to us in a passage from van der Roxas's biography of Sporck of 1715 referred to earlier. To quote from p. 23: 'His other noble delectation was Music, in the cultivation of which it is possible to say without excessive praise that he knew no rival in Bohemia. The hunting-horns or so-called Waldhörner were introduced into this kingdom for the first time through his Excellency's agency and made known in his often noble, yea princely performances, whereby the Glory of the Princes of the Kingdom, the Honour of the entire Nobility and the Renown of the Land were greatly enhanced.' From this oblique and swollen prose (the style of

---

[1] Preserved in the Basle and Leipzig collections respectively. These instruments will be dealt with more fully in the following chapter.

[2] These collections of hunting-songs did not actually appear in print until a good ten years after they had become popular. They were issued as supplements to Sporck's theological publications such as *Christliche Gedancken auf Alle Tage des Monaths* (Prague, (Wickhart), 1701); and *Geistliche Wochen* (Prague, 1708). Most popular among these songs was the 'Bon-Repos Aria', named after Sporck's hunting-retreat: a French par-force-hunting melody whose text had been translated at Sporck's behest by the poet Gottfried Benjamin Hancke. By about 1700 this tune had already become a folk-song, and may still be heard in Bohemia and Saxony today. The Bon-Repos Aria was set by J. S. Bach to a text by Picander in his *Peasant Cantata*, with an accompaniment of violin, viola, continuo, and horn. Later these hunting-songs were printed as separate collections. One of these editions, the *Geistreiche Gesänge* (Schweidnitz, 1725), included verses of the Gospels set to the Bon-Repos Aria: these were to be sung in churches 'in Accompagnirung einiger musicalischer Instrumenten' as a means of imparting Scripture to the illiterate. We may with reason assume that the horn was amongst the accompanying instruments.

which was to lead Würzbach, writing in 1887, to dismiss van der Roxas as 'das geschmacklose Buch') it is clear that Sporck, after bringing the horn to Bohemia, made it known to the public through his 'noble, yea princely performances'. We are given no information as to the nature of these performances, of course, but presumably the elaborate ballets and concerts of instrumental music, for which Sporck was so well known, are meant here.[1] The early date of this biography lends credibility to van der Roxas's statement, and in view of the circumstances already described, together with the confirmation afforded by later evidence, we may safely accept this account at face-value. It is thus the earliest mention of the horn in a performing context in a German-speaking court, assuming that these first 'princely performances' were given in the early 1680s, as indeed this passage clearly implies.

Recently, two further records of the horn's early indoor employment have come to light, both of which are connected with Sporck.

Our first piece of evidence appears in the form of an opera libretto from the year 1708. It appears in a collection of poems, song lyrics, and libretti by the poet Johann von Besser entitled *Schrifften in Gebundener und Ungebundener Rede*, published at Leipzig in 1720. The title reads as follows:

The Marriage of Alexander and Roxana, presented in a Comic Opera at the Wedding of His Royal Majesty of Prussia and Her Highness Sophia Luyse, Duchess of Mecklenburg, etc., on 28 November 1708.

The actors in the Prologue are then enumerated, each group led on by a consort of instruments:

Six Macedonian Heroes, led on by six Hautboys ... [names follow, all courtiers] Six Persian Heroes, which are led on by six Waldhörner . . . The Music and Symphonies to the Opera composed by Herr Stricker,[2] Royal Chamber-Musician.

At the end of Act I the stage directions clearly show that the horns and oboes are meant to play together:

Roxane and Cleone leave the stage. The Macedonian and Persian Heroes draw up for the dance, the former led on by six Hautboys, the latter by six Waldhörner.

These twelve characters then unite in the 'entre act danse', probably with their counterpart instruments playing from the pit or behind the scenery—for to dance with any accuracy while playing a wind instrument is wellnigh impossible.

---

[1] Korrespondenz, 26 October 1724; 6 and 21 January 1725; 1 and 4 February 1725. See also Benedikt, op. cit., pp. 127–42.

[2] Bach's predecessor at Cöthen. He collaborated with Finger on the score of *Sieg der Schönheit über den Helden*.

Thus we have one of the very earliest records of horns and oboes being played together in a ballet ensemble. The likelihood that the horns in such a performance derived from Sporck's example is strengthened by his association with the author. Von Besser had spent some time at Bad Kukus a few years before, at one point enjoying Sporck's patronage:[1] and it is evident from many letters that Sporck was a frequent hunting-guest at the Prussian Court from the early 1680s onward.[2]

The second record of Sporck's precedence in using the horn in a mixed ensemble appears in connection with J. S. Bach's *Peasant Cantata*, in the form of several supporting documents. In the air, 'Es nehme zehntausend Ducaten', Bach sets the melody of Sporck's 'Brandeiser Jägerlied'[3] to a text by Picander, the Silesian poet whose verses had formed a part of Sporck's first edition of *Das Christliche Jahr* in 1725 (see page 15, footnote 1). The accompaniment of horn, violin, viola, and continuo which Bach uses in this

Ex. 5. a)   the 'Brandeiser Jägerlied' melody.

b)   'Es nehme zehntausend Ducaten' from Bach's Peasant Cantata.

Horn
in G

setting is that which Enders[4] cites as Sporck's favourite accompaniment for the arias sung to his bathing-guests at Bad Kukus[5] (Ex. 5). Recently yet another corroboration of the Waldhorn's early use as an accompanying instrument in these serenades has come to my attention. Christian Hofmann von Hoffmannswaldau, in discussing Hancke's translation of the French text

[1] Enders, op. cit., p. 23. Korrespondenz, 13 June 1730.

[2] Sporck's letters contain numerous entries concerning invitations to 'Jagdlustbarkeiten' on various hunting *reviers* belonging to Augustus the Strong. Sporck was his personal guest at the grand hunt following the Campement at Mühlberg. See the Korrespondenz for 20 June 1730.

[3] This tune appears repeatedly in Sporck's collections of hunting-songs and hymn melodies (see page 21, n. 2). It was printed on the back of the title-page to *Das Bonrepos-Büchlein* (Prague, 1721); appears with the 'Bon-Repos Aria' in *Kurtzer Begriff Derer . . . Schuldigkeiten, welche . . . alle Liebhaber Chiens Courrants oder Parforce-Jagd zu beobachten haben* (Prague, 1723); in *Der Gefangene und doch Vergnügte Jäger* (Prague, 1723), with Hancke's German text; and in the *Geistreiche Gesänge*, set to a sacred text. The complete set of twelve verses may be seen in *Gottfried Benjamin Hanckens . . . Weltliche Gedichte* (Dresden, 1727), pp. 144–7. This melody is well known in Saxony and Bohemia as the folk-song 'Frisch auf zum fröhlichen Jagen'.

[4] Enders, op. cit., p. 36. Also given in Benedikt, op. cit., p. 381, n. 26.

[5] This is further confirmed by Benedikt, op. cit., p. 381, from the archives of Sporck's personal correspondence. At Kukus the continuo was played on the harp.

of this hunting-melody, recalls: 'I have heard this [another hunting-song] as well as a French Hunting-Song which begins,

> Pour aller à la Chasse
> Faut être matineux

very often sung at Bad Kukus,[1] and in the French song there occurs the following Tutti:

> Tayeu, ho, ho, ho, ho,
>   bricolt mireau tous les
> Chiens qui nous faut.

This is sung at the end to the accompaniment of Waldhörner.' Hence there can be no doubt that this melody was sung to the accompaniment of horns in the serenades at Kukus.

We know that Bach was acquainted with Sporck and therefore doubtless knew the provenance of this melody. (Spitta tells us that Bach sent Sporck a copy of the Sanctus from the B Minor Mass in 1735.[2] Picander, in his dealings with Sporck, would have known the tune as well: and since the appearance of the horn in this obbligato context is unique at this period, we can but conclude from the circumstances that its inclusion with this particular melody was a deliberate tribute to Sporck on Bach's part.

The evidence presented in the foregoing pages suggests that Sporck may reasonably be accepted as the originator of consort horn-playing. It must be remembered that his part in bringing the horn indoors was solely that of a sponsor—though fortunately a sponsor whose lead in recognizing the horn's aptness for both hunting-field and concert-room was quickly followed by his peers. The musical credit for this innovation, as Benedikt has pointed out, is owing largely to Sporck's 'Capell-Meister und Küchel-Schreiber' Tobias Seemann. Professor Benedikt has kindly brought to my attention a letter of Seemann's in which mention is made of the Waldhorn in the house serenades at Bad Kukus, and of its use in the Sporck house orchestra from the earliest years.[3]

---

[1] The song referred to here is the so-called 'Brandeiser Jägerlied' which Bach used.

[2] Philipp Spitta, *Johann Sebastian Bach* (Leipzig, 1880), ii, pp. 523 ll., and pp. 656 ll.; also Friedrich Smend, 'Kritischer Bericht der neue Ausgabe der H-Moll Messe', in *Neue Ausgabe Sämtlicher Werke J. S. Bachs* (Kassel, 1956), Serie II, Band I, p. 124 and p. 166.

[3] Tobias Seemann to Count Friederich Grossa, 24 February 1727. Federal Archives, Prague, 24 chart. in cod., 1727. Seemann describes on p. 611 a volume of fifty arias about which Grossa had written to enquire, and remarks that these tunes, including the 'Bon Repos Aria' are used as settings for the Epistles and Gospels in Sporck's private chapel on Sundays and holy days. These airs are sung to the accompaniment of the organ 'and musical instruments such as the double bass, harp, violin, viola and violin-cello; the Hubertus-aria, however, is sung to sets of wind instruments and horns, which all together make a most agreeable harmony'.

In following these two decades of the horn's history from Sweda and Röllig's first lesson at Versailles in 1680 to the serenades at Bad Kukus and Lissa, we have witnessed not only the beginnings of the horn's orchestral career, but the founding of a style of horn-playing as well. With Sporck's return to Bohemia in 1681 the course of artistic horn-playing had begun. The cor-de-chasse was to remain solely a hunting-instrument in France; in fact, not until about 1750, when Bohemian descendants of Sporck's first horn-players reintroduced the transformed orchestral instrument, was the horn to appear on a permanent basis in French orchestras.

We must now take up the thread of the development of the cor-de-chasse as an instrument in the workshops of Vienna.

II

THE DEVELOPMENT
OF THE VIENNESE HORN
TO 1750

The Leichnambschneider brothers

THE role of the instrument-maker is highly important in the matter of instrumental style. He must translate the wishes of both player and composer into the instrument itself: and upon his interpretation the player, the composer, and finally the listener, are directly dependent for the sum total of nuances which we recognize as style in instrument-playing. Thus, through the instrument, the maker himself is responsible in a large measure for the tone quality which distinguishes a particular school of playing.

As in earlier years the great schools of violin-playing had each adopted a particular type of instrument for its characteristic sound—the Bolognese virtuosi choosing the brilliant and powerful Cremonese fiddles, the Viennese preferring the quieter sweetness of the Stainer and Tyrolean instruments for their more lyric style—so the Bohemian and Austrian horn-players were to build their style upon the Viennese Waldhorn of Johannes and Michael Leichnambschneider.

The Austrian school, and indeed all later Germanic horn-playing, stands greatly in the debt of these first Viennese horn-makers. In their hands the trenchant cor-de-chasse was transformed into the full-throated Waldhorn of the Austrian Baroque. Theirs were the first orchestral horns, and the first crooks; and they were the first makers to favour the keys of E flat and F as the most suitable and characteristic for the horn. Through two and a half centuries both players and makers of the Austrian school have kept to the basic horn tone which these gifted artisans established in the early 1700s. In this sense the brothers Leichnambschneider may be considered the first modern horn-makers.

Michael and Johannes Leichnambschneider were born in Osterberg, a village near Memmingen in a part of Swabia later allotted by Napoleon to Bavaria, in 1676 and 1679 respectively.[1] The parish church register does not

[1] Pfarrkirche Osterberg (Pfarramt Oberroth), Taufmatrikeln, Fol. I, pp. 30 and 43. Especial thanks are due here to the Vicar of Osterberg, Pater Franz Wanke, for making these documents available. The name Leichnambschneider appears in several variant spellings, such as Leichamschneider, Leichnamschneider, Leicham Schneider, etc.; but

record the trade of their father, Georg: and although Memmingen had enjoyed some importance as a centre of wind-instrument-making in the sixteenth century,[1] it is unlikely that the elder Leichnambschneider would have worked as an instrument-maker at this late period. In all probability he was an independent artisan belonging to a metal-working trade, for there was a strong tendency for families to keep to related crafts. This likelihood would strengthen the supposition that the Viennese copper-engraver Johann Leichnambschneider[2] was a relative of the Osterberg family, and might well have arranged for Johannes and Michael to come to the now-prospering Imperial capital to learn the trumpet-maker's trade. That the brothers served out their apprenticeships in Vienna is virtually certain; and from all indications they were most probably bound to the master trumpet-maker Hanns Geyer (c. 1640–9?).[3]

In their provincial origin the Leichnambschneiders typified the Viennese artisan of the later seventeenth century. Attracted by the prospect of plentiful jobs and easy money, artists and craftsmen of every description now flocked to Vienna from the fourteen nations of the Habsburg Crown, and indeed from all over Europe.[4] The source of this attraction lay in the Imperial city's new-found prosperity. With the final banishing of the Turkish hordes in 1683 Vienna embarked upon a programme of jubilant rebuilding, much as Prague had done half a century earlier. New palaces, churches, and

---

the spelling used in the text is that of the parish birth records. A medieval surname meaning literally a tailor to an undertaker (*Leichnam*=corpse or body, *Schneider*= tailor). By the seventeenth century the name Leichnambschneider had become rare, a fact which helps to trace our horn-makers.

[1] See Adolf Layer, 'Memminger Blasinstrumentenmacher des 16. Jahrhunderts' in *Memminger Geschichtsblätter* (Memmingen, 1961), p. 16.

[2] This third Viennese Leichnambschneider is known only through a passing entry in the parish marriage register of St. Stephen's Cathedral, dated 22 May 1747. 'Johann Leichnamschneider, Citizen and Copper-engraver, is a marriage-witness for Joseph von Hartmann, Lieutenant.' The original document is missing; but it is given in Albert Startzer (ed.), *Quellen zur Geschichte der Stadt Wien*, I. Abt., VI. Band (Vienna, 1908), No. 9128.

[3] See Langwill, op. cit., p. 39. To Langwill's list of instruments by Geyer should be added a tenor trombone dated 1687, now in Lambach Monastery, Upper Austria.

[4] Windisch-Graetz, in listing the nationalities represented by the enrolments in the Vienna Academy, points to this diversity of national origins as an index to Vienna's importance as an artistic centre during this period. 'In the first two years (following the establishment of the "Free Royal Academy of Painting, Sculpture, and Architecture" in 1726) there were 137 (students) from the Habsburg Crown Dominions, 43 from the Holy Roman Empire, 6 Swiss, 11 Italians, 2 Frenchmen, one Spaniard and three from the Low Countries. In the two succeeding years we meet 144 Habsburg subjects, 56 from the Empire, 4 Swiss, 12 Italians, 5 Frenchmen, two Spaniards and two Netherlanders, one Turk, and, remarkably enough, an American; as well as 21 of uncertain origin.' Franz Windisch-Graetz,'Jakob Christoph Schletterer, Die Plastiker Des Donner-Kreises und Die Wiener Akademie', in Feuchtmüller, R. (ed.), *Katalog der Paul Troger Austellung* (Vienna, 1963), p. 27.

government buildings sprang up within the city walls and on the meadows outside the gates. Graceful onion-towers and copper-green cupolas joined the remaining medieval spires and sedate gables of the older Vienna. Her importance as an architectural centre now eclipsed that of Rome; her attraction as a seat of art and music surpassed even Paris. Overnight, Vienna had become the cross-roads of a far-flung empire, where languages, blood-streams, and traditions met and mingled to form a culture as vibrantly original as it was astonishingly versatile. Small wonder, then, that it was a magnet to the provincial craftsman of the time.

It was to this buoyant Vienna that Michael and Johannes Leichnamb-schneider came in about 1695. No record of their apprenticeship has as yet come to light. It is likely, however, that Hanns Geyer was their master, if only from the fact that his manner of ornamenting mouthpipes with multiple scores, and collars with a double *cavetto* bordered by multiple scores, is much in evidence on the early Leichnambschneider instruments. Following their five or six years of apprenticeship, the brothers appear to have set up shop together in about 1700—Michael would have been 24, Johannes 21 years of age. (It is, of course, possible that Michael may have come to Vienna a few years before Johannes, completed his apprenticeship and established himself about 1697. At any rate, they appear to have joined forces by 1700.) Their shop and living-quarters were in the Naglergasse, the traditional street of the trumpet-makers.

Trade must have grown quickly for the brothers, for in 1701 we have the first evidence of independence and professional solidity: Michael, now a free citizen, marries one Maria Thallheimer. The marriage is recorded in the parish register of St. Stephen's Cathedral (Nr. 7164. 1701, Oktober).[1] 'Michael Leichnambschneider, Bürger und Trompetenmacher, zu Osterberg in Schwaben geb., Mariam Thallheimerin, eines Bäckers Tochter.' As the parish records for this period are practically complete, it is reasonably certain that the younger brother, Johannes, did not marry, and that the trumpet-maker Franz Leichnambschneider was therefore the son of Michael.

The Waldhorn and the cor-de-chasse compared

It was in about the year 1700 that the Leichnambschneiders evolved the first Viennese Waldhörner from the cor-de-chasse, a development which proved to be the most important single contribution of their career. (Caution must, of course, be taken in assigning too precise a date to a process so organic as the development of a musical instrument: but there exists sound documentary and historical support for the assertion that the basic Waldhorn model was arrived at within a few years of the beginning of the eighteenth century.) Before examining the circumstances underlying this transforma-

[1] Also cited in Startzer, op. cit., vol. VI.

tion, however, let us briefly outline the principal differences between the Waldhorn and the cor-de-chasse, and acquaint ourselves with their basic properties.

When the two types of instrument are compared physically, there appears to be little difference between them (Plates IIIa and IIIb). Upon closer inspection, however, it is immediately evident that the cor-de-chasse is the narrower and more slender of the two, and that the Waldhorn presents a more robust aspect generally. This impression is borne out when the instruments are compared in detail. (A sufficient number of instruments of the period 1700–30 from which to arrive at a true average of measurements is not available. The following dimensions are therefore taken from some typical examples.) There is a noticeable difference in the size of the mouthpipe opening between the two types. The cor-de-chasse mouthpipe inlet is smaller in diameter, measuring 5·5 mm. (Cretien, c. 1720, Paris Conservatory C 578 E 890) as against the Viennese prototype's 7·7 mm. (M. Leichnambschneider, 1718, Basle, Historisches Museum 1878.22). Since the tubing in the corpus of both types is conical throughout its length, it is difficult to speak of the bore as such; but the tubing of the Waldhorn is proportionately larger in diameter, as a glance at the photographs will show.

The most striking difference between the two instruments, however, will be observed in the profile of the bell. In the cor-de-chasse the neck of the bell leaves the corpus of the horn as a cylindrical section, beginning a gradual expansion just above the stay; from the stay downward the throat forms a steep cone which expands in an unbroken parabola to the bell rim. The Viennese bell exhibits a markedly different profile. At the point where the upper end of the neck leaves the corpus it is noticeably larger than that of the cor-de-chasse. Unlike the French bell, there is no cylindrical section; instead, the neck opens gradually to join the throat just below the stay. The throat itself is considerably wider than that of the cor-de-chasse. The expansion through the throat is more rapid; and although this section at first glance would appear to be a straight cone, as is the cor-de-chasse throat, the faintest curve continues through its length. At the lower end of the throat the abrupt flare of the bell mouth begins. This is a distinct section in itself, as opposed to the mouth of the cor-de-chasse bell, which expands as a constant parabola, continuing the curve of the lower throat until it reaches the bell rim. The curve of the Waldhorn's bell mouth is swept sharply outward until it is caught by the rim, by which point the curve approaches a perpendicular to the axis of the tubing. These contours have a pronounced effect upon the musical properties of the instruments, and in their respective differences lies the origin of the tonal qualities for which each type is distinctive.

The tone of the cor-de-chasse is brilliant, penetrating, trenchant, evocative of the trumpet's martial quality. The Waldhorn, although it shares

much of the French instrument's brilliance at this early period, is nevertheless considerably broader and darker in sound, having fewer overtones in its
tonal spectrum (modes or partials in the acoustician's language) than the
cor-de-chasse. This darker and softer quality was to become more pronounced in the Viennese horn as time went on. Because of its affinity with
the growing romanticism of the later eighteenth century, this quality was in
a large measure responsible for the popularity which the horn enjoyed as a
solo instrument during that period: and in its ultimate development in the
valve horn of the early Romantic period, the Viennese horn tone became the
ideal upon which the modern Germanic styles are based.[1] But, as we have
said, the germ of this ideal was already evident in the first Leichnambschneider Waldhörner. With the appearance of these instruments the
supremacy of the Viennese model in the German-speaking lands seems to
have been established from the outset. The French instrument as such was
abandoned, and the Viennese pattern adopted increasingly by makers in
other cities as time went on. Let us now examine the circumstances, both
historical and musical, under which the transformation of the cor-de-chasse
came about.

The development of the Waldhorn

When we consider that Count Sporck had established the cor-de-chasse in
Bohemia and its neighbouring dominions by the mid-1680s, it is surprising
that no Austrian model of the instrument was developed until 1700: especially so in view of the fact that the Bohemian nobles, and indeed all the
provincial aristocrats, came to Vienna to attend at Court while the Emperor
was in residence from October to April.[2] For this purpose the nobility
maintained substantial palaces at Vienna, to which they transferred the
entire staff of their country residences for the season, including, of course,
the house orchestra. Sporck, with his high rank and important connections
at Court, made no exception to this practice, as the correspondence shows;
and with his horn-players thus spending several months of the year in the
capital, there would have been ample opportunity for the Viennese trumpet-
makers to acquaint themselves with the cor-de-chasse, and ultimately to
evolve their own model. Indeed, it is only in terms of these facts that the
origin of the Viennese Waldhorn may logically be explained. It is beyond
doubt that the cor-de-chasse first came to the Leichnambschneider workshop
(or more probably to that of their master Hanns Geyer) in the hands of
Sporck's horn-players, Röllig and Sweda.

However, the events of Sporck's career at this period help to account

[1] Under this heading we may include the present-day German, Dutch, American,
Italian, and possibly the Russian schools of horn-playing.
[2] Vehse, op. cit., pp. 291 ff.

for the Viennese horn's late development. He was named Viceroy of Bohemia in 1690 and created Privy Counsellor to the Emperor in 1691. Only
then did he begin to take up residence in Vienna during the Court season.[1]
Thus Sporck's significant connection with the Viennese Court begins within
a few years of the first extant Leichnambschneider horns. This fact, coupled
with the evidence afforded by the surviving instruments, suggests that the
advent of the Viennese Waldhorn falls within the decade before 1700; and
leaves little doubt that it was he who first brought the cor-de-chasse to
Vienna.

When comparing the Waldhorn's properties with those of the cor-de-
chasse, the question quite naturally arises as to the musical reasons underlying the changes which are evident in the Viennese instrument. Why did
the Leichnambschneiders consider it necessary to redesign the cor-de-
chasse, and to change its tonal character to such a marked degree? The
answer lies in the basic tonal ideal of the Austrian Baroque, to which contemporary stringed instruments can provide us with a reliable guide. If we
compare a violin by any of the prominent Viennese violin-makers with a
a Cremonese or Brescian instrument of the period, we are immediately
aware of its much quieter and darker tone. The same is true of the lower
stringed instruments. A double bass by Antony Posch, for instance (lute- and
violin-maker to Joseph I and Charles VI from 1705 to c. 1739), has not the
silken clarity of an Amati bass: its rounder, more velvety sound is rather the
'dicker Klang' of which Mattheson speaks.[2] This preference for softness as
against brilliance in orchestral timbre was perhaps best typified by the
stringed instruments of Johann and Andreas Stainer, as witnessed by the fact
that virtually every major monastery throughout the Crown lands possessed
a complete set of their instruments during this period. But perhaps the soft
consonants and dark vowels of the Austrian speech are as sure a proof as any
of this natural inclination towards softness in instrumental sound.

To the Austrian, and particularly to the Viennese ear of the time, the
cor-de-chasse would have been too bright in tone colour. While the French
horn made an admirable effect as a hunting-instrument or when sounding
fanfares in the orchestra, its tone quality was too incisive to blend with
the *Klangkörper* of a Viennese instrumental consort of this period. This

[1] Correspondence, 1691, to Count von Vrbna; to the Stadthalterei, 14 July 1700; and
Benedikt, op. cit., pp. 78 ff.

[2] Johann Georg Mattheson, *Das Neu-Eröffnete Orchestre* (Hamburg, 1713), p. 286.
The proximity of the principal horn desk to that of the principal double-bass has given
the writer the opportunity for a first-hand comparison of the two instruments mentioned.
The one, an Andreas Amati dated 1587, belongs to Signor Giuseppe Landi of the Palazzo
Pitti chamber orchestra at Florence; the other, made by Antony Posch in 1730, is in the
possession of Count Nikolaus d'Harnoncourt at Vienna, and is used regularly in the
Concentus Musicus ensemble. Especial thanks are due to the owners of both these instruments for permission to examine them in detail.

discrepancy in colour would no doubt have concerned the Leichnamb-schneiders; and in carrying out their first commissions to copy the newly popular 'Jäger-Hörner' (whether at Sporck's behest or for a Viennese noble is not known—these first Waldhörner may well have been ordered for the hunting band of Leopold I), they set about reconciling the instrument's sound with the tonal ethos which they knew.

The development of the Waldhorn appears to have won immediate recognition for the Leichnambschneiders. Early in their career the brothers began to receive commissions for this new instrument from the rich Lower Austrian monasteries. This may be inferred from the fact that many of the extant documents concerning the Leichnambschneiders' trade are to be found in the archives of the monasteries Zwettl and Göttweig. The appearance of these records in this connection is in itself significant, for the great monasteries spared no expense in obtaining the best possible instruments for their orchestras. In their inventories names such as Stainer, Amati, Haas, and Denner appear side by side: thus it is an index to the quality of the Leichnambschneider instruments that the surviving documents relating to them should appear in three of the most musical of the great Austrian monasteries.

It is generally agreed that interchangeable crooks for altering basic pitch were first applied to the horn in Vienna. No basis for this assumption, however, has been known up to now, apart from the general practice of referring to the earliest system of master-and-coupler terminal crooks as 'Viennese crooks'. Furthermore, no date for the introduction of crooks to the horn has as yet been authenticated; but Blandford, with characteristic insight, says in his article, 'The French Horn in England',[1] that 'proper concert horns with crooks . . . appear to have originated at Vienna before 1718; and Bach had a set at his disposal at Cöthen, if the inventory of the Capelle can be trusted'.[2] Indeed, the place and date of the first use of crooks on the horn has been a matter for considerable discussion amongst both scholars and horn-players.

A document which contains what is undoubtedly the first mention of crooks as applied to the horn has recently come to hand. It is a bill to the Abbot of Kremsmünster, dating from the year 1703 and written in Michael Leichnambschneider's own hand. The bill reads as follows:

[1] *Musical Times*, August 1922.
[2] See Rudolph Bunge, 'Johann Sebastian Bach's Kappelle zu Cöthen und deren nachgelassene Instrumenten' in *Bach-Jahrbuch* (Leipzig, 1905). On p. 38 a list of horns is given. Blandford here refers to the item, 'Krummbogen, Setzstück sind im Hirsch'. (The Hart: an inn with a concert-room where the instruments had been kept for some years before this inventory was made.) Exactly how long a set of horns with crooks had been in the orchestra at Cöthen is not stated in the inventory: but one sees no reason to mistrust it.

List

What I have made as follows

Firstly 1 pair great new Hunting-Horns [Jägerhorn] at 34 Gulden
Item 4 new double Crooks ['Krumbögen']   7 Gulden
Further 4 new Shanks ['Stickel' = Stücklein: tuning shanks]
Further 2 new mouthpieces, each one 30 Kreuzer makes 1 Gulden
    For the case thereto is 1 Gulden.
                     Summa 43 Gulden 36 Kreuzer
Honorius Abbot   Michael Leichnamschneider
                                  Burgher, Trumpet and Horn-Maker

A pair of 'great new' horns, a set of four new 'double crooks', a pair of mouthpieces and tuning-shanks for the set, all fitted in one case: there can be no possible doubt that the crooks (no doubt doubly wound) are intended for these horns and no other instruments. Not only does this document contain the first mention of horn crooks as such, but it represents the first known reference to the orchestral horn as well, at a date much earlier than that commonly ascribed to the appearance of the horn as an orchestral instrument.

It is interesting to note that the term 'Jägerhorn' is used here to mean an orchestral horn with crooks. This would furnish additional proof that the High German term 'Waldhorn' had not as yet supplanted the dialect word 'Jägerhorn' in the horn-makers' vocabulary at this time:[1] a further deterrent to those who would impose an iron-clad nomenclature upon these terms.[2] It must be stressed that the horn with crooks was devised solely and exclusively for use in the orchestra or instrumental ensemble. The mounted horn-player has no need to change the pitch of his horn while playing in the hunt: in fact, a crooked horn would be a decided inconvenience to him while controlling his horse, as crooks tend to come adrift even when the player is stationary. (The author's own experience with playing crooked horns in both of these situations has borne out the truth of this statement!) The crooked horn, having no place in the hunting-field, was purely an orchestral instrument from the outset.

[1] The Lower Austrians seem to agree on the use of the term 'Jägerhorn', at this date at least, as is apparent from the following records (Arch, Gott., loc. cit., Nr. 93): 'several Trombones, Trumpets, and Horns [Jägerhorn] repaired—.51' (Rent Amts Rechnung, 1709, Nr. 93): 'April 1709: . . . further, two Horns [Jägerhorn] repaired . . . —.30.   Joh. Wäbl
                                                 Registered Plumber.'
(Wäbl was a plumber in Krems, a town on the bank of the Danube opposite Göttweig. His repairs were no doubt of an elementary nature; indeed, the practice of giving out simpler brass-instrument repairs to a local plumber seems to have been fairly common in provincial courts.)
[2] See *Galpin Society Journal*, No. XVI, pp. 33 ff.

The second document again concerns a pair of 'Jagerhörner'. They were made for the Prelate of Zwettl, and this is a receipt for payment. The entry reads: 'Zwettl Archive, addenda to the Viennese invoices, 24 November 1708. Joannes Leichnambschneider, Trumpet and Horn-maker, acknowledges the receipt of 28 Gulden for two Jägerhörner supplied to the Prelate.'

Another bill to the Abbot of Göttweig from the year 1709 shows that Leichnambschneider's new model was establishing itself in the best monastery orchestras.

Statement

I the undernamed have completed
for His Grace my Lord the Prelate
of Göttweig the following articles
As
1. 6th September 1709. One pair Hunting-
        Horns...............32 Gulden
2. One pair Crooks [Krumpögen] .... 2 Gulden
               —————
           Total 34 Gulden

This invoice has been paid   Michael Leichamschneider
to me with thanks by the   Trumpet and Horn-maker manupropria
 Paymaster.

Here again the designation 'krumpögen' (Krummbögen-crooks) is unmistakable. It can only mean a pair of wound terminal crooks for the pair of horns listed. The possibility that the crooks might have been intended for use with a trumpet is ruled out by the fact that the horns and crooks are both referred to in pairs, made up as a matched set and delivered on the same date, 7 September.

In the light of these records Michael Leichnambschneider appears not only as the probable originator of horn crooks but as the possible inventor of the orchestral horn. Although the bill from the year 1703 cited above is the first written record of these innovations, the practice of fitting crooks to the horn may well have preceded this date by two or three years. Crooks, after all, had been used on the trumpet since well before Praetorius's day,[1] and the principle of changing the basic pitch of a brass instrument by means of inserted lengths of tubing was well known.

Michael Leichnambschneider's orchestral horn did not immediately supersede the Waldhorn of fixed pitch, although the crooked horn appears to have found widespread acceptance early in the period. Horns of fixed pitch continued in general use until well after 1750, as the Cöthen inventory

---

[1] *Syntagma Musicum*, II (Wolfenbüttel, 1619), Tafel VIII, Fig. 13.

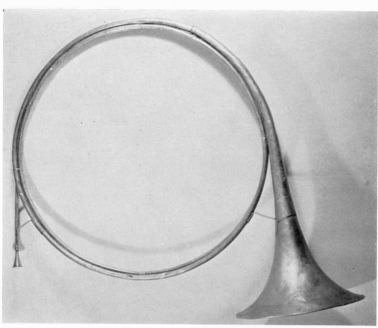

III (b) Parforce-Jagdhorn, Johann Grinwolt, Prague, 1735. (*National Museum, Prague*). See p. 29.

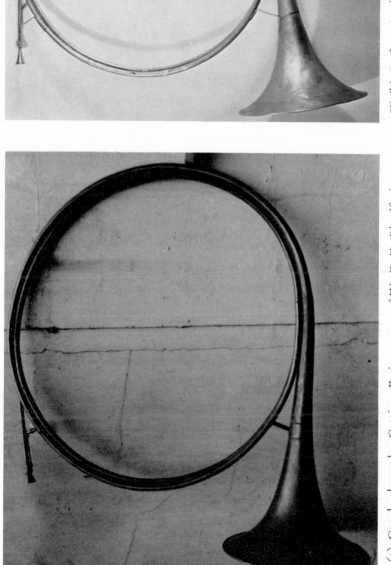

III (a) Cor-de-chasse by Cretien, Paris, *c.* 1720. (*W. F. H. Blandford per Eric Halfpenny*). See p. 29.

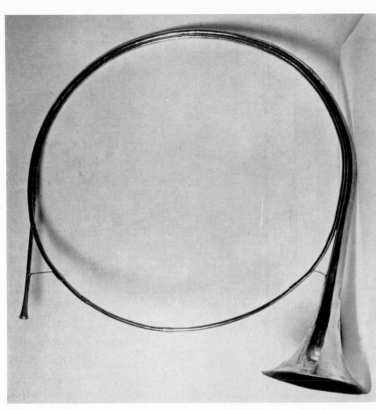

IV (b) Parforce-Jagdhorn in F, Johannes Leichnambschneider, Vienna, 1710. The earliest Viennese horn known to survive. (*Kunsthistorisches Museum, Vienna*). See p. 35.

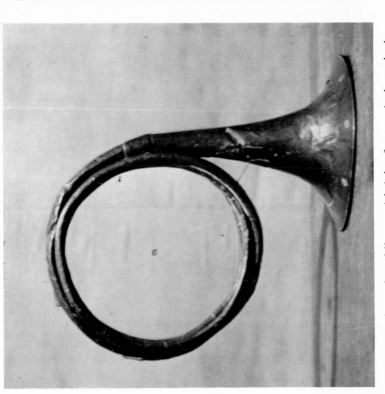

IV (a) Orchestral Waldhorn with inlet for terminal crooks by Michael Leichnambschneider, 1721. Possibly one of Johannes Thürrschmidt's instruments. (*Dr. Volcker von Volckamer, Schloss Harburg*). See p. 35.

shows.[1] A crookless orchestral model of fixed pitch was soon evolved, of which an example by Michael Leichnambschneider dated 1721 exists (Plate IVa). This type differed from the grand Parforce-Waldhorn in that it was quadruply wound in order to obtain the smaller coil diameter which made for convenience in indoor playing. It should be noted that the large-hooped hunting-horn, the crooked orchestral horn and this smaller horn of fixed pitch all were built on the same bell pattern: and apart from the slightly softer quality which resulted from winding the tubing several times upon itself, there was no difference in the basic sound of these three types.

The Character of the Waldhorn

The Leichnambschneiders continued to make the large-hooped Parforce-Waldhorn as well as the two orchestral types. The year 1710 furnishes us with an excellent example of this basic Viennese Waldhorn, now in the Sammlung Alter Musikinstrumenten of the Kunsthistorisches Museum in Vienna (No. 118511). It is made of brass and bears on its bell garland the inscription, 'MACHT JOHANNES LEICHAMSCHNEIDER IN WIENN 1710'. It is worth our while to examine both the physical and musical properties of this horn in some detail, for it occupies an important place in the history of the instrument. This Leichnambschneider horn is the earliest dated example of the Viennese type, and may be considered the archetype of the Baroque Waldhorn.

This superb instrument is built in the F of the period, a fact whose significance in connection with the music of the time will be discussed in a subsequent chapter. Recently the restoration of this instrument was completed by the Viennese horn-maker Anton Cižek, with this writer advising on historical points. The mouthpipe was missing, but the gradation of the tubing pointed unmistakably to a mouthpipe inlet of 7.8 mm. in diameter. The bell diameter is 21.5 cm. The profile of the bell is typical of the Leichnambschneider cut, and may be clearly seen on Plate IV(b). The inside of the bell is lacquered black. (Here it is interesting to note that the elaborate floral decorations and geometric designs with which the later French horn bells

---

[1] The Cöthen inventory of 1773 lists the following horns of fixed pitch:

30) 2 G Horns, J. G. Eichendopf, 1733.
31) 2 E flat Horns, J. H. Eichendopf. (Eichendorf)
32) 2 Hats containing Horns [explained in Morley-Pegge, op. cit., pp. 14 and 145].
33) 2 E Horns.
34) 2 C Horns, wound in black cord.
35) 2 F Horns, wound in black.

The fact that these horns appear in the inventory of the house orchestra, as opposed to that of the hunt, would indicate that they are orchestral horns of fixed pitch. (Herzogl. Haus- und Staatsarchiv, Cöthen, St. 12, Nr. 68. Quoted in Bunge, op. cit., pp. 38 and 39.)

were frequently ornamented are not to be found on the Austrian bells at any period. As in this example, the early Austrian bells were lacquered black—a practice carried over from the early cors-de-chasse—but later in the century, when the French bells glowed with gilt decorations on coloured-lacquer backgrounds, the Austrians left their bells plain.)

There has long been a tendency amongst writers to dismiss the tone of the Baroque horn as a less-than-pleasant shriek. This notion seems to have originated with Gerber as early as 1789. Referring to the instrument of the pre-hand-horn period, Gerber remarks, 'Im Zimmer es aber hören zu lassen, dazu war damals sein Ton noch viel zu rauh.'[1] Blandford speaks of the Baroque horn's 'Handelian blare',[2] and even Morley-Pegge relaxes his usual careful sympathy with the early horn when he refers to its 'eldritch screech'.[3]

None of these writers seems actually to have heard a Baroque horn, however: and with the exception of Gerber, they appear to have constructed their ideas of the early horn's qualities upon latter-day attempts to play the Baroque parts upon modern valve instruments. Their censure is all the more understandable in view of the fact that only in the past few years has the value of contemporary musical instruments as documentary evidence in the performance of earlier music come to be appreciated. While historical instruments of other categories have been studied in performance, particularly the strings, no detailed examinations appear to have been carried out on the horn of the pre-1750 period.

This writer has had the good fortune to conduct extensive performing trials both in private and on the concert platform, using the Leichnamb-schneider horn described above and other horns of the period. It is hoped that the results of these trials, which will be recorded here and in the following relevant chapters, will serve to clear away much of the misunderstanding which has grown up around the horn of Bach's time. The information gained from playing the Leichnambschneider horn under discussion here is of particular value because of its position as the earliest surviving example of the Viennese Waldhorn.[4]

Once the author's embouchure had accustomed itself to the old mouthpiece and instrument, the fallacy of these negative judgements was obvious. The tone of this Leichnambschneider Parforce-Waldhorn is clear and surprisingly full. Although the sound is distinctly more evocative of the hunting-field than of the music-room, it has none of the harshness for which the Baroque horn has been so often condemned. This is undoubtedly the quality

[1] See Appendix, p. 221.   [2] op. cit., p. 9.   [3] op. cit., p. 86.

[4] Especial thanks are due to Direktor Dr. Victor Luithlen, curator of the Sammlung Alter Musikinstrumenten in the Kunsthistorisches Museum, Vienna, for his kind permission to use the photograph of this instrument given on Plate IV, and to use the instrument itself in making these trials. A mouthpiece of *c.* 1720 was used.

of Mattheson's 'lieblich-pompeusen Waldhörner'.[1] Although some of the brassy qualities of the cor-de-chasse are present here, the tone of this early Leichnambschneider horn is nevertheless unmistakably distinguished by the broad, soft quality which has marked the Austrian sound down to the present day.

Each register of this early instrument's compass has its own character. The lower octave is distinctly bassoon-like in the grainy texture of its tone; the smoothness of the middle octave forespeaks the hand-horn quality; and the upper range is bright and round. So distinctly horn-like and individual is the character of this upper register that there can be no question of the horn's substitution for the trumpet on the grounds of identical tone quality, as has so often been assumed. The horn and trumpet were separate and distinct instruments in the Baroque period, as indeed they were in all periods; and a comparison of contemporary instruments will quickly prove, even to the untrained ear, that the horn and trumpet were by no means identical in tone, even though they may have been musically interchangeable to a certain degree. The Baroque, with its insistence upon contrast as an aesthetic principle, would not have tolerated any blurring of the demarcation between one instrumental quality and another, especially as this fidelity of colour was so vital to the essentially polyphonic texture of the contemporary orchestra.

This Leichnambschneider horn seems to respond best when played within the dynamic range between forte and fortissimo. (These markings are relative: the decibel value of each dynamic degree is much less on instruments of this period than on modern instruments.) This preference on the early horn's part for being played at the louder end of its dynamic scale would bear out Döbel's remarks quoted in Chapter I.

It is interesting to note that the eleventh partial lies slightly flat and the thirteenth slightly sharp. Especially with horns made before about 1750, this feature seems to reveal a conscious effort on the part of the maker to aid the intonation of the f″ and a″ (written pitch) at a time before hand-stopping was used, if known at all. This characteristic is not so pronounced on later horns.

When considering the opulent brilliance of the early Waldhorn's tone in connection with the contemporary philosophical ideals of courtly chivalry or *Tugend* discussed in the first chapter, it is readily seen why the horn became so popular within a few years after this model was introduced. Indeed, the excellence of the Leichnambschneider instruments must have done much to spark the popularity which the Waldhorn enjoyed in Vienna. Lady Mary Wortley Montague, in describing her experiences in the Vienna of 1717, tells us that 'they (the ballrooms of the great houses) are very

[1] Mattheson, op. cit., p. 267.

magnificently furnished, and the music good, if they had not that detestable custom of mixing hunting horns with it, that almost deafen the company. But that noise is so agreeable here, they never make a concert without them.'[1] Whatever Lady Mary's opinion of the horn's merits, her remarks leave no doubt that the horn had already won a position of prominence in Viennese musical life at that time.

The next document concerning the Leichnambschneiders dates from 1710, the same year as the Parforce-Waldhorn we have just examined. Although this document does not concern the brothers' horn-making trade specifically, it is nevertheless worth quoting. It affords a last brief glimpse of their private lives; but it requires comment and comparison if it is not to be construed as a source for confusing the identity of the two brothers. Again we draw upon the parish records of St. Stephen's Cathedral in Vienna (Heiraths-Urkunden, 1710, Nr. 7890). The entry is dated 15 June. 'Franz Pecler, Painter, born at Neudorf in Bohemia, residing in Butiani's house in the Renngasse, [marries] Maria Catharina Koch, of the same address, daughter of Peter Andreas Koch, Painter and Citizen, and Maria Cunegunda. Witness, Johann Michael Leichnambschneider Trumpet-maker.'

At first glance it might appear from this record that Johann Michael Leichnambschneider was one person, particularly as the designation 'Trompetenmacher' appears to be in the singular, as does the word 'Zeuge' (witness). It must be recalled, however, that in early eighteenth-century German the singular and plural of nouns often took the same form. (An example of this usage already noted occurs in the case of the word Horn, whose plural at this period is simply Horn, as against the later plural form of Hörner). Should any doubt arise as to the separate identity of Johannes and Michael Leichnambschneider, attention is once again drawn to the record of christening in the Osterberg parish church which unmistakably identify each brother under his respective Christian name (see page 26).

From the year 1713 two instruments survive, both by the elder brother, Michael. The first is in the Sammlung Alter Musikinstrumente in the Museum für Hamburgische Geschichte at Hamburg. This horn is listed in Schröder's catalogue[2] as 'Waldhorn. Twice-wound. On the bell the designation, "MACHT MICHAEL LEICHAMSCHNEIDER 17 WIENN 13".' The only information we have concerning this instrument, which was destroyed in the hostilities of 1939–45, appears in Schröder's description and measurements. He gives the diameter of the coils as 47 cm., and the diameter of the bell as 23·5 cm. It may be estimated that the horn was pitched

---

[1] Lady Mary Wortley Montague, *Letters of the Right Honourable Lady M——y W——y M——e* (London, 1763), I, p. 108 (Letter XX, 10 January 1717).
[2] Hans Schröder, *Verzeichnis der Sammlung Alter Musikinstrumente* (Hamburg, 1930), p. 54.

in the F of the period; and this would again point to the Leichnambschneiders' preference for this key.

In the Conservatoire collection in Brussels are two Waldhörner by Michael
Leichnambschneider, again dated 1713. Although the writer has not as yet
had the opportunity to examine these instruments, it is evident from
Mahillon's description that they are of exceptionally fine workmanship.[1]
Some unclarity has arisen concerning the identity of these instruments, both
on Mahillon's part and on that of Wilhelm Kleefeld.[2] Kleefeld writes, 'The
Brussels collection contains two Trompes de Chasse in E and E flat which
bear the mark, "Macht Michael Leicham Schneider in Wien 1713". According to Mahillon we have here the form of the hunting trumpet as it appeared
shortly after the time of its introduction into Germany. Considering the
unstable pitch of the period, it is possible that both were issued as D
trumpets. Mahillon considers the designation "Tromba" to be more accurate
than "Horn" since these instruments are strongly reminiscent of Praetorius's "Jäger Trommet".'[3]

It should be obvious to us today that two instruments made in Vienna
in the same year and pitched a semitone apart could not have been 'issued'
as having the same pitch. The question, of course, arises as to the sources of
the original commissions for these instruments: we do not know whether
they were both intended for use in Vienna, or each for a separate court whose
orchestral pitch may well have been a law unto itself. It is to be hoped that
more information as to the provenance of these horns may be forthcoming;
for the present, however, we must accept these pitches at face-value, that
is, a semitone apart in the contemporary Viennese tuning of F and E.

Kleefeld refers to these instruments as 'trompes de chasse', as does
Mahillon. Although Mahillon gives us no measurements to help in identifying these instruments, it is clear from the French designation that these
horns are undoubtedly Parforce-Waldhörner of the standard Leichnambschneider type. Their resemblance to the Jäger-Trommet of Praetorius lies
solely in their coiled form.

A document from the year 1714 in Michael Leichnambschneider's own
hand has come to the author's attention through the kind offices of the
Stiftsarchivar of Göttweig Monastery, Pater Emmeran Ritter, O.S.B. It
dates from the year 1714, but mentions a service rendered to the monastery
in the preceding year.[4]

[1] Victor Charles Mahillon, *Catalogue Descriptif et analytique du Musée Instrumental du
Conservatoire Royal de Musique de Bruxelles* (Brussels, 1896), II, p. 389.
[2] Wilhelm Kleefeld, 'Das Orchester in der Hamburger Oper, 1678–1738, in *Sammelbände der Internationalen Musikgesellschaft* (Leipzig, 1900), Band I, Theil 2, pp. 279–83.
[3] Michael Praetorius, *De Organographica (Syntagma Musicum*, II) (Wolfenbüttel, 1619),
Tafel VIII, Nr. 11.
[4] Arch Gott RAR, 1714.

Statement

What I the undernamed have made for his Grace my Lord the Prelate of Göttweig, as follows	fl	xr
1713: The 28th April 2 brass Mouthpieces	1	//
1714: The 26th June a pair of Horns repair'd, for which	//	54
The 30th ditto a pair of Horns repair'd	/2	15
The 10th April a Trumpet repair'd, and a new Crook made	//	51
The 14th ditto a new pair of Horns made	32	//

This has been properly paid   Total 37 Gulden

Michael Leichamschneider

manupropria

Registered Trumpet and Horn Maker
at Vienna in Nailsmith's Lane.

This autograph is important on several counts. It provides us with information about Michael's activities as a horn-maker at this early period; it confirms this writer's supposition that the Leichnambschneider workshop was located in the Naglergasse; and it proves that the material of which a mouthpiece was made was of importance to the maker. But perhaps most importantly this bill, together with the document from the year 1709 cited earlier, furnishes a valuable insight into the character of this gifted and original artisan by virtue of the fact that both appear in his own hand. When the author showed this bill to Dr. Roberto Kayselitz of the Kunsthistorisches Museum in Vienna, he estimated its date at first glance to be after 1780. After closer inspection which disclosed the dates 1713 and 1714 in Leichnambschneider's hand, his reaction was one of admiration at the progressive and, for that period, modern form which the letters of Michael's script exhibited. Indeed, the artistic quality and fineness of form in this handwriting are unmistakable: we cannot but recognize the creative mind behind it.

Johannes Leichnambschneider, the younger brother, comes to our attention again at this point through the agency of an invoice dated 1718. This document appears in connection with the monastery at Zwettl. As the original is missing, recourse was had to the Österreichische Kunsttopographie in which it is reproduced.[1] '20 August. Johannes Leichnambschneider, Trumpet Maker, acknowledges that he has received 29 Gulden for a pair of Trumpets.' While this invoice does not relate specifically to Johannes'

[1] Paul Büberl (ed.), *Österreichische Kunsttopographie* (Vienna, 1940), xxix, p. 309. See also p. 307.

horn-making trade, it does point to the fact that he continued to receive commissions from the major monasteries. We have already noted Johannes' great skill as a horn-maker in the foregoing description of his Parforce-Waldhorn dated 1710. Let us now examine a similar instrument by Michael Leichnambschneider which dates from the year 1718.

This later horn is now in the Historisches Museum at Basle (No. 1878.22). It bears the inscription, 'MACHT MICHAEL LEICHAMSCHNEIDER 17 IN WIENN 18'. The instrument is notable not only for its fine workmanship but for its exceptional state of preservation, and thus affords an unusually complete working example of the Leichnambschneider model.[1]

The workmanship of this horn is of a very high order, as we have observed before, and its general appearance would suggest a slight advance over the example dated 1710 by Johannes, if only because of the larger bell and twice-wound corpus. The dimensions, however, fall within the standard limits of the Viennese model. The diameter of the coils is 45·6 cm. The mouthpipe inlet measures 7·7 mm.; and as the mouthpipe is the original one, this measurement may be taken as an indication of the standard mouthpipe for this type and period. The bell diameter of 24·6 cm. represents an increase of 3·1 cm. over the earlier instrument of 1710. The horn is pitched in the F of the period.

The musical characteristics are much those of the Johannes Leichnamb-schneider instrument of 1710. But here again this horn appears to represent a decided development over the earlier instrument in that it is capable of taking a true fortissimo without overblowing or 'cracking'. This characteristic, as well as the darker tone quality of this horn, results from the larger bell diameter. An interesting feature of this horn was its ability to retain its basic tone quality regardless of the mouthpiece used. This is in a large measure due to the conical profile of its tubing. This integrity of tone is not so marked in later instruments, the conical profile of whose tubing is interrupted by the cylindrical sections necessary to accommodate tuning-slides and other addenda. Attention is called to the fact that all partials sounded perfectly in tune when the instrument was played with the contemporary mouthpiece. There was no discrepancy between the fifths and octaves, and the intonation of the scale in the third and fourth octaves was perfect (excepting, of course, the eleventh and thirteenth partials, which again exhibited the characteristics described earlier). The musical properties bore witness to the fine craftsmanship of the entire instrument.

That Michael Leichnambschneider continued to enjoy widespread patronage as a horn-maker is shown by a Waldhorn in the Städtisches Museum at

[1] The writer here records his thanks to Dr. Schneewitt and the Direktion of the Historisches Museum for permission to reproduce the photograph of this instrument which appears on Plate V, and for kindly lending the horn for playing and study.

Brunswick, dated 1719 (No. 71 in Hans Schröder, *Verzeichnis der Instru-
mentensammlung des Städtischen Museums in Braunschweig*, Hamburg, 1928).
Schröder's description (page 20) reads: 'Parforce Horn in C. Vienna 1719.
Brass, twice-wound. On the bell, a double eagle and the inscription:
MACHT MICHAEL LEICHNAMSCHNEIDER 17 IN WIENN 19.
Mouthpiece missing. Diameter of coils 31 cm.; bell diameter 25·5; length
about 313 cm.'

The bell diameter is again larger than that of the 1718 horn at Basle.
This would indicate a definite tendency towards enlarging the bell without
changing its essential profile in order to obtain a greater dynamic range.

A possible historical connection is suggested between this horn and the
ducal house of Brunswick. Duke Ludwig Rudolf, father of Empress Amalie,
was an ardent huntsman and music-lover. He was a frequent hunting-guest
of Sporck's,[1] and maintained a magnificent hunt and opera house at Brunswick, where Gottfried Caspar Schürrmann was Capellmeister. Schürrmann's
appointment to this post in 1697 was secured largely through the recom-
mendation of the Hamburg opera composer Reinhard Keiser, whose opera
Octavia (1705) was the first German score to employ the horn. The Duke's
position at the Viennese Court as the reigning Emperor's father-in-law took
him frequently to Vienna. This fact, coupled with his friendship with Sporck
and connection with Schürrmann and Keiser, both of whom wrote for the
horn, suggests strongly that this Parforce-Waldhorn by Michael Leichnambschneider may have been commissioned by the Duke himself for use in the
Brunswick hunt and house orchestra. (The provenance of this instrument,
as far as can be ascertained, is a Ducal bequest; but the records have been
destroyed.)

The Leichnambschneiders' fame as horn-makers is further attested to by
two silver horns made for Sir William Morgan, Lord Tredegar, in 1725.
Mention is made of these instruments in Blandford's article, 'The French
Horn in England':[2] 'When Sir William Morgan Lord Tredegar, (who
adopted as his supporters two huntsmen properly accoutred and wearing
trompes) wanted silver horns, he got them from Vienna. These horns, for
particulars of which the writer is indebted to Lord Tredegar, were made by
Johannes Leichnambschneider in 1725 and are decorated on the bell rim with
engravings of hunting scenes and Sir William's crest and arms. These horns
are also in F (by estimation), but having a 9½-inch bell of a more modern
type than Bull's horn.' (The reference here is to the horn by William Bull
dated 1699, now in the Horniman Museum.)

---

[1] Sporck decorated the Duke of Brunswick with the Order of St. Hubert (the
exclusive hunting-order of his own founding) in 1724, following a grand Parforce-hunt
held to celebrate the coronation of Charles VI in Prague. See the Correspondence to
Grossa, 19 and 30 September 1724.

[2] *Musical Times*, August 1922.

Whether the Viennese horn-maker Johannes Leichnambschneider came to Sir William's attention through his contemporary Lady Mary Wortley Montague is not known; but it is significant that when this noble sportsman required horns of exceptional quality he should look to a maker so far afield as Vienna. This fact may be taken as attesting to the known excellence of the Leichnambschneider instruments. It is also interesting that the horns should bear the mark of Johannes, as opposed to Michael Leichnambschneider, and comprise the last known record of these makers. The bell diameter of 9½ inches (24·8 cm.) would indicate that the size of the bell had become virtually stabilized by this later period in the Leichnambschneiders' working lives.

These superb instruments are now in the possession of the present Lady Tredegar at Cannes, where the writer recently examined them with her kind permission. Apart from the features of design which Blandford records (though he never actually handled the horns), the small mouthpipe inlet and comparatively compact corpus which these instruments show are distinctive. The mouthpipe inlet of 7 mm. is smaller than that of the standard Viennese inlet of the period. One can only surmise that it was made with an eye to the English huntsmen (or Welsh, more properly) who were to play these horns, making allowances for the smaller shank of the French mouthpiece then currently in use in the British hunting-fields. It is possible that this dimension was taken from the mouthpiece of one of Sir William's retinue, for although there is no record of his activities during this period, it is presumable that he would have taken the Grand Tour and come across the Leichnambschneider horns in the course of it. The 18-inch diameter of the coils would suggest that these horns were worn on, but not over the shoulder.

On the shell-bordered garlands of these superlative instruments are three scenes engraved on gilt panels, depicting the stag, hare, and boar hunt. In each scene two mounted huntsmen are playing horns. The style of these engravings is unmistakably that of Michael Heinrich Renz, an example of whose work appears on Plate VI. Sporck had commissioned many plates from this well-known artist for his countless books, and Renz and his fellow engraver Montalegre were retained by the Prague Court. That his work should appear on a Leichnambschneider horn made for a British nobleman is not surprising when we remember that Sporck had played an important part in this instrument's early development. Nor is it improbable that the Tredegar horns came to Renz's hand through Sporck. A further connection between Sporck and Sir William has yet to come to light; but it is enough that Tredegar's patronage of Leichnambschneider and Renz resulted in a pair of the most beautiful and perfectly made examples of the valveless instrument.

During the twenty-five years of the Leichnambschneiders' working careers of which we have record they may be credited with a number of contributions to the development of the horn. Among these were the redesigning of the cor-de-chasse which resulted in the prototype Viennese Waldhorn: the first application of crooks to the horn; the creation of the first orchestral horn; and a decided preference for the basic key of F, which not only had its effects upon the horn-music of the time, but which led the way for later makers in establishing F as one of the most suitable and characteristic pitches for the horn.

The Leichnambschneiders' Viennese model was to remain the basic pattern for the horn until well after 1750, when the influence of hand-stopping began to make itself felt in the design of the instrument. It may strike us that the Leichnambschneiders exercised an unusual monopoly over the horn-maker's trade in Vienna during these early years, as no other names of makers who worked in this early period have as yet come to light. But when we consider that there was relatively little demand for these instruments in the earliest years; that they were costly; and that the quality of the Leichnambschneiders' horns was of a surpassing standard, it is not surprising that they should eclipse, in the eye of posterity at least, all other contemporary horn-makers. In the following section we shall see how after 1730 makers in other German-speaking countries adopted the Leichnamschneider pattern and rang their own changes on it. As far afield as England and Italy, the Viennese model remained in much its original form until nearly 1800; and in Vienna itself the demands of a changing musical style in the seventies were met by departing as little as possible from the early prototype.

An impression of the horn's progress in countries outside the main Austrian tradition is best formed by first retracing our steps for a moment to Nürnberg in 1680.

Horn-makers in Germany, England, and Italy

Surprisingly enough, makers at Nürnberg do not appear to have made any substantial contribution to the development of the horn as an orchestral instrument. This might seem to be something of a paradox when we recall that Nürnberg had supplied the courts of Europe with brass instruments of the highest order since the early sixteenth century. But the ranks of the trumpet-makers' guild had thinned out noticeably after the middle of the seventeenth century. This was no doubt a result of the Thirty Years War, for the town's records show that Nürnberg, standing at the hub of the conflict between Catholic South and Protestant North, had lost upwards of 10,000 lives. By the close of the century, when the horn began to emerge as an orchestral instrument, the art of brass-instrument-making was in a state of decline, due not only to the effects of the war but to a succession of city governors who had deprived the guild of many of its revenues and rights.

Thus when the horn entered its first phase of development in the early 1700s Nürnberg was no longer able to make the contribution to its growth which she undoubtedly could have done a century earlier.

Of the surviving horns bearing the marks of Johann Wilhelm Haas (1648–1723), Wolf Wilhelm Haas (1681–1750), Ernst Johann Conrad Haas (1723–92), Friedrich Ehe (1669–1743), and Johann Leonhard Ehe II (1664–1724), all are hunting-horns of the Parforce-Waldhorn type. No purely orchestral instruments survive from their hands, nor is there any documentary evidence to suggest that they produced concert-horns with crooks. Although the superior craftsmanship traditionally associated with Nürnberg brass instruments is abundantly present in these horns, they show no impress of the developments in design which the Leichnambschneiders were carrying out in Vienna.

Six horns have come down to us from the Haas workshop, seven from that of Ehe. Like their Viennese counterparts, the earliest of these Nürnberg horns are an adaptation of the cor-de-chasse, and show its parentage clearly. This is particularly so in the case of the J. W. Haas and H. L. Ehe horns; the later examples by Friedrich Ehe and W. W. Haas generally have a wider bell throat and somewhat smaller coils.[1]

In fact, the earlier Haas and Ehe Parforce-Jagdhörner may well represent the first steps toward a German version of the cor-de-chasse, anticipating the Leichnambschneider brothers in this process by a good ten years. We cannot accept this as proven, however, for only one horn bearing a date earlier than 1700 survives which is not of the small sixteenth-century Jagdhorn type. This is the horn listed as No. 1661 in Kinsky's catalogue of the Heyer collection at Leipzig. It bears the date 1698, but no name. I have not seen this instrument, and Kinsky's description does not say whether it is of the large-hooped Waldhorn type. It is possibly a Nürnberg horn, but this is only conjecture. Apart from this example we know from Weigel's description of the trumpet-maker's art in that same year that makers at Nürnberg were producing larger or 'double' horns before the Viennese did so. 'The Wald-Hörner', he observes, 'are both large and small, and moreover coiled in various ways. The larger, or so-called "double" horns, are as big as a

---

[1] The three instruments cited in support of this argument are a singly wound 'Jagdhorn' in A altissimo by Wilhelm Haas dated 1682 (Basle, Historisches Museum, No. 15); a 'grosses Jagdhorn' in B flat (Heyer-Leipzig, No. 1661), said to be by a Nürnberg maker; and the 'Waldhorn' in B flat alto, dated 1698, by Hanns Leonhard Ehe in the Pfälzisches Gewerbemuseum at Kaiserslautern. The writer has had the opportunity of examining only the Haas instrument: and while it is of a decidedly Germanic design, its narrow bell throat is more that of the cor-de-chasse type than of the Viennese. The Ehe horn in Kaiserslautern appears from illustrations to follow the pattern of the Haas. There remains the anonymous Waldhorn of the Heyer collection: but it would be difficult to authenticate the origin of the Waldhorn on the sole basis of an anonymous instrument.

sizeable bowl, and give out a strong, far-carrying tone.' On this evidence it does seem likely that the first Germanic version of the cor-de-chasse was made at Nürnberg.

These first Nürnberg horns were obviously modelled on those cors-de-chasse which Sporck's horn-players brough back from Versailles. In all probability they owed their existence to his commission. It is not inconceivable, of course, that the Leichnambschneiders at Vienna first saw the new instrument, not in its original French form, but in the version which the Nürnberg makers had devised, and so came to base their design instead on the pattern laid down by Haas and Ehe. Yet when the early Nürnberg and Vienna horns are compared point for point, this seems unlikely. Despite certain similarities in the cut of the bell, the Viennese instruments differ noticeably in tone quality from those of Haas and Ehe, sounding altogether sweeter and more compact. The Nürnberg horns by contrast have a greater breadth and volume of sound. Both are derived from a common source, but not the one from the other. If the Leichnambschneiders had taken their cue from the Nürnberg instruments, it seems inevitable that there would have been enough conversation between the two centres, if only through the medium of Sweda and Röllig, for Haas and Ehe to have heard of the Viennese makers' new system of crooks. Evidently this did not happen, so we must conclude that each centre evolved its own design independently. The main historical fact is, however, that whereas the Leichnambschneiders established a tradition of horn-making which has continued unbroken to the present day, the Nürnberg design, except for sporadic examples by E. J. C. Haas, did not survive much beyond the death of Friedrich Ehe in 1743. Even Werner's Inventionshorn, which we shall meet in a later chapter, based its innovations on the Viennese model.

Before turning from the Nürnberg makers, a widespread misconception about a horn by Johann Leonhard Ehe II ought to be set to rights. A Parforce-Jagdhorn in B flat by this maker now in the Brussels Conservatoire (No. 3152) is equipped with a terminal crook. This had led many, including members of informed musical circles on the Continent, to assume that Ehe was one of the first to fit crooks to the horn.

Nothing could be further from the truth. On careful examination it was immediately evident that the bell had been added to this singly wound corpus at a point some 15 inches above the rim; that the metal of the bell section was of a different colour from that of the main body of the horn; and, what is most important, that the terminal socket was actually the garnish from the first yard or mouthpipe of a contemporary trumpet which had been split at the bottom and crimped to form a crude soldered joint on to the abbreviated mouthpipe of the horn! Not only does the manner in which this trumpet garnish has been attached violate every principle of sound construction, but it interrupts the crucial taper of the mouthpipe at a point which affects the instrument's playing characteristics.

There are other earmarks of forgery. The entire corpus is covered with tiny file marks, something which no eighteenth-century maker who hoped to sell his instruments would have allowed to pass. The marks of the file teeth are exact and regularly spaced, showing that the file was machine-made. (Files made before the Industrial Revolution were cast in hand-made moulds.) The bell by contrast shows the typical shaving-marks found on all well-finished instruments of the period before the introduction of emery cloth in about 1840. A distressing addition has been made to the bell garland. Over the engraved turk's head which was the mark of Johann Leonhard Ehe, a cast turk's head of nineteenth-century origin, possibly French, has been brazed on above Ehe's name. This has been clearly applied from the outside without removing the garland, for the metal of the garland itself has softened and run slightly in the heat of the operation. At four other points round the garland, cast heads of alternating full-face and profile views of a Roman general intrude between the opposing terminal scrolls of the engraved floral pattern. Each of these heads has been brazed on from the outside, and round each the metal has distorted and run. The finish of the garland has been irretrievably lost through buffing on a coarse wire wheel for a matt effect.

The crook itself is neatly made and retains the original mouthpiece inlet sleeve. In position, its loop falls on the right-hand side of the corpus, a fact in itself not remarkable, except that its tenon crosses the main coil to engage the socket on the left-hand side of the body. An eighteenth-century maker would hardly have equivocated on this point; crooks were either right- or left-handed. But the final proof of this crook's spurious origin is the fact that it has no stay, nor has it had one: the file-marks where the feet of the stay would have been attached show no trace of solder.

Quite apart from this physical evidence, there is the question of the use to which the horn was to be put. The corpus of this instrument measures $21\frac{3}{4}$ inches across the coil. Surely the whole point of fitting crooks was to enable the body to be made small for convenience in a crowded opera pit or on a packed platform, with the crooks further saving space by removing the necessity for a whole set of horns of different pitches. A crook on a large hunting-horn is a contradiction.

Obviously this horn is an amalgam of two separate, though contemporary, instruments dating from the early eighteenth century. All of its components are old. Even the trumpet garnish which takes the crook displays the familiar spiral turning and fleur-de-lis collar of the Nürnberg instruments of this period. But it does not take an expert to see that these various elements did not start life together.

The fact that such an obviously counterfeit instrument should be taken as the model for modern reproductions for use in public performances proves that much more research into early brass instruments is needed. That such reproductions should be used in reputable circles urges this need still more strongly. A forgery on this scale would never be accepted in the world of stringed or keyboard instruments. Be that as it may, the evidence of the Brussels example does not furnish proof that Johann Leonhard Ehe applied the principle of terminal crooks to the horn.

Elsewhere in Germany proper horn-makers are only occasionally met with at this period. Johann Georg Eichentopf (Eichendopf or Eichendorf) appears to have made horns of quality at Leipzig, and indeed supplied them to the Court orchestra at Cöthen, where Bach was Capellmeister. The Cöthen inventory[1] lists '2 G Hörner, J. G. Eichendopf 1733' and another pair in E flat bearing his name. A similar pair in E flat, twice-wound and having a fixed mouthpipe, survive at Prague as Nos. 85 and 86 in the National Museum. Except for minor differences of detail, they are identical in design to the orchestral horn by Michael Leichnambschneider at Schloss Harburg dated 1721, and bear further witness to the widespread influence of the Viennese pattern at this time. One A. F. Sattler was also working at Leipzig during the first half of the century. Morley-Pegge mentions J. C. and W. M. Müller working at Roda, from whom two horns dated 1713 and 1779 respectively have survived. One can only hope that fresh evidence will come to light and broaden our knowledge of these early German makers.

In London, William Bull was making 'ffrench Hornes' by his own advertisement from 1681 until about 1707 (see Introduction, p. 7), but to judge from the example dated 1699 in the Horniman Museum and the illustration on his trade card of c. 1700, these were not concert horns. An amusing sideline at this time was the sportsman's helical horn, coiled tightly so that it could be worn inside a hat. Hats containing these instruments could evidently be had in various head-sizes. Whether Bull was the originator of this diverting variation we cannot be sure; but certainly the idea was English. The hat-horn enjoyed some favour in Germany as well. Mattheson tells us of one Gleichmann, the organist at Ilmenau in the Thuringian forest, who offered for sale amongst other instruments 'English cors de chasse, e.g. horns hidden in hats so that one can put them on and wear them'.[2] The Cöthen inventory for 1768 lists 'A Pair of Hats wherein are A Horns', and 'A Pair of Hats containing Horns' is mentioned in the inventory for 1773, but presumably these are identical with the earlier pair. Again, these

[1] Herzögl. Haus-und Staatsarchiv Cöthen st. 12., nr. 68, quoted in *Bach-Jahrbuch*, Leipzig, 1905, p. 38.

[2] J. G. Mattheson, *Critica Musica*, Hamburg, 1722, I, p. 254. . . . engelländischen Cors de chasse, it . . . solche Wald-Hörner, die in Hüten, so man aufsetzen und tragen kann, verborgen sind. . . .'

are not concert horns, but it is interesting that they should appear amongst the horns used in the Cöthen orchestra.

Mention should be made of a product from the one known horn-making workshop in northern Italy at this period. This is a Jagdhorn in G marked 'P. L. Crema', now in the Kunsthistorisches Museum at Vienna. This horn is of late seventeenth- or early eighteenth-century workmanship; and in its fairly small single coil (10¾ inches) and wide-throated bell (diameter at rim 7¼ inches) embodies elements of both the small sixteenth-century Jagdhorn and the orchestral horn of the early eighteenth century. The sound of this attractively made horn is soft and full in the Austrian manner; yet it is obviously a hunting-instrument, having been fitted out by the maker with rings for attaching the baldric. Crema is a town in Lombardy which was under Venetian rule at this period. Is it too fanciful to suppose that P. L. might be a Leichnambschneider? After all, members of the Eberle family of violin-makers were working at Venice and Padua.

This, then, was the horn as it evolved from the cor-de-chasse into the orchestral Waldhorn, and was taken up in its Viennese form by makers in other countries. Before pursuing its further development in the second half of the century, let us first turn to the music written for it and meet some of the first concert horn-players.

III

THE GROWTH OF
THE BOHEMIAN SCHOOL
TO 1770

The first orchestral horn-players

THE horn-players of the first two generations were nearly all of Bohemian birth and training. A few came from Saxony, Lower Austria, and the neighbouring Dominions, and appear to have learned the instrument from the Bohemian players attached to the provincial courts. These early horn-players were a special sort of men, marked out by a singular mixture of bloodstreams, languages, and talents. In them the inborn musicality and wander-lust of the Bohemians united with the natural vitality of the Sudeten Germans. To this unusual combination of native traits was added a rigorous musical training in the Jesuit and Benedictine monasteries. The end product was a race of horn virtuosi which included some of the greatest players the instrument has ever known, and whose members established the horn as an orchestral and solo instrument throughout the civilized world of the eighteenth century.

Most of the early players were sons of huntsmen and foresters on the estates of the great nobles, and from a childhood in the out-of-doors gained a hardiness which was more than a match for the physical demands of the horn. (Some, like Matiegka and Ziwiny, retained their full powers for more than half a century.) Underlying this natural vigour was a thoroughly mixed ancestry, a result of the Austro-German migrations into Bohemia during the seventeenth century. Thus in glancing through the names of these early players one encounters pure Czech surnames such as Beda, Cžermak, and Schindelarž; Sudeten German names like Messing, Schindler, and Nagel; while many such as Steinmetz (Stamitz), Steinmüller, Zeddelmayer, and Seydler, point to an Austrian mountain origin. Yet all were German-speaking, save those whose Czechdom was proclaimed by their Christian names, and all were Austrian in point of schooling and general culture.

The first generation of horn-players, whose working period covers the years 1680 to *c.* 1725, included the first teachers and travelling virtuosi. Contemporary accounts leave no doubt that it was Sporck's horn-players, Sweda and Röllig, who first taught their fellow Bohemians the art of horn-playing. The new instrument caught on quickly, and soon Prague became a centre of horn-playing to which resident teachers and professional players were drawn in increasing numbers.

Early in the period a few names begin to emerge. Hermoläus Smeykal, *c.* 1685-1758 (see page 97), was the first major professional teacher. Born in the provincial town of Kuttenberg, he was trained in the Jesuit monastery there, and was already active as a player and teacher in Prague before the death of Sweda. It was Smeykal who first raised the pedagogy of the horn to a formal, though not written, plane; and as the tutor of Joseph Matiegka and (most probably) Anton Joseph Hampl he emerges as an important early figure who founded the central teaching tradition of the Austro-Bohemian school. Thus a continuity was established quite early in the century, a full forty years before the date at which horn pedagogy was generally thought to have begun.

Horn tutoring of a fair quality appears to have been available in Bohemia in the decades before Smeykal's day, however; for no matter how assiduously Sweda and Röllig may have given themselves to passing on their art, they alone could hardly have been responsible for the surprising number of players of evident ability who appeared very early in the century. (Some, we must remember, were self-taught, and many received their early training on the trumpet or trombone; but the high level to which such players as Zeddelmayer, Rossi, and Otto attained as early as 1715 would point to a certain amount of sound idiomatic training at some stage.) Indeed the number of instances during the first two decades in which the horn made an appearance in an ensemble proves that these early horn-players had achieved sufficient skill to make it acceptable as a concert instrument.

As early as 1704 we have record of travelling horn-players in London: German-speaking, and almost certainly Bohemian. In a concert bill of 1 June 1704 we are told of a performance to be given at Chelsea College.

CONCERT

Music. By the best Masters, together with
seven young Hautboys lately come over from Germany,
who will perform several Entertainments on the
Hautboys, Flutes, and Hunting-Horns, to great Admiration.
At the desire of several Persons of Quality.
At 6 P.M.   Tickets 5s.[1]

Dart[2] gives the dates of other concerts by this popular band on 3 April and 31 May of the same year, advertising themselves as playing on 'Hautboys, Flutes and German Horns' in the earlier performance.

[1] Emmett L. Avery, *The London Stage 1660–1800*, vol. I, part ii (Carbondale, 1960), p. 68.
[2] 'Bach's Fiauti d'Echo' in *Music and Letters*, xli (October, 1960), p. 339.

These 'seven young Hautboys' had been brought to England by Gottfried Pepusch, Johann Christopher's younger brother, who had been Court
composer to the Elector of Brandenburg and King of Prussia, Frederick
William the First. Gottfried and many of his orchestra had been dismissed
late in 1703 as a result of the Prussian monarch's active dislike of music.[1] The
Dictionary of National Biography, xv (London, 1909), p. 799, quotes Burney in
saying that J. C. Pepusch set some pieces for this group in 1704, a fact which
must have accounted in part for the great popularity which they enjoyed.

The inclusion of a pair of horns in a travelling band at this early date in
company with flutes and oboes would suggest that they were employed to
musical ends, however rudimentary. It is significant, too, that these players
should come from 'Germany'; for Bohemia was the only German-speaking
country at that time which was producing horn-players of sufficient ability
to arouse great admiration.

The year 1704 marks a curiously related instance of horn-playing activity
in the distant Pomeranian city of Stettin. Gottfried Pepusch's teacher,

Ex. 6.   F. G. Klingenberg: Aria, 1705: Ritornello.

Johann Gottfried Klingenberg (*c.* 1658–1720), held the post of resident
organist and composer at the church of St. Philip and St. Paul from 1699
until his death. Stettin was under the rule of the Brandenburg Court at
Berlin between the years 1678 and 1710. Frederick William's dismissing the
greater part of his Capelle may well have been responsible for the appearance
of horn-players in this Pomeranian outpost in 1704; for Klingenberg's aria,
'Die Singende Liebe', for bass, two horns, two oboes, bassoon, and continuo
dates from that year. Unfortunately the music is lost; and our only knowledge of the piece stems from Freytag, who, in his *Musikgeschichte der Stadt
Stettin* (Greifswald, 1936), tells us that it was set with ritornelli for these
instruments. Fortunately, however, a surviving example of Klingenberg's
unusually early use of horns dates from the following year. His occasional
aria, 'Die aus dem Markt nach Pommern wandernde Liebe', first performed
on 1 September 1705 (see Ex. 6), features a separate ritornello for the full
ensemble of oboes, horns, bassoon, and cembalo. Remarkable for their early
idiomatic treatment of the horn, these parts demand considerable facility and

[1] Sources disagree as to exact date; but see *Die Musik in Geschichte und Gegenwart*, x
(Kassel, 1962), p. 1030.

were obviously written for skilled players. Klingenberg's horn-players, like Pepusch's, probably hailed from Bohemia or Saxony; and it is amusing to consider that both of these pairs may well have set out upon their respective travels from the common starting-point of Frederick William's Court. It is to be regretted that the London pieces which J. C. Pepusch wrote for his brother's group have not survived, for the style of his horn parts would undoubtedly resemble that of Klingenberg's aria.

The year 1705 has hitherto been regarded as marking the beginning of the horn's orchestral career, for it was in that year that Reinhard Keiser first wrote for the horn in an operatic setting in the fanfares of his *Octavia*. But in view of both Klingenberg's and Pepusch's ensemble settings of 1704, and in view of Sporck's early use of the horn in his house serenades at Bad Kukus and Lissa, we must now regard *Octavia* rather as the first instance where the horn becomes a full-fledged member of the opera orchestra.[1]

It is entirely possible that the horn-player Johann Theodorus Zeddel-mayer took part in the *Octavia* performance in 1705, for Opel[2] sees Zeddel-mayer's appointment at Weissenfels the following year as a result of Keiser's offices on his behalf. Whatever Zeddelmayer's origins, he was evidently not a doubler upon the trumpet, as is shown by both Keiser's fanfares and the *Jagdcantata* horn part which J. S. Bach wrote for Zeddelmayer and his second, Anton Fiedler.[3]

[1] This is not strictly speaking the first appearance of the horn in opera. See pp. 5–6. In Cavalli's first opera, *Le Nozze di Teti e di Peleo*, of 1659, there is a remarkable fanfare in five parts, marked 'Ciamata alla Caccia'. It appears as an interpolation in the Coro di Cavalieri ('All' armi, all' armi'), and the instrumentation for the scene, according to the score in the Vienna Nationalbibliothek, calls for 'Corni e Tambouri, Trombe'. Gold-schmidt ('Das Orchester der Italienischen Oper im 17. Jahrhundert', in *SIMG* ii Leipzig, 1902, p. 40) sees in this passage the first appearance of the horn in opera. Piersig (*Die Einführung des Hornes in die Kunstmusik*, Halle, 1923, p. 28), with much pursing of histori-cal lips, warns against taking the title of the fanfare as an indication of the instruments required, and guardedly suggests that it was played on trumpets. Morley-Pegge (op. cit., pp. 80–4) gives a sound and practicable explanation of how it could have been played on horns of the period, but once intimated to the present writer in private that he thought it was for strings in imitation of horns. The author concurs with both Goldschmidt's view and Cavalli's scoring. In his dealings with the French Court, Cavalli certainly would have known the cor-de-chasse, and indeed *Le Nozze* itself was performed at Paris in 1654. The awkward low E for the third horn might simply arise from the fact that Venetian composers at that time had little contact with instruments other than strings, let alone horns. Goldschmidt adds that horns are encountered in other operas by Cavalli and Cesti; but this writer has not come across them. Even so, their presence as occasional instruments in early Venetian and Viennese opera need not detract from the historical importance of Keiser's score. There the horn is for the first time truly integrated, although as an obbligato colour instrument, into the orchestral fabric.

[2] *Neue Mittheilungen aus dem Gebiet histor. und antiquärischen Forschungen für Schwaben und Neuburg*, xv, 2 (Halle, 1882), p. 499.

[3] Active from 1709 to 1717. See Chapter IV s.v. 'Zeddelmayer'.

A lesser-known work from the year 1705 which calls for horns is Buxtehude's *Templum Honoris*, written to celebrate the accession of the Holy Roman Emperor, Joseph I. Since many of the outside instrumentalists required for Buxtehude's 'Extraordinairen Abendmusiken' at the *Marienkirche* at Lübeck were recruited from the Hamburg opera, it is equally possible that Zeddlemayer was present amongst the horn-players on this occasion as well. However that may be, this last work of Buxtehude's is interesting as the first full-scale cantata to call for a chorus of horns.

Although the music is lost, the libretto is preserved in the St. Anne Museum at Lübeck, where it came to the writer's attention.[1] *Templum Honoris* is set 'nach der Operen Art' with choruses, arias, recitatives, and instrumental ritornelli. The instrumental forces are in keeping with the occasion, and are comprised of two choruses of drums and trumpets, a chorus of oboes and a chorus of Waldhörner; the exact number of each instrument, however, is not given.

After the first verse of the text to the aria, 'Unsterbliche Ehre', we find the printed instruction, '*Ritornello* mit 2. Chöre Waldhörnern und Hautbois, *concert*irende'. The appearance of horns in context with the affection or concept of Honour further bears out the point made in Chapter I, where the horn was shown as an instrument which symbolized princely valour and *Tugend*.

The following year, 1706, marks the first recorded engagement of a horn-player as a permanent member of a court orchestra. Johann Theodorus Zeddelmayer (*c.* 1675-*post* 1736 already met with in Hamburg and Lübeck) was appointed 'Waldhornist' under Johann Philipp Krieger in that year by Duke Christian of Saxe-Weissenfels. A detailed discussion of his background and activities can be found on pp. 92–4. Duke Christian was fond of music, and in addition to maintaining a flourishing opera kept a hunting-band which consisted of the usual pairs of oboes, horns, and bassoons. Krieger's *Lustige Feldmusik* of 1704 included 'ouvertures' for this combination, but it is doubtful whether Zeddelmayer was as yet on hand to take part in their performance.[2] In 1716, however, the young Weimar Capellmeister Johann Sebastian Bach wrote his cantata, 'Was mir behagt, ist nur die muntre Jagd', in celebration of Duke Christian's birthday, which fell on 23 February. As this work was performed at Weissenfels, the horn parts were without doubt composed with Zeddelmayer and his second, Anton Fiedler, in mind. The first horn part to this work presents Zeddelmayer as a player of a high degree

[1] The libretti of both *Templum Honoris* and its preceding sister-work, *Castrum Doloris*, are reproduced in facsimile in Georg Karstädt, *Die 'Extraordinairen Abendmusiken' Dietrich Buxtehudes* (Lübeck, 1962). It is from this study that the information concerning the extra instrumentalists in Buxtehude's concerts has been drawn.

[2] See Arno Werner, *Städtische und Fürstliche Musikpflege in Weissenfels* (Leipzig, 1911), p. 119.

of virtuosity whose style of playing was remarkably idiomatic for the time (see Ex. 7). It is further significant that Duke Christian was a frequent hunting-guest of Count Franz Anton von Sporck: and it may well be that Zeddelmayer was brought to Weissenfels from Lissa or Bad Kukus. The emulation which Sporck's hunting-music aroused amongst his noble neighbours has already received comment. Duke Christian's permanently employing a horn-player at this early date further attests to the popularity which the horn was rapidly gaining.

Meanwhile the art of horn-playing had been cultivated in the Bohemian monasteries since the opening years of the century. Smeykal, the noted

Ex. 7.   Bach: Jagd cantate, BWV 208.

Prague teacher, first learnt his instrument in the Jesuit monastery at Küttenberg; and though records for this period are sparse, we do encounter references which leave no doubt that the horn was coming into use as an orchestral instrument in the larger seminaries and colleges of the religious orders in Bohemia and Lower Austria. The Cistercian monastery at Osseg in Bohemia, for example, possessed a complete *instrumentarium* which included virtually every orchestral instrument of the Late Baroque. An inventory of the instrument chamber at Osseg, dated 1706, was published by Paul Nettl in his article 'Weltliche Musik des Stiftes Osseg im Siebzehnten Jahrhundert'.[1] The register is headed, 'Specificatio Instrumentorum Musicalium'; and amongst the wind instruments we find the entry, 'Litui vulgo Waldhörner duo ex Tono G'. Both Nettl and Sachs[2] regard this use of the term

[1] *Zeitschrift für Musikwissenschaft*, vi, 4 (Leipzig, 1921), p. 357.
[2] 'Die Litui in Bachs Mottette "O Jesu Christ"' in *Bach-Jahrbuch* (Leipzig, 1921), p. 96. 'This evidence is unequivocal, and gains added significance from the fact that it not only falls within the period of Bach's creative activity, but comes to light in a

'Lituus' as conclusive proof that the Waldhorn was in fact the instrument for which Bach wrote in Cantata 118.

Duke Anton Ulrich of Brauschweig-Wolfenbüttel was quick to follow the example of his neighbour at Weissenfels, and by 1710 his orchestra at Wolfen-

monastery which lies scarcely a dozen kilometres from the Saxony border.' The use of Latin names for instruments was assuredly obsolescent amongst composers in Bach's time, but persisted in theoretical writings until as late as the eighties. (Forkel, in his *Allgemeine Geschichte der Musik*, Leipzig, 1788, i, p. 415, gives a list of Greek names for the trumpet family, including Lituus as an equivalent for Salpinx.) Walther (op. cit., p. 367), writing in 1732, a date nearer that of the motet in question, says Lituus is 'Tubam curvam, meaning a military horn'.

One of the earliest seventeenth-century sources to speak of the lituus as an equivalent term for the contemporary cor a plusiers tours is Mersenne's *Harmonicorum Libri* (Paris, 1635), Lib. ii, prop. 17; and indeed this may well be the first modern application of the term to the helical horn. It is most likely, however, that Bach's use of Lituus to mean Waldhorn has its source in Athanasius Kircher's *Musurgia Universalis*, a widely read theoretical and acoustical treatise published at Rome in 1650. In the section, 'De Fistulis et Lituis', Kircher illustrates the principal wind instruments of the Hebrews, amongst which the helical *Lituus retortus* appears (Lib. ii, p. 54: see Fig. 1(a).) The

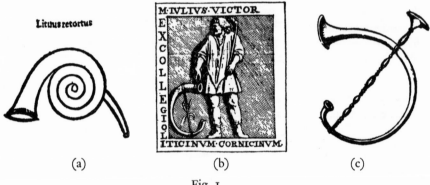

(a)   (b)   (c)

Fig. 1

symbolic aptness of the name of this horn-like Old Testament instrument for the Waldhorn in a motet whose textual subject was Christ is readily seen, and undoubtedly appealed to Bach.

Another treatise on wind instruments which may have come to Bach's attention, though perhaps less well known than Kircher's more general work, is Caspar Bartholinus's *De Tibiis Veterum* (Amsterdam, 1697). His illustrations of the Lituus, Fig. 1 (b) and (c) leave no doubt as to the possible derivation of Bach's term, and his discussion of that instrument (p. 404) is equally revealing. 'Extat in horto domus quondam *Advocati Ronconi* e regione S. Isidori Hebernensium & hominem exhibet cum lituo, ad cujus pedes Cornu inflexum, tale fere ac in columna Trajana, cum hac inscriptione: M IULIUS VICTOR / EX COLLEGIO / LITICINUM CORNICINUM.' See Fig. 1 (b).

'Fuit aliud Buccinae genus incurvum, *Lituus* veteribus dictum, ex *Festo*, gracilem edensvocem, quo in bello utebantur, qui eo canebat *Liticen* dictus est. *Priscianus* lib. I. *Liticen, Liticinus, ex Lituo, quod est genus Tubae minoris.* Unde & soni fuit acutioris, quemadmodum apud *Statium*: Et lituis aures circumpulsantur acutis. *Lucanus* Lib. I.: "—Stridor lituum clangorque Tubarum".'

Kircher was one of the standard theoretical writers of Bach's day, and Bartholinus appears in the libraries of Prague, Vienna, Nuremberg, and Leipzig: a fact which may

büttel also featured a permanent horn-player. Georg Laurentz Reichel appears in the church register for 2 April 1710 as 'Waldhorniste u. Violischellniste bey Ihr Herrschftl Durchl Capell'.[1] In 1717 Reichel, the son of a town musician from Ronneburg, a watering-place on the Saxon-Bohemian border, was joined in 1717 by a second horn-player. That year the Wolfenbüttel Capellmeister, Georg Caspar Schürmann (1672–1751), set a cantata, 'Komm, O Tröster', for voices with two obbligato 'Corn de Chas'. As the music is lost, we can but speculate as to the playing style of Reichel's second, Johann Georg Hildebrand. But an impression of Reichel's considerable virtuosity is readily gained from Schmidt's description (p. 448) of the concertante solo horn part to the tenor aria, 'Grosser König Du Krone der Helden', which Schürmann wrote for Reichel in his opera *Clelia* in 1730. The obbligato horn line reveals this early player's command of his instrument in its 'quick triplet runs, quaver staccatos and a sustained high trill.' Reichel and Hildebrand both appear to have died or retired by 1731.

The engagement at Wolfenbüttel of horn-players at such an early date may well be a result of Duke Anton Ulrich's frequent intercourse with Sporck, roughly his contemporary, at whose hunts he was a regular guest. Sporck, on the occasion of the royal hunt at Lissa on 3 November 1723, decorated both Reichel's and Zeddelmayer's lords with the Order of St. Hubert, the hunting-order of Sporck's own founding.[2]

In 1711 the electoral orchestra of the Saxon Court at Dresden appointed as resident 'Hoff-Waldhornisten' Johann Adalbert Fischer and Franz Adam Samm. The two Bohemians began their duties with the opera there on 26 October of that year.[3] From that date a continuous tradition of Bohemian-schooled horn-playing flourished until the bombings of 1945.

It was Sporck's lifelong boast that his Jägerchor had sung before Augustus the Strong at Dresden. In his younger days as Elector of Saxony, Augustus III[4] and Sporck hunted frequently together; and it is to this association with the Dresden Court that the timely appearance of regular horn-players there is no doubt owing.

The horn appears to have been a favourite instrument with the young monarch, as indeed its predominance in the known major musical events of his life suggests. The ceremonies attending his marriage in 1719 to Maria

be taken as proof that his work was known in learned circles at least. In the light of these authors' agreement on the meaning of the term Lituus, it is easily seen why it should be used as the nearest Latin equivalent for the horn, both by Bach himself and by the inventorist at Osseg monastery.

[1] G. F. Schmidt, *Die Frühdeutsche Oper* (Regensburg, 1933), pp. 123 et seq.

[2] See the Korrespondenz, 30 November 1723; and Chapter I, p. 42, footnote 1.

[3] Moritz Fürstenau, *Geschichte der Musik und des Theaters am Kurfürstlichen Hofe zu Dresden* (Dresden, 1862), ii, p. 80; see also p. 96.

[4] 1696–1763: succeeded Augustus the Strong as King of Poland 1733.

Josepha, daughter of the deceased Austrian Emperor Joseph I, were enlivened by frequent horn fanfares; and as a finale Lully's *La Princesse d'Elide*, with its evocative horn flourishes, was performed.[1] J. S. Bach composed his Mass in B Minor for Augustus's accession to the Polish throne in 1733. The horn solo in the Quoniam, itself a high-water mark in the Baroque horn repertory, was to all evidence played by one of the Bohemian brothers Schindler, who succeeded Fischer and Samm as Court horn-players. Bach's cantata No. 208a, 'Was Mir Behagt, ist nur die Muntre Jagd,' originally written for Duke Christian of Weissenfels, was performed in an altered version on the King of Poland's name-day in 1735. It was at Augustus's behest that both Hampl and Haudek came to reside in Dresden: thus the Saxon king, through his interest in the horn and in music generally, did much to stimulate horn-playing towards the perfection to which it attained during his lifetime. His signature can be seen next to that of Charles VI in the opened book of Sporck's Order of St. Hubert in the frontispiece.

The electoral orchestra at Düsseldorf had horn-players in 1711 as well. The 'Quatierlisten des Churpfälzischen Hofstaates bei der Kaiserwahl Carls VI. zu Frankfurt' for 1711 include amongst the fifty-two musicians of the electoral band '2 Beyde H. Jagdt Hornisten'.[2] In 1716 the Elector Palatine, Johann Wilhelm, died, and certain players were dismissed. His successor, Carl Philipp, brought with him a select band from his orchestra at Innsbruck; and in the orchestra register of 1718 a 'Walthornist Pangratz' and a 'Walthornist Hoffmann' are listed. This is the first list to show the horn-players' names; but they are probably identical with the two who had played at the Imperial coronation. In 1719 another horn-player was added, and an ensemble of fifty-three members was maintained under the composer Johann Hugo Wilderer until 1723. It was this group which became the nucleus for the famous Mannheim orchestra when the Palatinate Court removed to the new palace there in 1724.

Of Pangratz's and Hoffmann's provenance we know nothing. Certainly the very date of their appearance as professional horn-players is almost reason enough to assume that they were Bohemians. If they came with Philipp Carl in 1716, then their Bohemian origin is virtually assured, for the new Elector had brought with him a number of Bohemian musicians to Innsbruck;[3] but it is significant that horn-playing had been established at Mannheim for three decades before the arrival of Johann Stamitz.

[1] This ballet was originally written as the *entr'acte* to Molière's play *Les Plaisirs de l'isle enchantée* in 1664.

[2] Quoted in Gerhard Steffen, *Johann Hugo Wilderer* (Cologne, 1960), p. 89.

[3] Friederich Walter, 'Karl Philipp als Statthalter von Tirol' in *Mannheimer Geschichtsblätter*, ii (1928), p. 28. 'He had taken this band with him to Innsbruck, and with it presumably a number of Bohemian musicians, the majority of whose successors later enjoyed such fame in the Mannheim orchestra.'

Vienna and Naples

It was not until 1712 that the Imperial orchestra at Vienna appointed its first regular horn-players. This date seems surprisingly late when we consider that the Leichnambschneiders had already begun to attract widespread attention there as horn-makers a good ten years before, and that the smaller electoral and princely courts to the north had been accepting the horn as a permanent member of their orchestras since as early as 1706. Certainly interest in the horn had not been wanting in Vienna, nor had there been a lack of players, to all evidence. But no significant additions to the Hofcapelle had been made during the last years of the ageing Joseph I's reign; and it remained for the succeeding Emperor, Charles VI, whose love

Ex. 8.   J. J. Fux: 'Trionfate, Cacciatore' from *Elisa.*

for both music and the hunt met, as did Sporck's, in the horn, to dignify his favourite instrument with a place in the Court orchestra.

Accordingly the names of Wenzel Rossi (*c.* 1685–1740) and Friederich Otto (1686–1718) appear for the first time as 'Jägerhornisten' amongst the personnel of the *Staats- und Stands-Calendar* register of the Imperial orchestra for 1712. Though no record of their origins remains, their names are typically Viennese: Rossi's Bohemian Christian name and Italian surname represents a mixture common both in Bohemia and Austria at the time. The archives are equally silent on the matter of their early training. If, however, we recall that Charles VI while Archduke had sent huntsmen to Sporck at Lissa to be trained; and that Sporck's horn-players, Sweda and Röllig, came to Vienna with their lord for four months of the year from 1690 onwards, it then seems

likely that these first Imperial horn-players were taught by the two Bohemians.

It was for Rossi and Otto that Johann Joseph Fux wrote the highly
idiomatic horn parts in his opera *Elisa* of 1715 (see Ex. 8. The reader is
referred also to the record which accompanies this book). As nearly as can
be judged from the few remaining scores of this period which include horns,
Elisa marks a turning-point in the style of writing for the horn. The martial
character of earlier trumpet-derived horn parts is entirely absent here; and
the flowing six-eight hunting-call figures imbue the hunter's scenes with a
romantic quality which directly anticipates that of von Weber's *Der Freischütz* by more than a hundred years. Fux's horn passages are further
remarkable in that they confine themselves to the most sonorous and characteristic part of the instrument's compass, never ascending above the written
g". Here is no 'eldritch screech': rather Fux's fanfares reflect the darker,
round-toned Waldhorn quality for which Rossi and Otto were undoubtedly
distinguished, and which has set the Viennese style apart from all others
down to the present day.[1]

In the year following Rossi and Otto's appointment to the Hofcapelle at
Vienna, Johann Georg Mattheson published his *Das Neu-Eröffnete Orchestre*
at Hamburg. It is in Mattheson's work that the horn is described as an
orchestral instrument for the first time. 'The soft and stately Horns', he

[1] Fux called for two horns in F to sound the fanfares in the Overture to the ballet
music which he set for Ziani's opera *Meleagro* of 1706. These flourishes (Ex. 9a; see p. 61)
bear more than a passing resemblance to those in the first movement of Bach's Brandenburg Concerto No. 1, written some thirteen years later (Ex. 9b). Both figures are based
on a greeting-call which was in fairly common use in this period (Ex. 9c), and both Fux
and Bach adapt it in much the same way. A comparison of these two passages can be
heard on the accompanying record. Although it was in his later years that Bach
placed Fux at the head of the list of those composers whom he most admired (J. N.
Forkel, *Über Joh. Seb. Bachs Leben und Kunst*, Leipzig, 1802, p. 68), there is no reason why
he should not have come across this early ballet by Fux in the course of studying the
works of the Viennese opera composers, amongst whom Ziani was at this time a prominent figure. In fact, the similarity between these two horn passages is so close as to
suggest that the earlier piece was possibly the blueprint which suggested this use of the
greeting-call to Bach.

The dotted quaver-semiquaver on the third beat of the call in the Fux example
would, of course, be the equivalent of a crotchet-quaver in a triple bracket in modern
notation, this device being as yet unknown in Fux's time. This figure, and the triple-
rhythm character of the original call, suggest that the first two beats be played in
unequal dactyls as well. Although one hesitates to apply indiscriminately the principle
of inequality to Viennese music of this period, the result in this case is effective. It
sounds convincing in performance, lending rhythmic consistency to the horn-call
figure and calling attention to it by contrast with the equal quavers in the strings.

There is, in fact, much to be said for performing the horn calls in the Brandenburg
in this way (Ex. 9d). Here too, the call takes on a rhythmic unity and is more easily
heard through what Tovey has called the orchestral forest. The cross-rhythms are
bracing in their effect, and serve to highlight the return of the A section at the end of
the movement.

Ex. 9.

J. J. Fux: Overture from the Ballet Music
to Ziani's Opera *Meleagro* (1709).

Corni
da
Caccia
(F)

J. S. Bach: Brandenburg Concerto No. 1, first movement (1719).

Corni
da
Caccia
in F

Greeting-Call, probably Saxonian, but general in the
early eighteenth century in German- speaking countries.

Suggested way of playing opening fanfare.

Breath legato in third movement, bar 95 et seq.

writes on page 267, 'Italian Cornette da Caccia, in French Cors de Chasse,
have come very much into fashion at the present time: partly because their
nature is not so rude as that of the trumpets, and partly because they can be
played with more agility. The most practical pitches are F, and C with the
Trumpets. The Horns also sound fuller and fill in better than the deafening
and screaming Clarini (in the hands of a good player, that is), since they

stand a whole fifth lower in pitch.' Clearly Mattheson was describing the tone quality of the Waldhorn as he heard it from such players as Zeddel-mayer, for his remarks could hardly be considered applicable to the contemporary cor-de-chasse.

Writers on orchestration and instruments since the nineteenth century have almost universally regarded the horn of this period as a second-best substitute for the trumpet, dismissing its tone as considerably less than musical. Mattheson's account forcibly refutes this misconception. Not only is the line between the horn and the trumpet sharply drawn, but the descriptive 'lieblich-pompeus' points unmistakably to the soft and noble sound which even at that early date was a hallmark of the horn.[1]

During the second decade of the century Vienna became increasingly important as a centre for disseminating horn-players to the far corners of Europe. The Imperial diplomats maintained elaborate courts in the cities to which they were assigned, whether outposts of the Imperial government or capitals of foreign countries. The Austrian emissaries invariably took with them their house orchestras, which at this period began to include horn-players, usually of Bohemian origin. It was through these channels that Austrian musicians went to take up positions in cities as far removed as Brussels, St. Petersburg, and even Constantinople.

The appearance of four 'Jägerhörner' in the royal orchestra at Naples in 1714 is a typical example of this kind of broadcast through diplomatic contact. The *Capella Reale* had been attached to the Court of the Viceroy since the Austrian conquest of Naples in 1680. This office was awarded by the Emperor to a high-ranking member of the Imperial Court; and was held from 1706 until his death in the December of 1719 by Count Johann Wenzel Gallas. As the head of one of the most influential of the great Bohemian musical families, Gallas maintained a sizeable house orchestra both in Prague[2] and at Campo, his country palace; and from amongst its members the nucleus of the Neapolitan Capella was drawn. Thus it stands to reason that the four horn-players who come to our attention at Naples in 1714 were

---

[1] A detailed discussion of this point with reference to an actual Leichnambschneider horn of the period can be found in Chapter II, pp. 35–37.

[2] Zedler, *Universal-Lexicon*, x (Leipzig, 1735), p. 154; xix (1739), p. 1846. Both the Martinitz and Gallas families maintained large hunting-bands and house orchestras at Schmetschen and Campo respectively; both were leading members of the prominent musical circles in Prague and Vienna throughout the eighteenth century; and both names appear amongst the trustees of the Prague Conservatory and the Gesellschaft der Musikfreunde in Vienna more than a century later. The Gallas family were noted for the quality of their house orchestra. The scene of many of their musical evenings was the *Stadtpalais* Gallas in Prague, a gem of Baroque architecture worth mention in its own right. It was built by Johann Bernhard Fischer von Erlach in 1713, and is considered an outstanding example of its period. A fuller description may be found in H. Auren-hammer, *J. B. Fischer von Erlach* (Vienna, 1957), p. 47.

amongst those musicians whom Gallas had brought from Bohemia in his retinue.

The Empress Elisabeth Christina's birthday fell on 28 September, and that year a grand open-air serenade was held in her honour in the Piazza before the viceregal palace. The music was by Giovanni Battista Bononcini (1672–c. 1750), who had composed many operas for the Court at Vienna. A mammoth orchestra of sixty-two violins, twelve contrabasses, twelve violoncellos, two oboes, four horns, three lutes, and two cymbals had been assembled to lend pomp to the occasion, together with a vast chorus. Unfortunately the music to this serenade has been lost, and its exact title is not known. The orchestral list has survived, however;[1] and the isolated appearance of four 'Jägerhörner' at this date in a city situated so far to the south of the horn's breeding-ground immediately suggests the agency of a musical noble who knew and liked the instrument.

It is by no means a coincidence that both Bononcini's serenade and Fux's opera *Elisa*, also written to commemorate the Empress's birthday, should be embellished with horn fanfares. Elisabeth Christina was the daughter of Duke Johann Adolf of Braunschweig-Wolfenbüttel. Her uncle, Duke Anton Ulrich, was a passionate huntsman and music-lover, and has already figured in the present study as one of the first nobles to install horn-players in his opera orchestra at Wolfenbüttel.[2] The young Empress evidently inherited his love for the hunt and his musical interests, which she shared with her husband, Charles VI. The inclusion of horns in two scores which were written expressly for her birthday a year apart suggests that she was partial to this instrument; and it is not at all impossible that the appointment of Rossi and Otto as 'Jägerhornisten' to the Imperial orchestra was a result of her in-fluence as well.

Horn-players appear to have become a permanent department of the Neapolitan chapel royal, for in 1715, the year following the Bononcini serenade, Alessandro Scarlatti brought out his opera *Tigrane*. This score calls for a pair of horns, as does his *Telemaco* of 1718.[3] Scarlatti's German pupil

---

[1] Quoted in Benedikt, *Das Königreich Neapel unter Kaiser Karl VI* (Vienna, 1927), pp. 624–7.

[2] See page 57 in this chapter, and Chapter II, p. 42.

[3] See Edward Dent, *Alessandro Scarlatti* (London, 1905), pp. 127 and 157 respectively. Dent remarks on p. 125 that 'In the later operas they [the horns] nearly always have passages of some length to play by themselves unaccompanied, so that their charac-teristic tone might be heard to the best advantage. Probably they were played by the trumpeters, just as now the cor anglais part is often played by one of the oboe players, since the horns and trumpeters are never used together.' In the light of the probable Bohemian origin of these early Neapolitan horn-players, it would appear that Dent's theory is now subject to reconsideration. The horn parts themselves argue against the identity of the horn-players with the trumpeters, since they are not clarino parts, but keep rather to the second and third octaves of the horn's range.

Johann Adolf Hasse learned to write for horns while at Naples, and included a pair of them in his first opera, *Tigrane*, performed there in 1723. His Viennese operas often call for horns, and *Cleofide* (1730) has important parts for F horns throughout.

In 1732 the oratorio *Il Giasone* was performed in the Palazzo Reale with the composer, Scarlatti's pupil Nicola Porpora (1686–1766), conducting. Here again the orchestra included four horns.[1] Pairs of horns are met with in *Sta. Elena al Calvario*, Leonardo Leo's oratorio of 1734, and again in Francesco Durante's oratorio *Abigaile* of 1736, a piece remarkable for its use of stopped notes. Durante's pupil Nicola Jommelli scored for a pair of horns in his opera *Odoardo* (Naples, 1738); and in almost all of his later operas written at Vienna and Stuttgart. Thus the horn was adopted early in the century as a regular, if infrequent, embellishment in the orchestration of Scarlatti and his pupils at Naples. Except for slight variations amongst individual composers, the style in which the Neapolitans wrote for the horn differed little from that of their Viennese and German colleagues: a feature which suggests that nearly all the orchestral horn-players of this period shared a common provenance.

Meanwhile at Vienna the horn had been gaining steadily in popularity since its formal début in 1715. We have noted earlier that in 1717 Lady Mary Wortley Montague was 'deafened' by the horns which enlivened the music at every public ball. Two years later Antonio Caldara called for a pair of horns in his opera *Sirita*. Caldara's fanfares, however, are not so well wrought for the instrument as were those in *Elisa*, partaking rather more of the trumpet idiom. This may well reflect the fact that Otto's death in 1718 had broken up the Imperial opera's leading pair of horn-players, and that Caldara had to make do with trumpeters who doubled on the horn. But the mere fact of their inclusion points to the increasing use which the horn now found.

The Baroque style matures

Towards the end of the second decade of the century the Baroque style in horn-playing reached its full perfection. Both the instrument and its technique had by this time matured sufficiently to invite confidence on the part of composers in assigning to it full-length obbligato parts which abounded with exposed solo passages of great difficulty. Bach, Handel, and Telemann,

[1] Benedikt, op. cit., p. 627. The composition of the orchestra on this occasion is interesting in that it furnishes an index to the normal strength of the Capella Reale in all departments: four contrabasses, two violoncelli, two lutes, one bassoon, thirty-two violins, six violette, four 'Jagdhörnern', two trumpets and six oboes—a total of fifty-nine players. Each musician received two ducats, Porpora 45 lire. It should be noted here that although the portrait of the royal Neapolitan orchestra under Mancini (Vice-capellmeister under Scarlatti) in Palais Harrach at Vienna does not depict wind-players, Benedikt's lists clearly show that oboes, horns, trumpets, and bassoons performed frequently with the ensemble; they were in all likelihood part of its permanent personnel.

the giants of that day, began to accord a position of increasing prominence to the horn; and it is amongst their works that we find some of the most valuable and definitive records of the pre-hand-horn style. In most of these instances the music is our only source. There are a few cases, however, where the identity of the actual horn-players is either known or can be inferred from surrounding evidence. A case in point is the First Brandenburg Concerto of J. S. Bach.

Most authorities agree that 1719 was the year of the First Brandenburg's composition. The actual date of its first performance, however, has up to now been a matter for conjecture. It is clear from three entries in the Cöthen Court archives that the appearance there of the two horn-players Hans Leopold and Wenzel Franz Seydler on 6 September 1721 most probably marks the date of the new concerto's first hearing.[1] The Cöthen orchestra had no regular horns of its own, and although Seydler and Leopold were readily available from the near-by Court at Barby, it is obvious that they would only be called in for a work which specifically required a pair of horns.

Not only do the horn parts in Brandenburg No. 1 demonstrate the remarkable advancement in technique which horn-playing had reached by this time, but they provide a concrete record of Leopold's and Seydler's playing style. In point of sheer facility these parts show a considerable gain over those of the *Jagdcantate* which Bach had written only three years earlier for Zeddelmayer and Fiedler. Both the first and second parts abound with long chains of florid semiquavers; both make liberal use of the third octave; both parts bristle with leaps of fifths and octaves; and both require a degree of endurance which gives pause to even the best players of our own day. (See the accompanying record.) It is not in this virtuosity alone, however, that the significance of these parts may be seen to lie. Their true importance is rather in the elements which they share with the earlier horn music of the period. The hunting-call opening, as in the *Jagdcantate*, invokes the virtue *Tugend* in a salute to the princely patron and establishes at once the hornistic idiom; the abundance of thirds and sixths for the pair of horns provides the intervallic settings in which they sound best; and the tessitura lies in the second and third octaves of the horn's compass, the most sonorous part of its range, never exceeding C'''. Thus the Brandenburg horn parts reflect a developed horn idiom, and not, as has been assumed, an application of a style borrowed from the trumpet. These characteristics would further prove not only that Leopold and Syedler were players of the highest order but that their virtuosity was based on a fully evolved horn technique. Accordingly there is little doubt that they, like Zeddelmayer and Fiedler, did not double on the trumpet. It is no coincidence that Bach wrote his most genuinely horn-like obbligato parts for horn-players who were attached to various neighbouring courts

[1] See page 98.

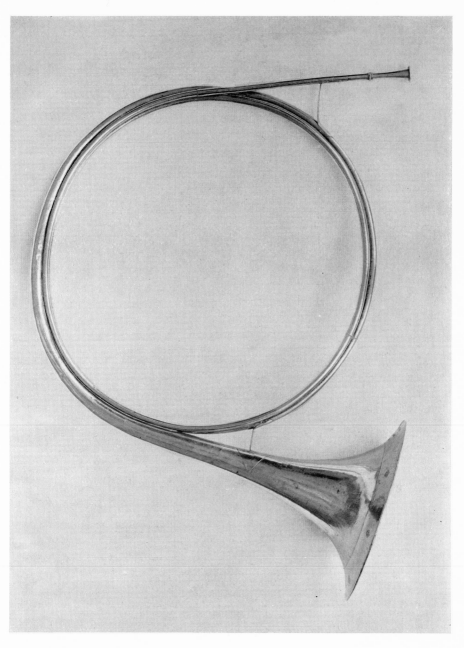

V Parforce-Jagdhorn in E by Michael Leichnambschneider, Vienna, 1718.
(*Historisches Museum, Basel*). See p. 41.

VI A Boar Hunt, from a series of hunting prints by Michael Heinrich Renz, 1728. The upward-pointing position of the horn is clearly dictated by the triangular composition of the central group. Renz received many commissions from Sporck; the horn-player might well be Sweda or Rölig. See p. 83.

in that capacity: the *Jagdcantate* for Zeddelmayer and Fiedler at Weissenfels; the First Brandenburg Concerto fot the two Barby horn-players; and the Quoniam from the B Minor Mass for one of the Schindlers at Dresden.

The practice of doubling on the trumpet and horn was part and parcel of the horn technique of the Baroque, and indeed the instances of specialist horn-players which have been discussed up to this point form rather the exception than the rule. Only the more affluent courts could support both an opera and a hunt of sufficient stature to occupy even one or two horn-players the whole time; and it was common practice, especially in the case of the town musicians or *Stadtpfeifer*, for trumpeters to take up the horn when occasion required it. Indeed, the high clarino horn parts of Bach and Handel would be unthinkable except in terms of this doubling technique, and the fact that many of the early horn-players received their training on the trumpet has already received comment. It was because this reciprocal technique was so prevalent that the horn and trumpet remained more or less inter-changeable in many composers' minds until quite late in the period: a circumstance which has contributed to the erroneous present-day belief that the two instruments were identical in tone quality. But it was for the few players who could afford the luxury of specializing that the most characteristic horn music was written; and it is in these exceptions to the general situation—the court horn-players and soloists, and the music written for them—that we find the development of the horn's proper idiom.

Trumpets and horns frequently played the same parts side by side, as a glance through the works of Bach and Handel will show. It is in this capacity that we meet the brothers Schindler[1] at the festival performance of Fux's opera *Constanze e Fortezza* on the occasion of the coronation of Charles VI as King of Bohemia at Prague in 1723. The score of this work[2] does not call for horns specifically. Yet Dlabacž[3] tells us that these two horn-players from the Dresden Court played 'with great distinction'. From this it is evident that they simply doubled the trumpet line in the absence of expressly written horn parts. The style of one of the Schindlers is immortalized, how-ever, in the Quoniam of the B Minor Mass, a point which will be amplified further on.

During the twenties and thirties composers began to avail themselves of the highly developed technique which had become common amongst horn-players. From this point on an increasing number of prominent obbli-gato parts for solo horn begin to appear in the repertory, and the horn had

[1] The two Bohemians had been brought by Augustus the Strong to Dresden in 1720 from Prague, whence he recruited many of the virtuosi for his Court. There is a strong possibility that the Schindlers were pupils of Hermoläus Smeykal, the leading horn teacher at Prague during the early decades of the century.
[2] Reproduced as Vol. XVII of *Denkmäler der Tonkunst in Österreich*.
[3] op. cit., iii, p. 43.

virtually cast off the stylistic shackles which bound its idiom to that of the trumpet. Flowing six-eight rhythms which derived from the calls of the mounted hunt; conjunct semiquaver figures in long legato lines; melodic fifths and octaves; and the absence of marcato repeated notes now became the hallmarks of a natural style which enabled the horn to speak in its own right.

By the third decade horn-playing had advanced sufficiently in the acceptance of the public to admit of certain innovations and indeed sleight-of-hand variants within the framework of orthodox practice. Again we turn to the Cöthen Cammerarchiv for 1725,[1] where we read of a concert performed by one Beda, whose stock in trade was the curious feat of playing on two horns at once. '18 August. To the horn-player Beda, who plays on two horns at once, 6 Gulden in final payment.'

A number of theories have been assayed in explanation of Beda's ambidexterity; but failing more detailed contemporary accounts, we must content ourselves with the Cöthen record as it stands. It must be remembered that cornettists for well over two hundred years had used a side-placed embouchure like that presumably required to play two horns simultaneously: thus the technique itself was not new. Morley-Pegge's conjecture that a similar feat performed by a blind horn-player at Hamburg in 1713[2] represented an early attempt at horn chords does not apply here if the Cöthen account is to be taken at face-value. What does strike our attention, however, is that the only comment in the record concerns the novelty of the performance. We may therefore conclude that the appearance of a solo-horn recitalist was a fairly common occurrence by this date, whereas one who could boast his own accompaniment was a remarkable fellow indeed.

Handel and horn-players in England

The earliest example of the full-blown Baroque solo style occurs in Handel's opera *Giulio Cesare* of 1723 in the brilliant horn obbligato to Cesare's aria 'Va Tacito e Nascosto' in Act II. Here all the resources of the Baroque horn idiom are exploited to the fullest. Repeated notes, legato figuration in semiquavers both conjunct and disjunct, and triadic outlines are notably present, as is the characteristic breath legato (♩ ♩ ♩ ♩). (See the accompanying record.) The melodic fifth, derived from the *Jagdanblasen* call, recurs frequently; and the cadential flourish forecasts a convention which was to become especially popular with the Mannheim composers later in the century. It is unfortunate that the name of the virtuoso who first performed this remarkable piece of bravura horn-writing is not known.

[1] Quoted in Smend, op. cit., p. 154.
[2] Mattheson, *Der Vollkommene Capell-Meister*, p. 53.

Indeed, virtually nothing is known about Handel's horn-players, and apart from a shadowy Mr. Winch no actual names have come to light. Two points of evidence, however, strongly suggest that the early Handelian horn-players were Bohemians: the flood of German-speaking musicians which poured into London in the wake of both Pepusch and Handel; and the horn parts themselves, which resemble markedly those of Bach, Fux, and Telemann. It is worth our while to pause here and consider in detail the question of who Handel's horn-players may have been.

Ex. 10.

Handel: *Aci, Galatea e Polifemo* (1708).

Undoubtedly Handel's first contact with the horn came when as a boy he visited the Weissenfels Court; and it was at Hamburg in 1705 that he first experienced the horn as an orchestral instrument in Keiser's opera *Octavia*. Horn-players, as we have seen, were to be had in Naples as well; and it is no coincidence that the Naples serenata, 'Aci, Galatea e Polifemo' of 1708 (Ex. 10) included a pair of horns. When this passage is compared with the Klingenberg aria quoted in Ex. 6, a decided similarity in the handling of the two horns is unmistakable, particularly with respect to the frequent third-fifth-sixth sequence and the movement in consecutive thirds. While it is difficult to impute a direct influence on Klingenberg's part upon the early horn-writing of Handel, this example does point towards the fact that Handel learned to orchestrate for horns within the milieu of the North German composers of the day, all of whom, as we have seen, wrote for the early Bohemian and Saxon horn-players.

Ex. 11.

Handel: *Rinaldo*

Nor did Handel change his style of writing for the horn when he came to England: and the fact that it continued to develop in the direction followed by his continental contemporaries would further suggest that he was writing for horn-players of the Austro-Bohemian school. As early as 1711 we encounter a truly Mozartean use of thirds and fifths in the two F horn parts accompanying Armida's aria, 'Combatti da Forte' in Act I of *Rinaldo* (Ex. 11).

The sinfonia to Act III of *Floridante* (1721: Ex. 12) contains a horn call which evokes much of the same atmosphere as that in Fux's *Elisa*, written seven years earlier (Ex. 8). In their spacing, independent movement and use of intervals, the two F horns in the Chorus to Act III of *Admeto* (1727: Ex. 13) follow the general lines of those which signal the arrival of Neptune's ship

in Scarlatti's *Telemaco* of 1718 (Ex. 14). There is a surprising similarity between the horn parts which accompany Oronte's aria 'Dell'onor' in Act II of *Riccardo* (1727: Ex. 15) and those in the third movement of J. S. Bach's Brandenburg Concerto No. 1 (1719/21: Ex. 16). The same is true of the hunting-call patterns in the Allegro movement of the Concerto for Double

Orchestra No. 29 (1740: Ex. 17) when compared with the solo horn parts of the Vivace from Telemann's *Musique de Table*, 3me Production (1733: Ex. 18). It is significant that although Handel had used this identical horn melody ten years earlier to accompany Rosmira's aria 'So segno so fiero' in Act I of *Partenope*, the characteristic ascending dactyls which open the Telemann piece, and which figure prominently in the later Handel example (a

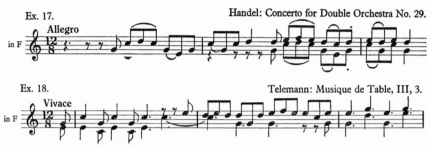

Ex. 17.   Handel: Concerto for Double Orchestra No. 29.

Ex. 18.   Telemann: Musique de Table, III, 3.

stylized adaptation, incidentally, of the Austrian 'Jagdanblasen' call) are not present (Ex. 19, a and b). As it is well known that Handel borrowed the Overture of the *Musique de Table* for the Occasional Oratorio (1746) and the 'Postillions' for *Belshazzar* (1745), we may assume that the horn-call figure was a direct borrowing as well. Yet the overall design of the horn parts in the earlier *Partenope* aria agrees with that of the Telemann parts: so much so that their common idiom would suggest a contact on the part of both Handel and Telemann with horn-players of a common stylistic schooling.

Ex. 19.   Telemann: first horn figure.
     a)   (as above).

     b)   Jagdanblasen call, Austrian, late 17th century.

It is often argued that Handel depended upon either French players for the performance of his horn parts or upon gifted English players who were primarily trumpeters, both of whom would have been familiar with the French hunting-calls and would have used the French instrument; and that this would account for the horn calls which abound in his music. While it is true that certain of the hunting-figures in Handel's horn parts may be traced to French origins, the fact remains that the greater number of hunting-call motives appear as stylized versions of Austrian calls: and it cannot be denied that in their general effect these calls are more evocative of *Elisa* than of *La Chasse du Cerf*.[1]

[1] A 'divertissement' by J. B. Morin, 1679–1745, performed before Louis XIV on 25 August 1708, is often cited as one of the first instances in which the horn appears in the orchestra in France. The hunting-fanfares which it contains consist merely of primitive repeated-note figures. See Piersig, op. cit., p. 39. A copy survives in the British Museum.

So far as the instrument is concerned, all the evidence indicates that Handel wrote for the terminally crooked model which the Leichnamb-schneiders had evolved in Vienna at the beginning of the century, and which was in common use amongst the Austro-Bohemian horn-players of Handel's day. A large number of his horn parts calls for horns in the higher keys of G and B flat. Horns in these keys were virtually unknown in France, the classic pitches for the cor-de-chasse being C and D. Furthermore, frequent changes of pitch are called for in the same piece (from movement to movement), and in many instances Handel anticipates the later practice of writing for four horns in two pairs of differing pitch, usually the tonic and dominant, in order to increase the available number of open notes. It has been assumed up to now that complete sets of French horns in various pitches were used to play these frequently changing parts. The factor of expense alone would rule out this practice, for a man could live comfortably for a year on the amount a single horn cost. If sets of instruments were used, then the cost would of necessity have been borne by the theatrical companies or by Handel himself; and there are no records of horns (or any other orchestral instruments, for that matter) bought by any of the London theatres or by Handel. Rather these key changes point clearly to horns with crooks, a feature which was not introduced in France until nearly 1750; and even at that time crooked horns were not well known before Johann Stamitz's arrival in Paris in 1754.[1] It was in England that Handel first came to know the concert horn, for he had left the Continent in 1711, a bare eight to ten years after the Leichnamb-schneiders first brought out their orchestral model with crooks in Vienna (see Chapter II, pp. 32–4); and it is reasonably certain that the crooked horn

[1] The first mention of the crooked horn appears in the *Mercure de France* for September 1749, where attention is drawn to 'les deux nouveaux cors de chasse allemands'. Yet this innovation made little impact at first. Rousseau, in a letter to Baron Grimm of 1750, still speaks of 'quatre grands cors de chasse' ('Sur l'opera italien', 1750, MS. Biblio-thèque de Neuchatel, Carton E; also reproduced in Jansen, *J. J. Rousseau als Musiker* (Berlin, 1884), p. 462). In 1750 the musical amateur, Riche de la Pouplinière, engaged horn- and clarinet-players from Germany for his private band. The horn-players were Syyryneck and Steinmetz (discussed in Chapter IV), who brought with them their crooked horns. It was not until 1754, however, when Johann Stamitz introduced these new instruments to Parisian audiences at La Pouplinière's concerts, that they caught on. (See George Cucuel, *La Pouplinière et la Musique de Chambre au XVIIIe Siècle*, Paris, 1913, pp. 320, 330–1.) The *Mercure de France* for October of 1754 (p. 185) brings to notice a 'symphonie nouvelle à cors de chasse et hautbois de la composition de M. Stamitz, directeur de la musique instrumentale et maître des concerts de S.A.E. Palatine', which had been played at a Concert Spirituel on 8 September of that year. The following March the *Mercure* (April 1755, p. 181) again comments on the novelty of 'une sym-phonie de Stamich avec clarinets et cors de chasse'. Gossec later confirms that Stamitz and his patron had ushered in horns and clarinets in a remark to his friend Marmontel about the year 1757: 'M. Le Riche de la Pouplinière qui le premier amena l'usage des cors à ses concerts d'après les conseils du célèbre J. Stamitz.' (Quoted in M. Brenet, *Les Concerts en France sous l'ancien Regime*, Paris, 1900, p. 221.) Even so, the Paris Opera did not feature a pair of regular horns until 1759 (Morley-Pegge, op. cit., p. 16).

had not yet come into widespread use, or at least to Handel's attention, by that date.[1] Thus the presence of crook changes in his horn parts of the following decade may be taken as an additional proof that the Waldhorn was introduced into England by horn-players of the Austro-Bohemian school. Viewed in this light, Burney's statement that 'The Messings were the first who pretended to perform in all keys in England, about the year 1740' is now subject to reconsideration.[2]

In the foregoing musical examples a decided predominance of the keys of F and E flat will have been noticed. Here again Handel follows the practice of his colleagues on the Continent, for there had been an early tendency on their part to settle upon these keys for exposed passages which were distinctly hornistic.[3] It is no coincidence, then, that the solo obbligato parts both in *Giulio Cesare* and *L'Allegro*[4] are pitched in F and E flat respectively.

Certainly the internal evidence offered by Handel's horn music itself makes out a strong case for the introduction of the crooked concert horn into

[1] Yet the Viennese innovation reached even Hamburg in a very short time, for Mattheson (*Das Neu-Eröffnete Orchester*, Hamburg, 1713, I, p. 267) remarks 'moreover, such horns can be tuned higher or lower by means of shanks and crooks.' Even so, this was two years after Handel had left Hamburg.

[2] This would further account for the decidedly Viennese design, tone quality and playing characteristics observable in certain crooked horns made in England about mid-century. These Austrian features are present to a striking degree in the English instruments of that period which have so far been examined by the writer, e.g. four horns by John Christopher Hofmaster (Johann Cristoph Hofmeister, who himself could well have been an immigrant Viennese maker), and two by Nicholas Winkings (Plate XIV). The Leichnambschneider instrument was itself known in England early in the century, as is revealed by the item, '2 French Hunting Horns made by Johann Leicham Schneider, Vienna, 1711' in J. C. Pepusch's catalogue of the Duke of Chandos's instruments, dated 23 August 1720. (Quoted in Otto Erich Deutsch, *Handel, A Documentary Biography*, London, 1955, p. 109.) Nor must we omit the two silver horns bought of Johannes Leichnambschneider by Lord Tredegar in 1725 (see p. 42). The six English-made horns which have come to light so far show a direct influence on the part of the Viennese makers; and the probability that the first concert-horn-players in England were Bohemians has already been explored above. On the strength of this combined evidence it now appears that the foundations of artistic horn-playing in eighteenth-century England were not French, as is commonly held, but rather Austro-Bohemian.

[3] Musical commentators of the same time in northern, middle, and southern Germany agree upon F as the horn's basic pitch. Mattheson says of his 'lieblich-pompeusen Waldhörner' that 'The commonest are pitched in F and C, the latter having the same compass as the trumpet.' Handel frequently doubled horns and trumpets in C. (*Das Neu-Eröffnete Orchestre*, Hamburg, 1713, I, p. 267.) Eisel confirms that 'they are most commonly pitched in F' (*Musicus Autodidactus*, Erfurt, 1738, p. 74); and Majer's *Museum Musicum* (Schwäbisch Hall, 1732), p. 41, unabashedly quotes Mattheson.

[4] Reference here is made to the air, 'Mirth, admit me of thy crew', from *L'Allegro, Il Pensieroso ed Il Moderato* of 1740. Another high-water mark in the Baroque solo repertory for horn, this highly characteristic obbligato part is in many ways more forward-looking than its counterpart in *Giulio Cesare*. Its short cadenza could well be used to good effect in the finale of many classical horn concerti. See Ex. 20.

Ex. 20.   Handel: *L'Allegro.*

England by players of Bohemian birth or training: but is there sufficient record concerning the players themselves to support this argument?

We have seen how the first Bohemian horn-players of whom record remains arrived in England with Pepusch's travelling 'Hautboys' as early as 1704. The horn had certainly been known in this country before that date, and is in fact thought to have come from France at the time when the Royal Buckhounds were refounded in the reign of Charles II. The very term 'French Horn', which was applied alike to instruments of both the cor-de-chasse and later Waldhorn genres, indicates an early acquaintance with the French instrument.[1]

It is clear from the scanty surviving sources, however, that the French horn, even though it was greatly developed and refined by English makers such as William Bull,[2] was not used as a concert instrument by native players here. Rather it served to embellish the polite serenades of the nobility, and 'to accomodate Sports-men with the delightful Harmony of Hunting'; and, in fact, any mention of the French horn in the English literature of the period up to 1750 is concerned mostly with its function as a hunting instrument.[3]

[1] See Pepusch's catalogue in footnote 2 on the preceding page.

[2] William Bull was trumpet- and horn-maker to William and Mary and to Queen Anne. His only surviving horn is a splendid example dated 1699, now in the Carse collection at the Horniman Museum. Patterned on the French model, it is made of copper with brass garnishings, and has a fine, ringing tone. It is not, however, a concert instrument.

[3] See also p. 7. The passage quoted is from Ned Ward's journal, *The London Spy,* for April 1699, hitherto thought to be the earliest reference to the horn in England. (See Blandford, 'The French horn in England', in *Musical Times,* October 1922, p. 697.) But there exists yet an earlier reference to the horn than that quoted above, if we accept the retrospective dating in the passage from Daniel Defoe's *The Fortunate Mistress* (1724) quoted on p. 7 footnote 2, which refers to events in 1695.

If the 'Trumpets in Hunting' which Daniel Purcell calls for in his setting of Dryden's *The Saecular Masque* of 1700 are, in fact, horns, then this is their first entry into concert music in England. The parts themselves, however, are cast unequivocally in the idiom of the trumpet: so that even if horns were implied they would undoubtedly have been played by trumpeters. Thus this music discloses nothing concerning the playing style of whatever concert horn-players may have been active in England at that date.

Later allusions to the growing favour which the horn enjoyed as the century progressed concern the hunt and its attendant serenades; but of native concert-horn-players no mention is made. By the second quarter of the century it had become the fashion amongst persons of quality to station a pair or more of horn-players in their gardens to regale guests whilst walking. On one occasion in 1729 the Duke of Newcastle visited Queen Caroline at Richmond Palace. '. . . . her Majesty sent us word that she

Just as every continental noble boasted his hunting-band, so the English aristocrat of the day appears to have considered a pair or more of horn-players to be a necessary part of his household staff. But these early hunting-horn-players, unlike their German-speaking counterparts, appear not to have developed their playing technique beyond that required for simple marches and hunting ditties:[1] and it is doubtful whether even the famous 'Cato'[2] could have done justice to the more difficult of Handel's horn parts.

As regards the Bohemian virtuosi and concert-horn-players, on the other hand, written record for the first third of the century is meagre indeed. After the appearance of Pepusch's 'young Hautboys' in 1704 there is a

was agoing to walk in the garden', wrote a member of the party, which then hastened to join the Queen. They 'walked till candlelight, being entertained with very fine French Horns' (Greenwood, *Lives of the Hanoverian Queens of England*, London, 1909, i, p. 310). If the writer of the passage quoted is, as R. Morley-Pegge believes, Sir Robert Walpole, then it is probable that 'Cato', the legendary negro horn-player then in Walpole's service, was amongst the 'very fine French Horns' that evening.

Even as late as 1750 the horn was to make its first impression on Dr. Johnson as an open-air instrument. Boswell, in his *Life of Johnson*, writes on page 896: 'Mr. Langton and he [Johnson] having gone to see a Freemason's funeral procession, when they were at Rochester, and some solemn musick being played on French horns, he said, "This is the first time that I have ever been affected by musical sounds;" adding, "that the impression made on him was of a melancholy kind." Mr. Langton saying, that the effect was a fine one,—Johnson. "Yes, if it softens the mind so as to prepare it for the reception of salutary feelings, it may be good; but inasmuch as it is melancholy *per se*, it is bad".' Boswell remarks in a footnote: 'The French horn however, is so far from being melancholy *per se* that when the strain is light in the field there is nothing so cheerful!'

[1] Whereas most of the early Bohemian virtuosi were the sons of foresters and bonds-men, many later achieved an independent livelihood as concert soloists, using a career in music as a passport to wider professional horizons and as means of raising their station in life. In England, however, the horn remained very much a servant's instrument, and such avenues for bettering one's lot appear not to have been available to the native retainer horn-player, as the following advertisement from the *Daily Advertiser* for 26 December 1747 confirms:

THIS is to acquaint any Gentlemen that are desirous to learn to play on any Musical Instrument, that they may be taught at the George in St. Mary Axe, every Monday and Thursday, at a very reasonable Rate. Gentlemen's Servants may be taught the French Horn.

This may be taken as a further indication that such virtuosi and concert players as there were would have come from abroad.

[2] Cato was a negro horn-player in the service of Sir Robert Walpole, from whose retinue he passed to that of the Earl of Chesterfield in the 1730s. In 1738, according to J. P. Hore's *History of the Royal Buckhounds* (London, 1893), p. 321, 'The Prince and Princess of Wales and young George and his little sister arrived at Cliefden House "for the summer season", where they received a present from the Earl of Chesterfield, "of Cato (his Black), who is reckon'd to blow the best French Horn and Trumpet in England". . . . His portrait was painted in a group of hunting celebrities by Wooton and is here (Hore, p. 322) engraved from the original picture in the possession of Walter Gilbey, Esq., at Elsenham Hall, Essex. The Prince of Wales appointed "Cato" head gamekeeper at Cliefden, and afterwards at Richmond Park.'

puzzling absence of horn-players from the concert bills and journals until 1729, when the Bohemian virtuoso and one-man duettist, Joachim Friede-rich Creta, arrives from Hamburg,[1] 'to blow the first and second treble on two French horns in the same manner as is usually done by two performers'.[2] There is a gap of twenty-five years between Pepusch's horn-players and Creta; and not until the forties do Mr. Charles and the Messings begin to give their solo recitals.

But it is remarkable that these players, aside from the nebulous Mr. Winch, were the only ones known so far to have attracted notice as concert players; and that they were all exponents of the Austrian style of horn-playing, as indeed Mr. Winch himself now appears to have been.[3] The gaps between these sporadic notices must not be taken to mean that horn-playing had stopped altogether, except for the orchestral trumpet-players who doubled on the horn. It is still true today that prominent orchestral players are rarely mentioned in the Press, and this was even more the case in Handel's time.

The great number of idiomatic horn parts in Handel's operas and orato-rios, however, requiring players who were familiar with the crooked horn and who confined themselves to the best part of the horn's range, unequivo-cally suggests Bohemian players. Moreover, it has been shown that the stylistic counterparts to Handel's horn pieces are to be found in Scarlatti,

[1] Mattheson's *Der Musicalische Patriot* (Hamburg, 1728), p. 26, contains a notice on Creta's Hamburg concerts, which earned him only just enough to pay his lodging bill (cf. p. 99). It is perhaps kindest not to take Creta's slender box-office as an index to his ability. He must have fared better in subsequent concerts, for he was able to travel to London the following year.

[2] *Dictionary of Musicians* (London, 1824), p. 87.

[3] Further support is given the possibility that Mr. Winch was of German-speaking origin by the following advertisement on p. 46 of the *Dublin Mercury* for 2–6 March 1742. 'For the Benefit of Mr. THUMOTH/ At the Theatre in Smock-Alley, on Friday the / 12th of March 1741-2 / A GRAND CONCERT / of Vocal and Instrumental MUSIC . . . Mr. Winch will Perform a Concerto compos'd / by Signor Hasse, with Barberini's Minuet on the French Horn.' The concerto in question was undoubtedly written for the Dresden horn-players after Hasse had taken up residence there in 1731. Mr. Winch, if indeed he hailed from Bohemia or Saxony, may have brought the piece with him. It appears to have been a standard item in his repertory, and was probably the 'Concerto' which 'the celebrated Mr. Winch, who has perform'd several Years in Mr. Handel's Operas and Oratorios', played between the acts of King Lear at the Smock Alley Theatre on 22 October of the previous Autumn (*Dublin Mercury*, 8–15 October 1740/1). In this context it appears not unlikely that Mr. Winch may have come with Handel to London, or at any rate followed him, perhaps from Hamburg, where Hasse's music was much played. On the other hand, if Winch was an English-man, he would obviously have obtained the Hasse concerto (probably a suite or trio sonata with a concertante horn part) from an immigrant hornist: in this case most likely his teacher. We must not forget, however, that the name 'Winch' could easily be an anglicized form of the German surname Wünsch or even Winschermann; just as 'Mr. Charles' owed his style to the difficulties of pronunciation which his Hungarian name evidently posed to the eighteenth-century Briton.

Fux, Telemann, and J. S. Bach, all of whom were writing within the main-stream of the Austro-Bohemian style. In view of the number of German-speaking musicians which flocked to London during Handel's lifetime, there is no reason to doubt that his horn-players were products of the parent Austrian school as well.

Bach's later horn parts and players

Returning to the Continent, a word about Bach's horn parts of the Leipzig period and the players for whom he wrote is owing here. The subject of these altissimo parts has already received far too much comment from writers who have no first-hand knowledge of the horn or, for that matter, of any brass instrument; and the problem has become rather a windmill at which music-ologists find it fashionable to tilt. We know that Bach had no wind-players permanently available in the orchestra at the Thomaskirche, and was there-fore constrained to call in his winds as the occasion demanded from outside sources. Principal among these, as Schering, Terry, and Carse have pointed out,[1] was Leipzig's band of *Stadtpfeifer*. It was common practice for trum-peters in these municipal bands to double on the horn; and it was for such players that the majority of Bach's cantata horn parts were written. From time to time Bach appears to have had one or two genuine horn-players at his disposal, as the characteristic lines in Cantatas 1 and 65, for example, clearly show. For the most part, however, the difficulty of the cantata parts lies not in their technical complexity but in their extremely high tessitura; and to the trumpeter-horn-player equipped with the broad-rimmed mouthpiece of the time these parts would have presented few terrors.[2]

---

[1] Arnold Schering, *Musikgeschichte Leipzigs* (Leipzig, 1911), p. 47; and 'Zur Gott-fried Reiche's Leben und Kunst' in *Bach-Jahrbuch* (Leipzig, 1921); C. S. Terry, *Bach's Orchestra* (London, 1932), p. 9; Adam Carse, *The Orchestra in the Eighteenth Century* (Cambridge, 1940), pp. 42 and 162.

[2] The typical Baroque horn mouthpiece, which is discussed in the chapter on mouth-pieces, is in itself a record of this doubling technique. The rim is broad and flat, identical to that of the trumpet mouthpiece of the time. The cup, however, is conical, with straight sides leading to a small bore; and it was this feature which enhanced, as much as was possible under the circumstances, the characteristics of the horn's tone. With this mouthpiece the normal first-horn-player can sound the written d″ of Cantata No. 1 with comparatively little strain on the contemporary F horn. (Those who would have it that this or that instrument or mouthpiece enables players to sound notes in the altissimo register 'with ease' simply expose their unfamiliarity with the actual business of playing the horn: all notes above the sounding f″ require a certain amount of effort.)

The writer is firmly convinced that Cantata No. 65 is intended for horns in C basso. Quite apart from the markedly hornistic character of the parts, the pastoral quality of the piece calls for the softer timbre of the traditional C Waldhorn; the absence of drum parts further indicates that the martial brilliance of the C alto horn is not desired; and the spacing of the string parts is decidedly sympathetic to the lower horns. The author has himself taken part in performances of this work using both modern and contem-porary instruments in both the C alto and C basso readings. To his ear the lower pitch

It was when writing a solo horn part for a particular player that Bach set some of his most characteristic lines for the instrument. The horn obbligato to the first chorale of the early Leipzig cantata, 'Erforsche Mich, Gott' (*BWV* 136) displays every convention of the Baroque style described earlier. In fact, so strong is its idiomatic flavour, even in terms of the concerto style of the later Classical period, that its first five bars invite comparison with bars 112–20 of the finale of Mozart's Second Horn Concerto (Ex. 21). The name of the gifted player for whom Bach wrote this part has not come down to us. He may have been a visiting virtuoso from a near-by court, possibly one of the Schindlers from Dresden. In view of this piece's high pitch and tessitura, however, it is not impossible that the soloist may have been

Ex. 21.   Bach: Cantata, BWV 136.

Mozart: Concerto, K. 417, 3rd movt., bars 112–120.

Gottfried Reiche himself, the famous principal clarinist of the Leipzig *Stadt-pfeiferei*, for whom Bach set so many of his high trumpet parts.

The identity of the horn soloist in the 'Quoniam' of the B Minor Mass, on the other hand, may be inferred from the circumstances of its composition. As has been pointed out before, the Mass was written to commemorate the accession of Augustus III as King of Poland, and was performed on 21 April 1733 in his private palace chapel at Leipzig by members of the royal chapel orchestra and of the Court opera. Andreas Schindler, the elder of the two Bohemian brothers of that name, was to all evidence the principal of the pair; and it was his rather personal style of playing around which Bach wove the stately octaves and sparkling chains of semiquavers which distinguish this masterpiece of solo writing for the Baroque horn. Indeed, the 'Quoniam' displays all the characteristic devices of the early florid horn style

is indisputably more in keeping with the affection of the piece, and the general effect is best with the earlier instrument. On the accompanying record the subject of the cantata is recorded on a pair of horns made before 1770 using C basso crooks.

to such a degree of perfection that it may be said to mark a musical high point of the pre-hand-horn period.[1]

The years of transition, 1740-1770: some leading players

From the 1740s onward the annals of the Austro-Bohemian School record in increasing numbers the names of players and teachers whose accomplishments have come down to us through the more lasting medium of contemporary writings, rather than through the tenuous agency of court ledgers or the circumstances underlying the odd horn part. Our knowledge of these horn-players and tutors owes much, of course, to the fact that the art of horn-playing had by this time developed sufficiently to form a tangible part of the musical scene of the day. But we owe still more to their actual contributions to the horn and its music, which in the eyes of their peers were great enough to win for them lasting recognition, even if later ages were to be less grateful.

It was during these transitional decades up to the seventies that horn-playing took several long strides forward. The old clarino technique advanced to become the style which the early symphonists handed on to Haydn; and these years were to witness a revolution in tone and technique, sparked by the genius of Hampl, which gave us the horn as we know it today. This period marks as well the emergence of several virtuosi who, in founding the renowned families of soloists which bore their names, projected the Bohemian tradition forward through three generations. Thus these thirty years of mid-passage saw both the working-out of the old Baroque style and the founding of the new; and while the first major virtuosi began to fill the music-rooms, a teacher at Dresden was evolving the technique of hand-stopping which was to become the cornerstone of modern horn-playing. Our study of the Baroque style closes with a glance at the careers and contributions of those virtuosi who represented its final flowering.

Shortly after the Bohemian brothers Messing 'pretended to perform in all keys in England, about the year 1740'; while Mr. Winch was acquainting London audiences with a 'Concerto compos'd by Signor Hasse'; and about the time when Mr. Charles, 'the Hungarian Master of the French Horn' came to Dublin 'to shew the Beauty of that Instrument', the Bohemian virtuoso

---

[1] A comparison of the horn part of the 'Quoniam' with that of the equally remarkable and effective obbligato to the aria 'Mirth, Admit Me' in Handel's *Acis and Galatea*, discussed earlier, points up the more forward-looking character of the later piece. Although written only seven years after the 'Quoniam', the *Acis* obbligato has already cast off the floridity which was part and parcel of the Baroque horn style, and in its triadic simplicity and flowing six-eight rhythm forecasts the *rondo à la chasse* which was to become so popular in the horn concertos of the Classical period. In this instance may be seen reflected the larger differences in musical outlook and historical position which distinguish these composers from one another.

Johann Schindelarž went to Mannheim. Schindelarž had already won recognition at Prague as principal horn-player to Prince Mannsfeld during the late thirties; and it was at the festivities attending Maria Theresia's coronation as Queen of Bohemia in 1741 that his playing appears to have attracted the notice of the Elector Palatine, Carl Philipp, who forthwith engaged him for the Mannheim orchestra. On the same occasion Johann Stamitz was appointed leader and Court composer to the Elector, and the two Bohemians may well have arrived at Mannheim together.

Schindelarž appears to have led the field in what the present writer has called the early symphony style of horn-playing. This idiom grew out of the florid clarino style of the late Baroque. It was generally less decorated, tending rather towards sustained cantabile melodies in the third and fourth octaves of the horn's range, and abounding in rapid leaps of octaves and fifths. Although this manner of playing became common amongst the high-horn-players of the middle decades, it may well have found its first expression in Schindelarž's playing: for we find its earliest musical reflection in the horn parts of Johann Stamitz's youthful Mannheim symphonies (Ex. 26, p. 112). Indeed Schindelarž's playing left its impress upon Stamitz's manner of writing for the horn throughout his Mannheim period, and it was this style which Haydn later embraced when writing for Thaddäus Steinmüller, the Bohemian horn-player who was active at Esterhazy.

To all evidence Schindelarž was the first to teach this last refinement of the Baroque style. He left behind in Prague his gifted pupil Carl Haudek, who in 1744 went to join Hampl as principal horn at Dresden. According to Dlabacž, Haudek ranked among the foremost virtuosi of the century, and the beauty of his cantabile was a constant credit to his teacher. Hasse's Te Deum of c. 1750 contains an obbligato for two horns which portrays Haudek as a principal of exceptional attainments. The general style of this part mirrors many elements which Haudek's playing shared with that of his tutor (Ex. 28, p. 116); and it is probably to his lessons with Schindelarž in the sixties that Punto owed his later mastery of the high resgister.

From about 1750 onwards the horn began a Ulyssean return to the country of its birth, but in altered form and in the hands of Bohemian soloists. In 1751 a spiritual descendant of Beda and Creta, one Mr. Ernst, edified an audience at a Concert Spirituel with the old trick of playing a concerto on two horns at once. 'Cette nouveauté a paru plus singulière qu'agréable', the *Mercure de France* commented wryly; but the 'nouveaux cors de chasse Allemands' quickly caught the public fancy, and soon a veritable immigration of Bohemian horn-players poured into Paris to answer the rapidly growing demand for accomplished players. In 1754 two travelling virtuosi, Syryyneck and Steinmetz, who had a few years previously been imported by the musical amateur Riche de la Pouplinière, performed a double concerto at another Concert Spirituel with great acclaim. We do not know their stature as players; but the efforts of these first Bohemians served to establish the horn as a concert instrument in France to a degree that when Stamitz arrived to produce his new symphonies that same year, he found waiting for him horn-players with whose style he was already familiar.

It should be remarked in passing that the 1740s and 1750s saw the horn carried to the corners of the civilized world in the hands of Bohemian players. We have already followed its progress in Naples and London. By mid-century the brothers Hosa were established at Brussels; Maresch had gone

Ex. 22.   Haydn: 'Horn Signal' Symphony.

off to St. Petersburg as a Court virtuoso and had evolved his Russian horn band; and Kölbel had first delighted the Turkish ear with his playing at Constantinople. The activities of these players lie more on the periphery of our study of these decades, however; and the reader is referred to Chapter IV for a fuller account of their adventures.

Haydn's horn parts in several instances reflect the influences of two of the most prominent exponents of the early symphony horn style, Steinmüller and Thürrschmidt. Thaddäus Steinmüller was a Bohemian virtuoso of formidable attainments. Formerly in the service of Count Nostitz at Prague, he joined the Esterhazy ensemble as principal horn in 1762. The first-horn part of the 'Hornsignal' Symphony (Ex. 22) not only demonstrates Steinmüller's astounding mastery of the altissimo range, but in its similarity to many of Stamitz's horn parts points up the influence which both Steinmüller and Schindelarž exercised upon the horn-writing of the Viennese and Mannheim symphonists. Further monuments to the Esterhazy virtuoso's prodigious technique appear in Haydn's Concerto for first horn, written for Steinmüller in the year of his appointment, and in the extraordinary Divertimento a Tre of 1767, in which the horn part ascends to the twenty-second partial of the E flat horn. Steinmüller evidently possessed great talent as a teacher as well, for his three sons, Johann, Joseph (Haydn's namesake), and Wilhelm, were much appreciated as soloists in the eighties and nineties.

If Haydn did, in fact, write his Symphonies Nos. 46, 47, and 48 for Prince Kraft Ernst of Oettingen-Wallerstein,[1] then the first-horn part of the 'Maria Theresia' in particular is an eloquent testimony to the playing style of the Wallerstein orchestra's first horn, Johannes Thürrschmidt. (Haydn would have come across Thürrschmidt and his second, Joseph Fritsch, in Vienna, where they occasionally appeared in performances given by the Wallerstein musical intendant, Ignaz von Beecke, himself an amateur composer.) Although nothing is known of Thürrschmidt's career before he was appointed to the Wallerstein orchestra in 1750, the three symphonies in question display the unmistakable trade-marks of the early symphony style. The remarkable high cantabile line in the first-horn part of the 'Maria Theresia's' slow movement reflects what appears to have been Thürrschmidt's strong point, judging from the parts which Anton Rossetti wrote for him at Wallerstein: and the horn parts of all three of these symphonies differ, in their predilection for a more legato style of playing, from the earlier horn part which Haydn wrote for Steinmüller at Esterhazy.

The elder Thürrschmidt was the last exponent of the Bohemian early symphony style of whom record remains. Steinmüller left the Esterhazy Court in 1772; Schindelarž evidently retired in 1778; but Thürrschmidt, even though he retired officially in 1780 at the age of 55, continued to play until his death in 1800. With him ended the tradition of the old high-horn virtuosi which had begun with Smeykal's pupils in the twenties, and which had established the horn as a concert instrument throughout Europe. Like his contemporary, Steinmüller, Thürrschmidt's gifts as a teacher were reflected in the playing of his sons and grandson. We shall meet his elder son, Carl, as one of the major virtuosi and innovators of the next generation.

The technique of the high-horn players

Before leaving the high-horn style of the Baroque, a note on the actual technique of these altissimo-register players is due. We have already touched

---

[1] See p. 119 for a discussion of the circumstances surrounding the composition of these symphonies.

VII (a) The horns and continuo department of the Imperial Opera orchestra at Vienna in 1758. Detail from a Canaletto engraving of a dress rehearsal for the ballet *Le Turc Généreux*. Instruments of the old fixed-mouthpipe model are shown being played left and right-handed. See p. 83.

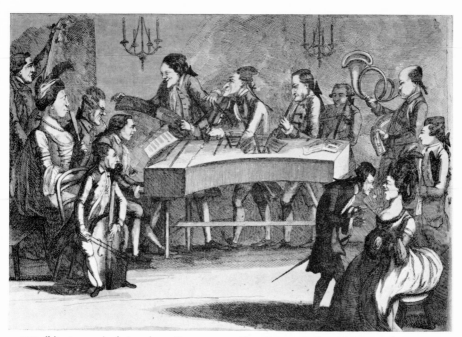

VII (b) A musical Sunday afternoon at Dr. Burney's house in 1782. Burney himself is seen in the right foreground; Fischer, the celebrated oboist, is standing behind the harpsichord. The horn-player is Monsieur Pieltain, a pupil of Punto. The satirical nature of Loraine Smith's drawing appears to have suggested the playing position of the horn. (*The Trustees of the British Museum*). See p. 83.

VIII Detail of a gold-ground silhouette of *c.* 1785 showing the wind-players
of the Wallerstein court orchestra. The horns are Josef Nagel and Franz
Zwierzina. See pp. 84, 161, 203.

upon the characteristic first-horn mouthpiece of the period; and it should be stressed that the embouchure of the pre-hand-horn style differed from that of the later period. Its placement was that of the trumpet embouchure, with two-thirds of the rim opening resting on the lower lip and one-third on the upper. This position made for ease in the upper register, although it restricted facility and fullness of tone somewhat in the bass octave.

Hand-stopping, of course, was virtually unknown in the earlier decades, and was little used by high-horn-players of the older generation even after stopping had been adopted by most low-horn-players after the middle of the century. By the forties, however, the occasional written a″ and b″ does appear in both first- and second-horn parts, and Bach and Handel both differentiate clearly between the f″ and F sharp, often in the same bar. Thus there is reason to suppose that a few horn-players knew how to use the hand in the bell to help them over certain notes: and the writer wholly agrees with Morley-Pegge's assertion that Hampl did not invent hand-stopping *totus porcus*. The core of the matter is that no one really knows when hand-stopping was invented, and in all probability no one ever will. It was a naturally evolved answer to the question of the false notes in the horn's partial scale, and it just grew. To those who would see in the potentially hand-stopped notes of Fantini's trumpet method of 1636 the beginnings of the right-hand technique, there is Tans'ur's statement of 1772 that 'D, F, A, and B are left out, by reason such *Notes* are not properly called *Trumpet* or *Horn Notes*; and when these sounds are set in a Piece of *Musick* they generally *rest* at these *Notes*, or use others in their stead, so as to make Harmony in the Concert, &c. And such as sound the 2d *Trumpet* or *Horn*, often perform the lower *concording Sounds* by the same Scale.'[1]

Mention should also be made here of the standing debate concerning the position in which the horn was held before the advent of hand-stopping. One viewpoint, supported by such authorities as Morley-Pegge and Janetzky, is that the horn was held with its bell pointing upwards when played. At the root of this assumption are the hundreds of illustrations which show the horn being played in this attitude. Typical examples may be seen in prints ranging in date from the early part of the century, such as the Rentz hunting-print of 1728 on Plate VI, to those of the middle decades, such as the Canaletto engraving of a scene mounted at the Hoftheater at Vienna in 1759, reproduced on Plate VII(a). Even as late as 1782 an English print shows the horn being played in this position by Mr. Pieltain, a pupil of Punto, at one of Dr. Burney's musical afternoons, Plate VII(b); and Blandford[2] has already mentioned in this context the Rowlandson and Hogarth prints which date from the close of the eighteenth century.

[1] William Tans'ur, *The Elements of Musick Display'd* (London, 1772), iii, p. 97.
[2] 'The French Horn in England' in *Musical Times*, August 1922.

The horn may well have been played in this vertical position in its early years, and even today horn-players are required to point their bells skyward for certain effect (for which the passage is marked 'Bells in the air', 'Schalltrichter hoch', or 'Padiglione in l'aria'). But in the writer's opinion, these illustrations represent a convention on the artist's part in the interests of showing the instrument to better advantage. The early orchestral players, to judge from all available accounts, were too much concerned with tone quality to sacrifice it to the upper air; and there remains what to the author's mind is the overriding consideration of practicality: that anyone who attempts to perform a difficult florid part holding the instrument in this precarious manner will soon be convinced that it is inadvisable to do so. The more plausible playing attitude of the pre-hand-horn-player is that adopted by the player in the centre of the right-hand group on Plate IIa; and on Plate VIII may be seen the typical position of the hand-horn period, which is also that of our own day.[1]

Hampl and hand-stopping

Much has been written about Anton Joseph Hampl, the Bohemian horn-player and teacher whose system of hand-stopping transformed the whole art of horn-playing about the middle of the century. Since Eichborn's *Die Dämpfung Beim Horn* (Berlin, 1887) first brought Hampl's importance to the attention of modern readers, virtually every writing on the horn has made some mention of him. Yet in spite of his widespread fame, not only as a teacher but as a virtuoso and inventor, there exists surprisingly little contemporary record of his accomplishments and discoveries, and indeed virtually nothing of his early life is known. The best account by an eighteenth-century writer is that of Gerber, which is reproduced on p. 226; and the most accurate present-day writing on Hampl's contributions is to be found in Morley-Pegge.[2]

All of these writings, save the last-mentioned, share the same misconceptions concerning Hampl's career and teachings. Most credit him with the outright invention of hand-stopping about 1770, some twenty years after this technique was known; most consider him a singular phenomenon who appeared suddenly at Dresden to revolutionize horn-playing *in toto*; and none discuss in any detail his accomplishments as a player. If, however, we look at him from the perspective of the Austro-Bohemian school of which he was so genuinely a product, not only do many of the anomalies concerning his life and works resolve themselves, but his historical position becomes

---

[1] Two authorities have kindly supported the writer in this view: Dr. Ernst Paul, author of the treatise, *Die Entwicklung des Hornes vom Natur- zum Ventilinstrument* (University of Vienna Dissertation, 1932), and Eric Halfpenny, of the Galpin Society.

[2] op. cit., pp. 88 ff.

clear as well. Seen against the backdrop of those horn-players who preceded and followed him, Hampl emerges as a central figure in eighteenth-century horn-playing.

That Hampl was a pupil of Smeykal, the major teacher of the first generation, is virtually certain. We know that Joseph Matiegka, Hampl's contemporary, who was a teacher and virtuoso of nearly equal significance, did study with Smeykal at Prague. The great similarity of style between the hand-horn pupils of both Hampl and Matiegka points unequivocally to a common schooling, as does the fact that Matiegka evidently sent Punto to Hampl at Dresden. Hampl appears to have come to the Dresden Court directly from Prague as a young man, and this would further confirm the external evidence: for it was from Prague that Augustus III recruited most of the principal instrumentalists for the Dresden opera to expand the orchestra under Hasse's new directorship. It is therefore more than likely that Hampl took up his post as second horn there as early as 1731. In view of these circumstances, Domnich's remark of c. 1808 that 'il vivait à la cour de Dresde, il y a environ soixante ans' takes on added authority.[1]

The importance of hand-stopping to the artistic development of the horn is generally agreed upon, as is Hampl's role as the first to present this technique in systematic form both in practice and on paper. The writer has said before that he is convinced that Hampl was not the sole inventor of the right-hand technique, but that he rather modified and organized a logical method of bridging the gaps in the horn's natural scale at which certain

[1] Heinrich Domnich, son of the Hungarian-born first horn at Wallerstein (see Appendix), later became the first professor horn-playing at the Paris Conservatoire. His *Methode de Premier et de Second Cor*, published at Paris in 1808, and later at Mainz with French and German texts, gives the first complete account of how Hampl reputedly evolved the technique of hand-stopping.

A la même époque, le Hautbois, bien éloigné du point de perfection où il est parvenu de nos jours, était un instrument aigre, criard et peu propre à l'accompagnement d'un chant gracieux ou d'un morceau d'expression. Quand on l'employait à cet usage, on avait coutume pour l'adoucir, d'introduire du coton dans la concavité du pavillon. Hampl, un des plus célèbres cors du tems conçut l'idée de substituer cette méthode à celle des sourdines. Il fit un tampon de coton disposé de manière à remplir l'objet qu'il avait en vue. Sa surprise fut extrême, la première fois qu'il s'en servit, d'entendre que son instrument était haussé d'un demi-ton. Ce fut pour lui un trait de lumière, et son génie entendant rapidement une découverte due au hazard, il vit le moyen, en présentant et retirant alternativement son tampon, de parcourir sans interruption l'échelle diatonique et chromatique de toutes les gammes. Alors il composa pour le Cor une musique nouvelle, où il fit entrer des notes qui jusques-là lui étaient étrangères. Quelque temps après, ayant remarqué que le tampon pouvait être avantageusement remplacé par la main, il cessa de se servir du tampon.

This, then, is one explanation, written certainly nearer the time than any other; but it seems unlikely that a player as intelligent as Hampl would be surprised at the effect of the cotton pad, especially as partial-stopping with the hand appears to have been known for some time before these experiments.

attempts had already been made. Accepting this postulate, there remains the question of how early Hampl began to use the new system, and when he started to teach it.

It is frequently maintained, even by modern writers, that Hampl 'discovered' hand-stopping in the 1770s. Not only may this theory be refuted by the fact of Hampl's death in 1771, but the appearance of the written a″ and b″ in the horn parts of Haydn and Stamitz during the sixties clearly points to an earlier knowledge of hand technique. Both Punto and Wiesbach left Matiegka's tutelage at Prague to study under Hampl shortly after the cease-fire of the Seven Years War in 1763. Since it is unlikely that the Dresden teacher could have evolved his new method during the period of Prussian bombardments and occupation (during which, it may be noted, activity at the Court opera was suspended), we may with reason conclude that he had brought it to a practical stage of development during the previous decade. (Domnich's account of how Hampl chanced upon hand-stopping is given in the preceding footnote.) This is further borne out by contemporary accounts (Gerber and Dlabacž) of how Punto, when living as Hampl's pupil at the house of the principal horn, Haudek, amazed the entire Court with his performances of Hampl's difficult second-horn concertos: clear proofs that by the early sixties Hampl had got as far as writing concertos embodying the new right-hand technique. (It is impossible to play a melody in the second-horn range without using the right hand; and indeed the whole genre of the cor-basse style was a direct result of hand-stopping.)

A helpful clue, not only as to the date of hand-stopping, but to Hampl's considerable prowess as a player, is furnished by one of his second-horn concertos which is preserved in the University Library at Lund (Sweden). Three such concertos by Hampl are listed in the Breitkopf catalogue for 1764, and two in 1769. Its melodic resemblance to the autograph *Lection Pro Cornui* of c. 1755–60 now in the Paris Conservatoire Library,[1] and its similarity in point of harmony and texture to the symphonies and overtures by Hasse and the Grauns from this period[2] strongly suggests Hampl's authorship and Rasmussen[3] has pointed to this piece as possibly the first extant concerto of the second-horn genre. The writer entirely agrees with this supposition, and with Miss Rasmussen's implied conjecture that it is of

[1] Hampl's *Lection Pro Cornui* is the earliest tutor to incorporate stopped notes. A number of autograph studies and an Arioso for three horns by Hampl are also preserved in this collection, and were no doubt presented by Punto himself. Excerpts from these pieces are reproduced in Morley-Pegge, op. cit., Appendix 4; and in Ex. 25a.

[2] See the musical examples in Carl Mennicke, *Hasse und die Brüder Graun als Symphoniker* (Leipzig, 1906), Chapter IV.

[3] 'The Manuscript Kat. Wenster Litt. 1/1–17b (Universitetsbiblioteket, Lund). A Contribution to the History of the Baroque Horn Concerto' in *Brass Quarterly*, Vol. V, No. 4 (Durham, New Hampshire, 1962).

an earlier date than the concertos listed in the Breitkopf catalogue. There has been no opportunity to study this work except from microfilm; but even without the confirmation which watermarks and other physical evidence might afford, it is safe to estimate the date of this concerto as falling between 1750 and 1760.[1]

Ex. 23.
a) from Hampl's *Lection pro Cornu*
b) from the D Major Concerto, 1st movt.
in D
c) D Major Concerto, 2nd movt.
in D

For the most part, only occasional stopped notes are met with in this work, and its musical worth is negligible. Passage-work such as that given in Ex. 23b comprises the bulk of its melodic content. But despite the monotony of these acrobatics, the piece affords an idea of the working vocabulary

Ex. 24. Haydn: Concerto for Second Horn, 1st movt.
in D

of the early second-horn style: and invites comparison with the second-horn concerto which Haydn wrote in 1767 for the Silesian horn-player Karl Franz (Ex. 24).

[1] This dating is suggested by a comparison with certain of Hasse's horn parts which were written for Hampl and Haudek at Dresden. Neither the Concertos for Violins, French Horns or Hoboys, written between 1736 and 1740 and published by Walsh in London *c.* 1742, nor the Te Deum in D of *c.* 1750, also written at Dresden, show any influence of Hampl's hand-stopping technique. We may therefore deduce that the cor-basse concerto under discussion was written after 1750 and before 1760, when the bombardments began and the Court orchestra broke up. It is unlikely that he wrote the piece during the three years when Dresden was under continuous siege.

Both historically and musically, the most significant moment in Hampl's concerto is the demisemiquaver scale in the cadenza of the second movement (Ex. 23 c). This curious passage is undoubtedly the earliest known instance of a diatonic scale in the horn's first and second octaves. It points both to Hampl's originality in the use of the right hand and to his own considerable virtuosity as a performer; and further strengthens this writer's conviction that Hampl began to make public use of hand-stopping as early as *c.* 1750.[1]

Hand-stopping brought about a virtual revolution in horn-playing which had far-reaching consequences. At one stroke the right hand gave the horn a complete chromatic scale in the first three octaves of its range; and because the hand now rested permanently in the bell of the instrument it had the important auxiliary effect of damping out the upper overtones in the horn's tonal spectrum, thus imparting that veiled, dark quality which still distinguishes the horn from the other brass today. Since it was no longer necessary to confine melodic playing to the extreme fourth octave where the natural tones of the horn lie a semitone apart, the first horn could now make use of the second and third octaves, thereby availing himself of the most pleasant and characteristic part of the horn's upper range. For this reason hand-horn players in the sixties began to replace the players of the old open-horn style of the Early Symphony period in the first part. By the following decade the change-over was virtually complete, and the clarino-based first-horn technique was, apart from the exceptions mentioned before, completely superseded. (Even established players and teachers like Matiegka, Hampl's counterpart at Prague, who had started his playing career as a clarino horn-player, now adopted and taught the new hand technique. The horn parts in both the 'Prague' Symphony and *Don Giovanni*, which Mozart wrote for Matiegka and his second, Schebka, embody stopped notes.)

The art of second-horn-playing also derived great benefits from hand-stopping and underwent sweeping changes as a result of its introduction. The line of demarcation between first and second horn, largely a legacy from the old trumpeters' guilds, now became clearly drawn. Before Hampl's technique had crystallized, high- and low-horn parts had overlapped to a great degree, and little if any use was made of the first octave. But with a chromatic scale now available in the lower register it was no longer necessary to press the mouthpiece so hard against the lips, as had been done to obtain the higher range. With this lightening of mouthpiece pressure, coupled with the downward-pointing position of the instrument which resulted from placing the right hand in the bell, the upper lip was now free to encompass

---

[1] Gerber, in his remark about the horn's bass octave (cf. p. 226), mentions this date as falling in about the year 1750. Gerber's dating, we may recall, errs on the late side; but here, since it concerns a person whom he actually knew, we are justified in accepting his statement within broad limits.

the larger vibrations of the notes in the lowest register; and accordingly the second horn's range was extended downwards by a full octave.

A corollary effect of this new playing position, one which affected both the high- and low-horn genres, was a change in embouchure. With the lighter pressure and free upper lip, the broad trumpet-type mouthpiece rim now gave way to the typical narrow rim of the present-day Viennese horn mouthpiece. This rim fostered a new embouchure placement, wherein the upper lip occupied two-thirds of the mouthpiece opening, instead of one-third its circle as in the clarino-horn embouchure. More will be said about this new embouchure in the chapter on mouthpieces: but it was the final result of the hand-stopping revolution, and if Hampl himself was not the first to teach it, we may be sure that the Bohemians were the first to adopt it.

Thus Hampl, in the light of his revision of the whole art of horn-playing, stands astride the line dividing the two periods. One of the last virtuosi and teachers of the Baroque, he paved the way by his mechanical and pedagogical reforms for the great hand-horn virtuosi of Mozart's day. In this sense he was at once the last great figure of the second generation and first major figure of the third. He was a product of that first era of horn-playing which had seen the horn win its place in the opera and chamber orchestra and impress its idiom upon the music of the principal composers of the time. His own generation had accomplished the ultimate refinement of the Baroque horn style. By the time of his death the horn had become an accepted solo instrument. His countrymen had established the horn at every court in Europe; and he himself had planted the seeds which were to bring about the great flowering of the hand-horn period.

IV

REGISTER OF
PLAYERS

Part One

First and Second Generations
1680–1760

THIS Register is intended to cover those horn-players of the Austro-Bohemian School of whom records remain. It is cast in chronological form, and embraces all the biographical material available concerning each player from the major virtuosi down to the humblest orchestral horn-players.

Such a register cannot pretend completeness, but it is the first attempt to put on record the Austrian horn-players of the pre-valve period. Thus while it may seem superfluous to include here the names of minor players about whom nothing is known apart from passing mention in orchestral lists, they nevertheless give a more complete picture of the scope of the school.

For convenience of reference the players have been divided into four generations: two for the pre-hand-horn or Baroque period, two for the Classical or hand-horn period.

The first generation includes the first players and teachers of the horn, whose birth-dates fall between 1640 and 1690 approximately. The youngest members of the second generation appear to have overlapped the playing lives of the eldest members of the first, and it is they who represent the height of the old clarino technique of horn-playing. This second generation (born *c.* 1700–*c.* 1735) includes a few players who later in their careers became the first teachers of hand-stopping, such as Hampl, Matiegka, and Haudek. The third generation spans the rather longer period between *c.* 1735 and *c.* 1775. It represents the zenith of the hand-horn, and the heyday of the great eighteenth-century virtuosi. The fourth and last generation embraces the period of the hand-horn's orchestral prominence after the decline of the virtuosi. Its youngest members were the last of the Austro-Bohemian School to receive their early training entirely on the valveless horn. The birth-dates of this last generation range from *c.* 1775 to as late as *c.* 1810. To sum up the four generations according to their working periods:

I.   1680–*c.* 1725
II. *c.* 1720–*c.* 1760
III. *c.* 1750–*c.* 1800
IV. *c.* 1795–*c.* 1830

Obviously these divisions are not absolute. Not only do they overlap one another, but in cases of long-lived players such as Matiegka (1728–1805) they break down altogether. It is best, therefore, to use each generation only as a rough guide to the players it includes, and as an aid to tracing the chronological development of the school.

Generation I: 1680–1725

SWEDA, *Wenzel, c.* 1638–*c.* 1710 (Swida, Sweida). One of the first Bohemian horn-players, and very probably the first teacher of the horn. A *Cammer-Jäger* and bondsman of Count Franz Anton von Sporck, he and his fellow huntsman, Peter Rölig, were chosen by Sporck from amongst his retinue to learn the horn whilst at Versailles. Contemporary accounts imply that it was Sweda, rather than Rölig, who passed on the art of horn-playing to his countrymen; and as he was much the elder of the two, this was probably so. Dlabacž[1] credits Sweda outright with founding the Bohemian school.

Swida, Wenzel, born at Lissa in Bohemia, travelled in 1680 with his learned lord, Franz Anton von Sporck, to Paris, where the horn was invented in that same year [Dlabacž shares this notion with Gerber, from whom he probably got it: cf. Appendix, paragraph C]. Through him the horn became so well known in his native country that even at that time one met Bohemian players who excelled all other nations on this difficult instrument. He died in Sporck's service in an unknown year.

The year of Sweda's death can be estimated roughly from a letter from Sporck to Count Lamberg dated 26 July 1703. In response to Lamberg's request for two fully trained huntsmen who could play the horn, Sporck expresses his regrets at not being able to oblige Lamberg, 'for I myself have only two huntsmen who play the horn. Both have families; one of them is already hoary with age and will not be in service much longer: so that at the moment I know of no other to fill his post in order to maintain my musical personnel at full strength'. Sweda's name does not appear next to Rölig's on the list of witnesses concerning a hunting offence in 1715: we may therefore assume the date of his death to be about 1710. (See also von Riegger, *Statistik von Böhmen,* vol. XII, p. 288; Anton Voigt, *Abbildungen der Böhmischen u. Mährischen Gelehrten u. Künstler,* Prague, 1775, II, p. 117; J. W. Buchmayr,

[1] op. cit., pp. 244–5.

Böhmische Oden und Fabeln, Prague, 1798, III, p. 47; Joseph Schiffner, *Gallerie der Interessanten und Merkwürdigsten Personen Böhmens*, Prague, 1802, V, p. 266; Benedikt, op. cit., p. 262. The present writer disagrees with Benedikt's supposition that Sweda was present at the *Brandeiser Kaiserjagd* in 1723, thereby outliving Rölig. Not only would he have been in his seventies, far too old to play the horn on horseback, but there is no further mention of Sweda in the Sporck records after 1703.)

RÖLIG, Peter, c. 1650–1723 (Röllig, Röhlich, Ralik). Rölig, like Sweda, was a *Cammer-Jäger* who travelled in Sporck's train of servants on the *Cavalier-tour*, and was taught the horn at Versailles. His role seems to have been that of second and desk-partner to Sweda, though the sources are vague. His name appears amongst the witnesses to be questioned in connection with a hunting offence with which Sporck was charged in 1715 (the complete document is reproduced in van der Roxas, op. cit., p. 281):

SPECIFICATION

Deren jenigen Personen / welche auf allergnädigsten Ihro Kayserl. und König. Majestät Befehl bey dem Königl. Craiss-Ambt in gewissen Sachen examinirt werden / und sie den 6. May allhier erscheinen sollen,

Als:

Johann Georg Wiesner, Stallmeister
Johann Georg Jacobez, Cammer-Diener
Tobias Seemann, Capellmeister [Composer of the *Brandeiser Jägerlied* borrowed by Bach in the *Peasant Cantata*]
Franz Osio
Franz Smrzeck
Peter Röllig, Jäger
Franz Ferdinand, Jäger [Possibly Sweda's successor—though not conclusively so in this context]
Heinrich Jechte, gemester Reutschreiber zu Lyssa
Johann Nitsch, Küchelschreiber.

Rölig's treatment at the hands of contemporary authors differs little from that of his companion, Sweda, except that we are told that he was born in Konoged, a village belonging to Sporck. (See Dlabacž, op. cit., p. 586; Buchmayr, loc. cit.; von Riegger, op. cit., XII, p. 277; and Schiffner, loc. cit.)

ZEDDELMAYER, Johann Theodorus, c. 1675–*post* 1736. The first horn-player to receive a permanent appointment, Zeddelmayer was engaged at Weissenfels by Duke Christian of Sachsen-Weissenfels in 1706. Unfortunately the Court records from which both Kleefeld[1] and J. O. Opel[2] worked have been destroyed; and apart from passing references by these writers nothing

---

[1] 'Das Orchester der Hamburger Oper 1678–1738', in *SIMG* I, 2 (1900), p. 280.
[2] *Neue Mitteilungen aus dem Gebiet Historischen und Antiquärischen Forschungen*, xv, 2 (Halle, 1882), p. 499.

further of Zeddelmayer is known. Kleefeld and Opel see Zeddelmayer's appointment as a result of Reinhard Keiser's influence: 'Vielleicht durch Keiser's Beziehungen zu Weissenfels erklärt sich, das Engagement des Waldhornisten Joh. Th. Zeddelmayer am dortigen Hofe in 1706.' Keiser had used horns in his opera *Octavia* at Hamburg the year before, and it may well be that Zeddelmayer was amongst them.

In 1716 Duke Christian held a grand hunt in celebration of his thirty-fifth birthday, which fell on 23 February. Duke Wilhelm Ernst of Sachsen-Weimar, an intimate friend of Christian's, contributed a hunting-cantata as his share in the festivities. The text was written by Salomo Franck, and set to music by Wilhelm's Kapellmeister, Sebastian Bach. 'Was mir behagt, ist nur die muntre Jagd', Bach's first cantata (*BWV* 208), was performed as a table music following the hunt on Christian's birthday, in the residence at Weissenfels.[1] Werner mentions that the performance was conducted by J. A. Kobelius, Krieger's successor at Weissenfels.[2]

Since there were as yet no resident horn-players in the orchestra at Weimar, there can be no doubt that the horn parts in the *Jagdkantate* were written for Zeddelmayer and an unknown second. It is interesting to note that neither of these parts ventures into the clarino register—the highest note in the first horn is a written a″ which is only touched in passing—and that the parts have a distinctly horn-like look on the page, much like those in Fux's opera *Elisa*, which was written the previous year. Wellesz has pointed out the connection between Bach and Fux at this period;[3] and the possibility that these horn parts were modelled upon those of *Elisa* has been discussed in Chapter III. What does strike our attention, however, is the fact that these highly idiomatic horn parts should be written for players resident at a court which boasted one of the strongest traditions of trumpet-playing in Europe: for it was Weissenfels which nurtured Gottfried Reiche and the Altenburgs. (See Arno Werner, 'Die Thüringer Musikfamilie Altenburg', in *SIMG*, vii, 1, Leipzig, 1905, p. 119.)

This is clear evidence that at Weissenfels, at any rate, the line of demarcation between horn and trumpet was clearly drawn; and that Zeddelmayer was not required to double on the trumpet, for there were trumpeters available in plenty. Most writers have dismissed the horn as a second-best substitute for the trumpet at this early date. The facts given above, however, would call for a revision of this verdict. For out of the evidence of Bach's *Jagdkantate* and the musical scene at Weissenfels, Zeddelmayer emerges as a player of ability whose style of playing was idiomatically horn-like.

[1] Philipp Spitta, *J. S. Bach* (Leipzig, 1880), i, 558; Friederich Smend, *Bach in Köthen* (Berlin, 1951), p. 13.
[2] *Städtische und Fürstliche Musikpflege in Weissenfels* (Leipzig, 1911), p. 119.
[3] *Fux* (London, 1965), cf. p. 10.

The cantatas and opera scores of the time only called for the horn occasionally, however, and like all horn-players of this early period Zeddel-mayer filled in much of his time by playing in the hunt. At Weissenfels the music of the chase appears to have been cultivated to a degree equalling that of the house orchestra. In a ducal celebration of 1730 we read of the favoured position which the hunting-musicians enjoyed, following closely upon the Duke's own carriage. ' . . . the Prince's Government . . . a Corps of Trumpets and Drums . . . the various Cavalry . . . then his Highness the Prince in his Carriage drawn by six Horses . . . the Swiss Guard . . . followed by the entire Hunt with the Grenadier Guards playing resounding Music . . .' This hunting-band was modelled upon the royal Jagdmusik of Christian's cousin at Dresden, Augustus the Strong, and consisted of oboes, horns, and bas-soons.[1] Presumably Zeddelmayer took part in this celebration, for it is reasonably certain that he remained in the Duke's service until the house orchestra was dissolved in 1736 as a result of his brother's military excesses. (See Gustav Schmidt, *Die Frühdeutsche Oper*, Regensburg, 1934, ii, p. 84.)

REICHEL, *Georg Laurentz*, appears in the register of Duke Anton Ulrich's band at Wolfenbüttel in 1710. The parish records for the Court contain an entry dated 2 April 1710, which describes Reichel as a 'Waldhorniste u. Violischellniste' in His Highness's Orchestra; presumably his actual engage-ment had not long been in force. A later entry from the year 1713 gives full particulars concerning his origins and duties, and casts a welcome ray of light on the activities of a horn-player whom we can but assume was typical of this early period. He was the 'son of the late Laurentz Reichel, Town Musician at Ronneburg, Violist and Horn-Player in the Court Orchestra, Horn-player in His Highness's private Band and Palace Guard, Court Musician here, 1713'.

The fact that Reichel's doubling instrument was the violoncello rather than another brass instrument would suggest that he was trained in a monastery and not under the town-guild system of which his father was evidently a product. The *Stadtpfeifer* tradition, strictly governed by guild laws, was that apprentices should learn three instruments of a given genre, either wind or string; and in practice the town musicians usually kept to instruments of one class, such as brass or woodwind. On the other hand, the monasteries stipulated that novices should be proficient on one other instru-ment beside their principal medium. If the main instrument was a string, then the second instrument must be a wind, and vice versa; in addition to which a mastery of the rudiments of singing and composition were required. Reichel's native town of Ronneburg was a watering-place in Saxony on the Bohemian border; and as Saxony was Catholic under Augustus the Strong

[1] Krieger's *Lustige Feldmusik* (1704) contains 'overtures' for this combination.

(who had embraced that faith in order to secure the throne of Poland), there was ample opportunity for Reichel to enter a monastery for his musical training in his native province, if not in Bohemia.

Thus Reichel's proficiency as a 'Violischellniste' made him a useful addition to the Wolfenbüttel orchestra. When the occasion demanded, of course, he was also available for duty in the palace guard band: an office which he held in common with his counterparts at Weissenfels and Dresden.

By 1717 Reichel had been joined by a second, presumably Johann Georg Hildebrand. Although Hildebrand's name does not emerge in the Court records until 1721, a pair of obbligato 'Corn. de Chas.' are called for in the cantata 'Komm, O Tröster', set by the Wolfenbüttel Capellmeister, Georg Caspar Schürrmann, in 1717. Unfortunately the music is lost, and only the text remains.

In 1721 a third horn-player, Martin Margraff, appears listed in the Court calendar as 'Waldhornist bey Fürstl. Capell'. Assisted by two extras named Jaresch and Statz, this trio held forth at Wolfenbüttel until 1731, when Reichel's name no longer heads the list of horn-players in the list entitled, 'Auf Ostern 1731 die Fürstl. Capelle bezahlt'. On that occasion Hildebrand and Margraff each received thirty-seven thalers. In the 'Hochfürstl. Braun-schweig-Wolfenbüttelschen Capell-Etat, wie der die letzte Zeit (1735) gewesen', both 'Mr. Hildebrand' and 'Mr. Margrave' are listed for the last time.

Neither Hildebrand's nor Margraff's playing appears to have moved Schürrmann to write solo parts for them; but a horn obbligato written for Reichel in 1730, the last year of his active life, deserves mention here. The tenor aria 'Grosser König Du Krone der Helden' from Schürrmann's opera *Clelia* calls for a concertante solo horn in F. Reichel's virtuosity has received a lasting tribute in this difficult part, which Schmidt describes as decorated with 'fast triplet runs, quaver staccatos, and a long high trill'. (G. F. Schmidt, *Die Frühdeutsche Oper und die Musikdramatische Kunst Georg Caspar Schürrmanns*, Regensburg, 1933, p. 448. The orchestra lists are reproduced on pp. 123–7.)

PANGRATZ and *HOFFMANN* appear to have been regular members of the electoral orchestra at Düsseldorf by 1711, if indeed not earlier. The 'Quatier-listen des Churpfälzischen Hofstaate bei der Kaiserwahl Carls VI zu Frank-furt' for that year includes amongst the fifty-two musicians of the Elector's band '2 Beyde H. Jagdt Hornisten'. It is fitting that a pair of horns should be a part of the orchestral music performed for the new Emperor's coronation, for, as we have already remarked, the horn was his favourite instrument. The reigning Elector, Prince Johann Wilhelm of Jülich-Berg, died in 1716 and certain members of the original band were dismissed. It was not until 1718 that the succeeding Elector, Carl Philipp, published a register of the orchestra.

Amongst the winds we find a 'Walthornist Pangratz' at a salary of 600 fl., and a 'Walthornist Hoffmann' whose salary as second horn was 480 fl. It is reasonably safe to assume that these players were the two who had taken part in the musical exercises of 1711. This seems even more likely when we remember that horn-players of orchestral quality were still something of a rarity at that time.

In 1719 another horn-player was added and the number of musicians increased to fifty. This larger band was regularly maintained until 1723, when Carl Philipp succeeded to the throne of the Elector Palatine. The orchestra wintered at Heidelberg, and in 1724 removed with the Electoral Court to its new seat at Mannheim. It was this ensemble which became the nucleus of the famous Mannheim orchestra; and it is apposite that when the Bohemian horn virtuoso Schindelarž arrived with Stamitz in 1742 he found a tradition of horn-playing which had flourished since 1711. (For the orchestral lists in which Pangratz and Hoffmann appear see Georg Steffen, *Johann Hugo von Wilderer*, Cologne, 1960, pp. 89 and 93.)

FISCHER, *Johann Adalbert*, and *SAMM, Franz Adam*. Engaged as principal and second horn respectively in the Dresden Court orchestra in 1711. In 1719 they distinguished themselves in the horn fanfares of Lully's *La Princesse d'Elide*, performed for the royal festivities at Dresden on 10 September.[1] Both Fischer and Samm were Bohemians,[2] and it is a matter of interest that the same Court where Hampl, another Bohemian, was later to discover hand-stopping, should also have been one of the first to engage horn-players as a permanent feature of its orchestra.

ROSSI, *Wenzel*, *c*. 1685–1740. Principal horn in the Imperial Court orchestra at Vienna from 1712 until 1740 under Fux during the reign of Charles VI. The combination of a Bohemian Christian name with an Italian surname suggests Vienna as Rossi's birthplace. Köchel[3] gives 1739 as the year of Rossi's death; but he is listed in the *Staats- und Stands Calendar* as Jäger-hornist until 1740. The horn parts in Fux's *Elisa* (1715) were doubtless written for Rossi and Otto (see below); and it is not beyond the limits of plausible speculation to assume that they had a hand in developing the Viennese Waldhorn with the Leichnambschneiders. Although not mentioned by Walther, Rossi played in the performance of *Constanza e Fortezza* for Charles's coronation at Prague in 1724.[4] The appointment of Rossi and Otto

[1] See Moritz Fürstenau, *Geschichte der Musik und des Theaters am Hofe zu Dresden* (Dresden, 1861), ii, pp. 58, 80; and *Dressdenisches Diarium auf den Monat September* (Dresden, 1719).

[2] The *Dresdnischer Hof- und Staats-Calendar* (Dresden, 1715) lists 'Zwey Hoff-Wald-hornisten ex Böhmen'.

[3] *Die Kaiserliche Hof-Musikkapelle in Wien 1573–1847* (Vienna, 1869), p. 80.

[4] See below, *s.v.* 'Schindler'.

as regular members of the *Hofkapelle* was in a large measure due to the Emperor's fondness for the horn. During Charles's reign the *Kaiserliche Jagd-musik* flourished, a band of eight selected players for whom the monarch himself wrote fanfares, and in this ensemble Rossi and Otto would have played the leading parts.[1] It is somehow a fitting coincidence that the deaths of both Charles and his first *Jägerhornist* should fall in the same year, 1740.

OTTO, Friederich, 1686–1718. Rossi's second in the Vienna *Hofkapelle* from 1712, the year of their appointment, until 1718, when Otto died at the age of 32. No suitable replacement seems to have been available, for Rossi is listed alone in the *Hofkapelle* register from this date onward. Perhaps the fact that Otto's death deprived Fux of his regular pair of horn-players explains the absence of specifically designated horn parts in the later operas. Shadowy though the careers of both Rossi and Otto may be, they occupy a place of historical importance as the first permanently engaged orchestral horn-players of whom record remains in the form of music written expressly for them in an opera (see p. 59).

SMEYKAL, Hermoläus, c. 1685–1758. The first major teacher of the horn, and the first to establish a teaching tradition within the Bohemian school. Born in Kuttenberg, he received his education and musical training at the Jesuit monastery there, taking orders as a lay priest. He then went to Prague, and for many years played in the orchestra of St. Wenceslas' Jesuit Seminary. There he taught Joseph Matiegka, who was to become one of the great eighteenth-century teachers of the horn and who may well have tutored Josef Hampl (q.v.). He died in Prague in 1758. (See Dlabacž, *Allgemeines Historisches Künstlerlexicon für Böhmen*, Prague, 1815, p. 123; and *Catalogus Personarum et Officiorum Provinciae Bohemiae Societatis Jesu*, Prague, 1758, p. 442.)

WECKER, Johann Gottfried, c. 1685–*pre* 1750. Horn virtuoso of the first half of the eighteenth century, born in Gebhartsdorf, Upper Lausatia. Wecker was also an accomplished violinist and keyboard-player. This is not sur-prising in view of the requirement laid down by the monasteries that all wind-players should master at least one stringed instrument, and vice versa. (See Ferdinand Simon Gassner, *Universal Lexicon der Tonkunst*, Stuttgart, 1847, p. 886.)

AN ANONYMOUS BLIND VIRTUOSO, fl. 1713. Mattheson's mention of this blind horn-player in 1713[2] is one of the earliest records of a travelling horn soloist. It goes without saying that this player was a Bohemian, as were

---

[1] These fanfares have disappeared, unfortunately, but the group has been refounded as the *Lainzer Jagdmusik*, and carries on under the able direction of Dr. Ernst Paul.

[2] *Der Vollkommene Capell-Meister*, p. 53.

virtually all of the travelling musicians of the time; but regardless of his origin, his appearance as a soloist at so early a date does suggest that horn-playing had reached a high degree of presentability much earlier than is commonly supposed. 'Apart', writes Mattheson, 'from mentioning the noble Horn, upon which a blind man recently played at Hamburg; he produced more Tones than an Organ has, though admittedly without mathematical Precision.' Could this be an early instance of using the right (or left) hand in the bell?

ONDRATSCHECK, Johann (c. 1685–1743) was appointed first horn to the Electoral orchestra at Mainz in 1717. This is the date given by Schweikert (see below); and it is confirmed by Gottron,[1] who adds that after his escape from Bohemia to Mainz that year Ondratscheck later studied composition under Fortunato Chelleri (1686–1757) at Würzburg. Ondratscheck was promoted to the position of leader in 1724, a post which was not uncommon amongst horn-players in the eighteenth century. His only surviving composition, a string trio, may be viewed in the Stadtbibliothek at Mainz. He died on 26 April 1743.

VEDULANG, Johann Wenzel, also a Bohemian, was engaged as Ondratscheck's second the same year at Mainz. (See Karl Schweikert, 'Die Musikpflege am Hofe der Kurfürsten von Mainz im 17. und 18. Jahrhundert', in Beiträge zur Geschichte der Stadt Mainz, ii, 1913, p. 22.)

LEOPOLD, Hans, and SEYDLER, Wenzel Franz. Horn-players in the service of Duke Heinrich of Saxe-Halle at Barby in the 1720s. They may well have taken part in the first performance of Bach's Brandenburg Concerto No. 1. Although there were no resident horn-players in the orchestra at Cöthen, the Kammerrechnungen show that horn-players were occasionally brought in from near-by courts. (Barby lies not quite fifteen miles from Cöthen.) On 6 September 1721 these records list a payment for 'zwei Waldhornisten'. It is not known when the First Brandenburg Concerto made its début. Bach's dedication is dated 24 March 1721; and it is entirely possible that the occasion for which a pair of horn-players was required early in the following autumn was that of giving the new concerto its first hearing. The Kammerrechnung reads:

1721. 6 September two Horn-Players.
1722. 6 June two Horn-Players.
1724. 10 May the two Horn-Players Hans Leopold and Wentzel Franz Seydler from Barby, who played here, 24 Gulden in final payment.

It is clear from the note 'in final payment' ('zur Abfertigung') that Leopold

---

[1] Adam Gottron, Tausend Jahre Mainzer Musikleben (Mainz, 1960), Abteilung III, 44.

and Seydler are the subject of the anonymous entries of 1721 and 1722, as this is the customary term to denote the closing of a standing account, which in this case referred to the earlier performances. This is further borne out by the fact that all later entries specifically describe the players to whom they refer, as:

1724. 31 August. To the Landgrave of Cassel's horn-player who performed here for a time, 24 Gulden.

And again:

1725. 18 August. To the two horn-players from Barby in final payment, 20 Gulden.[1]

BEDA, a travelling virtuoso whose stock in trade appears to have been a curious ability to play two horns at once. In this respect he and his contemporary, Creta (see below), were the forerunners of the mysterious Mr. Ernst, who performed the same feat at a *Concert Spirituel* in 1751 (see below, under 'Ernst'). Beda appeared at Cöthen in 1725. 'To the Horn-Player Beda, who plays on two horns at once, 6 Gulden in final payment.' (*Cöthen Kammerrechnung*, 18 August 1725. Quoted in Friederich Smend, *Bach in Köthen*, Berlin, 1951, p. 154.)

CRETA, Joachim Friederich, like Beda, was a travelling one-man duettist. Judging from the account just quoted, and from Mattheson's note on Creta's Hamburg concerts of 1728, this strenuous speciality was not very rewarding in terms of hard cash. Mattheson writes: 'Here in Hamburg we have just witnessed the fact that honest Creta (who blew two horns at once) was able to rake together seven Thalers in his first Drill-House concert; and in the second, secretly abetted by friends, he conquered just enough to pay for his quarters and pack his bags in peace. Thus does Art earn bread, my dear Patriot!'[2] Nevertheless, Creta evidently collected enough to pay his passage to England, for in a London concert bill of the following year he was announced 'to blow the first and second treble on two French horns in the same manner as is usually done by two performers'. (*Dictionary of Musicians* [anonymous], London, 1824, p. 87.)

There have been attempts on the part of some writers to assign to these exhibitionists a place in the history of horn-playing. Morley-Pegge has indeed raised the possibility that Creta's feat (Beda is not mentioned) represents the first performance of horn chords in public.[3] The present writer

---

[1] These records are reprinted in Smend, *Bach in Köthen*, pp. 153–4.

[2] *Musicalischer Patriot* (Hamburg, 1728), p. 26.

[3] R. Morley-Pegge, *The French Horn* (London, 1960), p. 87. Chords may be produced upon the horn by simultaneously humming one member of a triad and playing another: the third member and an octave doubling of one or two of the others will then sound in sympathy, depending upon the register of the player's voice and the member selected.

does not subscribe to this theory, however, for the reason that these accounts clearly state that two horns are played upon at once in each case. Furthermore, the trick of playing two horns at once, one on either side of the mouth, becomes less inconceivable when we remember that cornettists had been using the off-centre embouchure since the fifteenth century; the technique itself was nothing new.

It is admittedly difficult to discover what effect the singular demonstrations of these virtuosi had upon the horn-playing technique of the time, if any at all. Perhaps they are best regarded as indications of the popularity which the horn was gaining as a solo instrument at an earlier date than is generally supposed. If the horn had been totally unknown to the musical public of the time, Beda and Creta would not have been able to raise an audience at all, however poorly paid.

PRAMEYER, Leopold, appears as a cornettist in the Hofkapelle at Vienna according to both the Staats-und Stands-Calendar for 1726 and Walther.[1] Dlabač, however, calls him a Waldhornist;[2] and it is just possible that he might have doubled on the horn to replace Friederich Otto. At any rate, he was present at the Prague performance of Fux's Constanza et Fortezza in 1723.

Generation II: c. 1720–c. 1760

STRÖHL, Johann Adam, 1703–post 1750. A blind horn-player of some reputation, attached to the Court orchestra at Gera. According to Gassner (Lexicon, p. 807), he was born at Tüllstedt (Thuringia) in 1703.

SCHINDLER, Andreas and Johann Adam, horn-players in the Dresden Court orchestra from c. 1720 to c. 1745. They were Bohemians, and probably came to Dresden from Prague, whence Augustus the Strong recruited many of his virtuosi. The Dresdnischer Hoff- und Staats-Calendar for 1721 lists Andreas and Johann Adam Schindler as 'Hoff-Waldhornisten', and we may conclude from this that they were engaged the previous year.

Dlabač[3] tells us that the Schindlers played with distinction in the coronation performance of Constanza et Fortezza at Prague in 1723. He also quotes Johann Schindler's marriage record from the parish register of St. Mary under-the-Chain in Prague: '1725 die 16. Septembris copulatus est D. Joannes Adamus Schindler Reg. Maj. Poloniae Musicus Camerae.' That Schindler should be referred to here as a chamber musician to the King of Poland is helpful. Augustus the Strong kept a picked household band, the Königliche Harmonie, which attended him in his capacity as King of Poland both at Dresden and at Warsaw. This royal chamber group appears to have

---

[1] *Musicalisches Lexicon* (Leipzig, 1732), p. 494.   [2] *Künstler-Lexicon*, ii, p. 496.
[3] iii, p. 43.

been quite separate from the larger orchestra of the Electoral opera, though some of its members evidently played with the opera when the King-Elector was in residence. His successor August III maintained this private band until 1763. The brothers Schindler were regular members of the royal ensemble, as Walther[1] further confirms: 'In the year 1729 both Andreas and Johann Schindler stand in the service of the Royal Orchestra and Chamber Ensemble as Horn-Players at Dresden.' It is to be regretted that more detailed information concerning these evidently exceptional players is not available, but an examination of the horn parts in the Dresden operas of Porpora and Hasse during the period of the Schindlers' service might well reveal certain aspects of their playing style.[2] It was for one of the Schindlers, probably Johann, the elder, that J. S. Bach wrote the monumental horn obbligato to the Quoniam of the B Minor Mass. The Mass was written to celebrate the succession of Augustus III as Elector of Saxony and King of Poland in 1733; it was performed in the Court chapel at Leipzig on 21 April that year. This highly idiomatic and virtuosic part is one of the land-marks of the Baroque horn repertory, and marks Schindler as a player of exceptional gifts.

CZERMAK, two brothers, horn-players in the band at Dresden, where Dlabacž tells us they flourished about the year 1746.[3] One of the two was Glöckner's teacher (see below). They died in about 1750.

MARESCH, Jakob, 1709–post 1770. A horn-player at the royal Court at St. Petersburg in Russia, where indeed the orchestra consisted mainly of Bohemians. Schantl[4] gives the date and place of Maresch's birth as 1709 at Chotieborž in the Czaslau district of Bohemia. Maresch, like his desk-partner at St. Petersburg, Kölbel (see below), had an inventive mind. In the idea of combining two horns of different pitch by means of a common mouthpiece in order to facilitate a scale of open notes, Maresch anticipated Claggett by about twenty years. Whereas Claggett's 'Cromatic Trumpet and French Horn' of 1788 consisted of two instruments pitched a semitone apart, Maresch's earlier device employed two horns differing by a minor third in pitch. The principle in both cases was the same: by means of a valve in a chamber serving both mouthpipes, the air-stream from the mouthpiece was channelled into one horn or the other, enabling the player to select the appropriate overtone.[5]

[1] *Lexicon*, p. 552.
[2] Attention is drawn here to Alexander's aria, Act I, scene 2, in Hasse's *Cleofide* of 1731. The accompaniment consists of strings, two oboes, and two horns. See Fürstenau, op. cit., Beilage A.
[3] *Künstlerlexicon*, i, p. 306.   [4] *Die Österreichische Jagdmusik* (Vienna, 1886), p. 9.
[5] See p. 99, note 3; and Morley-Pegge, *The French Horn*, pp. 26 ff.

Maresch's principal contribution to horn-playing, however, was the codification of the so-called 'Russian horn music'; and while this ancillary development has nothing to do with orchestral or artistic horn-playing as such, it is worth mentioning as an outgrowth of the Bohemian school.

Dlabacž[1] describes the Russian horn band as consisting of thirty-seven horns of varying lengths and pitches, each sounding only one note, chromatically encompassing three full octaves. With these single-note horns sounding singly in succession or in combination, scales and complete chords were produced, much to the evident amazement of the onlooker. The effect was as much a visual spectacle as it was a musical phenomenon, and the art was developed to a high degree. Gerber[2] reports that these bands were capable not only of playing hunting-pieces at great speed, but also marches, arias, and entire symphonies replete with brilliant scales and passage-work.[3] The Russian horn bands were popular throughout Europe until late in the nineteenth century.

MESSING, Frederick, and brother were active as virtuosi and orchestra players in England from about 1740 until 1763, perhaps even later. Contemporary accounts give us no information about the country of their birth; but the name suggests Sudeten German origin. (*Messing* means brass: the name is occasionally encountered, not inappropriately, in the Erzgebirge, the ore-bearing mountains dividing Bohemia and Saxony.)

Dr. Burney, in his article on the horn in Rees's *Cyclopedia*,[4] relates that 'the Messings were the first who pretended to perform in all keys in England, about the year 1740'. Lysons, writing in 1812, recalls that amongst the star virtuosi on various instruments in 1755, Frederick Messing was 'an eminent performer on the chromatic French horn'.[5] The term 'chromatic' here refers to the use of crooks. 'Attempts at *chromatic* horns', says Burney, 'have been made early in the last century, in Germany.'[6] Hand-stopping was unknown in England until Punto's first performances in 1770 or 1771. The crooked horn, however, was hardly a novelty here by 1740, though the Messings may well have made it popular as a recital instrument.

Frederick Messing was a prominent soloist, and gave recitals from time

---

[1] *Künstler Lexicon*, ii, p. 258.

[2] *Lexicon*, 1792, ii, p. 4.

[3] This is confirmed by Meusel's *Teutsches Künstlerlexicon* (Lemgo, 1808), vii, 2, p. 11. See also Stählin, *Notice sur la Musique en Russie* (Leipzig, 1770), p. 74.

[4] London, 1819, xviii: the article itself was written in 1803.

[5] *History of the Origin and Progress of the Meeting of the Three Choirs* (Gloucester, 1812), p. 183.

[6] See Chapter II. The work of the Leichnambschneiders was evidently known in England through examples other than the horns made by Johannes for Lord Tredegar and the Duke of Chandos. The Germany of Burney's day, it is well to remember, began at Ostend and ended at Trieste; but here he clearly means the Viennese horns.

to time. 'This gentleman occasionally gave concerts at the Devil Tavern,' Lysons continues, which he advertised in the following whimsical way:

Mr Messing

Goes to the Devil this present Thursday, to prepare a polite serenade, both vocal and instrumental, for the entertainment of his well-wishers and bene-factors.—To begin at half an hour after six o'clock. Tickets to be had at the place of performance, the Devil Tavern, Temple-Bar; and of Mr. Messing, at the Golden Acorn, in James-Street, Covent Garden. Red, 5s, White, 3s.

Note. One of the vocal parts by a lady who never performed in public.

Further mention of Frederick Messing occurs in connection with the Three Choirs Festival at Worcester and Hereford in 1755 and 1756. He also appears in a benefit concert given by eminent virtuosi at Cheltenham in the same year. Again to quote Lysons, 'The other performers mentioned in the advertisement of 1756 are Mr. Wass, Millar, Adcock, Messing and Thomp-son' (p. 186). Frederick Messing is listed in Mortimer's *London Directory* of 1763 in the capacity of violinist as well as that of horn-player.[1] This appears to be the last record of either of the Messings. Whether they died shortly thereafter or retired and returned to their native country is not known.

The Messings, and particularly Frederick, did much to make the horn popular in England, as is shown by the number of horn-players who begin to appear in concert bills during the 1750s. They were the first members of the Austro-Bohemian school of playing to reside in England for any length of time; and in so doing acquainted audiences here more fully with the horn as a concert instrument, thus preparing the way for Punto and the many virtuosi who followed him later in the century.

Mr. CHARLES came to England about the same time as did the Messings. Burney, Reese, and contemporary writers do not mention him, and it appears that his influence was less than that of the Messings; although he delighted audiences here and in Ireland with solo recitals, duets by himself and his anonymous 'second', and trios with his wife on third.

His first British appearance is recorded in the *Dublin Mercury* for 24 to 27 April 1742 (No. 28, fol. 101).

> At the MUSIC-HALL in Fishamble-Street
> On Wednesday the 12th of May 1742,
> will be performed
>
> ### A GRAND CONCERT OF MUSIC
>
> By Mr. CHARLES, the HUNGARIAN, Master
> of the French Horn, with his Second; accom-
> panied by all the best Hands in this City

[1] See R. Morley-Pegge, *The French Horn*, p. 88.

First Act.

1. An Overture with French Horns, called,
   new Pastor Fido;
2. The 6th Concerto of Signior Geminiani;
3. A Solo on the French Horn, by Mr. Charles,
   to shew the beauty of that Instrument;
4. A Concerto on the Clarinet.

A footnote adds: 'NB. The Clarinet, the Hautbois de Amour, and Shalamo, were never heard in this Kingdom before.' Mr. Charles played these novel instruments himself, as we gather from the following advertisement from the *London General Advertiser* for 23 April 1744.

For the Benefit of Mr. CHARLES
AT Mr. Hickford's Great Room in Panton-
Street, near the Haymarket, on Wednesday next,
will be perform'd a Grand CONCERT of

MUSICK

In which Mr. Charles, Mrs. Charles, and Son,
will perform Variety of choice Pieces on the
French-Horn; Mr. Charles will like-wise
perform Concertos and Solos on the Clarinet,
and on the Haut-boy-Amour. To conclude with
the TURKISH MUSICK, in the original Taste, as
perform'd at Constantinople.

Not only do these notices point up Mr. Charles's quite remarkable versatility, but they furnish us with a number of clues as to his origins, age, and identity. It has been thought up to now that he was probably a Bohemian. 'The identification was close enough for those days, and Hungarian names rarely occur in lists of horn-players', Blandford wrote in 1922. A plausible deduction, this: but had Mr. Charles's real name, whatever it was, been that of a German-speaking Austrian from the Hungarian province, he would no doubt have been billed simply as a 'German', especially as there were plenty of them about in those days. Rather the stage name 'Mr. Charles', and the designation, 'the Hungarian', expressly set off with commas (the punctuation is reproduced neither by Blandford nor by Morley-Pegge), strongly suggest to the present writer that our 'Hungarian' horn-player was, in fact, a Hungarian gipsy.

Anyone who has experienced the gipsy bands which may still be heard in the old inns of Vienna, Budapest, and the Burgenland province will have been impressed by the ability of these players to excel on several instruments; and he will have remarked that these bands are almost always made up from members of a single family, often with three generations present at

once. In the second concert bill Mr. Charles is to appear with his wife and
son, and will further demonstrate his versatility on the Clarinet and the
Hautboy-Amour, not to mention the Shalamo which he had played in the
first programme. The connection is obvious, particularly when we remember that the father of Heinrich Domnich, the famous teacher of the next
generation, came to Wallerstein as a schooled horn-player from Buda in
Hungary. Mr. Charles's anonymous second was probably a relative as well,
whose blood tie was either too tenuous or too complex to warrant mention
in a concert bill.

One item in the first programme particularly attracts our attention. The
'Overture with French Horns, called, New Pastor Fido' was none other than
the opening symphony to Handel's opera *Il Pastor Fido*. This work, revised
in 1734, was brought out in Dublin some months before Mr. Charles's concert, and had scored an immediate success there. The instrumental scoring of

Ex. 25.   'The Early Horn' by Mr. Winch / Galliard.

the new version of *Il Pastor Fido* differed from that of the earlier edition of
1712 in that the orchestra now included a pair of horns. The parts in the
overture require players of some skill, and in their style disclose unmistakably the characteristics of the Austro-Bohemian school. Considerable thema-
tic material is entrusted to the horns, which are frequently allowed to shine
in unaccompanied passages. Thus Handel's new overture would have been an
effective opener for just such a programme, especially as both *Pastor Fido* and
Mr. Charles were at the height of their popularity.

Exactly which solo Mr. Charles played to 'shew the beauty' of the horn
we do not know; but a staple item of his repertoire, and one which was no
doubt performed in the concert of 1744, was a piece for two horns called 'The
Early Horn'. Set, as we are told in the Thompson edition of *The Compleat
Tutor for the French Horn*, by Mr. Winch (see below), the piece was a favourite
amongst the drawing-room horn virtuosi of the day, and affords a good idea
of Mr. Charles's fluent command of the high register (see Ex. 25). Morley-
Pegge has pointed out that the technique of pieces such as this was that of

the trumpet. This is strictly speaking true, but the point to be observed is that the musical idiom is that of the horn, and agrees in its style with the horn parts of Handel and his continental contemporaries. It is fair to assume that its composer and players were therefore of Austro-Bohemian origins or training.

The scant remaining music of Mr. Charles's own composition furnishes us less with an impression of his playing style than of his nationality. In *Apollo's Cabinet: or the Muse's Delight* (Liverpool, 1757) a set of 'twelve duettos for the French Horns, composed by Mr. Charles' appears, together with some unenlightening 'instructions for the French Horn', the latter presumably by Mr. Winch. The twelve duettos make no technical demands upon the player, but their musical style is suggestive of early Haydn. A Concerto in D by 'Sig. Charles' appears in the musical library of Sir Samuel Hellier (*c.* 1746–84) at Wombourne Wodehouse, Staffordshire, where it is still preserved. A note in Sir Samuel's hand tells us that 'This Concerto is Either for French Horns or Trumpetts', and the character of the solo parts is suitably ambivalent; but the style of the composition, though perhaps less distinguished, is similar to that of Dittersdorf's early period, and points to an Austrian schooling. This would further confirm my own supposition that Mr. Charles was a Hungarian gipsy. From the evidence of this concerto, he may have played the trumpet in addition to the clarinet, shalamo and Hautboy-amour; but the horn was his major instrument, and he obviously played it well.

The fact that Mr. Charles arrived in Ireland in 1742 with a wife and a son old enough to take part in horn trios would suggest that he was between 35 and 40 years old himself. This would establish the date of his birth as falling somewhere between 1705 and 1710: near enough to identify him as a member of the second generation of the Austro-Bohemian school. His activities following the London concert of 1744 are obscure. Blandford (loc. cit.) tells us that he is met with at Edinburgh in 1755, and again in Dublin in 1756. Sir Samuel Hellier began his music collection while at Exeter College in 1753. It is possible that Mr. Charles either played at Oxford about this time or visited Wombourne Wodehouse for one of Sir Samuel's house concerts. The concerto described above appears amongst the earlier items in Sir Samuel's library, and probably dates from between 1753 and 1756. Mr. Charles is no more heard of after his last concert in Dublin that year. Presumably he returned to his native Hungary to join other members of his family in regaling guests in some country inn with gipsy music and his own feats on the horn. History does not tell us.[1]

[1] The writer here records his grateful thanks to Miss Evelyn Mary Shaw-Hellier of Wombourne Wodehouse for her kind permission to study at length Mr. Charles's concerto.

Mr. WINCH is first met with by name in a concert bill in the *Dublin Mercury* for 22 October 1741, where a performance of *King Lear* is announced to be enlivened between the acts with a concerto played 'by the celebrated Mr. Winch, who has performed several years in Mr. Handel's operas and oratorios'. This concerto must have been identical with that which Mr. Winch played at the Smock-Alley Theatre on 12 March 1742, for the *Dublin Mercury* for 2 March tells us that 'Mr. Winch will Perform a Concerto compos'd by Signor Hasse, with Barberini's Minuet on the French Horn'.

The circumstance of Mr. Winch's performing a solo concerto by Hasse greatly strengthens the present writer's conviction that this shadowy horn-player was, in fact, a Saxon or Bohemian, and that he most probably came to England with Handel either from Hamburg or from Hanover. Hasse wrote his most prominent horn parts for Hampl and Haudek at Dresden, and it was there that his five concertos, op. 4, for two horns were most probably composed, although they were published in London by Walsh about 1742. It is doubtful that the concerto in question is one of the opus 4 works, as no mention of a second player occurs in either of the announcements concerning Mr. Winch. It is likely that Hasse wrote a concerto for solo horn, for his contemporary at Dresden, Karl Heinrich Graun, composed a fine trio-sonata for Haudek with a most rewarding horn part. Mennicke, however, lists no such concerto in his table of Hasse's music; and it may be that Mr. Winch came upon this piece in Hamburg, where Hasse's works were much performed.[1]

If Mr. Winch's piece, 'The Early Horn' (Ex. 25), is a faithful reflection of his playing style, then we may without hesitation include him in the parent Austro-Bohemian school of horn-playing. The likelihood that Handel's horn-players were, in fact, Bohemians is discussed fully in Chapter III; and the possibility that Mr. Winch's stage name may be an anglicized form of 'Wünsch' or 'Winschermann' receives a supporting discussion in the section on Handel's horn-players. Indeed, if he was known for his performances for 'several years in Mr. Handel's Oratorios and Operas', it is not improbable that he was the soloist in the great horn aria in the first act of *Giulio Cesare*; but substantiating evidence has yet to be found.

KÖLBEL, c. 1700–8(?) is remembered chiefly as the inventor of the *Amorschall*. In the year 1730 Kölbel was already active as a virtuoso of the second-horn genre at the Imperial Court at St. Petersburg. He thereafter played for a time in Vienna, whence the Dutch ambassador took him to Constantinople with his band. In 1754 Kölbel returned to St. Petersburg, and spent the

[1] See Mennicke, *Hasse und die Brüder Graun als Symphoniker* (Leipzig, 1906), Anhang ii. The Graun trio-sonata is preserved in the Wenster collection of the University Library at Lund, Sweden; the Hasse opus 4 concerti at Oriel College, Oxford.

following ten years in perfecting the *Amorschall*. This was, in fact, not a new instrument, but an ordinary orchestral horn fitted with keys along the neck and throat of the bell. The *Amorschall* was evidently equally as difficult to describe as it was to play, for contemporary writers give widely differing accounts of the instrument's curious mechanism. Dlabacž[1] prudently quotes Gerber's description.[2] Although far from precise, Gerber's account does afford us an idea of Kölbel's mechanism. 'Towards the mouthpiece the tubing was fitted with keys like those of the oboe, whose openings were formed like a ball cut in half; over which another half-ball fitted, having in it several small holes.' (Er brachte endlich 2 Hörner zustande, die an der Röhre nach dem Mundstück zu, mit Klappen, wie die Hoboen versehen, und deren Schallöffnungen wie eine halbe Kugel gestaltet waren, worauf eine andere Halbkugel passte, an welcher etliche kleine Löcher befindlich waren.) The object of these keys, whatever their design, was, of course, that of providing the horn with a chromatic scale at a time when hand-stopping was not generally known, at any rate not in St. Petersburg. In this Kölbel's contrivance seems to have been successful, although the results were perhaps less satisfying to a later ear. 'And after practising diligently with his son-in-law Hensel', Gerber continues, 'he presented duets in F minor and E major on this new instrument to the applause of the entire Court, including even the Principal Conductor Galuppi.' (This performance fell within the two-year period (1766–8) of Baldassare Galuppi's residence at St. Petersburg.) 'Had the good Kölbel', comments Gerber, 'but heard the great Palsa and Thürschmied play in these keys today without such aids, he would have spared himself the trouble.'

The *Amorschall*, which made its début in 1758[3] is interesting as being the first of a series of mechanical attempts over the latter half of the century to bridge the gaps in the horn's natural overtone scale. Weidinger's keyed trumpet of 1800 may be regarded as the ultimate outgrowth of Kölbel's idea.[4] Bernsdorf includes as part of the *Amorschall*'s standard equipment a mysterious 'half-round lid, which fitted exactly on the bell'. In a later article Gerber speaks of a 'lid on the bell to make the tone itself softer' (see Appendix, paragraph 1). This was presumably a sort of mute.

FRITSCH, *Christoph*, horn-player in the service of Count Philipp Karl of Oettingen-Wallerstein *c.* 1730–47. In 1747 Fritsch went to Vienna, where he was arrested 'because of a misconduct'.[5] His son Joseph (q.v.) later attracted some notice as second horn to the elder Thürrschmidt at Wallerstein. The

---

[1] *Künstler Lexicon*, II, p. 84.   [2] *Lexicon*, 1792, p. 742.   [3] Gerber, op. cit., ii, p. 80.
[4] See also von Riegger, *Materialen zur Alten und Neuen Statistik von Böhmen* (Prague, 1788), xii, 247; and Bernsdorf, *Neues Universal-Lexicon der Tonkunst* (Dresden, 1856), p. 225.
[5] Wallerstein Archives, 10 February 1747.

Wallerstein Court was remarkable for its hunting-music, which in Fritsch's time had played for Charles VI. Later in the century the orchestra there was to feature some of the finest wind-players in Europe. (See below, Nisle, Nagel, Thürrschmidt, and Zwierzina: also Ludwig Schiedermair, 'Die Blütezeit der Öttingen-Wallersteinischen Hofkapelle' in *SIMG*, Leipzig, 1907, ix, 1.)

HAMPL, Anton Joseph, c. 1710–71. (Also more commonly Hampel. While the writer is aware that it is pointless to quibble over the spelling of German proper names at a period when a standard orthography was as yet unknown, he prefers the form which Hampl himself no doubt originally used. The name is still met with in Moravia and Lower Austria in this form. It derives from *Hamplmann*, a medieval mummer, and survives in present-day Lower Austrian dialect as a jocular term for an unreliable person, or dunce.) Hampl ranks as one of the major figures of the Bohemian school, both as a player and a teacher; and in the latter capacity he has influenced horn-playing down to the present day. It was he who first modified hand-stopping and the systematic use of the right hand in the bell, and there is good reason to believe that he was also the first to teach the setting-in type of embouchure. A detailed discussion of his contributions both as a teacher and as a composer will be found in Chapter III. The following notes are confined to his innovations in the design of the horn as described in contemporary texts, and to the known facts concerning his life.

Although mention of Hampl can be found in virtually every writing on the history of the horn, surprisingly little contemporary record is available concerning him. Even the meticulous Dlabacž makes no mention of Hampl, a fact which might suggest that he left his native Bohemia at an early age. Fürstenau[1] gives the year 1737 as the date marking Hampl's entry into the royal orchestra at Dresden: 'In that same year Johann Adam (Hampl's younger brother, a viola-player) and Ant. Jos. Hampel joined the orchestra.' Hampl's engagement could well have fallen in 1731, however; for in that year the orchestral forces of the Dresden opera were greatly expanded following the appointment of Johann Adolf Hasse as Court composer.[2] Both Gerber and Gassner (whose text follows)[3] find Hampl already active at Dresden in 1748. In 1744 Karl Haudek (q.v.) had been brought from Prague as first horn, and together the two Bohemians built up an international reputation as

[1] *Zur Geschichte der Musik und des Theaters am Hofe der Kurfürsten von Sachsen und Königen von Polen* (Dresden, 1862), p. 226.

[2] The gaps in the *Dresdnischer Hof- und Staats-Calendar* from 1730 to 1741 in the Prague University Library copy admittedly furnish latitude for this supposition; but if issues for these years were available, it is suspected on the external evidence that they would confirm it.

[3] *Lexicon*, p. 397.

duettists and teachers: Haudek teaching the alto horn technique, Hampl the
basso.

Following the bombardment of Dresden by the Prussians in 1760, the
royal opera was suspended and many of the singers dismissed. In 1763 the
Electoral revenues fell to Frederick the Great, and the Saxon king had no
choice but to release Hasse and his wife, Faustina Bordoni, without pension.
But Hampl did not suffer the fate of his Kapellmeister, nor did he follow
Hasse to Vienna, as some have maintained. The year 1764 found him still at
Dresden, drawing a salary of 300 Thalers.[1] As this figure represents roughly
half the normal orchestral player's pay at this period, we may conclude that
Hampl's retirement dates from that year.

Both Gerber and Gassner report that Hampl was still living in 1766;
Forkel[2] includes him in the Dresden orchestra register for 1782; and the
anonymous *Dictionary of Musicians* (London, 1824), p. 317, keeps him alive
until as late as 1784. The Sächsisches Staatsarchiv, however, records the
date of his death as 30 March 1771.[3]

Even if Hampl had not possessed the great pedagogic gifts which were to
mark him as one of the finest horn teachers of all time, his contributions to
the mechanical evolution of the instrument would have sufficed to win for
him lasting recognition. About 1753 he devised, together with the Dresden
maker Johann Werner, the model which became known as the *Inventionshorn*.
(This is described more fully in the section on Werner in Chapter V, p. 127.)
In principle Hampl's innovation was that of incorporating the interchangeable crooks into the corpus of the horn. In this way the position of the instrument relative to the player's mouth would remain constant and not
change with each key as it did with terminal crooks of differing length. The
concept was a sound one, and the *Inventionshorn* found widespread acceptance.
It was quickly taken up by other makers in Germany, copied for a time in
Vienna, and adopted in France some thirty years later by Joseph and Lucien-
Joseph Raoux as the basis for the *cor-solo*. Although various improvements
were subsequently made on Hampl's first idea, it laid down the form for the
modern horn in France and Germany. Indeed, in the latter country Hampl's
design was to remain unaltered in substance until the recent outcrop of
multiple-valved altissimo instruments at Mainz.

The other invention by which Hampl is remembered is one whose descendants may be found in the possession of every horn-player today: the
non-transposing mute. It is well known that Hampl experimented with
various pads and plugs in the course of working out his system for the right

[1] Sachsisches Staatsarchiv, quoted in Eitner, *Quellen-Lexikon*, v (Leipzig, 1905), p. 11.
[2] *Almanach*, 1782, p. 145.
[3] See Eitner, loc. cit. This date is given in Profeta, *Storia e Letteratura degli Strumenti musicali* (Florence, 1942), p. 564, but without authority; and in Morley-Pegge,
French Horn, p. 153, who cites Profeta.

hand. The effect of inserting a plug into the bell was to alter the pitch of the horn, Domnich tells us.[1] The same plug hollowed out and slightly enlarged would not change the instrument's pitch when introduced into the bell, but produced a most convincing echo effect. It was thus as a corollary to his main experiments that Hampl hit upon the principle of the non-transposing mute: and so added to his already imposing list of achievements and inventions a device which greatly enriched the horn's palette of tonal colour. The echo effect was to become one of the most popular items in the later eighteenth-century virtuoso's bag of tricks, and contributed much to the horn's popularity as a solo instrument. With few alterations it has come down to us intact from Hampl's own hand.

The exact dates of Hampl's inventions will probably never be known. It is possible, however, to estimate the period of his inventive activities as falling between the years 1748 and 1760. His system of hand-stopping could hardly have been completed much before 1750, although Fröhlich clearly states that both the hand technique and its by-product, the mute, date from the first half of the century.[2] It is clear from Gerber's text that the prototype of Hampl's Inventionshorn made its appearance in 1753 (see below). It is unlikely that any of these discoveries were made later than 1760, however, for an atmosphere filled with exploding Prussian shells would hardly lend itself to invention and study. Soon after the cease-fire in 1763 Punto and Wiesbach (q.v.) came to study with Hampl, and apparently found him with his new technique fully worked out.

The most reliable contemporary account of Hampl's life and works is that given by Gerber.[3] The information contained in this article came to Gerber from the horn virtuoso Carl Thürrschmidt, as did most of the material in Gerber's writings on the horn. Particularly as this article deals with Hampl's inventions, it is appropriate here to quote it in full.

Hampel, Anton Joseph, Second Horn in the Royal Polish Orchestra at Dresden about the year 1748, still under Hasse's conductorship, was one of the great masters of his instrument and a thinking artist. Not only did he train many fine pupils, amongst whom J. W. Stich, called Punto, is mentioned above; but he was also the one who invented the earliest and best kind of Inventionshorn, and commissioned the first of these from the Dresden maker Johann Werner about 1753 to 1755. I have already given a more exact description of this discovery in my other Lexicon. [See Appendix.] After Werner's death his apprentice Leithold took over his workshop; but his instruments

---

[1] *Methode de Premier et de Second Cor* (Paris, *c.* 1805); see also below, Domnich, Heinrich, p. 207.

[2] Joseph Fröhlich, in Ersch und Gruber, *Allgemeine Encyclopädie der Wissenschaften und Künste* (Leipzig, 1834), ii, pp. 4–11.

[3] In his *Neues Historisch-Biographisches Lexicon der Tonkünstler* (Leipzig, 1813), ii, p. 493.

were not so much applauded as those of his master. A master at Vienna by the name of Körner see p. 131 was more successful, soon afterwards making horns of this type in a quality equal to Werner's. Apart from this valuable and generally useful invention Hampl also devised sordines or mutes which neither raised nor lowered the horn's pitch. This information came from the hands of that outstanding master Carl Thürrschmidt, whose death was unfortunately so premature. Hampl was still alive in the year 1766.

Since the appearance of this monograph a great deal has been written about Hampl, based on both fact and conjecture; but it was Gerber who paid him the highest tribute when he characterized this great teacher as a 'thinking artist'.

SCHINDELARŽ, Johann, c. 1715–7 (?). A Bohemian virtuoso of some note who earned recognition as a teacher through his pupils Haudek (q.v.) and Punto (q.v.). He was principal horn in the Mannheim orchestra under Johann

Ex. 26.   J. A. Stamitz: Symphony in G: Minuet, Trio.

Stamitz from 1742 to 1756. There Schindelarž's style of playing exercised a decisive influence upon Stamitz's manner of writing for the horn. This idiom of writing frequent octaves and conjunct melodies in the altissimo register was taken up by all the early symphonists, who patterned themselves on Stamitz's models. In this way Schindelarž's playing left its stamp on the clarino-horn style of the third quarter of the eighteenth century. A typical example of his style as reflected in Stamitz's writing may be seen in the Symphony in G (*DTB* III), given in Ex. 26. Many of the later parts embrace the written a″ and b″, which would indicate that Schindelarž was acquainted with hand-stopping.

    With regard to the details of his career, Schindelarž remains a shadow-figure, owing mainly to the fact that the relevant archival material for both the Mannheim and Munich orchestras begins too late to include him. Dlabacž finds him in Prague as 'Principal Horn to Prince Mannsfeld in 1738, where he taught Karl Haudek, later to become famous, to virtuoso standard.

After that he left his native country, and was appointed to the Electoral Orchestra at Mannheim as virtuoso and leader.'[1] In point of fact his career followed closely that of Johann Stamitz, for Schindelarž, like Stamitz, attracted the notice of the Elector Palatine, Carl Philipp, by his playing at the coronation of Maria Theresia in Prague in 1741. He appears to have come with Stamitz to Mannheim at Carl Philipp's behest, and was no doubt on hand during the musical festivities which filled that eventful week in 1742 preceding the crowning of the Elector's cousin Charles Albert as Charles VII. From 17 to 24 January the Emperor-elect was at Mannheim. 'Tous ces jours se passèrent en fêtes, il y eut un opéra magnifique. . . .'[2] It was during these performances that Stamitz's playing aroused a storm of applause, and not at Frankfurt, as Riemann supposes.[3] The fact that the celebrations in question had originally been planned for the double marriage of both the Archbishop of Cologne, Charles's nephew, and the young Prince Palatine suggests that Stamitz and Schindelarž had been engaged in Prague with this event in mind. But by 1756 Schindelarž had left to take a post in Munich, and Marpurg's list of the Mannheim orchestra for that year finds Joseph Ziwiny as first horn.[4] Shortly thereafter, about 1760, Punto came to Munich to study with the famous Bohemian: '. . . then to Munich to join the class of the famous Schindelarž . . .'[5] Whether Schindelarž retired to Bohemia or ended his days in Munich is not known. He is not mentioned in Leopold Mozart's list of the Mannheim orchestra in 1778 (the Mannheim ensemble had that year been transferred to Munich when the Elector Palatine succeeded to the throne of the Elector of Bavaria). All things being equal, death probably claimed him in the early seventies, as it had his contemporary, Hampl.

STRYYNECK (Širineck) may well be a brave attempt on the part of the French to spell Škrizuwanek or Schrywanek (q.v.), with whom he may be identical. Syryyneck appears as principal horn in the Paris Opéra orchestra about 1750, and was one of the first Bohemian horn-players to come to Paris in mid-century.[6] The *Mercure de France* (Mai 1754), p. 182, mentions that in a Concert Spirituel of 16 April 'M. Syryyneck et M. Steinmetz jouèrent un Concerto de Cors de Chasse'. This would suggest that Širineck and his partner had been travelling duettists before settling in Paris. The *Etat de Paris* for 1757 mentions them as 'les deux cors de chasse de M. de la Populinière'. They had joined the famous musical amateur's private band in about

---

[1] *Künstler-Lexicon*, iii, p. 42.
[2] *Tagebuch des Kaiser Karls VII*, ed. K. Heigel (Munich, 1883), p. 44.
[3] Preface to vol. xiii of *DTB*, p. xv.
[4] F. W. Marpurg, *Historisch-Kritische Beyträge zur Aufnahme der Musik* (Berlin, 1753–7), ii, p. 567.
[5] Dlabacz, op. cit., iii, 209.
[6] See *Almanach Historique du Théâtre* (Paris, c. 1770).

1750. Whether Syryyneck and the Viennese Širineck are one and the same is open to question; but see p. 203, under Skrižuwanek.

SCHMIDT, an orchestral player in the Comedie Italienne at Paris in 1756, probably of Bohemian origin. He is listed in the *Almanach Historique* together with Bremer (q.v.) for that year.

HOSA, Thomas, c. 1715–86, and *Georg*, c. 1718–87. Bohemian horn-players in the service of Prince Charles of Lorraine in the orchestra of the Electoral opera at Brussels. The two brothers were accomplished players who, according to Bernsdorf, had already attracted notice as virtuosi in Bohemia.[1] They set out on a tour of Germany at an early age, ultimately settling in Brussels as the permanent horn-players of Prince Charles's flourishing opera. They may well be credited with bringing the Austrian style of playing to the Netherlands, and it is virtually certain that Othon Vandenbroek (q.v.) was their pupil. The Hosas amassed a considerable fortune, in itself a remarkable feat for any orchestral horn-player, and according to Dlabacž, Thomas left to his poor sister in Bohemia the sum of 15,000 Gulden. His younger brother inherited his 'costly wardrobe' and his instruments.

Gretry: *Zemire et Azor*, III, iv, bar 17 passim.

Ex. 27.

No horn-player is immune to the occasional 'off-day', and the Hosas were no exception. It was on just such an occasion that the ubiquitous Dr. Burney heard them while in Brussels in 1772. Burney attended a performance of Grétry's opera *Zemire et Azor*. 'The orchestra', he reports, 'was admirably conducted, and the band, taken as a whole was numerous, powerful, correct, and attentive. But in its separate parts, the horns were bad, and out of tune, which was too discoverable in the capital song of the piece, when they were placed at different distances from the audience, to imitate an echo, occasioned by the rocks, in a wild and desert scene.'[2] When considering the fine reputation which the Hosas enjoyed, their dubious performance on that night would seem surprising. In fact, the solo parts of the piece in question (Act III, scene IV) are not at all taxing, and consist merely of a slow descending scale on the C horn's middle register (see Ex. 27). But given a bad lip, even the best of horn-players can slip up on a seemingly harmless passage. It is ironical that Burney of all people should have chosen that particular evening to hear these otherwise excellent players. (See Dlabacž, *Künstler-Lexicon*, i,

[1] Edward Bernsdorf, *Neues Universal-Lexicon der Tonkunst* (Dresden, 1856), ii, p. 453.
[2] Charles Burney, *The Present State of Music in Germany* (London, 1775), i, p. 26.

pp. 667–8; and his entry in von Riegger, *Materialen zur Alten und Neuen Statistik von Böhmen*, xii, p. 242.)

SCHADE is listed as third horn in the orchestra at Stuttgart for the year 1757. (Marpurg, *Historisch-Critische Beträge zur Aufnahme der Musik*, Berlin, 1754–7; also Carse, *The Orchestra in the Eighteenth Century*, Cambridge, 1940, p. 59.)

SPORNI was Schade's principal at Stuttgart under Jomelli in 1757. (See the foregoing references.) He was succeeded in the 1790s by Joseph Ziwiny (q.v.).

HAUDEK, Karl, 1721–*post* 1800. A Bohemian virtuoso, equally famous as both player and teacher, who began his career in Prague as a pupil of Schindelarž. Haudek was Hampl's desk-mate at Dresden for many years as principal horn. Nothing could give a better picture of the musician and the man than Dlabacž's extensive note on Haudek in the *Künstler-Lexicon* (i, p. 574).

Haudek, Karl, Principal Horn to the Elector of Saxony, was born in 1721 at Dobržich in Bohemia. In his seventeenth year he came under the tutelage of the famous horn-player to Prince Mannsfeld, Johann Schindelarž; and remained six years in the Prince's service. The extraordinary talent with which he handled his instrument opened for him the path to other orchestras. Thus in 1744 he was engaged by that great patron of music, Count Leopold von Kinsky; and after only two years he entered the service of Prince Johann Adam von Auersberg. A year later the King of Poland and Elector of Saxony called him to Dresden, appointing him a Court virtuoso in 1747. Here his companion was another Bohemian, the already-famous Anton Hampel, with whom he played the most difficult duets before the entire Court. The widespread fame which these two virtuosi earned for themselves moved Joseph Count von Thun to send both Johann Stich, later called Punto, and Franz Wiesbach to Dresden to be trained in their class. These pupils soon appeared as virtuosi in Prague; and the fame of their teachers soon spread throughout the kingdom. And to this day the name of Haudek is dear to every Bohemian artist: for he accomplished a great deal of good, and through these and many other pupils greatly stimulated the cultivation of this instrument amongst the Bohemians. A paralysis forced him to retire in 1796; but in the September of 1800 he was still living at Dresden at the age of 78, having served in the Electoral orchestra with great honour for 52 years.

The esteem which Haudek's exceptional gifts as a player and teacher won for him was heightened by his remarkable modesty. In 1800 he wrote as a footnote to the data which Dlabacž included in the above-quoted article:

Here you have, dearest friend, my insignificant life history. Why this? Should I, a little musical worm, be mentioned amongst men of great talents? No, I don't deserve it. Should you still wish to include this, strike out everything ostentatious, and make it so short as to be not worth reading. I am your friend and servant Haudek.

But in spite of his self-effacement he ranks as one of the important players of the mid-eighteenth century.

As a pupil of Schindelarž, Haudek developed at Dresden the style of florid clarino-horn-playing which his teacher took to Mannheim. This particular style was more suitable in playing octaves and stepwise melody in the altissimo register than was its more ornamented Baroque predecessor. It was this later idiom which the Stamitzes adopted as the characteristic horn style of the early symphony (see Ex. 26). This style may be seen in an example written for Haudek and Hampl—though in a more archaic musical context—in Hasse's Te Deum (Ex. 28). The point to be noted here, however, is that this

Ex. 28.   Hasse: Te Deum.

style of horn-playing was brought to Saxony and the Palatinate from that Bohemia which in those days was known as the 'heart and brain of Austria', by Bohemian players using horns made in Vienna.

EDER, *Andreas,* a tutti horn-player in the service of the Prince of Oettingen-Wallerstein under Anton Reicha's direction. In 1748 he was promoted to a salary of 20 Gulden monthly for 'good services rendered'. He was advanced from livery service. *Oettingen-Wallerstein Hofkammerrechnungen,* 1748.)

STEINMÜLLER, *Thaddäus, c.* 1725–1790, a Bohemian-born virtuoso and teacher, was for many years principal horn in the orchestra of Prince Esterhazy under Joseph Haydn. Quite apart from Steinmüller's exceptional brilliance as an orchestral player and his extraordinary command of the altissimo register, he deserves recognition as the teacher of his three sons, Johann, Josef, and Wilhelm (qq.v.). The Esterhazy archives record the payment of 600 Gulden 'dem Waldhornisten Thaddäus Steinmüllern aus Böhmen' in

1762.[1] This is the date given both by Pohl[2] and Hoboken[3] as the year of the elder Steinmüller's entry into the Esterhazy orchestra.

Steinmüller possessed a formidable technique to which Haydn gave free rein in a number of works written between 1762 and 1772. The first of these show-pieces was the Concerto for First Horn, composed for the Bohemian virtuoso in the year of his arrival.[4] The first horn part of the famous Symphony No. 31 'Mit dem Hornsignal' shows Steinmüller's outstanding mastery of the high register, and demonstrates the similarity between his playing style and that of Schindelarž. Both of these players wielded considerable influence in clarifying the clarino-horn style of the Mannheim and Viennese symphonists. (See Ex. 22, p. 81; these parts were written for the elder Steinmüller, Karl Franz [q.v.], and two other players, Oliva and Páner, also of no mean ability. The commonly held assumption that these parts were written for Steinmüller and his three sons is refuted by the date of the Hornsignal's composition, 1765. The eldest son was born in about that year.) Steinmüller's virtuosity is given a further tribute in Haydn's Divertimento a Tre of 1767 for violin, horn, and cello. Here the horn covers the quite astonishing range between the second and twenty-second partials of the E flat horn. The equally difficult Sextetto No. 14 (for horn, oboe, bassoon, violin, viola, and cello: written before 1781) embraces the third and nineteenth partials; but the Divertimento remains a landmark of the altissimo-horn style, and the supreme example of Steinmüller's monumental technique.

According to Pohl, he left the Esterhazy orchestra in 1772. Dlabacž[5] reports that Thaddäus and his three sons were members of Count Nostitz's orchestra in Prague in 1775. If, however, we accept Pohl's statement[6] that the three sons were born at Eisenstadt ('All three were born at Eisenstadt and lifted from the baptismal font by the Haydns'), the eldest son would have been less than 10 years of age in 1775. Surely Dlabacž means 1785. It is reasonably certain, at any rate, that Thaddäus Steinmüller ended his days in Bohemia. (See also A. Hyatt King, 'Haydn's Trio for Horn, Violin, and Cello' in *Musical Times*, December 1945, p. 367.)

FRITSCH, *Joseph*, son and pupil of Christoph Fritsch (q.v.), was engaged as second horn in the Wallerstein Court orchestra from 1752 to 1775. His desk-partner was Johannes Thürrschmidt. 'In the year 1752, on 12 April, Johannes Thürrschmied and Joseph Fritsch were appointed as Primarius and Secondario.'[7] According to Diemand[8] Haydn dedicated his Symphonies Nos. 46,

---

[1] Budapester Staatsarchiv, *Acta Musicalia*, 1676–1800, fol. 45, 1762.
[2] *Joseph Haydn* (Leipzig, 1880), i, 266.   [3] *Joseph Haydn* (Mainz, 1957), p. 535.
[4] See the accompanying record for examples of staccato scale-work and legato playing in the high register. The instrument on which these passages were recorded was made during Steinmüller's lifetime.
[5] *Künstler-Lexicon*, iii, 205.   [6] loc. cit.   [7] Arch. Wall.
[8] *Josef Haydn und der Wallersteiner Hof* (Augsburg, 1921), p. 72.

47, and 48 to Prince Kraft Ernst of Oettingen-Wallerstein, the latter being addressed to the Princess Maria Theresa. Indeed, the horn parts exhibit none of the dazzling virtuosity which Haydn came later to expect from the Steinmüllers at Esterhazy. Rather, these parts show a definite lyric quality and confine themselves principally to the second and third octaves.

In 1764 the Emperor Joseph II (then Archduke) visited Wallerstein. He was serenaded at table by Count Philipp Carl's *Jagdmusik* of clarinets, horns, and bassoons. This band was a descendant of the earlier group of horns and oboes which had regaled Charles VI, in which Fritsch's father Christoph had played.[1]

In 1775 Fritsch appears in the orchestra of the Prince Thurn und Taxis (brother of Princess Maria Theresa of Oettingen-Wallerstein) as second horn. The horn parts to a Symphony in D by Theodor von Schacht dated 1779 (Thurn und Taxische Hofbibliothek, No. 3) bear the names of the players: Rudolf, Fritsch, Weiss, and Stumm. These parts abound with lively passage-work which marks all four players as being of a very high standard. Forkel's list of the Regensburg orchestra has Weiss and Stumm change parts, but leaves Fritsch on second. 'Fürstl. Thurn und Taxische Kammermusik zu Regensburg. Waldhornisten. Herr Rudolph [most probably Anton Rudolph, q.v.] Fritsche. Stum. Weiss.'[2]

Mr. ERNST was probably a Bohemian. To all evidence he was a descendant, in spirit at least, of those shadowy double-horn virtuosi of the first generation, Beda and Creta. Mr. Ernst played a concerto for two horns, according to the *Mercure de France* of April 1751, at a Concert Spirituel in that year. 'Mr. Ernst, Allemand, a exécuté seul un concerto à deux cors de chasse. Cette nouveauté a paru plus singulière qu'agréable.' Mr. Ernst's performance, apart from its intrinsic singularity, was probably one of the first instances of a horn concerto being performed in Paris.

STAINMETZ (Steinmetz, Staimetz, or Slamitz), Franz, was one of the first to gain employment as an orchestral horn-player in Paris. He may well have belonged to the immigration of Bohemians who brought orchestral horn-playing to France about the middle of the eighteenth century. The *Almanach Historique du Théâtre* lists him as Syryyneck's second in the horn department of the Opéra orchestra in *c.* 1750. In 1754 we find him in the Opéra Comique, this time as a desk-partner to 'Hebert' (Herbert). He was also a member of La Pouplinière's private band, and may well have come to Paris with Johann Stamitz to introduce the first symphonies with clarinets and horns to be heard in that city.[3] In the April of 1754 Steinmetz and his first, Syryyneck

---

[1] Schiedermair, op. cit., p. 107.   [2] *Almanach*, 1783, p. 103.

[3] See Cucuel, George, *La Pouplinière et la Musique de Chambre au XVIIIe Siècle* (Paris, 1913), pp. 330-1.

(Širineck) played a 'Concerto de Cors de Chasse' at a Concert Spirituel,[1] a fact which casts a favourable light on their competence as duettists. The *Etat de Paris* for 1759, 1760, and 1761 lists one 'Slamitz, Rue du Chantre' under 'Musiciens'. According to Cucuel, no further mention of him is found in Paris after 1762.[2] This disappearance may well indicate that Steinmetz and the Viennese horn-player Staimetz were the same: in which case he ended his days as a supernumerary of the Viennese Court orchestra. (See s.v. 'Staimetz', p. 198.)

MICHEL, Joseph, c. 1720–90, was first horn and clarinist in the orchestra of the Strahow Monastery in Prague. Details of Michel's career are not known; but it is a matter of some interest that the archaic practice of the first horn's doubling on the high trumpet was carried on so late in the century. According to Dlabacž, Michel died in the year 1790 'at a great age'.[3]

THÜRRSCHMIDT, Johannes, 1725–1800 (variously Thürrschmidt, Thürrschmiedt, Dürrschmied, Türrschmied, Duirschmied, and Thurshmit), was the founder of a family of eighteenth-century horn virtuosi, of whom the most prominent was Carl Thürrschmidt, 1753–97 (q.v.) The elder Thürrschmidt was born at Leichgau in Bohemia on 24 June 1725. According to Gassner,[4] he was 'one of the foremost horn virtuosi of his time'.

No record remains of Thürrschmidt's early career; but in 1752 it is recorded in the Wallerstein treasury archives that on 12 April 'Johannes Thürrschmidt und Joseph Fritsch [q.v.] were engaged as Primarius und Secondario'.

If we accept Diemand's assertion that Haydn wrote his Symphonies Nos. 46, 47, and 48 for Prince Kraft Ernst of Oettingen-Wallerstein,[5] then the first-horn part in the 'Maria Theresia' is an impressive testimony to Thürrschmidt's exceptional cantabile in the upper register.[6] The fact that Thaddäus Steinmüller left the Esterhazy orchestra in 1772 further points to the likelihood that the three symphonies in question were written with the Wallerstein players in mind. A glance at the horn parts of these works shows that Thürrschmidt's style of playing differed little from his countryman and

---

[1] *Mercure de France*, loc. cit.   [2] *La Pouplinière*, pp. 330–1.
[3] *Künstler-Lexicon*, iii, 315.   [4] *Universal-Lexicon*, p. 849.
[5] 'Josef Haydn und der Wallersteiner Hof', in *Zeitschrift des Historischen Vereins für Schwaben und Neuburg*, xliii (Augsburg, 1921), p. 72.
[6] Diemand's statement can be supported on several counts. Kraft Ernst had met Haydn while a student in Vienna, and maintained contact with him through the Wallerstein musical intendant, Ignaz von Beecke; Princess Maria Theresia, Kraft Ernst's wife, was 21 in 1772, and the young Princess's birthday would have provided a more likely occasion for the dedication than one of the Empress Maria Theresia's visits to Esterhazy, especially as Haydn was on leave that spring; and to this day the exact year of the 'Maria Theresia' has not been conclusively proved, even by such authorities as Hoboken (op. cit.) and Robbins Landon (*The Symphonies of Joseph Haydn*, London, 1955).

contemporary at Esterhazy. If, indeed, conclusions can be drawn to such a fine degree on this evidence, it would appear that the Wallerstein virtuoso favoured a more lyric style; although the high-horn concertos written for him by Anton Rosetti attest to a remarkable technique and an exceptional fluency in both high and low registers (Ex. 29).[1]

Ex. 29.   Rosetti: Concerto for High Horn, c. 1775.

The elder Thürrschmidt retired in 1780 at the age of 55, but kept up his playing by standing in now and again for his successor, Joseph Nagel (q.v.). A note in the parish register archives at Wallerstein establishes the year of Thürrschmidt's death at 1800: '1801 sagt die Tochter dass der Vater vor einem Jahr gestorben ist.' This contradicts Gassner's date of 1780. He had completed forty-eight years' service at the Wallerstein Court.

Thürrschmidt's ability as a teacher was reflected in the playing of his son and pupil, Carl, who went on to win an international reputation as a soloist. His younger brother, Joseph, 'was in Paris and considered to be a good second horn in the year 1797'.[2] Carl in turn was the father and teacher of Carl Nicolaus (1776–1842), later a distinguished orchestral player in his own right. Thus Johannes Thürrschmidt stood at the head of a family tradition of horn-playing which spanned three generations.

Fig. 2

One of Johannes Thürrschmidt's instruments, an orchestral horn with fixed mouthpiece by Michael Leichnambschneider (Vienna, 1721, Fig. 2), is served in the Wallerstein library at Schloss Harburg.

[1] These concertos are preserved in the Oettingen-Wallerstein and Thurn und Taxis libraries. See the author's article, 'Anton Rösler', in *Die Musik in Geschichte und Gegenwart*, XI (Kassel, 1962), p. 619.
[2] *Dictionary of Musicians*, 493.

THÜRRSCHMIDT, Anton, 'younger brother of the preceding [Johannes], was also a good horn in the service of Prince Albrecht von Teschen (Bohemia)'.[1]

MATUŠKA, Johann, c. 1725–*post* 1800, is listed by Marpurg (Beyträge, ii, 567) as fourth horn in the Mannheim orchestra in 1756: 'Johann Matuška aus Böhmen'.[2] Dlabacž describes him as 'a famous horn-player, by birth a Bohemian, residing in 1796 at Stuttgart and Zweybrücken'. Sittard[3] mentions Matuška as being one of the prominent members of the Stuttgart ensemble about the turn of the century. He and his countryman Midlarž (q.v.) had joined the Duke of Württemberg's band in 1784.

BREMNER was one of the early German or Bohemian horn-players in Paris. He is listed by the *Almanach du Théâtre,* together with his second, 'Schmidh', as a member of the Comédie Italienne orchestra in 1756.

MATIEGKA, Joseph, 1728–1804, is remembered principally as one of the foremost teachers of the eighteenth century. A man of great intellect and possessing a deeply philosophical turn of mind, he was obliged by a freak accident to turn his exceptional powers to teaching and playing the horn. Dlabacž's account of his life is of such interest as to merit citing here complete: the more so in view of the fact that this great horn-player played under Dlabacž's personal direction in the Strahow monastery orchestra.

Matiegka, Joseph, a horn virtuoso in Prague. Born on 28 January 1728 at Obercerewitz in the Czaslau district, he went as a young child to Teltsch, where he won a scholarship at the Jesuit seminary, graduating in poetry and classics. He was thereupon engaged as a horn-player at the Seminary of St. Wenzel in Prague. Here he read philosophy and theology for several years, intending to enter holy orders as a lay brother. His ambition was not fulfilled, however, for a damaged finger on his left hand cost him the admission to the Archbishop's seminary. Matiegka now decided to seek his fortune through music. In this he succeeded well; and in a short time began to play the most difficult concertos and solos in church services and concerts with extraordinary facility and sweetness.

He was soon appointed as horn-player to the Theinkirche, the Church of St. Aegidius and, in 1754, to Prince Lobkowitz's Lauretta Chapel in the Hradschin Palace. In 1769 he was additionally engaged as Court musician to the unforgettable Prince Karl Egon von Fürstenberg, and in 1773 to the Prince-Archbishop of Prague, Anton Peter Count von Pržichowitz. From 1800 onwards he held posts at the Metropolitan Cathedral of St. Vitus, in the Opera, and at

---

[1] *Dictionary of Musicians,* 493.   [2] *Künstler-Lexicon,* ii, 280.

[3] *Zur Geschichte der Musik und des Theaters am Württembergischen Hofe* (Stuttgart, 1891), ii, 204.

the Strahow Monastery, at present under my musical direction; and fulfilled these appointments to everyone's satisfaction.

On 5 February 1804 this worthy and God-fearing man celebrated the fiftieth anniversary of his service to Prince Lobkowitz's Chapel with a solemn mass dedicated to the Almighty, in which the best Prague musicians and singers performed with the greatest feeling. Their Highnesses the Lobkowitz Family, as patrons of this holy place, crowned his service as an ageing and faithful servant with a special celebration led by the great conductor Franz Strobach.

Matiegka died the same year on 20 April at noon in the St. Lauretta Musicians' Residence at the Hradschin, aged 76 years, 2 months, and 24 days. He had lived as a devout Christian, tender father, outstanding artist, and law-abiding citizen; and was buried in the churchyard at Koschirž. He trained more than fifty pupils, amongst whom the famous Punto, Zalužan, and his own son Joseph (1767–1793) broadcast the fame of their master.

Matiegka was a pupil of Smeykal (q.v.) and was thus a product of the best tradition of the preceding generation. He was Punto's first teacher; and indeed it appears that every Bohemian horn-player of any note during the second half of the century came under his tutelage at some point. He no doubt influenced horn-playing in Vienna as well, for the Lobkowitz family maintained a sizeable palace there at which they passed the Court season each year. As a member of the Prince's private band, Matiegka would have accompanied his lord to the capital.

None of the actual music known to have been written expressly for Matiegka has at the time of writing come to hand, so it is not possible to comment on the particulars of his playing style. We may be sure, however, that it differed little from the general styles of his countrymen and con-temporaries, Johannes Thürrschmidt and Thaddäus Steinmüller. He was a high-horn player.

The fine quality of Matiegka's playing is evident from contemporary accounts. In a report of the most prominent virtuosi and singers of the day, the *Jahrbuch der Tonkunst*[1] declares that 'Matiegka has achieved great perfection on the horn'. Dlabacž's *Abhandlung von der Schicksalen der Künste in Böhmen*[2] praises Matiegka and Schepka (q.v.) as 'up to now the soundest horn-players in Prague'. In his *Teutsches Künstler-Lexicon*,[3] Meusel singles out Matiegka amongst the foremost German-speaking musicians of the period as a 'Virtuose auf dem Waldhorn zu Prag'.[4]

DAMNICH, Friedrich , c. 1728–90, was a tutti horn-player in the Waller-stein orchestra from 1746 to 1751. A letter in Count Philipp Carl's hand dated 29 April 1751 deals with a petition for release by Damnich, 'from Ofen

[1] Prague, 1796, p. 126.   [2] Prague, 1797, p. 35.   [3] Lemgo, 1808, ii, 17.
[4] See also Gassner, op. cit., p. 593.

[the Pest of modern Budapest], in his fifth year with us as a horn-player, wishing to seek his fortune elsewhere'. The petition was granted, as Damnich had shown himself 'devout, loyal, and sensible'. In Damnich we have a rare instance of a horn-player of Hungarian origin: a fact which points to the widespread popularity which the horn enjoyed throughout the Austrian dominions. Friedrich was the father of Arnold and Heinrich Damnich or Domnich, the latter a famous teacher and professor at the Paris Conservatoire (see p. 207).

ZOEBEL was fourth horn in Stuttgart, according to Marpurg's list of 1757.[1] When Jommelli was appointed *Kapellmeister* at Stuttgart in 1754 he insisted upon enlarging the forces of Duke Charles Eugene's orchestra to equal those he had known at Vienna. Zoebel may well have been a Viennese himself, as the name is common there, albeit in the form of Zöbl. (Marpurg, we will remember, was a Berliner, and so would have Germanized the spelling of such names.)

VOGEL, Joseph, is listed in Bernsdorf[2] as 'Thurn und Taxische Hofmusicus' and a member of the Regensburg orchestra about the middle of the eighteenth century. He was the teacher of the duettist-virtuosi Ignaz and Anton Boeck (q.v.) and of his son Johann Georg Vogel, who was principal 'Kammer-Cornist' at Ansbach in 1782.[3]

ŽIWINY (Žwini), *Joseph, Wenzel, and Jacob*, were Bohemian-born brothers who attracted some note as members of the Mannheim orchestra under Johann and Carl Stamitz from *c.* 1745 onwards. The eldest, Joseph, was Schindelarž's alternate in the principal-horn chair, and appears to have enjoyed a good reputation as a high-horn virtuoso. He joined the Mannheim orchestra in 1747, according to Walter.[4] In the seventies the team of brothers disbanded, and we find only Joseph in Forkel's list of the Mannheim personnel in 1782. The elder Žiwiny, together with his erstwhile fourth, Matuška, appears in Sittard's register of the Stuttgart ensemble in 1796.[5] This default of Žiwiny and Matuška from Mannheim to Stuttgart may well have resulted from Duke Charles Eugene's constant efforts to lure the more prominent players of the Electoral orchestra (which was the object of his bitter envy) to his own band by the promise of higher pay. In this he was only partially successful.[6]

[1] *Beyträge*, iii, 200.

[2] *Neues Universal-Lexicon der Tonkunst* (Dresden, 1856), i, 421.

[3] Forkel, *Almanach*, 1782, p. 137.

[4] Friederich Walter, *Geschichte der Musik . . . zu Mannheim* (Leipzig, 1898), p. 371.

[5] op. cit., ii, 204; see also Dlabacž, *Künstler-Lexicon*, iii, 447; Forkel, op. cit., 1782, p. 126, and Hugo Riemann's preface to *DTB* III, p. xv.

[6] See Yorke-Long, *Music at Court* (London, 1954), pp. 50–1.

HORŽIZKY, Joseph Ignaz, was principal horn in the royal band at Berlin under Karl Heinrich Graun. He and his second, Christian Mengis, are mentioned in Marpurg's list of 1754. A trio sonata for horn, oboe d'amore and continuo written for Horžizky by Graun (preserved in the University Library at Lund, Sweden) shows him as a player of uncommon ability. The style is that of the older florid Baroque tradition.

JOSEP(H), Joseph, was a member of Count Philipp Carl's hunting-band at Wallerstein in 1754.[1] He later became principal horn in the Electoral orchestra at Trier. (See Forkel, *Almanach*, 1782, p. 153; and *Musikalische Korrespondenz*, Speier, 1790, 24 November, p. 160.)

MIDLARŽ, c. 1730–post 1800, a Bohemian in all probability, joined the Stuttgart orchestra as a second horn in 1754. It was in that year that Duke Charles Eugene moved his Court to the new palace at near-by Ludwigsburg, and engaged Nicolo Jommelli as *Capellmeister*; he in turn enlarged the orchestral forces to include four horns. Midlarž is mentioned in Marpurg's list of 1757. Midlarž's career attained a length which it is often the privilege of low-horn players to enjoy; he held the post of second horn from 1754 until 1799. In his last years he shared his desk with Matuška (q.v.), another Bohemian, who joined the orchestra in 1796 succeeding Midlarž upon his death. (See Dlabacž, ii, 318; and Carse, op. cit., p. 59.)

NIEMECŽEK left the tailor's trade to become a pupil of Matiegka (q.v.). Dlabacž[2] describes him as 'ein guter Waldhornist'. (See also von Riegger, xii, 264.)

REINERT, Carl, 1730–9?, joined the band of the Prince of Schwarzburg-Sonderhausen in 1757, bringing with him a pair of Hampl-designed Inventionshörner made at Dresden by Werner and dated 1755. When Reinert left Sondershausen a few years later to become principal horn and *Cammer-Musiker* to the Duke of Mecklenburg at Schwerin, Prince Günther bought his horns 'for the Court orchestra's benefit' for 80 Thalers.[3] Later he served at Schwerin under Antonio Rosetti, who was *Capellmeister* from 1789 until 1792; but the horn parts which Rosetti wrote for him do not differ significantly from the normal orchestral writing of the period. (See also Dlabacž, ii, 557.)

RODOLPHE, Jean Joseph, 1730–1812, is mentioned here only because he is so frequently confused with the Bohemians Anton and Georg Rudolf (qq.v.) Rodolphe may be considered the first truly French player. An excellent biography appears in Morley-Pegge, op. cit., p. 153.

[1] Archive Wallerstein.   [2] ii. 389.   [3] Gerber, *NTL*, p. 146; see also Appendix, p. 223.

V

THE HAND-HORN
IN
VIENNA AND PRAGUE
1755–1830

Changing concepts of instrumental sound

HAND-STOPPING not only revolutionized the technique of horn-playing, but brought about distinct changes in the design of the instrument itself.[1] It soon became evident that the bell of the old Baroque horn was too narrow in the throat for the most effective use of the right hand. Accordingly the bell-throat was widened and the bore of the entire instrument increased proportionately. The mouthpipe inlet was opened slightly to admit the larger mouthpiece necessary to supply this expanded instrument with the greater volume of air which it now required. In some cases thicker metal was used for the tubing, presumably in order to retain something of the resistance of the older horn. Thus the introduction of the right hand to the bell, quite apart from the smoothing effect upon the tone produced by the hand itself, sparked off a series of changes in the instrument which left it with a tone that was undeniably darker and fuller than that of the Baroque horn; and this new quality accorded fully with the tonal ideals of the dawning Classical style in music.

Certain fundamental changes in musical style now increasingly separated the new period from the Baroque. Whereas the polyphonic textures of the Baroque depended for clarity upon the distinct and individual quality of each instrument in projecting its own line, the homophonic style of the

---

[1] Hampl's first mechanical experiments had resulted in the model known as the Inventionshorn (see Plate IXa), which the Dresden maker Werner had brought out in the early 1750s (see the present chapter, p. 127). The design of the Inventions-horn, however, was directed mainly toward a more practical system of interchange-able crooks which could at once alter the pitch of the instrument and provide a ready means of tuning within a given key. It appears to have preceded Hampl's hand-stopping innovations, and thus, so far as is known, the form of its bell did not reflect the influence of the right-hand technique. The basic idea of the Inventionshorn was nevertheless the first step in evolving a workable means of tuning for the orchestral player; and it was Hampl's principle of the movable crook in the centre of the horn's corpus which was incorporated by the Viennese makers into the famous Orchesterhorn.

new music relied upon a smoothly blended orchestral timbre in its more purely chordal harmonies.

Instruments were now built to sound fuller and smoother. Any auxiliary sounds from the vibrating material of which the instruments were made were now eliminated, with a consequent loss of overtones. The inevitable result of this gain in purity and resonance was that instruments began to approach one another in quality and to sound more alike: an effect which admirably suited the purposes of classical orchestration.

If this process of tonal change was to lend a new richness to those instruments which were destined to become the standard members of the symphony orchestra, it brought about the death of many others; and whole families of instruments fell by the way in the gradual sorting-out. The viols, for instance, gave way to the violin family; the cornett to the oboe and, to a degree, to the clarinet; the recorder to the transverse flute. By about 1760 the survivors had definitely been selected, and their construction showed the trend of the times. Oboe reeds had become thinner and narrower; bassoon bells unchoked; and the bells of the brasses enlarged over those of their Baroque counterparts. As the longer, concave bow gained favour the strings began to exhibit that ability to 'swallow up' one another which was later to temper the success of the fugal movements in Haydn's and Beethoven's quartets: for polyphony, however effective as a musical archaism, was hampered without the viols whose character it reflected. These far-reaching instrumental reforms, then, were not without their parallel where the horn was concerned.

It is unlikely that hand-stopping was evolved in answer to the changing concepts of instrumental sound which resulted in the homogeneous timbre of the Classical orchestra; but it is remarkable that this revolution in horn tone and design which the new hand technique brought about should occur at the very time when the other instruments were undergoing a marked revision in tone colour. As these changes began to exert themselves about mid-century, so the immediate effects of hand-stopping on the horn's design began to be felt by about 1755, when second-horn-players were gradually adopting the new right-hand technique. It is at Dresden that the actual design of the horn shows its first response to this new technique.

Johann Werner and the Inventionshorn—his influence in Germany—
Haltenhof at Hanau

It may strike us as curious that the one maker in the second half of the century who contributed most to the development of the horn should stand outside the main tradition. We do not know who Johann Werner's master was; certainly there was no continuous tradition of brass-instrument-making at Dresden such as existed at Nürnberg, however waning. Yet Werner's workmanship is said to have been of the highest order, and his position with regard to the evolution of the instrument is second only to that of Michael Leichnambschneider. It was Leichnambschneider who brought crooks to the horn and made it a concert instrument; it was Werner who, translating Hampl's ideas, rationalized their use and paved the way for the valve horn: for without Werner's design the valve would have taken much longer to apply to the horn. He was the father of the modern German horn, standing midway between Leichnambschneider and Stölzel.

Between 1750 and 1755 Hampl redesigned the orchestral horn so that the Viennese-type terminal crook was replaced by a straight tuning-shank, and the crook itself was inserted into sockets in the centre of the horn's corpus. These sockets were obtained by cutting one of the coils as it passed by the neck of the bell, and bending the two ends inward; they were then straightened to lie parallel some three to four inches apart and project into the circle described by the body of the instrument. Similarly the tenons on the crook which were to fit into these sockets were formed by bending tubing of the appropriate length (this varied, of course, with the pitch desired) into a coil some four inches across and allowing its ends to extend parallel at a distance corresponding to that separating the sockets. On the earlier model both sockets and tenons were short, and were described as having a slotted sleeve on the tenon which engaged a pin on the crook's tenon to lock it into place. Even so the whole device was prone to wear quickly and develop leaks; perhaps this is why no specimens of the prototype have survived. As a result the sockets and tenons were soon lengthened to form a tuning-slide.[1] With this improvement the horn could be tuned quickly and exactly. Wear was brought down to a minimum, and, what was perhaps the greatest boon to the player, a fixed mouthpipe could now be fitted. (See the drawings on pp. 35 and 39 of the writer's article in *Galpin Society Journal*, No. XVI.) It was Werner who worked with Hampl at Dresden to translate these concepts into practice. The model which resulted was known as the *Inventionshorn*, or horn with innovations or improvements. With characteristic disregard for exact

[1] J. G. Haltenhof of Hanau is often credited with the invention of the tuning-slide as such. It is true that his is the earliest surviving horn to incorporate this device; but then none of Werner's Inventionshörner have come down to us, and he made many. It seems unlikely that a maker of Werner's reported ingenuity would overlook the slide principle inherent in the socket-and-tenon arrangement.

A note on this term is owing here. Morley-Pegge takes the German word '*Zapfen*' in Gerber's text (rendered as 'plugs' in Bargans's article—see page 130) to mean a conical tenon of the kind used on terminal crooks. Like our own word tenon, this can mean any kind of tubular insert, whether conical or cylindrical. In the case of the terminal crook the conical or tapered tenon was fitted into a socket having a corresponding taper. It could be tightened with a twisting motion while pushing the crook home, ensuring an airtight seal. The tapered tenon-and-socket set-up would not work with the centrally inserted crook, for it would be impossible to turn the crook in order to seat it into the two sockets.

usage, makers and writers of the time soon called all crooks '*Inventionen*', whether terminal or inserted.

The obvious gain in convenience of tuning and crook changing which this new design offered caused it to be adopted speedily all over the Continent. The term is met with in musical writings and instrument lists with increasing frequency from about 1765 onward, and Gerber tells us that it was in use in all the major orchestras. This seeming ubiquity is somewhat open to question, however; for, as we have seen, the term Inventionshorn meant any horn with crooks.

But these improvements brought their drawbacks. In order to accommodate the crook and its slides, a certain amount of additional bracing was necessary in the construction of the horn; then, too, the tubing of the crook and tenons had to be cylindrical in profile. These changes combined to detract perceptibly from softness and freedom of tone. For these reasons apparently the Inventionshorn did not catch on with the Viennese, nor did it find favour at Prague, although a few examples were made there late in the period. Even though Werner's tuning-slide later was adapted to the Viennese *Orchesterhorn*, the earlier system of terminal crooks was retained. England, too, appears to have been unresponsive to the advantages offered by Werner's new system, for players here kept faithfully to the old Viennese master-and-coupler system of crooks until well into the nineteenth century. The tuning-slide was nevertheless adopted here in much the same form as at Vienna, a fact which suggests that the influence of the Austro-Bohemian tradition in England continued until well after Handel's time. The French appear to have got the idea of the tuning-slide from English players rather than from Germans or Bohemians, for La Borde, writing in 1781, makes a particular point of the advantages conferred by the tuning-slides of the new *cors à l'anglaise*.[1]

Johann Werner occupied the same historical position with respect to the horn-makers of this period as did Hampl in relation to its players. His earliest surviving instrument, a trumpet in the Brussels Conservatoire collection dated 1733, shows him to be a near contemporary of Hampl. Other dated examples from his hand suggest that he was producing continuously during the thirties and forties: a pair of Jagdhörner, dated 1735, Nos. 98 and 99 in the Bernoulli collection at Greifensee; and a Jagdhorn from the year 1740 in the Heyer collection (No. 1664) at Leipzig. Like Hampl, Werner was a member of the second generation who made a definitive contribution to the orchestral horn's development while the century was in mid-passage. His Inventionshorn marked a turning-point in the design of the instrument corresponding to the change which Hampl's hand-stopping marked in its technique. With each, the move from Baroque to Classical was accomplished.

[1] J. Ch. La Borde, *Essai sur la Musique*, II, ii, Paris, 1780, p. 254.

That it should come when a corresponding change was taking place in musical style was a fortunate coincidence from which the Classical orchestra was to gain.

The date of Werner's death is not known. He was still working in 1755, for Gerber tells us that Carl Reinert brought with him a pair of these new horns which Werner had made for him in that year: this was in 1757, when Reinert joined the orchestra at Sondershausen as principal horn. (See p. 124 and the Appendix, page 226.) Assuming that Werner would have set up on his own about 1730 or earlier, he would presumably retire about 1760 after a normal working span of thirty years or so. This is pure conjecture, for no records of Werner's life have come to light; but it has some support in the fact that his pupil Leutholdt appears to have survived him by some twenty-five years.

Of Johann Gottfried Leutholdt, or Leydholdt, Werner's pupil and erstwhile partner, we know even less. Bernsdorf[1] says that Leutholdt 'enjoyed a remarkable reputation in the second half of the previous century' and that his instruments were in use the world over. Gassner[2] confirms that Leutholdt enjoyed a world-wide reputation, remarking that the Saxon maker's instruments were everywhere 'sought, treasured and dearly bought'. Morley-Pegge (op. cit., p. 186) mentions a horn bearing the mark of the firm of Werner & Leydholdt and the date 1760. Leutholdt evidently set up with Werner in the latter's declining years and inherited his master's tools and patterns upon his death. According to Meusel,[3] Leutholdt died in 1788.

He in turn was succeeded by his pupil Friedrich Wilhelm Jacobi, who carried Werner's direct line into the early nineteenth century. Although Meusel, whose information was presumably fresh, gives 1754 as the date of his birth, the *Zeitschrift für Instrumentenbau* for September 1929 corrects this to read 1762 and cites 1813 as the year of his death. He evidently enjoyed the patronage of the Electoral Court at Dresden, for a horn dated 1804 in the Berlin *Musikinstrumentensammlung* bears the arms of the Elector over his name. Meusel tells us that Jacobi learnt his art from 'the famous instrument-maker Johann Gottfried Leuthold, to whom he was apprenticed for seven years until that master died. Jacobi afterwards inherited his patterns and established himself in the year 1788. Since that time he has made such progress that his instruments are equal to those of Leuthold in their artistry and finish.'

Meanwhile at Hanau on the river Main, from whose banks Southern and Middle Germany hail one another, another maker of the first water was working along the lines laid down by Werner. The earliest surviving horn

---

[1] *Universal-Lexicon der Tonkunst*, II (Dresden, 1856), p. 751.
[2] *Universal-Lexicon der Tonkunst* (Stuttgart, 1847), p. 539.
[3] *Künstler-Lexicon*, I (Lemgo, 1808), p. 429.

from the hand of Johann Gottfried Haltenhof, dated 1776, is preserved in the Paris Conservatoire collection. An example of the finest workmanship, this instrument is also remarkable for its unique system of crooks. The shorter crooks from B flat alto down to F are made each with its independent mouthpipe, and have only one leg of the crook fitting into the central socket. In this way each crook retains its integrity, having only one tenon which joins up with the main tubing of the horn at the lower socket. This tenon then slides in the socket for tuning. The remaining lower crooks are fitted in the usual Inventionshorn manner; the tenons of each have a graduated scale marked on them to assist in tuning.

This novel design of the higher crooks provided a neat though expensive way round a problem of intonation which was a major drawback to the Inventionshorn system. These high keys are badly out of tune when obtained by means of a common mouthpipe and successively shorter crooks of the *Invention* type. With Haltenhof's system each high crook had its own mouthpipe, thus retaining its proper scale intact, and was readily tuned with the slide.

Another record of Haltenhof's skill as a horn-maker survives in more conventional form in the collection of the Prince of Oettingen-Wallerstein at Schloss Harburg in Bavaria. This is a pair of Inventionshörner dated 1815. These instruments feature the graduated tuning-slide as well, a useful idea which appears to have originated with Haltenhof. It is occasionally met with on modern instruments. The date of the Paris horn, 1776, and that of the horns at Harburg, may be taken as a rough guide to Haltenhof's period of activity.

Haltenhof of Hanau is often credited with the creation of the Inventionshorn, in English-speaking circles at least. This notion has its root in an article by one Karl Bargans which appeared in *The Harmonicon* in 1830.[1] Written by a man with only a smattering of historical knowledge, it appears to have been translated literally by someone who had a nodding acquaintance with the German language and still less contact with brass instruments. Through it all Gerber's article is dimly discernible, especially Paragraph E of the Appendix (see p. 223), but the often-cited passage reads, ' . . . at length an artist in Hanau succeeded in producing improved horns, Inventions-Hörner, and upon their model, trumpets were soon after constructed.' This idea had indeed gained some currency by the time of Gerber's paper, but the translator does not mention that Gerber himself suspected it, and rightly assigned the credit for the Inventionshorn to Werner.

These Haltenhof horns, apart from furnishing an index to the stature of their maker as a craftsman and inventor, throw a welcome ray of light on

[1] Karl Bargans, 'On the Trumpet, as at present employed in the Orchestra', in *The Harmonicon*, VIII (London, 1830), p. 23.

horn tone in Germany proper at this time. With both the earlier and later horns, the pure intonation and easy response are what one would expect in the playing qualities of first-rate instruments. The sound in both cases is more compact than that of a Viennese horn of this period, yet rather softer than that of the contemporary French instruments—noticeably so when compared with the products of the Raoux family at Paris, which may be taken as the French norm. There is a noticeable edge in the forte, and it is this feature of the German horn tone which Gerber notes in his article of 1789. (See the Appendix, page 224.) These horns show that a distinctly German style of playing had emerged by the third quarter of the century. Although traces of Viennese influence were still to be seen in many instruments, the leading makers discussed here were now working confidently on their own versions of Werner's model. The German style of horn-playing, though as yet still an offshoot of the parent Austrian tradition, could now draw upon instruments which were suited to its own tonal requirements and made to the highest standards.

Mention should also be made of those makers of the German school about whom little has come to light. We know that J. F. Schwabe was working at Leipzig during the second half of the century. Morley-Pegge notes that J. G. Kersten was active at Dresden in 1775. Of A. F. Krause, Gerber remarks that 'Krause in Berlin made the best improved Inventions horns about 1796'. One C. F. Duirschmitt or Thürschmidt was making instruments at Neukirchen in 1800 or thereabouts; was he perhaps a relation of the famous horn-playing family of that name? Then there is C. G. Eschenbach at Berlin, from whose hand an Inventionshorn so marked is preserved in the Paris Conservatoire collection. When played it shows the same characteristics as the Haltenhof horns, though it is not nearly so well made. Morley-Pegge lists yet another Eschenbach who was known to be working at Markneukirchen in 1818. Or was this the Berlin Eschenbach removed to another address? Perhaps we shall know in time.

These, then, were the makers, major and minor, who followed after Werner in Germany. Let us now trace the effect of hand-stopping on the design of the horn in the hands of the Viennese makers.

Some leading Viennese hand-horn makers and their contributions
The first Viennese maker to depart from the traditional Waldhorn model of the Leichnambschneiders was Anton Kerner, or Körner, the elder (1726–1806). Kerner's earliest hand-horns appear to have been copied from Werner's Hampl-designed Inventionshörner, with which he was evidently quite successful. Gerber[1] tells us that Kerner made Inventionshorns to Hampl's design which were equal to those of Werner in refinement and workmanship.

[1] *Lexicon* (1813), iii, p. 89.

He confirms this good opinion of Kerner's instruments again when speaking of the Dresden maker Leuthold's failure to equal the quality of his master, Werner, in his Inventionshorn.[1]

The Inventionshorn appears to have found no great favour with the Viennese and thus to have exerted no lasting effect upon the design of the Viennese hand-horn. It is curious to find, therefore, that these instruments should cause such favourable comment from so far afield. According to Forkel, a maker named Geier was still producing Inventionshörner in 1776; but as no mention whatever of this model appears in any of the Viennese address-books, trade directories or Künstlerlexica, we must for the time being conclude that these horns were most probably made for the German trade, for it was at Berlin and Dresden that the Viennese horns of this type found their greatest appreciation.[2]

To judge from surviving examples of his work, Kerner's importance lies in the fact that he was the first to modify the crooked horn of the Baroque so that it conformed to the demands of hand technique whilst keeping its basic form intact. Whereas other makers indulged in various experiments with tuba-like bell throats and tightly coiled bodies, it was Kerner's model, with its twice-wound corpus and gracefully flaring bell, which became the standard concert instrument of the Austrian school until the advent of the valve. Even after the more practicable Orchesterhorn replaced Kerner's model for orchestral playing, the terminally crooked Waldhorn remained the favourite solo instrument, as it had been when Mozart and Haydn wrote their concerti.

The earliest instrument of this type bearing Kerner's name to come to this writer's attention is dated 1769. His inscription on the bell garland reads: 'ANTON KERNER/17 IN WIENN 69' (see Fig. 3). The device of a

---

[1] Ibid., p. 493.

[2] J. N. Forkel, *Musicalischer Almanach für Deutschland auf das Jahr 1782* (Leipzig, 1782), p. 205. The Geier in question was most probably the son of the trumpet-maker Hanns Geyer, under whom the brothers Leichnambschneider appear to have served their apprenticeship. No further record of him can be found; but it is worth quoting Forkel's article for its own sake, and for the light it may throw on the Inventionshorn's career at Vienna.

Geier (———) . . . In Vienna this kind of instrument is especially prized [Forkel has been speaking of brass instruments generally]. Amongst these Geier's horns are acclaimed the most, fetching 12 Thalers the pair. For six years or so one has been able to buy the so-called Inventions-horns as well, which have their crooks in the middle of the horn on extending sockets instead of on the mouthpipe. By means of this device a complete octave of pitches can be had on these horns. At first one paid 60 to 80 Thalers for this advantage; but now one can buy such Inventions-horns for 16 to 20 Ducats. The Viennese horns of this type are far superior to those made at Hanau [the reference here is to the German maker Johann Gottfried Haltenhof, who about 1770 devised an improvement on the Dresden maker Werner's crooks (see p. 129 and Morley-Pegge, op. cit., p. 22)]; and further prove that nowhere are better wind instruments to be found than at Vienna and Dresden.

Fig. 3

double eagle surmounted by the Imperial crown, which Kerner as 'Kayserlich-Königlicher Hoff Waldhorn-und Trompeten Macher' was permitted to stamp on his work, embellishes both the inscription and the garland. In its design and dimensions this horn represents the prototype of the Viennese open-hooped hand-horn with terminal crooks. Its bell diameter measured 25·6 cm. at the rim, approximately the same as the later Leichnambschneider horns, though its throat was somewhat wider; and its twice-wound corpus was 29 cm. across the coils. Although it played quite freely, this instrument was so battered as to defeat all attempts at measuring the diameters of its conical tubing; but the measurements of bell and corpus given above are encountered repeatedly in horns made by Kerner's contemporaries and successors at Vienna, and may be taken as standard for this type. The horn had been lent by an anonymous donor to a monastery in Upper Austria whose Abbot, true to the secrecy with which persons in those regions often feel they must cloak even the most straightforward matters, asked that its name be withheld. As might be expected in such circumstances, no photographs of the Kerner horn were permitted; but a good idea of its bell profile may be had from the photograph on Plate IXb of a parforce-horn by Kerner dated 1777 (Prague National Museum, No. 565), though the bell rim is of a slightly larger diameter.

Fig. 4

A later hand-horn of this type by Kerner dated 1794 (see Fig. 4) is preserved in the National Museum at Prague (No. 608 E). Its dimensions are identical with those of the 1769 horn given above; and apart from the individual differences peculiar to hand-made instruments, the playing qualities of this later horn are identical with those of its prototype. Each of the three instruments mentioned confirm the writer's initial impression that Kerner's horns are remarkable for their beautiful workmanship and superb playing qualities. The tone of the hand-horns is particularly noteworthy in that despite its softness and suppleness it possesses great carrying power, a feature which must have recommended Kerner's instruments strongly for solo playing. These are indeed instruments of the first water from which much can be learned about the Viennese ideal of horn tone in the second half of the century. It is fitting that the reputation of this great maker should outlive him; and there is much truth in Gassner's somewhat exaggerated encomium which described Kerner nearly fifty years after his death as 'a horn and trumpet-maker working at Vienna about the middle of the last century whose instruments were sought and treasured the world over, and commanded high prices'.[1] A remark in Lichtenstern's *Beschreibung des Erzherzogthums Oestreich unter der Ens* (Vienna and Leipzig), 1791, p. 189, implies that Kerner's international trade was based upon the excellence of his concert Waldhorn, for by this time the Inventionshorn had fallen out of fashion in Vienna. 'Viennese musical instruments, especially horns and trumpets by the late Stärtzer and his successor Kerner, are famous in foreign countries as well.'

A résumé of the elder Kerner's career is worth setting out briefly here, for a clear picture of the standing he enjoyed amongst his colleagues emerges from the principal events of his life. He took the oath of citizenship, and with it presumably attained to the rank of Master, on 27 January 1751, at the age of 26. As early as 1774 Kerner is listed in the *Staats- und Stands-Calendar* together with Carl Stärtzer (see below) as 'Cammer Waldhorn- und Trompeten-machere' (p. 499); though a bill to Zwettl monastery for 'zwei Posaunen samt Futteral' dated '15.xi.1767' is signed with this title. This added distinction furthered the reputation which his superlative instruments were by then earning; and in 1785 he bought the 'Hornmacherhaus' at No. 796 Dominikanerplatz (now Wollzeile 33). He held the title of horn- and trumpet-maker to the Imperial Court (see Fig. 5) until his death in 1806, when it passed to his two sons Anton II and Ignaz: although in 1792 he had tried to secure for them an appointment which had fallen vacant at the death of the basset-horn-maker Theodor Lotz (1748–92). That same year Kerner was successful in his protest against Joseph Huschauer (see below) for stamping his instruments with the double eagle and crown of the Imperial privilege without authority.[2] In 1794 he took on an agency for Turkish cymbals, according to the *Wiener Zeitung* for 29 October of that year. He

---

[1] Gassner, op. cit., p. 524. La Borde confirms this, saying that in 1780 'Les cors de Vienne en Autriche, faits par M. Kerner, sont les meilleurs pour les concerts'. La Borde, *Essai sur la Musique* (Paris, 1780), II, ii, p. 255.

[2] HR Fasz. 8: 347/1792.

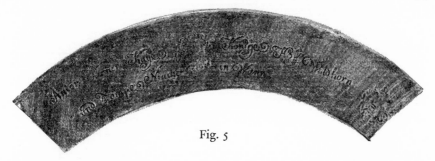

Fig. 5

became head of the horn- and trumpet-makers' guild in 1803, the last honour he was to enjoy before his death three years later. His sons Anton and Ignaz inherited his house and shop; and the other four children each received a generous portion from the great horn-maker's fortune.[1]

Carl Stärtzer or Startzer (1730–91) was presumably a contemporary of his colleague Anton Kerner, but does not come to light before 1770, when his name appears on a Waldhorn now in the Carse Collection of the Horniman Museum. The bell garland of this instrument bears the inscription 'CARL STATZER/1770 IN WIENN'. Upon close examination this garland has been rather crudely fixed to the horn at a later date; certainly the horn is not by Stärtzer. It bears a close resemblance to the Kerner horns, but is of an earlier cut and workmanship than his instruments. One can only conclude that it was near enough in appearance and playing characteristics to be passed off as a Stärtzer. Presumably it was made or repaired by one M. Anton Lausmann of Graslitz, whose name is engraved on the bell stay. Although it appears to date from between 1750 and 1760, this instrument conforms to the pattern of the Kerner horns described above. Its dimensions are in fact identical. The bell measures 26.5 cm. at the rim; the corpus, 29 cm. across the coils; and the inside diameter of the crook socket opening is 12.5 mm., which corresponds within half a millimetre to the crook opening of the Kerner horn of 1794. The playing characteristics of this horn differ from those of Kerner in that the eleventh partial lies slightly flat, and the tone is brighter and more silvery. No detailed record of Stärtzer's career or products has come to light apart from this one garland, a bill in his own hand to Göttweig monastery, and occasional mentions in the Viennese Court calendar and trade directory. Yet he was undoubtedly one of the foremost makers of handhorns at Vienna during the second half of the eighteenth century, a fact which his appointment as horn-maker to the Imperial Court confirms.

Only sporadic facts concerning Stärtzer's life have emerged. The *Wiener Commerzialschema* for 1779 lists him on page 146 under 'Trompeten- und

---

[1] See Helga Haupt, 'Wiener Instrumentenbauer 1791–1815', in *Studien zur Musikwissenschaft*, xxiv (Graz, Vienna, and Cologne, 1960), p. 149; and Ignaz de Luca, *Österreichische Staatenkunde im Grundrisse* (Vienna, 1798), p. 118.

Waldhornmacher' as 'Carl Starzer in der Naglergasse 186'. It is not at all unlikely that this address (now the Gasthof zum Braunen Hirschen, an inn dating from the mid-seventeenth century) had also marked the location of the brothers Leichnambschneider's workshop and lodgings, and that Stärtzer had taken over the business upon their death or retirement. The coincidence of these addresses, if any (Michael Leichnambschneider gives his address as simply 'in der Naglergasse', and the rate-books for this district have been destroyed), would further suggest that Stärtzer may have in fact learnt his trade from the Leichnambschneiders.

Not until 1774 or shortly before does Stärtzer appear to have received his appointment as 'Cammer Waldhorn- und Trompeten-Macher'. He first appears in that capacity in the *Staats- und Stands-Calendar* for that year together with his colleague Kerner (p. 499). This date may be taken as marking approximately his appointment to that office, pending further evidence; for although the horn described above bears the double-eagle stamp, it is signed without the title.

An interesting insight into Stärtzer's personality is afforded by the bill to Göttweig monastery referred to earlier. It is written in a bold and elegant hand whose characters are remarkable both for their clarity and their economy of design. The 'Stück' (pieces) to which Stärtzer refers were probably the inner tenons of the trombone slide, and the terminal crook sockets on the horns: the first parts in each case to give way or wear in normal use. The document is dated 14 April 1780.[1]

Stärtzer's worldly substance appears to have been considerably less than that of his fellow horn-maker Kerner. He did not marry, nor did he own his own house: for both the Court calendar and the trade directory mention that he 'logirt in der Naglergasse 186', whereas Kerner lived in his own

---

[1] The document reads as follows:

Statement

Repairs I have made as agreed
on Horns and Trombones
Namely
One Trombone and 4 Horns
repaired, and new Parts
fitted — — — 6 Gulden
Total 6 Gulden

Vienna, 14th April
   1780
This amount has been
correctly paid me

Carl Stärtzer Royal
and Imperial Court Trumpet
and Horn-Maker

I certify that the foregoing Six Rhenish Gulden has been paid from the Göttweig Treasury. Göttweig Monastery, 30th December 1780.

Pater Hartmannus
  Chamberlain
    manupropria.

Pater Marianus
acting Choirmaster
manupropria.

house. He died intestate in 1791, probably in January. In February of that year the horn-maker Huschauer took over his workshop and lodgings.

In the *Wiener Zeitung* for 19 February 1791 the following announcement appears:

Announcement for Music-Lovers

Joseph Huschauer, registered Trumpet and Horn-Maker, of No. 186, Nagler-gasse in Vienna, the premises of the late Royal and Imperial Court Horn-Maker Carl Stärtzer, commends to the nobility and musical public his instruments, which are of the purest intonation and offered at the lowest prices. Since he has worked more than twenty years at this address to the complete satisfaction of his master he is all the more assured of the confidence and favour of the esteemed Public. Instrument-Lovers can furthermore be served with instruments made by the late Horn-Maker Herr Stärtzer.

That Joseph Huschauer (1748–1805) had worked since about 1770 with Stärtzer is clear from his remark that he had been active 'more than twenty years at this address'. It is equally certain that Stärtzer had been amongst the masters who had expressed their satisfaction with his work, and it is most probable that Huschauer had at some point served under him as an apprentice. It now appears, however, that there was a Joseph Huschauer who worked at Vienna during the Leichnambschneiders' lifetime: for a terminally crooked Waldhorn bearing the inscription 'JOSEPH HU-SCHAUER/17 IN WIENN 23', and the device of a cockle-shell (Plate X(a)) has turned up in the National Museum at Prague. In all likelihood this earlier Huschauer was the father of the Joseph Huschauer who succeeded Stärtzer in 1791.[1] The similarity between the bell profile of the horn by Huschauer senior and that of the hand-horn of *c.* 1770 marked 'JOSEPH HUSCHAUER/IN:WIENN:', and displaying the device of a crossed horn and trumpet on a kind of weather-vane, suggests strongly that the younger maker learnt his principles of design from his father.

The writer was fortunate in having this fine Huschauer instrument in his possession for several months. During that time he had opportunity to examine and play it extensively,[2] and to try its qualities in a public performance of the Brandenburg Concerto No. 1 by J. S. Bach.[3]

[1] This instrument, in establishing the existence of another accomplished horn-maker during the first half of the century, helps to explain the riddle of the Leichnamb-schneiders' apparent monopoly. It comes as a relief to know that there was at least one other maker whose workmanship was of a standard equal to theirs, even though one very battered instrument is admittedly slender evidence.

[2] He here records grateful thanks to Count Nikolaus d'Harnoncourt, conductor of the Concentus Musicus ensemble at Vienna, for kindly lending the horn. It is one of a matched pair belonging in the first instance to an Austrian monastery whose name remains undisclosed for the same reasons as those which shield the owners of the Kerner horn discussed on pages 132–3 from public discovery.

[3] In the Konzerthaus at Vienna with the Concentus Musicus on 23 April 1963.

The tone of this instrument, when compared with the Kerner horns, is somewhat more masculine and compact. It is capable of infinite dynamic shading on the lower scale of volume typical of all mid-eighteenth-century instruments, and thus lends itself admirably to ensemble-playing, especially with instruments of this period. Huschauer's claim to 'purest intonation' for his instruments, mentioned in his advertisement of 1791, is fully justified, for this horn was absolutely true in the intonation of its fifths and octaves. The eleventh partial lay slightly sharp, the thirteenth slightly flat: a feature which made for accuracy of pitch on the f" sharp and a" flat. Both this instrument and its twin displayed a remarkable ease of response in the extreme high and low registers. It is no wonder that the players of the hand-horn period, equipped with instruments like this, rose to such heights of virtuosity.

The younger Huschauer was evidently subordinate to Carl Stärtzer during the latter's lifetime, and only after setting up on his own following the elder maker's death does he appear to have claimed his share of recognition. During most of his working life he was eclipsed in a further sense by the fact that both Stärtzer and Kerner held appointments to the Imperial Court. Yet in spite of the fact that Huschauer's horns were not amongst the most favoured instruments of the hand-horn period, the bell design which he carried on from his father nevertheless arouses historical interest on two counts. It was the only bell design which was adaptable for hand-stoppings without alteration because of its generous throat; and it was this feature which caused the early nineteenth-century makers Pechert and Uhlmann to incorporate Huschauer's bell form into their own horns. Thus, although Huschauer himself made no significant contribution to the design of the hand-horn, his importance to the continuity of the Austro-Bohemian school is assured by the fact that the bell pattern which he passed on to his successors was to enjoy well over a century's unbroken use. He died without issue in 1803 of 'inflammation of the lungs', the traditional disease of wind-instrument makers, at the age of 57; and in 1815 his business premises and tools were taken over by the horn- and trumpet-makers' guild.[1]

The only record of Nicodemus Pechert or Bechert which remains survives in the form of two superb orchestral horns of the late eighteenth century. On the earlier instrument Pechert signs himself as an 'Instrumenten Fabrik in Markt Gaunersdorf'. This village some forty kilometres north of Vienna (renamed Gaweinsthal in 1806), was an episcopal see in the later eighteenth century, and accordingly possesses extensive parish records; but no trace of Pechert's having been born or married there is to be found in them. The second instrument is of a later date, and is signed from Vienna. It represents a considerable advance in both design and workmanship over the other horn, and thus tells us not only of Pechert's move to the capital, but records an

[1] See Helga Haupt, *Wiener Instrumentenbau* um 1800 (Diss. Vienna, 1952), p. 126.

IX (a) Inventionshorn by C. Lobeit, Prague (?), *c.* 1785. The later type with fixed mouthpipe. (*Boston Museum*). See p. 147.

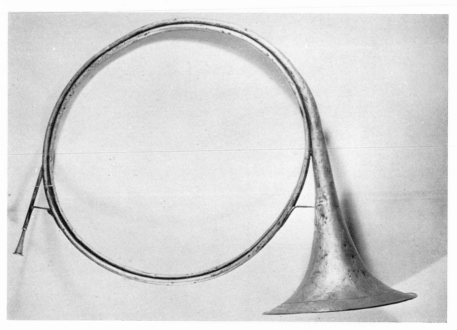

IX (b) Parforce-Jagdhorn, Anton Kerner, Vienna, 1777. (*National Museum, Prague*).
See p. 133.

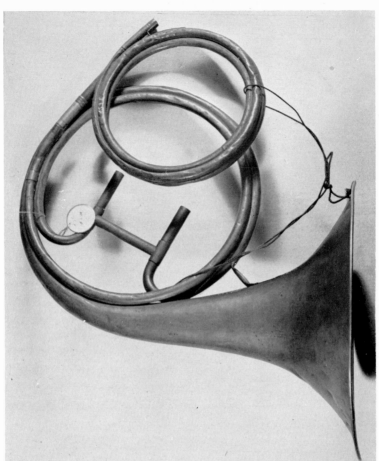

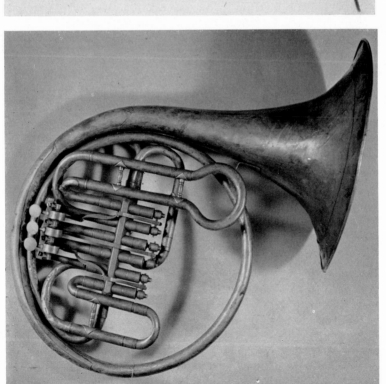

X (a) The corpus of an early orchestral Waldhorn by Joseph Huschauer the elder, Vienna, 1723. One of the earliest known sets of Vienna valves of *c.* 1820 has been added. (*National Museum, Prague*). See p. 137.

X (b) An anonymous Orchesterhorn with terminal crook, *c.* 1760. (*National Museum, Prague*). See p. 139.

XI (b) Orchesterhorn, Nicodemus Pechert, Vienna, c. 1795.
(*Author's Collection*). See p. 140.

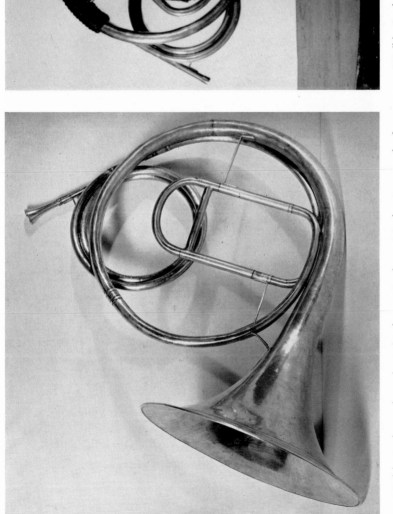

XI (a) Orchesterhorn by Nicodemus Pechert, Markt Gaunersdorf,
c. 1785. (*Kunsthistorisches Museum, Vienna*). See p. 140.

XII (a) Orchesterhorn, Leopold Uhlmann I, Vienna, *c.* 1810. The immediate forerunner of the Pumpenhorn. (*Author's collection*). See p. 142.

XII (b) Pumpenhorn or Vienna horn, Leopold Uhlmann II, *c.* 1875. Identical, except for refinements of detail, to the model based on the hand horn shown above. It was designed by the elder Uhlmann in about 1815 and continues in use in Vienna today. (*R. Morley-Pegge*). See p. 142.

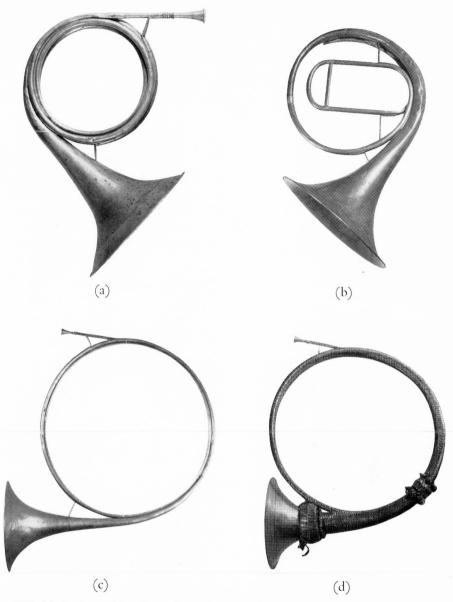

(a) (b)

(c) (d)

XIII (a) Orchestral Jagdhorn in E flat, Joseph Simon Anger, Graslitz, dated
1730. (*National Museum, Prague*). See p. 145.
(b) Orchesterhorn with terminal crooks, Franz Stöhr, Prague, *c.* 1800.
(*National Museum, Prague*). See p. 146.
(c) Parforce-Jagdhorn in C basso, Prague, dated 1735. (*National Museum,
Prague*). See p. 145.
(d) One of a pair of anonymous Parforce-Jagdhörner in C basso of the type of
c. 1750. (*National Museum, Prague*). See p. 147.

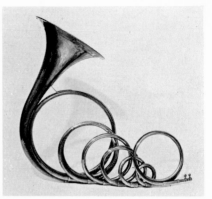

XIV (a) Concert horn, English, *c.* 1760. Terminal crooks are for B flat alto and G. A pair of small tuning bits appears to the left of the bell-rim. (*Guy Oldham collection. Photo: John M. Henshall*)

(b) Horn on the early Viennese pattern, English, *c.* 1760. Probably by Nicholas Winkings. Its complete set of master and coupler crooks and tuning bits are shown. (*Photo: John M. Henshall*). See pp. 73, 229.

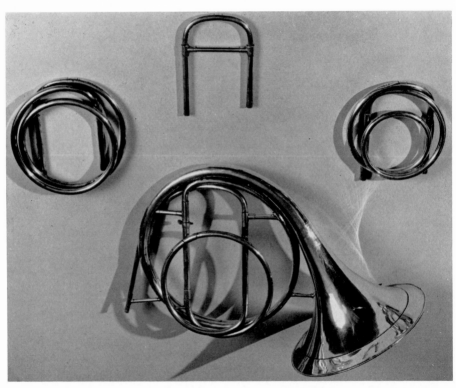

(c) Cor-solo by Lucien-Joseph Raoux, *c.* 1785. Crooks for D, E flat, and G are shown separately. Many of the great virtuosi took up this model for solo playing. (*R. Morley-Pegge collection. Photo: Dr. P. D. Watson*)

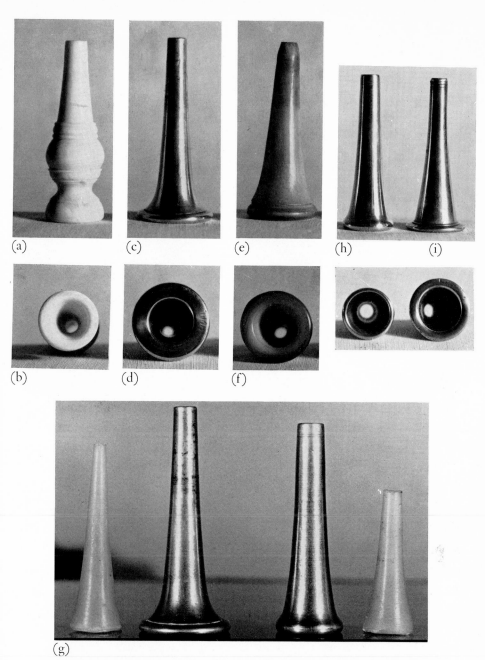

(a)   (c)   (e)   (h)   (i)

(b)   (d)   (f)

(g)

XV (a) and (b) Mouthpiece associated with the William Bull horn of 1699. English, *c.* 1690–1710. Copy made by the author. See p. 155. (c) and (d) Orchestral mouthpiece, brass, *c.* 1720. Presumably Viennese. See p. 156. (e) and (f) Soloist's mouthpiece of oxhorn, *c.* 1720. See p. 157. XV (g) Internal profiles of (left) the Viennese orchestral mouthpiece of *c.* 1720 and (right) a Viennese second-horn mouthpiece of *c.* 1770. These bees-wax castings show the difference between the longer, narrow Baroque type of cup and the shorter, wider cup of the hand-horn period. The backbores are not shown. (h) A Viennese second-horn mouthpiece of *c.* 1770. See p. 160. (i) A first-horn mouthpiece, Prague, *c.* 1790. See p. 161. This example probably belonged to a soloist. It is well to remember that, then as now, there were as many individual mouthpieces as there were players.

XVI (a) Giovanni Punto at the age of 35. See p. 173.

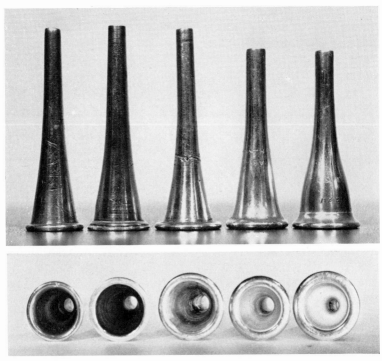

(b) left to right: Side and end views of mouthpieces (i) English, brass, 18th century, probably by Nicholas Winkings, whose initials are chased on the body. (ii) English or French, brass with silver rim, 18th century. (iii) French, silver, late 18th century, associated with a hand-horn by Courtois Neveu l'aîné. (iv) Modern English, silver-plated brass; the Aubrey Brain model. (v) Modern English silver-plated brass, showing German influence in its convex-sided cup.

episode of refinement which the Orchesterhorn underwent in the hands of one maker. In order to understand more fully these improvements, it is necessary at this point to review briefly the stages through which the Orchesterhorn had passed since its first appearance about 1765–70.

The Orchesterhorn

That the Orchesterhorn (or Kirchenhorn, as it is still locally known in Austria because of the favour it found with provincial church orchestras) grew out of the Hampl-Werner Inventionshorn as a Viennese adaptation is virtually certain, for its type is peculiar to makers at Vienna and Prague. It is difficult, however, to say when this model was first brought out, or by whom. Even an obviously early specimen such as that illustrated on Plate Xb bears no date, and no dated examples of the first models have as yet come to light. This particular instrument clearly shows the parentage of the terminally crooked Waldhorn and the Inventionshorn's central slide, however; and it is reasonable to estimate its date at *c*. 1760.[1] Although the tuning-slide is missing, this horn affords a good example of the earliest model to incorporate both features. It is signed 'Wenzel Landa in Prag': a photograph of a Viennese instrument of this type and date was not available at the time of writing.

The Orchesterhorn owed the next stage of its development to an improvement which the Franconian-born virtuoso Carl Thürrschmidt (1753–97) first applied to the Inventionshorn in 1781. This revision was the obvious one of crossing the tubes which received the central crook before bending them into the circle of the corpus. Gerber, who knew Thürrschmidt well and who based most of his information concerning the horn upon that virtuoso's first-hand knowledge, describes this improvement on p. 442 of his *Lexicon* of 1792:

In 1781 Carl Thürrschmidt improved the Inventions-horn by crossing the inward-curving tubes upon one another so that the air could pass through unhindered; for of the curved tubes which lie within the circle, one must bend abruptly right, then left, making the instrument more difficult to blow.

That same year Thürrschmidt had a horn built of silver by the famous Parisian maker Raoux which incorporated this design.[2] This one feature

[1] A further clue to its date is the grotesque enlargement of the bell throat which makers at this transitional stage felt was necessary to provide room for the stopping hand to perform its new functions. Both left- and right-handed models were made.

[2] This was the cor-solo, which was soon adopted by many of the leading virtuosi, including Punto, as the standard solo instrument. It was in effect an Inventionshorn with a fixed mouthpipe and a centrally inserted crook. The relationship of mouthpipe to bell was carefully set up for maximum truth on those crooks which gave the most popular solo keys, e.g. D, E, E flat, and F. The Cor-solo was not adopted by the Viennese, although a few were made at Prague.

appears to have been adopted immediately by makers throughout the German-speaking countries; and so furnishes a convenient means of dating approximately horns of this type.[1] An anonymous Orchesterhorn of this improved design bearing the mark 'Wien 1783', preserved in the town museum at Lunz in Lower Austria, attests to the ready favour which Thürrschmidt's idea found at the Imperial capital. The Viennese were quick to appreciate the convenience of the movable tuning-slide for general orchestral playing. They appear to have distrusted the Inventionshorn's fixed mouthpipe and heavy central crooks, though, and soon reverted to their traditional terminal crook, which, if less efficient, was decidedly better in tone quality. It is this point which represents the height of the Orchesterhorn's development; and in this form it came to the hand of Nicodemus Pechert.

The earlier Pechert Orchesterhorn appears to date from about 1785.[2] The bell is beautifully thrown (it measures 29·5 cm. at the rim as against the 26·5 cm. of the Huschauer bell upon which its form is based); but there are ungainly points in the design and workmanship which suggest that this was one of Pechert's earlier Inventionshörner. The tuning-slide tenons, for example, are imperfectly braced to the corpus; the slide itself does not reach across the entire circle and gives an impression of incompleteness when compared with the later horn; and there is an awkward brazed join just behind the upper slide stay which divides the bell section into three parts.

None of these defects of detail affects the horn's playing qualities, however. The tone is full and velvety, and is distinguished by the brightness and sheen which is characteristic of Viennese horns of this period. Its ease of playing, flexibility, and response mark it as an instrument of the finest quality.

The later of these two horns by Pechert not only shows certain improvements in design and craftsmanship but documents the preference for the increasingly darker and more mellifluous sound which led to the tonal ideals of the Romantic period. This instrument, a major item in the writer's collection and in daily use, dates from between 1795 and 1800, and is signed 'Nicodemus Pechert Instrumenten Fabrikant in Wien' (Plate XI(b)).

The fuller sound and generally freer playing characteristics of this instrument result from its greater internal volume. Although the bell rim is identical in size to that of the earlier horn, the bell throat is perceptibly

---

[1] Indeed, from this point onward the German makers north of the Main (a geographical boundary for separating the German provinces of the time from the Austrian Kulturraum proper) were to come increasingly under the influence of the Parisian makers; and from about 1790 a distinct German school of makers and players is discernible. See Appendix p. 224, paragraph G.

[2] The writer here records his thanks and acknowledgements to Dr. Viktor Luithlen of the Kunsthistorisches Museum, Vienna, for permission to examine and play this instrument and for permission to publish the photograph on Plate XI(a).

more open and the bore at the tuning-slide measures 11·8 mm. as against 11 mm. in the case of the other. This increase in bore reflects the gradual enlargement of the horn's interior dimensions which came in answer to the demand for an ever smoother and more homogeneous tone. If, for example, we carry this comparison back yet another stage to the Landa horn of 1770, we find that its bore is only 10 mm. in diameter: so that in these three representative instruments this trend is graphically illustrated.

The overall appearance of this later Pechert hand-horn is generally more symmetrical and finished, though perhaps less graceful than the 1785 model owing to its larger bore. The tuning-slide features a pair of tenons which insert into the sockets of the corpus. This modification allows the sockets to be braced with two stays in a manner which is both structurally sound and visually pleasing. The bell section is thrown in one piece; a compound curve leads the base of the mouthpipe into a plane with the upper slide socket, with which its parallel extension forms the lower socket; and the collars and bell garland are of nickel silver, the latter most tastefully engraved with a floral motive and a geometric border in the Louis XVI manner. These two instruments mark the Orchesterhorn at the height of its development, and point the way to the orchestral horn of Leopold Uhlmann.[1]

The name of Leopold Uhlmann (c. 1785–1850) is more properly associated with the valve; but he figures in the present study as the last major maker of hand-horns. In 1810 his elder brother Tobias was granted permission to set up a workshop for both woodwind and brass instruments,[2] which the

[1] Mention should be made here of the elder Kerner's sons, Anton (c. 1770–1848) and Ignaz (c. 1768–1813). Although they appear to have made no contribution to the advancement of the horn, nevertheless a few examples survive which attest to their fine workmanship. A pair of parforce-horns, one by Anton and one by Ignaz, hang amongst Count Eugen Waldstein's collection of hunting-implements at Schloss Carlslust in Lower Austria, together with a horn of the same model by Joseph Huschauer, jun. The date 1802 is stamped on the bells of these horns; but from the appearance of the characters it may indicate the year in which these instruments were first registered in the Carlslust inventory, rather than the date of their manufacture.

According to an article by P. E. Richter, 'Eine 2-ventilige Trompete aus d. Jahr 1800 und die Wiener Instrumentenmacher Kerner' (Zeitschrift für Instrumentenbau vol. 30 (1909–10), p. 36), the brothers Kerner were the first to apply valves to a brass instrument. This claim is substantiated by the supposed evidence of a two-valved trumpet bearing their name and dated 1806, now in the Museum des Altertumsvereins at Bad Tölz in Bavaria. From the photograph of this instrument with which the article is illustrated it is impossible to tell whether the valves are a retrospective addition or not: and until this is established we must withhold any final evaluation of the Kerner's place in the history of brass instruments. See Haupt in Studien zur Musikwissenschaft, xxiv, p. 150.

[2] Archiv der Stadt Wien HR Fasz 12, 467/1810. The address of this new shop is not given, but was presumably at No. 19 Laimgrube. He and his brothers Jacob and Leopold are listed at that address by Anton Redl's Handlungs-Gremien-Schema from 1811 to 1817. This directory gives the address of the Uhlmann lodgings as No. 595 Mariahilf from 1818 to 1821; from 1822 to 1831 as No. 189 Breitegasse (now VI, Breitegasse 4: the

three brothers evidently ran as a joint enterprise. Anton Ziegler's *Adressen-buch von Tonkünstlern* for 1823 (p. 54) describes them in the following entry: 'Uhlmann Herr Tobias, graduate of the National Conservatory (Clarinet), resident on the Spittalberg, Breitegasse No. 189. Uhlmann, Herr Jacob, gradu-ate of the National Conservatory (Oboe), address as above. Uhlmann, Herr Leopold, graduate of the National Conservatory (Horn), address as above.' From this we may conclude that Leopold was the youngest: a fact of some interest in itself, as his early life has up to now been virtually an unknown quantity.

In 1962 the writer acquired a pair of superb Orchesterhörner of quite unusual design which bear the inscription, 'Leopold Uhlmann in Wien'. The unique layout of the corpus of this model, arranged so that the tuning-slide points downward (Plate XIIa), not only results in a greater structural strength and less weight than the conventional design, but aids the removal of water by the position of the central slide, obviously dictated by the principle that water runs downhill. It was only when comparing this design with a later valve horn by Leopold Uhlmann II (*c.* 1830–98), however, that the full significance of its singular construction was borne home. A glance at Plate XIIb will reveal the similarity between the basic set-up of both the valved and valveless model. Thus Uhlmann's Orchesterhorn not only marks the very last refinement of the hand-horn but establishes the form to which the double-piston Vienna valve was immediately adaptable. This instru-ment was the prototype of the Vienna horn which is still used there today.

Uhlmann was granted a *K. K. Privilegium* for the Vienna valve in 1830; but the writer recalls seeing a valved horn by Uhlmann in the possession of the late Gottfried von Freiberg dated 1818, and the mechanism of that instrument was by no means the first of its type. The valve lies outside the scope of the present study; yet the existence of the basic valve-horn form in an instrument made no later than 1815 would suggest that perhaps Uhlmann had experimented with the valve as early as 1810.

As hand-horns these Uhlmann instruments provide a final document of the tonal concepts which closed the Classical era and ushered in the Roman-tic. These horns are quite remarkable for their veiled quality and soft volume of tone. They have little in common with the slender elegance of even Pechert's horns; and are much more suited to a Schubert symphony or Weber opera than to an orchestral work by Beethoven.

This more intimate sound appears to result from a bell which is smaller at the rim by 1 cm. than Pechert's; the combination of smaller throat with a somewhat more open neck (the section above the bell-throat which tapers

---

brass-instrument-making firm of Dehmal now occupies this site, so this may well have marked the location of the Uhlmann shop all along); and J. B. Schilling's *Adressenbuch* (Vienna, 1832–5), gives their address as No 22 Pelikangasse for those years.

into the corpus); and a bore of 10·5 mm. as against the 11·8 mm. bore of the later Pechert horn. In overall appearance as well as in tone, the Uhlmann Orchesterhorn reflects the style of the awakening Biedermeier period, that counterpart to the English Regency which gently welcomed the Romantic age.

The following additional makers worked at Vienna during the hand-horn period:

(1) Beyde, August. Active 1823.[1]

(2) Ferber, Anton. Parforce-horn dated 1748, No. 508 in the Kunsthistorisches Museum, Vienna.

(3) Harrach, Franz. 1750–1831. His son Melchior, also a horn-maker, was active in 1856.[2]

(4) Hofmann, Friedrich Christian,

(5) Hofmann, Franz and

(6) Hofmann, Johann, were all active as horn-makers in 1810. The latter two tried unsuccessfully to transfer their working licence from Floridsdorf to the Leopoldstadt that year; Friederich Christian's petition had failed two years previously.[3]

(7) Hofmeister, Johann Christoph, was active in London from about 1750 onwards as John Christopher Hofmaster, to be succeeded in 1763 by G. H. Rodenbostel. Nothing of Hofmaster's provenance is known. He is included under the Viennese school of makers because of the definitively Viennese characteristics and appearance of the pair of terminally crooked hand-horns which Sir Samuel Hellier acquired about 1760. They appeared in Day's catalogue of the Royal Military Exhibition, London, 1898, as No. 308, and are erroneously said to have been acquired by Hellier in 1735.[4]

(8) Naumann. Orchesterhorn in the Conservatiore Royal collection at Brussels, No. 1161. Signed, 'Machts Naumann in Wien, 1804'.[5]

(9) Mazzucato or Mazogato, Franz. c. 1779–1832. Licence granted 13 August 1812; shop in the Naglergasse.[6]

(10) Riedl, Josef Felix, c. 1785–post 1849. In 1812 he was granted a licence to move his shop from the suburb of Floridsdorf to Vienna. The trumpet- and horn-makers' guild refused his application to take over the premises of Joseph Huschauer in 1815. Three fine Orchesterhörner by him are in the Kunsthistorisches Museum in Vienna, Nos. 354, 355, and 356; they display much the same tonal qualities as the Uhlmann horns of the pre-valve period. Riedl made

---

[1] Ziegler, op. cit., p. 262.

[2] Arch. d. Stadt Wien, Totenprotokoll 1831; Bürgerbuch, 1792–1835, p. 136. Wr. Zeitung, 26 May 1802, Anhang, p. 64; Haupt, Diss., p. 124.

[3] Arch. St. W. HR Fasz 12, 444/1808; 265/1810; 739/1810; Haupt, Diss., p. 125–6.

[4] Lyndesay Langwill, *An Index of Musical Wind-Instrument Makers* (Edinburgh, 1962), p. 53; and Blandford, op. cit., p. 546.

[5] Mahillon, *Catalogue Descriptif*, ii (Gand, 1909), p. 38.

[6] Redl, *Handlungs-Gremien Schema* (Vienna, 1802), p. 150; Oscar Freiherr von Keess, op. cit., ii, p. 168 et seq; Haupt in St. z. Mw. xxvi, p. 160.

a five-keyed trumpet on Weidinger's system; but his greatest achievement was the invention of the rotary valve, which survives today in the same form as that which Riedl patented in 1832. He died after 1849, when he last appears in Franz Fray's *Allgemeiner Handlungs-Almanach*, Vienna, 1836–49.[1] A brother or near relation, Anton Riedl, worked at Graslitz.

Makers at Prague and in the Bohemian province

Whereas early in the century Prague had been the chief centre for horn-players, with Vienna supplying most of the instruments, during the hand-horn period a distinct school of horn-makers emerged in the Bohemian capital and province, while Vienna gained in importance as a focal point for players and teachers. The early predominance of Vienna in matters of horn-making, and the flourishing school of makers active there during the second half of the century, have led to the supposition that, generally speaking, horn-players came from Bohemia and horns from Vienna. Because of the very number of players active at Prague, however—and there were in the latter half of the century more than fifty permanent orchestras—[2]it has seemed most likely to this writer that there were a number of established makers working in the Bohemian capital at this time. The proximity of a source for good-quality brass at the famous Joachimsthal foundry would further point to this likelihood; as would the favourable working conditions which the Prague hand-workers' guilds fostered.

It is now possible to confirm these historical probabilities with actual instruments, for several Bohemian-made horns, representing some fourteen makers, have come to the writer's attention. These instruments cover the period 1730–*c.* 1830; and while the majority date from the hand-horn era, the earlier instruments are included in order to give a complete picture of this newly identified Bohemian school of horn-makers.

Although no two of these instruments are alike, the general impression to be gained from playing them was that the Bohemian ideal of horn tone inclined toward a darker and more fluid quality than did the Viennese: and in this tendency may be seen a reflection of the Bohemian virtuoso's tone at this period. (This preference is not surprising when it is remembered that many of the roots of the Romantic movement in music are to be found in Bohemia.) The basic sound of these Bohemian horns, however, is distinctly Austrian in character, as indeed one might expect. The Bohemians favoured a more open-throated bell of slightly larger diameter than the Viennese type established by Stärtzer, and they appear at one point to have adopted the Inventionshorn, some years after the Viennese had discarded it. Nevertheless,

---

[1] Arch. d. St. W. HR Dep M, 26941, 20800, 21098/1815; ibid., HR Dep M, 4691, 18394/1812; Bürgerbuch, 1792–1835, p. 389; Haupt, St. z. Mw., p. 126.

[2] *Jahrbuch der Tonkunst von Wien und Prag* (Prague), 1796, article, 'Herrschaftliche Hauskapellen'.

the pattern of the Prague bell and the size of the mouthpipe inlet remain true
to the Viennese model of each instrument's respective period. The Bohemian
school, then, may be said to form the principal subdivision of the Austrian.

(1) Joseph Simon Anger: Orchestral Jagdhorn with fixed mouthpipe in E flat,
signed 'Joseph Simon Anger in Graslitz 1730'. Prague National Museum (as
are all of the following instruments unless otherwise indicated), 743 E. Mouthpipe inlet 8 mm.; diameter of bell rim 21·8 cm.; across coils 21·5 cm. Unfortunately no musical impression could be had of this instrument, as the tubing was
blocked. Plate XIII(a).

(2) Johann Grinwolt (Grünwald): Parforce-horn in C basso, signed 'Macht
Johann Grinwolt in Prag, 1735'. 578 E. Mouthpipe inlet 7 mm.; diameter of
bell 25·5 cm.; of coils 59 cm. The playing characteristics of this instrument are
very similar to the Leichnambschneider horns of the period: free-blowing,
accurate in its intonation, and responsive in the extreme registers. Plate XIII(c).

(3) Johann Georg Frantisch (or Frantischek): Pair of orchestral Jagdhörner
with fixed mouthpipe in B flat alto. 'Macht Johann Georg Fratisch [sic] in
Prag 1752.' 83 E and 84 E. Mouthpipe inlet 8·4 mm.; diameter of bell 22·3
cm.; of coils 26·6 cm. The tone of these horns is exceptionally fine and clear,
being somewhat brighter(!) than the Viennese sound of this transitional
period; and the workmanship is of the highest order.

(4) Josef Petschmann: Orchesterhorn with terminal crook and tuning-slide,
c. 1750–60. 411 E. 'Josef Petschmann Instrumentenmacher in Karolinenthal'
(a surburban district named c. 1750; now Prague IX). Outside diameter of
tubing at foot of crook socket 11·8 mm.; bore of cylindrical section 10·6 mm.;
diameter of bell 29 cm.; of body 32·5 cm. An undistinguished instrument of
coarse workmanship. Its only merit is that it represents the normal mid-
eighteenth century type.

(5) Wenzel Umlauff: Orchestral Jagdhorn in E flat, 1770. 742 E. 'Wenzel
Umlauff in Prag 1770.' Mouthpipe inlet bent; diameter of bell 24·5 cm.; of
body 27·4 cm. An instrument of flawless workmanship and design. Unfortunately it was not in playing condition. The upper third of the body is wound in
the original woollen cord, a method of protection carried over from the hunting-
instrument. This horn appeared in the Prague exhibition (see Langwill, p.
251).

(6) Wenzel Landa: (I) Orchesterhorn with terminal crook and tuning-slide, c.
1765–70. 153 E. 'Wenzel Landa in Prag.' An early example of its type. Its
condition prevented accurate measurement.

(II) Orchesterhorn with terminal crook and tuning-slide. Pre-1781. 154 E.
'Wenzel Landa in Prag.' Bore 10 mm. at cylindrical section; diameter of bell
28·5 cm.; of body 25 cm.; this small body is achieved by coiling the tubing
twice upon itself. The normal Orchesterhorn is once-wound and has a larger
circle. Although the workmanship is mediocre to the extent of leaving off the
bell garland, this horn played well. One often finds horns of this quality among
the orchestral residue in less-than-affluent churches.

(7) M. I. G. Liebel: Waldhorn with terminal crook, 1777. 498 E. 'M. I. G.

Liebel in Neukirchen 1777.' In E flat without the crook. A section embodying a curious little loop has evidently been added to obtain this exceptionally low tuning, for such horns are usually built to C alto. Diameter of bell 26 cm.; of body 31 cm. The crook inlet was badly bent, making the horn unplayable. A very well-made instrument.

(8) Joseph Pieltz: Waldhorn with terminal crook, c. 1780. 406 E. 'Josebh [sic] Pieltz in Johannesberg.' Built to normal pitch of C alto without crook. Measurements identical to No. 7. An undistinguished instrument.

(9) Franz Stöhr: (I) Pair of Orchesterhörner with terminal crooks and tuning-slides, c. 1780–90. Munich Städtische Instrumentensammlung 41/313 and 41/314. 'Franz Stöhr in Prag.' Double-eagle stamp. Mouthpipe inlet on (original) A flat crook 8·2 mm.; bore 10·4 mm.; diameter of bell 29·5 cm.; of coils 33·5 cm. Both horns are cheaply made. There is no bell garland and the bells are spun separately and brazed on. Stöhr's name and stamp are engraved on a shield-shaped plate which is soldered on to the bell throat at the side. The work-manship of the plates is better than that of the instruments. The bell throat is narrower than the Viennese standard, but wider than the French. On all crooks the sixth partial was flat and the eighth sharp.

(II) Orchesterhorn with terminal crooks and tuning-slide, c. 1800 (Plate XIIIb). 3.30 E. 'Franz Stöhr in Prag.' Czech inscription in Cyrillic letters (i.e. in Old Church Slavic): 'To the Church of God in Tuchomyewitz.' Out-side diameter of slide tenons 13 mm. (slide siezed). The bore would be about 11·4 mm.; diameter of bell 30 cm.; of body 33 cm. Posts and stays ornamentally turned. A beautifully made instrument, accurate in intonation, responsive, and having a fine full tone.

A horn by Stöhr with three rotary valves appears in Fétis's Report on the Paris Exhibition; a four-valve tuba is in the Prague Collection. It would be safe to estimate Stöhr's working period at c. 1780 to c. 1840.

(10) August Wolf: Waldhorn with terminal crook, c. 1810. 407 E. 'August Wolf in Prag.' Built to D flat alto without crook. No measurements possible. Mediocre workmanship.

(11) Johann Adam Bauer: Waldhorn with terminal crook, c. 1810. 219 E. 'Johann Adam Bauer in Prag.' Diameter of bell 28·8 cm.; of body 30 cm. Built to D flat without crook. A late example of its type, as is No. 10. Leopold Ulhmann adopted this tuning in Vienna about 1800 to facilitate a shorter crook, which would place the date of these horns slightly later. Even this late in the period of the hand-horn Viennese influence was still felt in Prague.

(12) Anton Lippert: Waldhorn with terminal crook, c. 1820. 717 E. 'Anton Lippert in Prag.' Diameter of bell 29 cm.; of body 32 cm. Altogether wretched.

(13) [Anton] Hannabach: Pair of Orchesterhörner with terminal crook and tuning-slide, c. 1820. Private: Direktor Fritz Stradner, Klosterneuberg, Vienna. Diameter of bell 28·2 cm.; of body 30·5 cm. 'A Hannabach in Schön-bach Böhmen.' Fine examples of the later period. The dark Bohemian quality is quite pronounced in these instruments. Exceptionally good workmanship and flawless intonation.

(14) C[arl] Lobeit: Inventionshorn with fixed mouthpipe, c. 1785. Mason Collection, Boston (U.S.A.) Museum, No. 193 Plate IX(a). 'C. Lobeit.' Mouthpipe inlet 8 mm.; bore 11 mm.; diameter of bell 29 cm.; of body 32 cm. Silver alloy bell garland with floral engraving; tuning-slide spacing-posts ornamentally turned; stays spirally-twisted.

Lobeit has been included in the Bohemian school on the strength of the similarities between his instrument and those listed above. The bell profile is very much that of the Prague horns of this period, the throat being somewhat wide for a Viennese maker. The mouthpipe is fixed, a feature unknown to Viennese horns before c. 1880. This fact further suggests that the Lobeit is of Bohemian design. The ornamentally turned posts are similar to those on the second Franz Stöhr horn. A strong resemblance to the motifs used in Bohemian ornamental metalwork of the period c. 1775–90 is to be seen in Lobeit's spirally-twisted stays and floral engravings.

Bessaraboff[1] speaks of the Lobeit horn as German. Although this model was admittedly more popular with makers north of the river Main, the possibility of German origin is defeated on three counts. (1) The mouthpipe is larger than that of the German horns of this period, which have rather the narrower French mouthpipe. (2) The bell throat is more open than the German. (3) The tone is not German, but has the breadth and indefinable floating quality which distinguishes the Austrian horn tone.

(15) Anonymous: Pair of Parforcejagdhörner in C basso, c. 1750 581 E and 582 E. Plate XIII(d). Mouthpipe inlet 8·2 mm.; diameter of bell 25 cm.; of body 50 cm. approx. These exceptionally fine horns are typical of the classic Parforcejagdhorn of the early eighteenth century. They are wound in braided leather with tooled ornamental collars. Both the mouthpipe and bell garland are decorated with score-cuts in the fashion of Johann Leichnambschneider. Mouthpieces of spun sheet brass, evidently contemporary, are present on both horns. For their fine workmanship, rich tone quality, and the ease with which they play, these instruments are outstanding. If they are not the actual work of a Prague maker, they nevertheless typify the pattern which the Bohemian makers used.

A maker named Wieszeck, evidently of some importance, appears to have worked in Prague during the early eighteenth century. Apart from a passing mention by Fétis which is quoted in Kleefeld's article[2] little is known of Wieszeck.[3]

Mention should also be made of the maker Johann Anton Lausmann, of Graslitz, whose earliest known horn, dated 1791, is in the Heyer collection in Leipzig. Either he or a relative appears to have repaired a horn by Carl Stärtzer of Vienna dated 1770 (see p. 135). On the foot of the bell stay is stamped 'M. Lausmann Graslitz'. A pair of late-eighteenth-century

[1] *Ancient European Musical Instruments* (Boston, 1941), p. 181.
[2] 'Das Orchester der Hamburger Oper 1678–1738', in *SIMG* in I, vol. 2, p. 279.
[3] See Morley-Pegge, op. cit., p. 186; and Langwill, p. 125.

Orchesterhörner inscribed 'J. W. Lausmann in Linz' was discovered by the writer in the monastery at Lambach, Upper Austria. There may be a connection between these makers, if only one of kinship.

Viennese influence in the provinces

The work of the provincial horn-makers in the provinces bordering on the Crown Dominions bore the stamp of the Viennese pattern as well. Moving up the Danube, we find a maker of some importance named Ignaz Lorenz working at Linz from about 1827 to c. 1880. A pair of beautifully made Orchesterhörner dating from c. 1835 in the writer's collection form a well-matched quartet in point of tone quality with the Uhlmann horns made twenty years earlier. This provincial tendency to preserve the urban fashions of previous decades is even more marked in a hand-horn by Lorenz, also the property of the author, which must be one of the earliest instruments to come out of the workshop which he set up at Linz in 1827. Yet it differs in no respect in its playing qualities from the Kerner horns of c. 1770. The practice of making horns of the finest quality in a style thirty to forty years behind that of the capital persisted at Linz until the Second World War. Winter and Schöner, who succeeded Lorenz in the 1880s, produced superb instruments of the Pechert pattern; and recently an Orchesterhorn on Lorenz's model, signed 'Ed. Heidegger in Linz 1933', was brought to the writer's attention by the modern Viennese maker Herr Anton Cižek.

Munich came under Viennese influence in matters of horn-making during the late eighteenth century. This is not surprising when one considers that the Mannheim orchestra moved to Munich in 1778, bringing with it a department of Bohemian horn-players who no doubt used Viennese horns. Then, too, there was the fact that most of the provincial Bavarian courts had strong connections through their lords with the Imperial Court at Vienna, whence indeed they drew their artistic sustenance. Instruments from the Kaiserstadt often came through Augsburg, where it was possible to pay for them directly in Bavarian Gulden without the bother and expense of exchanging them for the Rhenish coinage used in Vienna. A bill from the Oettingen-Wallerstein treasury records dated '3. 9bris 1780' confirms this situation with its mention of money paid 'for the carriage of a chest with two horns from Vienna'.[1]

[1] The accompanying bill from the Nördlingen drayman Magnus Träubler throws further light on what was a common transaction.

I the undersigned certify that I paid out the following amounts for Horns at Augsburg:

to Herr Carli et Compani	8 Gulden 15 Kreuzer
My Drayage:	1 Gulden
Received from Colonel Böke at Wallerstein	(Ignaz von Beecke, Intendant of Music
Nördlingen, 3rd November 1780	under Anton Rosetti)

Thus with intercourse at all levels between the Bavarian province and Vienna, it is only natural that the work of the Munich horn-makers Philipp Schöller and Michael Sauerle should bear the impress of the Viennese design. An orchestral Jagdhorn, whose size would suit the hunting-field or the opera pit equally well, is preserved in the Kunsthistorisches Museum at Vienna (No. 247 8601 C. 257). Its bell follows the Kerner pattern faithfully, and its playing characteristics are similar to those of the Kerner horn at Prague dated 1777.

Similarly the Orchesterhorn by Michael Sauerle of c. 1775–80 exhibits many of the qualities observed in the Pechert horn of c. 1785. Thürrschmidt's improved design is not incorporated in this instrument, a factor which helps to establish its date as pre-1781. Its bell is larger at the rim than the Pechert bell by 1·4 mm.; and its bore of 11 mm. is identical with that of the Markt Gaunersdorf instrument.

It has been shown in this chapter that there was not only a continuity of hand-horn design amongst the Viennese makers but that this design was constantly changing to meet the demand for an increasingly darker and smoother tone. That the horn-makers in the Kaiserstadt and at Prague managed to meet this musical challenge is reflected not only in the high quality of many of the surviving instruments but in the spread of the Austrian design to other provinces, and indeed in the enthusiastic commentaries of writers such as Forkel and Gerber.

The mouthpiece itself also reflected the impact of hand-stopping, as had the instrument, and in its turn changed with the instrument as the period advanced. Let us now trace briefly the history of the mouthpiece as it follows the development both of the horn and its playing technique.

VI

THE MOUTHPIECE
AND ITS ROLE IN
THE BAROQUE AND
CLASSICAL PHASES

Some previous authorities' views

THE mouthpiece is the most important mechanical factor influencing horn tone and technique, excepting the corpus of the horn itself. It affects playing style in the same manner as the instrument; and some knowledge of its development during the Baroque and Classical periods is therefore essential to a complete picture of the pre-valve horn. The most accurate and direct source for this information would appear to be the mouthpieces themselves, and accordingly the following material has been collected by studying and playing actual historical examples. No previous writers seem to have approached the matter on this practical basis, however; so before turning to the mouthpieces themselves we must first acquaint ourselves with the theories and misconceptions which have been put forward.

Mouthpieces are never dated, and it is difficult to date accurately the few historical specimens which still exist. It is this lack of dated examples which both accounts for the fact that no detailed study of the mouthpiece as such exists, and has given rise to certain false notions which writers on the horn have mentioned in passing. Even Terry alludes only briefly to the horn mouthpiece;[1] and although Rühlmann,[2] Eichborn,[3] and Kunitz[4] give some space to their ideas on the subject, all save Terry share the belief that the pre-1750 horn mouthpiece was identical to that of the trumpet. This conviction stems, no doubt, from early illustrations of the coiled Italian clarino,

[1] C. S. Terry, *Bach's Orchestra* (London, 1934), p. 35.

[2] Julius Rühlmann, 'Das Waldhorn', in *Neue Zeitschrift für Musik* (Berlin, 1870), p. 291.

[3] Hermann Eichborn, 'Die Einführung des Hornes in die Kunstmusik', in *Monatsheft für Musikgeschichte* (Leipzig), xxi, 3, 1889, p. 84.

[4] Hans Kunitz, *Horn* (Leipzig, 1957), pp. 347 ff. For reasons which he does not explain, Eichborn dogmatizes: 'The funnel-shaped mouthpiece did not exist on the horn before 1753!' (*Die Dämpfung Beim Horn*, Leipzig, 1887, pp. 9, 15.) This notion is perpetuated by Kunitz, equally without substantiation, and has made its way into a number of modern books on orchestration.

an instrument which has been mistaken for an early form of the horn by more than one author.[1] Particularly since Eichborn was for a long time the only authority on the history of the horn, his insistence upon the similarity of the trumpet and horn mouthpieces strengthened the assumption generally held that the tone of the Baroque horn was the same as that of the trumpet: a premiss which we have already seen to be disproved by the evidence of both contemporary writings and instruments (see pp. 36 and 37).

The question of the mouthpiece in the Classical or hand-horn period has been for the most part passed over, probably because the horn parts of this era pose no great problems to the modern performer. Eichborn has dealt briefly with the hand-horn mouthpiece, again without evidence and with great inaccuracy, and here, too, his views have been kept alive up to the present day.[2]

Perhaps Eichborn's writings, whether first-hand or assimilated, prepared the way for the most recent confusion concerning the later eighteenth-century horn mouthpiece. H. C. Robbins Landon, in dealing with the problem of the high-horn parts in Haydn's symphonies in his book, *The Symphonies of Joseph Haydn*, describes his trials of the mouthpieces which he assumes to belong to some late eighteenth-century horns in Lambach Monastery. 'By using the much shallower and far less conical mouthpieces at Lambach the author was able to produce without difficulty the first five notes of the highest register on the D-alto horn.' The mouthpieces in question were in fact trumpet mouthpieces which had been mistakenly inserted into the crook sockets of the horns. That these were the subject of Dr. Landon's experiments was evident from their being stuck fast by the corrosion of many years. Clearly they have nothing to do with the mouthpieces used by Haydn's horn-players.[3]

[1] Two well-known illustrations of the Italian trumpet are those in Praetorius, *Syntagma Musicum* (Wolfenbüttel, 1619), ii, Tafel VIII, No. 13; and in the portrait of Bach's first trumpeter, Gottfried Reiche, reproduced on the frontispiece of the *Bach-Jahrbuch* (Leipzig, 1918).

[2] 'Die Einführung', p. 84: 'The horn mouthpiece was exactly like that of the trumpet; and it appears to me that not until much later, after the horn had long since been introduced into the orchestra and experiments had been made with the hand about mid-century to bridge the gaps of the overtone scale with a corollary refining effect upon the tone, were attempts made at lessening the well-known critical angle of the mouthpiece's interior where the cup meets the throat: that angle whose absence or near-absence marks the present-day horn mouthpiece.'

[3] H. C. Robbins Landon, *The Symphonies of Joseph Haydn* (London, 1955), p. 123. The diameter of the eighteenth-century trumpet mouthpiece at the point where it enters the mouthpipe is about 12 mm., and its taper allows it to fit perfectly into the crook socket of the contemporary horn. To be sure the upper partials of the horns to which these trumpet mouthpieces had accidentally become mated spoke easily; but the octave between the fourth and eighth partials on both instruments was augmented by a semitone, and the fundamental on each was three-quarters of a tone flat. (The horns at Lambach, incidentally, are built to the standard pitch of C alto without crooks. The

Only Morley-Pegge[1] succeeds in giving a plausible picture of what the later eighteenth-century mouthpiece was, and cites such authorities as Domnich, Duvernoy, and Dauprat. Helpful as his remarks are for understanding the French mouthpiece of the late eighteenth and early nineteenth centuries, the topic of mouthpieces as used by Austrian or Bohemian horn-players, whether Baroque or Classical, is not touched upon. Since our enquiry into the Austro-Bohemian mouthpiece is not to be satisfied by the existing writings on the horn, we must obviously turn to an examination of actual mouthpieces. But before taking up the historical and musical aspects which early specimens may reveal, it is well to fix in mind the function of the mouthpiece in playing, and the effects of both its design and material upon tone and style in horn-playing.

The function and basic features of the mouthpiece
The main office of the mouthpiece is to conduct air into the horn. It is rather the by-product of this basic process, however, which gives the mouthpiece its musical properties. This side-effect is the influence of the inner profile, and of the material from which the mouthpiece is made, upon tone quality and upon ease of playing in the several registers.

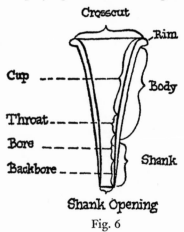
Fig. 6

Six basic elements combine to determine the playing qualities of a given mouthpiece, all of cardinal importance. They are: (1) the shape and breadth of its rim; (2) the size of its crosscut; (3) the depth and profile of its cup; (4) the width of its throat; (5) the diameter and length of its bore; and (6) the length and contour of its backbore (see Fig. 6 for a diagram of these components).

---

piano in the instrument-room was tuned a whole tone flat, a fact which possibly misled Dr. Landon. No horns in D alto survive, nor were there any parts written in this key.)

[1] Op. cit., pp. 102–5.

(1) A broad rim face supports the embouchure and increases endurance. But since it does encourage pressing against the lips, a wide rim tends to detract from sensitivity and accuracy. A narrow rim face furthers accuracy and sensitivity, as a smaller area is brought to bear upon the lips, but lessens endurance, especially in the high register. A deep rim cheek gives additional support, and is ideally suited to the setting-on type of embouchure where the rim is placed on the white of both lips. For the setting-in type of embouchure, where the rim is placed on the white of the upper lip and set within the red of the lower, a shallow cheek is essential for a feeling of purchase and security. A rounded inner shoulder makes for a softer tone quality and a smooth legato. But if the line of demarcation between shoulder and cup is not distinct, the embouchure will have no feeling of grip on the rim: the tone will be foggy and accuracy in the high register will suffer. A sharper shoulder aids endurance and furthers clarity of tone and attack, especially in the upper register. The sharp inner shoulder is a pronounced feature of pre-1750 mouthpieces.

(2) The size of the crosscut determines to a large extent the register for which the mouthpiece is intended. For first horn the crosscut ranges from 15 to 17 mm. in diameter, for second horn 18 to 20 mm. (Duvernoy, writing in 1800, recommends 16 and 18 mm. respectively.) Of course, individual variations within and exceptions outside these limits must be allowed for. The size of the crosscut seems to have increased steadily over the past two hundred years. The Alexander stock model for first horn today, for example, has a 17 mm. crosscut.

(3) The ultimate quality of the tone is almost entirely governed by the depth and profile of the cup. There are two general types: the older deep, straight-sided cup and the shallow, concave-sided modern type. A deep cup produces a velvety quality, a smooth legato, and a full low register. This type of cup requires more breath control and physical endurance. It is the basic format of the later eighteenth century, and survives in the modern Viennese mouthpiece. The shallow cup favoured today gives a brighter sound with more overtones. Its principal advantage lies in the ease with which the high register speaks. A powerful fortissimo may be had with a minimum of effort, and the pianissimo requires less mental concentration than with the older deep cup. The attack tends to be explosive and the legato dry with the shallower cup; but its advantages under modern performance conditions have found for it widespread acceptance in Germany and the United States, and increasing favour in England.

(4 and 6) An open throat makes for a soft tone and a full low register. A long, slightly tapered backbore aids the upper register and staccato, but is apt to harden the tone. A short, widely-flaring backbore is conducive to a rich low register and a smooth legato, but if this flare is too pronounced the

tone will lose its focus and become woolly. The backbore governs the intonation of the octaves and fifths. Both modern and pre-1750 mouthpieces have longer backbores than do those of the late eighteenth and early nineteenth centuries.

(5) The bore is a vital factor in determining tone quality and facility in the extreme registers. A darker timbre results from a larger bore, a brighter and harder tone from a smaller bore. The bore must be cylindrical for a length of at least 4 mm., for if this section is either tapered or without length the notes will not centre in properly and the pitch of each will waver. (General opinion would have it that ease in the high register is to be had mainly by narrowing the bore. From the author's experience with mouthpieces of various countries and periods, it appears rather to be the crosscut which exerts the greatest influence upon facility in the upper register.)

These six elements in the mouthpiece's make-up directly govern basic timbre, facility in the various registers and dynamic ranges, and quality of attack, staccato, and legato. They may be altered singly or in combination to suit a particular player's needs or a particular musical situation.

The material of which the mouthpiece is made influences tone colour as well, though to a lesser degree than the design of the integrants mentioned above, and in some cases may even determine the purpose for which a given mouthpiece is to be used. Metal, horn, and ivory are the materials most widely used during the period under discussion. Brass has over the years proved to be the most satisfactory metal for making mouthpieces, and was evidently used for the very earliest horn mouthpieces (see p. 40 for Michael Leichnambschneider's mention of 'zwey Mössingen Mundstück').[1] Silver has been preferred by many players in spite of its expense because of its resistance to evil-tasting tarnish. Punto is said to have used a sterling silver mouthpiece, as did many of the great soloists. Silver appears to have a slight brightening effect upon the tone as well.

Horn, whether ox or buffalo, is a highly satisfactory substance for making mouthpieces, and was especially popular in the first half of the eighteenth century. Because of its porosity horn has a softening effect upon the tone. Its fibres run the length of the piece, a feature which makes for especially good vibrating properties. The carrying power of the tone is thereby enhanced, and the tone acquires a silken quality of remarkable purity. It is the author's conjecture that mouthpieces made of horn were used by soloists and in small ensembles during the Baroque, as opposed to the metal mouthpieces played on by orchestral horn-players. Surely Michael Leichnambschneider's distinc-

[1] In fact the earliest brass-instrument mouthpiece known to the writer, a trumpet mouthpiece dating from the late fifteenth century in the possession of Herr Franz Cizek, the Viennese mouthpiece-maker, is made of brass. One of the most easily turned metals, brass possesses excellent acoustical properties as well: and is still the preferred metal for making mouthpieces, though nowadays it is frequently silver-plated.

tion of 'Mössingen Mundstück' points to a division of materials according to purpose.

Mouthpieces of elephant ivory were evidently in some fashion in the late seventeenth and early eighteenth centuries. Ivory was prized for its handsome appearance and its value as a material; perhaps, too, for the ease with which it could be worked in ornamental turning. But an ivory mouthpiece could not have found much favour amongst concert horn-players, for it is acoustically dead and has an unpleasant way of sticking to the lips. The few specimens which have come to the writer's attention have been richly ornamented and possessed rather inferior musical properties.[1] Surely the question of *instrumenti usati e non usati* might be raised with respect to these mouthpieces, especially as instruments which were intended solely for ornament or for use as theatre properties were frequently made of ivory. (A superb example of an ornamental ivory mouthpiece dating from the late seventeenth or early eighteenth century is preserved with the William Bull horn in the Carse collection at the Horniman Museum. See Plate XV (a and b.)[2] The mouthpiece owes much, then, to the material of which it is made.

The design and material of the mouthpiece affect not only the mechanical production of the tone, but both factors bear physically and psychologically upon the player himself as well. The mouthpiece forms the actual link between the player and his instrument and is the immediate receptacle into which he introduces the physical impulses which frame his musical ideas. Thus a correctly designed mouthpiece should emphasize the strong points

[1] It should be noted that these objections to stickiness and acoustical shortcomings apply only to the thin-walled horn mouthpiece whose rim rests for the most part against the red of the lips. Mouthpieces for trombones, serpents, and ordinary and curved cornetts were made of ivory with complete success, to judge from the number which have survived. With each of these instruments the mouthpiece is placed on the white of the lips while playing, and the problem of stickiness which so hampers the horn embouchure does not arise. Even when a centrally-placed embouchure was used in the case of the cornett (though the side-placed embouchure seems more to have been the rule), the cornett embouchure is less mobile than that of the horn, and an ivory mouthpiece's slight adherence would serve to steady rather than to restrict. In none of these instruments does the relatively shallow mouthpiece cup amplify the vibrating impulses to the same degree as the conical cup of the horn mouthpiece: hence the non-vibrating property of ivory is not detrimental to tone quality.

[2] The author made an exact duplicate of this mouthpiece with the kind permission of the Curator. A tusk of antique ivory dated 1827 was used in order to approach as nearly as possible the condition of the original's material. The tone of the Bull instrument (1699) when played with this copy (the original is not playable) was very much that of the contemporary cor-de-chasse, but a certain brittleness was inescapable. An eighteenth-century brass mouthpiece from Vienna was then duplicated in both the antique ivory and in modern seasoned ivory. In each case the tone was hard and much inferior to that of the brass original; and the rim stuck to the lips in a most exasperating manner. To prove the point once and for all the author then copied his own mouthpiece in ivory and played on it in a public concert (Wadham College, 23 February 1963). The results were disheartening.

in a given player's technique and bolster its weaknesses, if any, and should enhance his characteristic tone.

When the foregoing factors, both mechanical and human, are taken into account, the importance of the mouthpiece as a formative element in playing style becomes apparent. It is because of its significance in this capacity that an investigation of the mouthpiece's historical development belongs properly to a study of the Austro-Bohemian school. Let us now examine some actual mouthpieces from the Baroque and Classical phases.

The Baroque type, c. 1700–1760

Two horn mouthpieces of the Baroque period, one of brass and the other of oxhorn, have recently come into the writer's possession. From the circumstances of their discovery it may safely be assumed that both are Austrian; and both have been dated by reliable authorities at c. 1720. Each has a deep cup of conical profile, and a broad, flat rim. Quite apart from their intrinsic value, they are of great importance to the present study as documents which offer irrefutable evidence that the horn mouthpiece at this time was distinct and separate in design and acoustical properties from the trumpet mouthpiece of the period.

The brass mouthpiece of c. 1720, illustrated on Plate XV(c and d), reveals the physical and acoustical attributes of what may well be the very earliest type of orchestral mouthpiece.[1] The wide rim (6·5 mm.) and the exceptionally deep (54 mm.) and narrow-angled profile of the straight-sided cup are at once the most striking and significant features of the piece's design. There

---

[1] The buttery colour of the brass of which this mouthpiece is made is in itself a clue to its date. This yellow cast almost always suggests the presence of calamine, a crude ore used in the manufacture of brass in the seventeenth and early eighteenth centuries. This crude ore was rich in zinc, which when alloyed with copper in a 70–30 ratio produced brass. Calamine contained various auxiliary ores, mostly lead and tin, and some sulphur; and it was these which were responsible for the golden colour. In about 1750 A. F. von Cronstedt discovered a process for extracting zinc in pure form, although Savot (see below) had recognized that brass was the product of zinc and copper as early as 1627. After Cronstedt's process became widely known in the eighties, pure zinc was much in use; and brass alloys of this later period tend to show a greenish tint. The old technique of cementation with calamine did not completely die out until well into the second half of the nineteenth century, however: so that colour is not an infallible guide for dating articles of brass.

The writer estimated the date of this brass mouthpiece at c. 1715–25. This dating was confirmed unofficially by Professor Lahner of the Federal Laboratory for Chemical Analysis at Vienna, and by Dr. Ernst Paul, technical adviser to the Vienna Philharmonic and author of the treatise, *Die Entwicklung des Hornes vom Naturzum Ventilinstrument* (Diss. Vienna, 1932). It was not until the Archaeological Laboratory at Oxford undertook tests of the alloy of the mouthpiece by bombarding it on a neutron screen that the dating could be established without doubt as falling near the end of the second decade of the eighteenth century. The writer here records his thanks to Dr. Aitken and his staff for carrying out these tests.

has been much argument on the question of whether or not the early high-horn-players doubled on the trumpet, even in the face of the many horn parts which partake of the trumpet's register and musical idiom. The wide rim of this mouthpiece, dating from the height of the late Baroque, when, as we have seen, the horn was just coming into vogue as an orchestral instrument, clearly points to this doubling technique.

In fact, only in terms of the reciprocal horn-and-trumpet technique are the clarino horn parts of this era to be explained. We know from present-day experience that when a trumpet-player changes to the horn he retains his high register for about six months, until his embouchure adapts to the lower pitch and to the more relaxed position required to produce the horn's softer tone. Hence the lip of the high trumpeter-horn-player would not be affected by the occasional change of octave when playing horn parts in one of the lower keys. Furthermore, record exists of several players who won considerable recognition as performers on both instruments.[1] Let us now apply the foregoing external evidence to the mouthpiece at hand.

If a player were to change frequently from trumpet to horn, he would certainly spoil his embouchure for both unless the rim and crosscut were identical on both mouthpieces. The theory that such a player would use the same mouthpiece for both horn and trumpet may be refuted on two counts. The shank of the trumpet mouthpiece is too large to fit into the horn's mouthpiece inlet; and the shallow-cupped trumpet mouthpiece will not function properly on the horn of this period, as we have seen in note 3, p. 151. The comparative ease with which the upper partials speak when this mouthpiece is played on a contemporary horn clearly shows that it was intended for this purpose. The wide rim is a considerable advantage here, as is the small bore (3·9 mm.). Yet the deep, conoid cup ensures that even when played by a trumpet-player, as actual experiments have proved, the horn retains its characteristic softness. The evidence of this mouthpiece, then, strongly contradicts the notion that the mouthpieces, and thus the tone, of the trumpet and horn were the same during the Baroque phase of the horn's artistic career.

The oxhorn mouthpiece, illustrated on Plate XV(e and f), is a rare example of what the present writer surmises to be a soloist's or chamber player's mouthpiece of the Baroque period. This distinction arises from the softening effect of the oxhorn upon the tone, for in its essential design this mouthpiece differs little from the brass example described above. It is undoubtedly Austrian, and is artistically turned from a solid piece of oxhorn, probably native. Except for the cupric oxide stains on the shank (which in themselves record the mouthpipe inlet sizes of the Austrian horn from c. 1710 to well

[1] See in Chapters 4 and 8: Bauers; Bernardon; Knechtel; Kohaut; Kail; Lissner; Michel; Risch; Winter; Zalužan; Žahradniczek.

after 1750), the piece has aged to a uniform brownish-yellow not unlike the colour of old meerschaum.

Establishing the date of this mouthpiece presented some difficulty. Oxhorn, being a living organic and therefore variable material, cannot be analysed chemically for dating purposes. A radiocarbon count could not be undertaken because of the expense. But from the colour of the horn and the oxidation present in the fine surface crazing, the Barockabteilung of the Kunsthistorisches Museum at Vienna agreed unofficially upon a date of c. 1720. This dating was likewise confirmed by Dr. Paul after trial and examination.

The suitability of this mouthpiece for playing in the altissimo register was abundantly apparent after a few minutes' playing on a contemporary instrument. Because of the material's softening effect upon the tone, there is no need for the exhausting restraint often necessary to produce a mezzo-piano in the high register on a modern mouthpiece; and with this horn mouthpiece tone was distinctly more velvety than with the brass example. The performer may thus play freely without fear of overbalancing the other instruments, a serious problem when playing high parts with the small ensembles which are typical of this period. The broad rim (5·3 mm.) bears evidence of having been cut down, so that it is reasonable to assume that it was probably as broad as the rim of the brass model.

Not only does the design of this oxhorn mouthpiece clearly show that it was intended for a high-horn-player, but its acoustical properties when played suggest that it was not intended for a low horn-player. The extreme upper partials are remarkably easy; and the lower partials, though perfectly in tune with one another, are not particularly full-sounding. A peculiar feature is the slightly convex throat, which appears to aid the intonation of the upper partials and prevent shrillness in the highest register. It would not be at all far-fetched to suggest that this was the type of mouthpiece on which Leopold and Seydler played the First Brandenburg Concerto.

We have thus far discussed these two Baroque mouthpieces only with respect to their importance in an orchestral context; but there is good evidence that the brass model, at least, found use in the hunting-field as well. The overall shape of both these mouthpieces corresponds exactly to that depicted in a number of prints and illustrations of the period. The mouthpiece on the Gross Jagd Horn illustrated on p. 174 of Hanns Friederich von Fleming's *Der Vollkommene Teutscher Jäger* (Leipzig, 1719) furnishes an exact likeness (Fig. 7). Still more convincing is the print of a horn-blowing huntsman in full regalia in *Jaeger und Falkoniers* by the Augsburg engraver, Johann Elias Ridinger (Augsburg, 1735). Plate II(b). This type of mouthpiece appears on the horns in Ridinger's hunting-scenes from c. 1720 to 1750.

No less important than the tonal evidence afforded by these mouthpieces is the information they provide concerning the embouchure. We have seen how the high-horn-players of the day doubled on the trumpet, and many of the second-horn-players on the trombone. Sources for the actual technique of horn-playing in this first period are therefore best sought in the trumpet tutors of the time, notably Speer and Altenburg.[1] Though neither writer states expressly the placement of the mouthpiece on the upper and lower lip, we know that the only admissible placement for the trumpet embouchure has always been that of one-third of the mouthpiece's circle on the upper lip, two-thirds on the lower: or in some cases, half and half. The broad rim of the trumpet mouthpiece precludes any other placement.

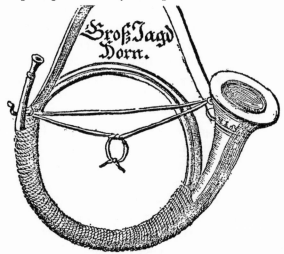

Fig. 7

By inference, the wide rims of the two horn mouthpieces just examined show that the Baroque horn embouchure was the same as that of the trumpet; and this is additionally borne out by the strong evidence for the doubling practice set out above. Hence these mouthpieces afford the first conclusive record of the pre-hand horn-player's embouchure as well. We pass now to the mouthpiece of the Classical phase, and to the changes in embouchure which Hampl's codification of hand-stopping brought about.

The hand-horn type, c. 1755–1830

It is difficult, of course, to pinpoint the actual date at which the hand-horn mouthpiece began to replace the older wide-rimmed model. The transformations which hand-stopping had brought to the instrument were soon reflected in the mouthpiece, as we have seen; and these changes resulted in

[1] Daniel Speer, *Grundrichtige Unterricht zur Musikalischen Kunst* (Ulm, 1697); and Johann Ernst Altenburg, *Versuch einer Anleitung zur Heroisch-Musicalischen Trompeter- und Pauker-Kunst* (Halle, 1795).

turn from the change in embouchure which the new hand technique had
engendered. The tonal ideals of the dawning Classical period mentioned
earlier played their part as well. The hand-horn mouthpiece owed its narrow
rim to the general lessening of pressure which resulted from the availability
of a chromatic scale in the middle register; and it derived its more open
throat from the general process of widening and enlarging of bell and bore
which the entire instrument had undergone in answer to the demand for a
softer and more homogeneous tone. The backbore was shortened pro-
portionally, enhancing both legato and flexibility: two elements in playing
style which distinguished the Classical phase from the Baroque.

Like all stylistic changes, this transition did not occur overnight, nor did
it represent a clean break with the Baroque tradition. We have seen how
players like Steinmüller and Thürrschmidt the elder carried their altissimo
style right up to the end of the century, using their old-fashioned mouthpieces to the last. On the other hand, it has been shown that Hampl must
have begun to teach the art of hand-stopping in the fifties, and that its
impress soon bore upon the design of the horn itself. It therefore stands to
reason that the setting-in embouchure, probably one of Hampl's innovations,
was known in practice amongst second-horn-players by *c.* 1755. (The
Baroque and Classical mouthpieces are compared on Plate XV(g).)

It is to be regretted that no mouthpieces from the early hand-horn period
appear to have survived, but it is doubtful whether the early Classical model,
once fully evolved, would have differed materially from the later specimens
which have come down. An example of the later hand-horn mouthpiece, a
Viennese model of *c.* 1770,[1] is illustrated on Plate XV(h). Its rim is extremely
narrow (2·4 mm.) and sharp, and is of a curious design with a deep and
rounded cheek, no doubt made up for a second-horn-player whose lower lip
was thick and whose upper lip narrow. The cup is typical of the period, being
straight-sided and measuring 44·7 mm. in depth, as against the 54 mm. of the
brass Baroque example discussed above. A marked increase in the size of the
bore over the 1720 model is evident when the two measurements are compared: 5·7 as opposed to the 3·9 of the earlier mouthpiece's bore. On the outside of the body the fine turning-marks which appear on all mouthpieces
made before the advent of abrasive cloth are clearly to be seen.[2]

---

[1] Here again thanks are due to the Archaeological Laboratory at Oxford for the
analysis which made this dating possible. It is interesting to note that lead and tin are
present in almost equal amounts, 4·8 and 5·8 per cent respectively; and to recall that
Krünitz (op. cit., p. 771) mentions that these metals may be added in small equal parts
'um den Messing geschmiedig zu machen'—to make the brass malleable.

[2] Hard abrasive or emery cloth as we know it was invented in about 1790, but was
not widely used until *c.* 1825, according to Dr. Willibald Machu, author of *Schleifen und
Polieren* (Vienna, 1958), a treatise on abrasives. Consequently earlier turned work made
of all but the softest metals often shows the marks of the finishing-tool. Brass polish was
known, of course, in various forms; and Christoph Weigel, writing in 1698, mentions

The acoustical characteristics of this mouthpiece when played reveal much about the playing style of the hand-horn period. Because of this mouthpiece's straight-through design, the attack is soft, the legato remarkably smooth, and the tone dark and velvety. As one might expect of a mouthpiece made for a low-horn-player, the lower register speaks easily with a full sound, although the upper register is secure and clear. This kind of second-horn tone must have been a valuable colour in the eighteenth-century orchestra's palette, particularly as it possessed great blending power in the middle register, and could support the entire ensemble with pedal tones in the bass range. This was much the quality upon which the great soloists built their fame, for most of them were second-horn-players: though for virtuoso playing a wider rim would have been required to give the embouchure the needed support.

A typical first-horn mouthpiece of this period, though slightly later, is that illustrated on Plate XV(i). It came to the writer's hand in Prague, and dates from c. 1790. Attention is particularly drawn to the rim, whose width (4·2 mm.) and design are typical of the model intended for the setting-in embouchure where the rim is set within the red of the lower lip. The bore is somewhat smaller (4·1 mm.) than that of the mouthpiece described above, and marks this Prague example as a mouthpiece made for a first-horn-player. Except that the tone is correspondingly brighter and the high register easier, the musical properties of this piece differ little from that of the Viennese example.

Mouthpieces of this later period do not lend themselves so well to illustration as do the wide-rimmed Baroque models. Nevertheless, a general idea of the form can be gained from the silhouette of a wind ensemble at Wallerstein dating from c. 1780. In the detail from this silhouette shown on Plate VIII, the horn mouthpieces may be seen with reasonable clarity.

Mention of the French mouthpiece is owing here. The period of orchestral horn-playing in France begins roughly at the mid-century mark, so the cor-de-chasse mouthpiece need not concern us here. From those examples of the French hand-horn mouthpiece which have survived from the second half of the century (and they are fairly numerous), it is clear that they derive their inner profile from that of the Austrian Baroque model. This is consistent with the fact that the earliest Bohemian players who arrived in Paris would have brought with them their pre-hand-horn mouthpieces.

---

that professional metal-polishers knew 'how to give a beautiful sheen and adornment by means of flint-powder, emery, blood-stone, zinc ash, and other specially-prepared secret polishing powders'. Though many of these materials were trade secrets, the horn-makers no doubt knew a few of them. But the turning-marks remained, and serve today as a hallmark of the pre-1800 mouthpiece. Cf. Christoph Weigel, *Abbildungen der Gemein-nützlichen Haupt-Stände* (Nürnberg, 1698), p. 374.

But by about 1780 a definitive French type appears to have evolved. Many were made of sheet metal, either brass or silver, with the rim turned separately and soldered on to the cup. The principal difference between the French and Austrian design at this period lies in its overall length, greater by some 1·5 to 2 cm., and its appreciably smaller bore. This latter feature arose from the narrower inlet of the French instrument: some 5·5 to 6 mm. as against the Austrian horn's mouthpiece inlet of between 7·5 and 8 mm.

The conformation of the French mouthpiece exerts a compressing influence upon the tone which both refines and brightens. In playing, its response is noticeably more immediate, and its general characteristics marry with those of the French instrument to produce that peculiar 'bursting' quality which both accounts for the intensity of the French sound and contributes to its unique beauty. If an Austrian player such as Punto or Thürrschmidt changed to a French instrument, he would have to adopt a tailored version of the French mouthpiece as well—the Austrian shank would not fit into the French inlet. This gives rise to speculation as to what the resultant sound might have been; but we may be sure that the leading virtuosi would have retained the breadth and softness of tone which was inherent in their style. The combined result must have embodied the best qualities of both French and Austrian schools.

Our knowledge of the instrument and mouthpiece which the great hand-horn virtuosi played on is now complete enough to lend meaning to a brief survey of their style of playing. We turn now to the period in which hand-horn-playing reached its greatest heights, and in which much of the finest horn music was composed.

VII

HAND-HORN PLAYING FLOURISHES AND DECLINES
1770–1830

UP to the middle of the eighteenth century our main records of horn-playing style have been the instrument itself and the music written for it. There were as yet no critical writers on musical performance as such, and even Mattheson's captious comments on the early horn-players leave us no clue as to how they sounded. During the Enlightenment, however, musical criticism began to acquire discipline and direction, and to emerge as a branch of literature in its own right: so that by the time the major hand-horn virtuosi entered upon the scene they found writers sufficiently versed in specialized knowledge to convey accounts of their exploits accurately and with understanding. Reviews of musical events appear in rudimentary form in certain of the London and Paris newspapers as early as the middle of the century; and Mattheson's literary descendants in Germany began to publish journals devoted exclusively to music in the 1770s and 1780s. The most valuable descriptions of the great horn soloists' performances, however, appear in the writings of the music historians and lexicographers of the latter third of the century, such as Burney, Forkel, Gerber, and Dlabacž. Their evidence, taken together with that afforded by the surviving instruments and by the music written for the prominent players of the day, provides us with a remarkably clear picture of what the famous horn-players played, how they played it, and on what instrument.

Some prominent soloists

It so happens that the first great hand-horn virtuoso to come to our notice through the agency of the Press is Ignaz Leutgeb, for whom Mozart wrote the four horn concertos, the Konzert-Rondo, K.371, and the 'Leutgeb' quintet, K.407. It is paradoxical that although these works have become the staple items round which every modern horn soloist's repertory is built (with the result that Leutgeb's name is virtually a household word) comparatively few facts concerning his personal life have come down to us. Yet despite this lack of accurate information about his early training and his career as such, it is nevertheless possible to form a definite impression of Leutgeb's playing style and qualities as a musician.

Shortly after joining the Archbishop of Salzburg's Court orchestra as principal horn, Leutgeb set out, presumably on a concert tour, for Paris. In the spring of 1770 he appeared twice at the *Concert Spirituel* as the soloist in three concertos of his own composition. His first performance on 1 April was heartily applauded, as the critic of the *Mercure de France* reported:

M. Liekhgeb, de la musique de M. le prince évêque de Salkbourg, a reçu les applaudissemens dûs, au talent supérieur avec lequel il a donné un concerto de chasse de sa composition.[1]

Apparently Leutgeb's second concert in May was even more successful, for the *Mercure*'s often trenchant commentator was moved to describe his playing in glowing terms:

M. Seikgeb, premier Cor de Chasse de S A S Monseigneur l'Archevêque de Salkbourg, a donné deux concertos avec tout l'art possible. Il tire de cet instrument des intonations que les connoisseurs ne cessent d'entendre avec surprise. Son mérite est surtout de chanter l'*adagio* aussi parfaitsment, que la voix la plus moëlleuse, la plus intéressante et la plus juste, pourroit faire.[2]

From these remarks it is evident that Leutgeb's musicianship was of a very high order, for he evidently possessed some skill as a composer in addition to his superior gifts as a player. But it is the Parisian critic's comment on Leutgeb's ability to sing an adagio 'as perfectly as the most mellow, interesting, and accurate voice' which strikes our attention most. Not only does it provide us with an eyewitness account of the Salzburg virtuoso's arrestingly beautiful tone, but points to the high degree of perfection to which the art of hand-horn-playing had attained scarcely two decades after Hampl's first experiments.

Looking ahead for a moment to the works which Mozart was to write for his friend Leutgeb in the eighties, it becomes apparent at a glance that mere beauty of sound was by no means that player's only strong point. Even in the technically unprepossessing First Concerto, K.412, Mozart departs from the conservative cast of his first venture in this medium[3] to furnish Leutgeb with some latitude for his facility in the chains of semiquavers in bars

[1] *Mercure de France* (Avril 1770), ii, p. 141.

[2] Op. cit., (Mai), p. 164.

[3] Apart, of course, from the 'Waldhornstückl' which he wrote about 1766 for Martin Grassel, a horn-player-*Cammerdiener* in the service of Prince Breiner, Precentor of the Salzburg Cathedral. The piece itself, K.33 h, is lost. See Leopold Mozart's letter of 16 February 1766.

113–15, and 130–6 of the first movement (Ex. 30). The opening statement of
the solo horn in the first movement of the Second Concerto, K.417, shows
that Leutgeb had a formidable technique at his disposal, for the second
semiquaver scale in bar 132 ascends to the sixteenth partial of the E flat
horn (see accompanying record); and indeed the entire movement makes
considerable demands on the soloist's endurance, flexibility, and command

Ex. 30.   Mozart: Concerto, K. 412, 1st movt.

of the second and third octaves. Of particular interest is the return of the
second theme in the solo part in bar 151. Here the utmost control of the
upper register is required, as well as a fine tone and a smooth legato; and
the downward leap of a major sixth has been the downfall of many modern
horn-players (Ex. 31; see also accompanying record). Indeed, this ability to
cover wide intervals in cantabile passages appears to have been a prominent feature of Leutgeb's style. Mozart calls for frequent legato octaves and
tenths in the second movement of this concerto; and the whole of the Third
Concerto, K.447, embodies wide melodic intervals of this kind.

Ex. 31.   Mozart: Concerto, K. 417, 1st movt.

This predilection for wide legato leaps was not peculiar to Leutgeb,
however. We find these intervals frequently in other works composed both
for and by the great horn-players of the time: and this in itself is a revealing
insight into the fluent embouchure of the hand-horn phase—such intervals
would have been impossible on the wide-rimmed Baroque mouthpiece. Nor
was this feature found only in the horn technique of that day. Mozart's
arias abound with wide leaps, and these were very much a legacy from his
Venetian and Neapolitan forebears of the bel canto era. As the technique of
the horn was based directly upon vocal principles, it is not surprising to find
that it embodied the vocal device of the disjunct legato. It is remarkable that
this ability to slur smoothly and expressively over large intervals has remained a definitive feature of the Austrian horn-playing style to the present
day.

After the comparatively unvirtuosic Third Concerto, Leutgeb evidently asked Mozart for something more brilliant in character to balance up his repertory. This seems entirely probable, for of the four concertos it is the Fourth, K.495, which makes the greatest demands in terms of sheer technique. Rapid scales and cantabile lines in the high register abound, both a carry-over from the florid clarino style of the Baroque. Particularly effective use is made of the darker colour of the stopped notes, perhaps even more

striking here than in the previous concertos because of their contrast with the brighter open tones of the upper range. Especially in the relative minor (bars 97 ff., first movement: Ex. 32 and accompanying record) and in sequences through distantly related keys (bars 141–5, third movement: Ex. 33), Mozart appears to have consciously exploited the veiled quality of the stopped notes. He had done so in the earlier concertos as well, though to a less calculated degree. In the transition the return of the A subject of the second movement in the Second Concerto (bar 64: Ex. 34) he plays upon the

difference between the stopped and open qualities (a difference, be it noted, which was more pronounced on the Viennese instrument than on the French) and upon the hand legato with ravishing effect. The Romanze of the Third Concerto contains a most surprising and dramatic use of a stopped note played sforzando-piano which underscores a diminished ninth chord to spark off the dissonant transition to the restatement (Ex. 35). But in none of the first three concertos does Mozart make such controlled and telling use of stopped notes for colouristic and non-harmonic effects as in the Fourth.

It is clear from the foregoing instances that Mozart was writing not only in terms of Leutgeb's particular abilities, but that he was drawing as well upon the stylistic vocabulary of a highly developed tradition of hand-horn playing. One can only wish that Leutgeb had encouraged Mozart to write more for him than he did; but it is fortunate for us that Mozart should have befriended one of the major virtuosi of his time, and that this collaboration should have resulted in so many works of enduring beauty.

Hand-stopping was first brought to England by a virtuoso named Spandau, who to judge from his name, hailed from the Brandenburg forests. In 1773, only three years after Leutgeb's Paris début, Spandau amazed a London audience with the beauty of his tone and the perfection of his chromatic technique. 'In the beginning of the year 1773.' writes Burney,[1] 'a foreigner, named Spandau, played in a concert at the opera-house a concerto, part whereof was in the key of C, with a minor third; in the performance of which all the intervals seemed to be as perfect as in any wind-instrument . . .' In a later article[2] Burney wrote that Spandau 'contrived in his performance so to correct the natural imperfections of the horn, as to make it a chamber instrument. He played in all Keys, with an equality of tone, and as much accuracy of intonation in the chromatic notes, as could be done on a violin, by which means in his delicacy, taste, and expression, he rendered an instrument which, from its force and coarseness, could formerly be only supported in the open air, in theatres, or spacious buildings, equally soft and pleasing with the human voice.' These first-hand accounts by one of the most critical writers of the time strongly refute those modern scholars, including Carse, who would have us believe that horn-playing, and indeed all instrumental performance in the eighteenth century, was a haphazard and out-of-tune affair.

The Swabian critic and musical essayist Christian Schubart, writing about 1785, paid Spandau the tribute of calling him 'in the high horn genre the foremost player of our time. He draws the finest and most tender sounds from his instrument; only the notes often appear to split under his lips, an effect to which the horn takes not at all kindly in the high register.' But we must remember that then, as now, no great horn-player was immune to the occasional off-day. Whether Schubart heard Spandau when he was not on his best form, or at a time when his powers were beginning to decline, we do not know; but it is abundantly clear from his and Burney's remarks that Spandau was an artist of the first rank, and that Leutgeb was not alone in his early mastery of the hand-horn.[3]

[1] E. Chambers, *Cyclopedia, or, an Universal Dictionary of the Arts and Sciences*, ii (London, 1799).
[2] Abraham Rees, *The Cyclopedia*, xxxiii (London, 1819).
[3] C. F. L. Schubart, *Ideen zu einer Ästhetik der Tonkunst* (Stuttgart, 1785/1825), p. 237.

Shortly after Spandau had introduced the hand-horn to the London public, the celebrated Giovanni Punto came to England to score one of the early successes which marked his rise to lasting fame. Johann Wenzel Stich had been born a bondsman to Count Wenzel Joseph von Thun at Tetschen, now Jehusiče, a village in the German-speaking Czaslau district of Bohemia,[1] in 1747. Count Thun, recognizing the young horn-player's extraordinary talent, sent him first to Prague to study with Matiegka, then to Schindelarž at Munich, and thence to Dresden, where he learnt hand-stopping under Hampl and perfected his high register with Haudek. Stich returned to his lord and patron, but found livery service too much of a burden after the freedom he had enjoyed. With four other musicians he made good his escape into Germany, hotly pursued by minions of Thun, who in his fury at the loss of such a jewel from his orchestra, ordered them either to capture Stich alive or at least to knock out his front teeth. To avoid detection Stich translated his name to Giovanni Punto, and under this guise embarked upon a meteoric career which was to bring him recognition as perhaps the greatest player the horn has ever known.

Punto soon managed to find employment, entering the Court band of the Prince of Hechingen as principal horn about 1768. The lure of a better position shortly took him to Mainz, but after a year or so he resigned in high dudgeon when the Elector refused him the *Concertmeister*'s post. (Punto always saw himself as a great violinist, and one of his chief ambitions was to lead an orchestra. Gerber tells us, however, that his skill on his second instrument was far from sufficient to qualify him for this post even in the humblest band.) He then went to Würzburg as principal horn, and from there obtained leave to set out on his first extensive tour as a soloist.

It is at this point that we meet the first detailed account of Punto's playing from the pen of the ubiquitous Dr. Burney. In 1772 Punto, following his London triumph of the previous year (of which no notice has as yet been found in the London newspapers), had been engaged by the Elector at Coblenz. 'The Elector had a good band,' Burney reports, 'in which M. Ponta, the celebrated French horn from Bohemia, whose taste and astonishing execution were lately so much applauded in London, is a performer.'[2]

His reputation was by now legendary. From Coblenz he made extensive tours which spread his fame further afield to Hungary and Spain; and when he revisited England in 1777 the horn-players of King George's private band

[1] Jaroslaus Schaller, *Topographie des Königreichs Böhmen* (Prague, 1785–90), v, p. 192. 'The German countryman here seeks his livelihood from light agriculture, weaving . . . and trade in timber and grain.' Dlabacž, however (*Künstlerlexicon*, p. 213), mentions that Stich's mother tongue was Czech, a point which has been made much of by present-day nationalist writers. The fact remains that Stich, like all educated Bohemians of his day, was Austrian in schooling and general culture.

[2] C. Burney, *The Present State of Music in Germany* (London, 1775), i, p. 74.

were placed under his tutorship.[1] The spring of the following year found Punto in Paris, where his playing so impressed Mozart that he wrote the solo horn part of the Sinfonia Concertante, K.297b, for the great Bohemian. 'Now I shall write a Sinfonie Concertante for Wendling, flute, Ramm, oboe, Punto, horn, Ritter, bassoon', Mozart wrote to his father on 5 April; and in a later letter remarked, 'where else can 4 such people be found together?' 'Punto bläst magnifique,' Mozart had written in another letter of the same season, and indeed this was the opinion of the *Mercure de France* critic, who had heard the great virtuoso in his Concert Spirituel appearances the two previous years.[2]

Punto's friendship with the Franconian horn virtuoso Carl Thürrschmidt dates from his visits to Paris in the late 1770s, and it is from Thürrschmidt that much of what we know about Punto has come down. In 1781 the famous Parisian maker Lucien-Joseph Raoux made three silver horns on the model of Thürrschmidt's design for Thürrschmidt, for Palsa, and for Punto. This instrument was to win considerable renown in its own right as the *cor-solo*, so called because it was designed for optimum tone quality in the soloist's keys of D, E flat, E, F, and G, and was supplied only with these crooks. Owing to the ease with which it played and to its true intonation, the cor-solo became the solo instrument *par excellence*, and Punto adopted it as his regular instrument henceforth. Whether or not his tone was affected adversely from this changeover is a matter for conjecture, and although it calls to mind Dennis Brain's adoption of the wide-bore German horn in the mid-1950s, Punto's change of instrument arose from considerations of preference rather than of survival. To judge from surviving examples of the cor-solo, it would have lessened the discrepancy between Punto's stopped and open notes, a factor which may itself have prompted his change, and it would have made his tone somewhat brighter, as Fétis indeed remarked; but it is unlikely that his basic sound now differed much from that which he had made on his earlier horn, presumably a Viennese instrument by Kerner or Stärtzer. Punto's reputation up to this point had owed as much to the

---

[1] *The Quarterly Musical Magazine and Review* (London, 1818), i, p. 155. '. . . the King understanding that several of the persons selected (for the private orchestra) played well on stringed besides wind instruments, and perceiving considerable indications of talent among them, His Majesty placed them under masters of eminence at his own expence, and the result was such as to gratify his expectations. Moller and E. Kellner were consigned to the tuition of PONTO, the famous horn blower.'

[2] *Mercure de France* (April 1778): '. . . Les virtuoses, les grands talens ont été applaudis, principalement M. Punto pour le cor de chasse, M. Wendling pour la flûte, M. Raam pour le hautbois et M. Ritter pour le basson . . .'

Marie Antoinette herself heard Punto on 31 March 1777 at a Concert Spirituel. On that occasion concertos were played on the oboe, violin and horn by Lebrun, Jarnowick (Giornovici), and Punto. See M. Brenet, *Les Concerts en France sous l'ancien Régime* (Paris, 1900), p. 317.

beauty of his tone as to his technical facility, and it is improbable that he would have changed over to an instrument which would have markedly altered his basic voice-like quality.

Late in 1781 the Archbishop of Würzburg offered the Bohemian virtuoso a position in his Court band, which Punto accepted. But the next season the Comte d'Artois, later Charles X, bought him back with a life pension and the assurance of leave to continue his concert tours, and accordingly 1782 saw him again in Paris for a time. Punto then toured the Rhine in 1784, and played in Madame Mara's Pantheon concerts in London in 1788. Returning in 1789, he found the Revolution in full cry; and evidently availed himself of one of the many resultant vacancies to become director of the orchestra at the Théâtre des Variétés Amusantes, realizing at last his lifelong ambition to lead an orchestra as first violinist.

The horn did not lie idle, however, for between 1792 and 1795 he brought out the first edition of his tutor, the *Seule et Vraie Methode pour apprendre facilement les Elémens des Premier et Second Cors*, which he admitted on the title-page to be 'Composée par HAMPL / Et perfectionnée par PUNTO son Elève'.[1] In 1795 Punto charmed an audience at an extraordinary session of the Lycée des Arts with his playing, and set out on an extensive tour of Germany in 1798, which was to be his last, leading to Vienna and finally to Prague.

In the January of 1800 we find him in Munich. 'Punto, the most famous of

---

[1] There were at least three editions of Punto's tutor, the last being published, according to Fetis (*Biographie*, Paris, 1868, p. 136) in 1798. The first two bear the name of the publisher Naderman, and Kling, in his article, 'Giovanni Punto, célèbre corniste' in *Bulletin Française de la S.I.M.* (Paris, 1908), p. 1066, quotes the title-page of what was evidently the earliest edition. It is identical with that of the copy in the library of the Paris Conservatoire except for the dedication :'Dediée a la Convention Nationale par le Citoyen Punto, Professeur de Musique et de Cor' and 'Gravée par la Citoyen Oger'. From this it is clear that Kling saw the first edition, and that it appeared between 1792 and 1795, the dates of the assembly and dispersal of the Convention Nationale.

The only specifically technical instructions in the entire tutor appear on the title-page, and as such are worth quoting here:

1. De Prononcer en appliquant son premier coup de langue le mot DAON en frappant fort avec la langue et diminuant le son ensorte qu'il produise le même effet que le tintement d'une Cloche.
2. Pour bien executer le coup de langue sec il est essentiel de Prononcer en appliquant le coup de langue le mot TA.
3. Pour bien appliquer dans les Adagio le coup de langue doux il faut prononcer le mot DA.

Thus Punto on the three kinds of attack: but not a word is given as regards hand-stopping, which, as Morley-Pegge (op. cit., p. 93) points out, appears still to have been handed down from master to pupil by word of mouth. The exercises call frequently for stopping; but it is impossible to know which of them were edited or even added by Punto, and which were left intact as Hampl wrote them. Although these exercises may be taken as an index to Punto's formidable agility, they afford less information about his actual playing than do his concertos some of which are preserved in the library at, King's College, Cambridge.

all living horn-players, is now in Munich.' reported the *Allgemeine Musika-lische Zeitung*,[1] 'and enjoys the enthusiastic applause of the Court and public.' From Munich Punto went on to Vienna, where Gerber tells us he disgraced himself by playing the violin in a performance of Méhul's Sinfonie de Chasse. Fortunately for posterity, however, Punto returned to his proper medium; and his horn-playing so impressed Beethoven that he wrote for him the Sonate, opus 17, which he and Punto first performed in the old Hoftheater on 18 April 1800. The *Allgemeine Musikalische Zeitung's* on-the-spot account of the sonata's immediate success is worth reproducing here in full:[2]

The famous, and now probably the greatest horn-player in the world, Herr Punto, is at present sojourning in Vienna. A short time ago he gave a musical academy in which a Sonata for Fortepiano and Horn composed by Beethoven so excelled and pleased that despite the new Theatre Ordinance, which forbids loud applause and encores, the two virtuosi were compelled by loud clapping to start the piece from the beginning and play it through again.

Following this success at Vienna, Punto set out for Bohemia, the country of his birth, which Dlabacž tells us he had not set foot in for thirty-three years. There was no danger of capture now: not only was old Count Thun long since dead, but Punto's fame was by this time such that his countrymen cheered his progress on the roadsides and drank his health in the inns. New triumphs awaited him in Prague. On 18 January 1801 Punto gave a concert in the National Theatre which featured a concerto and a horn quartet with variations, both of his own composition. The critic of the *Prager Neue Zeitung* devoted several pages to an account of the Bohemian virtuoso's sensational performance, and from certain of these remarks a clear idea of Punto's style may be had:

The unanimous applause which this artist, whose genuine fame has come to him under the pseudonym of Punto, earned here when playing this concerto, was aroused by the incomparable perfection which he displayed in handling his instrument. Even the most respected connoisseurs were forced to admit that they had never before heard such a performance on the horn. His delivery on this normally difficult instrument was pure song in both high and low registers alike. In certain lyric-tragic cadenzas the artist even played double-notes and triads. The variations which he chose contained genuine musical innovations . . . [3]

Such unstinted praise speaks for itself. Two points to be noted, however, are the reference to the voice-like quality of Punto's delivery; and the comment on his equal command of both the high and low registers. This latter ability

---

[1] *Allgemeine Musikalische Zeitung* (Leipzig), xvii, 22 January 1800, p. 297.

[2] Op. cit., xl, 2 July 1800, p. 704.

[3] *Prager Neue Zeitung*, xxxix (1801), p. 473.

is also reflected in the concerti which Punto wrote for himself: and establishes him as the first horn soloist in the modern sense capable of absolute fluency in all registers of the instrument's compass.

In 1802 Punto was joined at Prague by the composer and forte-pianist, J. L. Dussek, his old friend from pre-Revolutionary days in Paris. Together the two Bohemians, both now at the height of their careers, embarked on a tour of their native kingdom. The country folk turned out to fête them at every village, and the two musicians were especially appreciated at Punto's home town of Tetschen, and at Czaslau, Dussek's birthplace, where they gave a benefit concert for the pianist's ageing parents.

It is fitting that this warmly applauded tour, in company with his old companion and so rich in early memories, was Punto's last. On the way back to Prague in the autumn of 1803 he was taken ill with a chest dropsy; and five months later, on 16 February 1803, he died at the age of 56. For days the newspapers were full of eulogies and tributes to Punto's greatness both as a musician and a man. Famous Bohemian-born artists came from all over Europe to take part in the performance of Mozart's Requiem at his memorial service. This was held on 26 February in the sumptuous St. Niklas Church, conducted by Dionys Weber and attended, according to the *Prager Zeitung*, by a greater throng of mourners than had ever been seen on such an occasion, even exceeding the four thousand who had heard Mozart's last rites there in 1791.[1] How appropriate that Joachim Cron, a priest from the Cistercian monastery at Osseg, which had been one of the earliest to embrace the horn in its orchestra, should set the Latin epitaph which still can be seen on Punto's tombstone:

Omne tulit punctum Punto, cui Musa Bohema
Ut plausit vivo, sic moriente gemit.

Having touched on the main events of Punto's extraordinary career, let us glance for a moment at the chief musical records of his playing style. The voice-like tone quality and legato which, as we have already noted, called forth such praise from the critics, were balanced by an astonishing facility of

Ex. 36.   Mozart: Sinfonia Concertante, K. 297b, 3rd movt., Var. IX.
in Eb

staccato technique in both high and low registers. Yet unlike Leutgeb, Punto's technical strength lay in rapid scales and arpeggios rather than in wide intervals. His preference for figures of this kind is clearly reflected in the solo horn flourish which opens Variation IX in the final movement of the Sinfonia Concertante, K.297b, where Mozart sets a musical autograph for each of the four solo winds (Ex. 36); and indeed the *à la chasse* character of the

[1] *Prager Neue Zeitung*, xxv (1803), p. 194.

concluding six-eight section may well have been suggested by the horn. This predilection for scalic passages is further shown in Punto's own First Concerto, now in the library at King's College, Cambridge, and in his F major Quartet. Although the great horn-player's ability as a composer appears to have been on a plane with his dubious talents as a violinist, his works nevertheless afford a valuable insight into the sort of passage-work which showed his horn technique to best advantage. His command of the extreme high register is recorded in the pieces he wrote for himself as well,

Ex. 37.   Beethoven: Sonata, Op. 17, 1st movt.

where in many instances the solo part ascends to the e''' of the E horn. Despite his exceptional high register, however, Punto was, like all the major soloists, a born low-horn-player. In the first movement of the Opus 17 Sonata which Beethoven wrote for him, the daring use of the factitious G between the fundamental and first partial of the horn's bass sub-octave (Ex. 37) points to a prowess in this register remarkable even for a second horn. Both in the final bars of the first movement and the bridge in the reprise of the last, Beethoven has added Punto's favourite arpeggios as an autographic underscore; and their difficulty is such that even present-day soloists rarely succeed in playing them neatly at full tempo (Ex. 38).

Ex. 38.   Beethoven: Sonata, Op. 17, 1st movt.

Op. 17, 3rd movt.

A final note is owing here on Punto the man. As a player and teacher his contributions to the advancement of horn technique speak for themselves, and it is abundantly evident from contemporary writings that his position as the greatest horn-player in an age of great horn-players was undisputed. But musical proficiency is not in itself enough to ensure lasting greatness as a musician: superior qualities as a human being are required as well. That Punto possessed these extra gifts is clear from the frequent tributes which his peers paid to him as a person. In the portrait which Miger made of this great virtuoso (Plate XVIa) at the age of 35 (1782) the traits which so endeared him to all whom he met speak out clearly. We see a remarkable

mixture of sensitivity, humour, intelligence, pride, integrity, and stubborn-
ness reflected in the aristocratic features of this striking face; and as a technical footnote, horn-players will recognize the conformities of a natural
setting-in embouchure. In view of these traits and his reputation, it is
tempting to agree with those who have called him the greatest horn virtuoso
of all time. He was without question the finest player of the eighteenth-
century Austrian school—and his portrait shows him to have been a true
statesman of humanity.

    Although the figure of Punto dominated the horn-playing world in the
later eighteenth century, there were other giants in those days as well.
Punto's friend Carl Thürrschmidt (1753–97) was a major virtuoso whose
contributions, both musical and mechanical, did much to advance the horn's
popularity as a solo instrument. Son and pupil of a great Bohemian-born
horn-player of the second generation, Johannes Thürrschmidt, Carl grew up
in the heady atmosphere of the Wallerstein Court in Franconia during the
years when Count Philipp Carl was beginning to attract prominent musicians
to his orchestra. Unlike his father, the younger Thürrschmidt was a low-
horn-player; and though he received the best training available at his
father's hand, there is good reason to believe that he may have been sent to
Dresden to study with Hampl. Carl's hand technique was the constant
wonder of the critics, and it is unlikely that he would have learnt the use of
the right hand from his father, a high-horn-player of the Early Symphony
period.

    Thürrschmidt's fame rested chiefly on his exploits as a duettist in company
with the Bohemian Johann Palsa, whom he joined at the age of 18 (see below).
He returned frequently to Wallerstein as a soloist, however. Anton Rosetti,

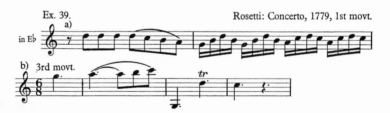

Ex. 39.   Rosetti: Concerto, 1779, 1st movt.

Capellmeister there from 1773 until 1789, wrote twenty-three horn concertos, of which five are for low horn, and bear the inscription, 'Pour Monsieur Durrschmied'. Gerber's remarks on Thürrschmidt's exceptional
right-hand dexterity have already been noted.[1] In the E flat concerto of 1779
Rosetti makes particularly effective use of the young horn-player's manual
agility, as can be seen from bars 115–20 of the first movement (Ex. 39a).
Thürrschmidt evidently shared Leutgeb's ability to cover wide leaps in a

[1] Gerber, *Lexicon*. See Appendix, p. 226.

quick tempo as well, to judge from the cadential figure in bars 84–8 of the Rondeau (Ex. 39b). A further insight into his style is afforded by many of the duets which he wrote for himself and his first, Palsa: here an admirable command of wide intervals in the low register is evident (Ex. 40). Gassner was more explicit about Thürrschmidt's tone than either Dlabacž or Gerber, who were dazzled by his hand technique, and commented that 'His fame had spread through half of Europe; and since his death few horn-players have

Ex. 40.   A Palsa—Thürrschmidt Duet.

been able to elicit such beautiful sounds from their instrument, nor possessed such facility as well. He was in truth a complete virtuoso and artist.'[1]

Like Hampl, Thürrschmidt had an inventive mind, and was much engaged with bettering the instrument mechanically. (This may be taken as another possible indication that he studied with Hampl, for he ranks second only to the Dresden teacher as an innovator and designer.) He improved the Orchesterhorn by crossing the tubes leading to the tuning-slide (see p. 127) and designed a cor-de-chasse, incorporating this principle, in conjunction with Raoux in 1781.

Thürrschmidt furthermore brought out an improvement on Hampl's non-transposing mute about 1795. By means of a ball on the end of a rod, the inside of the mute's neck could be stopped in the same way as the hand stopped the bell of the open horn. As a result the chromatic notes were available in muted colours, and with even less difference between stopped and open notes than in the case of the open horn. The echo effect, first used by the brothers Boeck (see below), was the delight of the drawing-rooms, and was much in vogue with the duettists of the day. It is easily seen how this additional colour greatly increased the horn's standing as a solo instrument; but Thürrschmidt's chromatic device must have caused a sensation.

This improved chromatic mute furnishes the only answer to the enigma of the stopped f″ in the first-horn part of the first movement of the Beethoven Rondino. The writer, using Bernsdorf's description and dimensions for this mute, made a reconstruction in seasoned acacia wood. Not only is the muted quality most pleasant on the natural horn, but the stopping device works with remarkable quickness and accuracy.[2]

[1] Ferdinand Gassner, *Universal-Lexicon der Tonkunst* (Stuttgart, 1847), p. 849. The article was written about 1825. Gassner says elsewhere that he had personally heard Thürrschmidt; so his account is valuable as first-hand information.

[2] Edward Bernsdorf, *Universal-Lexicon der Tonkunst* (Dresden, 1856), i, p. 646.

The leading duettists

As has been noted, Thürrschmidt's greatest successes were made together with Johann Palsa (1754–92), a Bohemian high-horn player with whom he toured extensively throughout Europe. Because of the horn's great range, tonal variety, and blend when used in pairs, horn duettists such as Palsa and Thürrschmidt were highly acclaimed by the audiences of the latter eighteenth century. It was undoubtedly this famous duo which Gerber had in mind when he commented that when a pair of horn virtuosi appeared in concert the effect was that of a flute accompanied by a gamba.[1]

Much of the popularity which the numerous horn duettists of the later decades of the century enjoyed resulted from the high degree of perfection which Palsa and Thürrschmidt brought to this branch of the art of horn-playing. They were the real pioneers in this field, for as early as 1770 they performed at a Concert Spirituel with great success.[2] If facility of execution was Thürrschmidt's strength, so Palsa was praised for the beauty of his tone: and the anonymous *Dictionary of Music* for 1824 quotes the 'editors of the French Dictionary of Music' as saying 'that it would be impossible to give an idea of the beauty and purity of the cantabile of Palsa, or the vivacity, quickness and skill of Türrschmidt'.

This testimony no doubt dates from their Paris period, when they were attached to Prince de Rohan-Guémenée's orchestra; but the fame of the two horn-players was to spread quickly after 1783, when the Landgrave of Cassel engaged them at an attractive salary and allowed them leave to tour. In 1784 Forkel heard them: 'There is nothing more beautiful', he wrote in his *Almanach*, 'than the little duets which Herr Palsa and his companion Herr Thürrschmidt play together on two silver horns, especially those in a minor key.' (The silver horns were the cors-solo which Raoux had made for them and for Punto at Paris in 1781.) In 1786 Palsa and Thürrschmidt came to London, 'where they were much admired', and attracted William Parke's attention at a Salomon concert the following year. 'The most striking part of their exhibition', Parke comments dryly, 'was their horns, which were made of silver.'[3]

The two partners no doubt had a hand in sparking off the sudden burst of double horn concertos which appeared in the 1780s; and it is perhaps not entirely a coincidence that Mozart's twelve horn duets, K.487, and the Musikalischer Spass, K.522, although written for Leutgeb and a companion, date from 1786 and 1787 respectively. The most popular key for double horn concertos was E major; and in this context the following comment on a

[1] Gerber, loc. cit. See Appendix, p. 225.
[2] *Dictionary of Musicians* (London, 1824); and Gassner, op. cit., p. 442. This concert appears not to have been reviewed by the critic on the *Mercure de France*.
[3] W. T. Parke, *Musical Memoirs* (London, 1830), i, p. 63.

performance by Palsa and Thürrschmidt at Cassel in 1786 is revealing: 'Accompanied by the orchestra of the theater of Cassel, they performed on their silver horns (mfd. at Paris, and each valued at one hundred louis d'or) two concertos in E major; and, in the Rondos, passed into the Keys of E minor and G minor with as much agility as performers on the piano-forte.'[1]

After the death of the Landgrave of Hesse-Cassel in 1786, Palsa and Thürrschmidt went to Berlin as the leading pair of horns in the Royal orchestra there. In 1792 Palsa died, like Punto later, of pneumonia, a common horn-player's disease in those days; he was replaced as Thürrschmidt's partner in the duo by Jean Le Brun (1759–1806).[2] As a pupil of Punto, Le Brun deserves mention here, for he was a great credit to his famous teacher. He appears to have been the only possible choice as a replacement for Palsa. Like the Bohemian, Le Brun had a fine singing tone, a prodigious technique, and could play with equal facility in all keys. Together the new partners were widely applauded as duettists: but not for long, as death claimed Thürrschmidt in 1797. Of Le Brun the Berlin critic of the *Allgemeine Musikalische Zeitung* wrote in 1799:

... until I met Thürrschmidt and especially Brun, I had always considered the horn to be quite useful and pleasant in the orchestra, but as a solo instrument rather limited if indeed not impractical. Never has an artist of any kind moved me as has this Brun. He is the complete master of his instrument. Never have I heard him miss anything, not even the tiniest detail. Every note, whether in fast passages or expressive sections, is clear and sure. His Allegro is beautiful, his Andante charms, and his Adagio has never failed to move me to tears. In short—Brun is a complete artist.[3]

This combination of expressiveness with technical perfection may serve to remind the modern horn-player of what heights his predecessors reached without the aid of machinery.

The Bohemian brothers Anton and Ignaz Böck or Boeck shared the honours with Palsa and Thürrschmidt as the leading duettists of the day. Their fame appears not to have spread beyond the borders of the German-speaking world, and unfortunately none of the music written for or by them has come to light; but their playing, to judge from the accounts of those who heard them, was some of the finest the horn has known. The Boeck brothers'

[1] *Dictionary of Musicians*, loc. cit.

[2] Although a Frenchman by birth, Le Brun falls within the framework of the Austrian school in that he was a pupil of Punto: and indeed all the prominent French soloists of the late eighteenth century invariably studied under Bohemian teachers, Punto, Domnich, and Kenn being the most prominent. Bohemian and German wind-players held sway in Paris until well after the first crop of native players had graduated from the Conservatoire in 1800. When Anton Reicha composed his brilliant horn trios, op. 82, there in 1818, he was writing for players of the Austrian style.

[3] *Allgemeine Musikalische Zeitung*, No. xxxix (1799), p. 621.

chief contribution was in the early use of the mute, which they featured in concert performances as early as 1775. It is most probable that Beethoven first met the muted horn at one of the Boecks' many performances in Vienna, where they were still much appreciated as late as 1815. The finale of the Sixth Symphony has a prominent muted solo: in fact, the Rondino, with its enigmatic *con sordino* passage, may well have been written for them.[1] Thürr-schmidt, Gerber remarks in 1815, knew and respected the Bohemian duet-tists, and most probably evolved his chromatic mute after they had shown him the possibilities of the earlier Hampl model which they used. This was a simple cone made of sheet brass covered with leather, and having an opening at the upper end.

Quite apart from the wonder which their muted effect always aroused, the Boecks' reputation rested on the polish and eloquence of their playing. One of the most detailed records of a performance by any of the late hand-horn virtuosi is contained in a glowing review of this duo's Berlin concert in the December of 1787. This account, too long to include here, but reproduced on p. 204, praises each point of their superb mastery of the instrument: their singing cantabile, accuracy in the extreme high and low registers, true intonation, and general artistry. When played with the consummate per-fection which the great eighteenth-century hand-horn-players brought to the instrument, it is easily seen why the horn commanded such a pre-eminent position as a solo instrument: and indeed so great was its popularity, Gerber tells us, that even the violin was forced to yield to the horn's over-whelming favour with the musical public of the day.

The virtuoso hand-horn style: some notes on technique

It is remarkable that the horn should have enjoyed such acclaim on the con-cert platform at a time when the violin, flute, clarinet, and oboe had each attained to a high degree of mechanical development, and were constantly heard in full perfection in the hands of some of the greatest performers these instruments have ever produced. In spite of the astonishing dexterity which the late eighteenth-century critics so admired in the major horn virtuosi, the horn remained by comparison an essentially limited instrument with respect to its technical scope. What, then, was the secret behind the magical effect which the horn obviously exerted over the concert-room audiences of the time?

All questions of echo effects and horn chords aside, it was the sheer beauty of the natural horn's tone which packed the music-rooms. In the hands of a fine player the sound of the horn had many affinities with the human voice, a fact which never failed to draw comment from the critics, as

[1] See the accompanying record. The mute was made by the writer to Thürrschmidt's specifications as quoted by Bernsdorf.

we have already noted in the case of the virtuosi discussed above. To the eighteenth-century listener the variety of colour, softness of quality, smoothness, and dynamic power of the horn's tone must have been impressive indeed; and in view of its pungent associations with the hunt and the noble country life which in those latter days was already threatened by egalitarian movements, the gentle-born concert-goer's heart would have been moved on hearing the horn.

The vocal quality for which the Austrian horn virtuosi were so justly famous resulted not only from their superb instruments but from a sound underlying discipline in the tone production which was handed down from the earliest days of artistic horn-playing. We will recall that one of the fundamental requirements for admission to a Jesuit or Benedictine monastery was a mastery of the rudiments of singing, and that the early teachers were without exception products of the Bohemian colleges and seminaries. So, too, were the teachers of the third generation: thus it is no coincidence that Punto, Domnich, and Fröhlich all advise the beginning pupil first to learn to sing correctly before taking up the horn, this being the best way to develop proper breathing, musical phrasing, and an accurate sense of pitch.[1]

Punto is said to have possessed what Dlabacž calls 'a very fine Basso voice', and is known to have taught singing as well. Punto's nephew, a Herr Jellauer, studied voice with him and sang an aria in the great horn-player's National Theatre concert at Prague in 1801.

Heinrich Domnich, son of the Hungarian-born virtuoso Friedrich Domnich (who combined the office of singing-teacher with his orchestral duties at Wallerstein), remarks in the Schott edition of his *Methode de Premier et de Second Cor* of *c*. 1828, that:

the relationship between horn-playing and singing is absolute. Everything one plays on this instrument must first be formed in the mind; if the inner concept is false or not clear, so the tone which results will sound accordingly. . . . The beginner, even before he first places the mouthpiece upon his lips, must already have acquired perfect facility in binding notes together in legato; in identifying intervals; and in matching the pitch of a given note: all learnt by practising Solfeggio. Although this grounding is useful when learning other instruments, it is indispensable in the case of the horn.[2]

Strong words; but if present-day horn-players would heed them we might be spared the dry legato and the crescendo-decrescendo on each note in melodic passages which have come to be accepted in much modern wind-playing.

Joseph Fröhlich was a horn-player himself, to judge from the accurate detail and practical common sense of his *Hornschule*, published at Würzburg

[1] The 1798 edition of Punto's *Methode* contains this advice in the first section.
[2] Heinrich Domnich, *Methode de Premier et Second Cor* (Mainz, 1808/28), p. 4.

in 1810; and in any case he consulted a number of leading players, including Punto, during its preparation. 'A singing style is the horn-player's principal grace, just as the choir-school is the only true training ground for those who in time hope to accomplish anything worthwhile on this instrument.' So Fröhlich counsels the prospective horn-player; adding that 'if in addition the pupil listens to many good singers, studies singing, and strives unremittingly to pattern his playing upon good singing technique, the resultng progress will quickly advance him so far in this field as to win him recognition as a true artist on his instrument'.[1]

Just as every correctly produced voice features a pleasant natural vibrato, so the vibrato appears to have enriched the tone of the virtuoso horn-players. The writer's experience has shown that, owing to its simplicity of design, the hand-horn's responsiveness is most conducive to an expressive vibrato—and indeed this essentially vocal element seems to have carried over into horn-playing from the basic schooling in singing upon which all horn-players at this period based their technique.

The vibrato appears to have been so intrinsically a part of the vocal tone quality and delivery of the great horn-players that it did not call forth separate comment from the critics: obviously if a player sang upon his horn, he sang with a natural vibrato. Yet one writer has singled out this feature as being responsible not only for the voice-like sound of the horn, but for its expressive powers as well. It is worth quoting in full this passage from the *Jahrbuch der Tonkunst von Wien und Prag* for 1796.

So far as the actual number of its notes is concerned this instrument is poor; but it is all the richer in its effect because of the roundness and fullness of its tone, and because of its vibrato. The composer who knows how to use the horn well can arouse remarkable sensations with it: by simple held notes and isolated accents he can depict love's complaints, repose, melancholy, horror, and awe, painting in the shadows as dark as he chooses. The vibrato, which is of such great effect in music, can be produced on no other instrument with such expressiveness and vigour as on the horn. The virtuoso has much to overcome in the way of embouchure and pitching, but he also has at his command a wonderful array of melting, floating and dying-away effects.[2]

[1] Joseph Fröhlich, *Vollständige Theoretisch-Praktische Musikschule* (Bonn, 1811), iii, pp. 17, 20. This section, 'Vom Horn', was published the following year under the title, *Hornschule nach den Grundsätzen der besten über dieses Instrument erschienen Schriften.* See also his article, 'Horn', in Ersch and Gruber, *Allgemeine Encyclopädie der Wissenschaften und Künste* (Leipzig, 1834), ii, pp. 4–11; and Otto Kade, *Die Musikalien-Sammlung . . . des Schweriner Fürstenhauses* (Schwerin, 1893), i, p. 280.

[2] *Jahrbuch der Tonkunst von Wien und Prag* (1796), p. 193. Further confirmation that the Bohemian virtuosi used vibrato may be seen in the fact that Russian horn-players, initially taught by eighteenth- and early nineteenth-century Bohemians, use vibrato to the present day. So do the French, another derivative school, although the vibrato was less rampant there before the Second World War than at present. In Austria and

Clearly the beautiful tone quality for which the great Austrian horn soloists were noted owed much to this thorough preliminary discipline in singing. In the opinion of the present writer there is yet another factor to be considered here as a decided influence on tone colour and its production— that of the language which these players spoke. It is well known that the various dialects of Austria, southern Germany, Bohemia, and Saxony have three features of pronunciation in common: soft dental consonants; long, resonant vowels; and a 'singing' inflection. Just as a person's musicality is reflected in his speech, so the musical nature of a people influences its language: thus it is no coincidence that since the eighteenth century Austria, Bohemia, and their surrounding provinces have continued to pro- duce horn-players, and indeed virtuosi on all instruments, who were remarkable for their softness of tone and voice-like legato.[1]

For all their enlightening remarks on tone production and phrasing, the eighteenth-century teachers are curiously evasive on the question of hand- stopping. Punto avoids the issue completely, even though both his *Methode* and *Exercice Journalier* call frequently for stopped notes, as we have noted; and both Domnich and Fröhlich give only the most rudimentary instructions for holding the hand in the bell, together with a rather elementary table of hand positions for each note, to which reference will again be made. This relative lack of explicit instruction is a matter for surprise to many: for the front-rank horn virtuosi owed their success with the musical public

---

Germany the vibrato is not encountered amongst horn-players today as a general rule, and has returned to the other winds, notably the oboe and bassoon, only in recent years. Richter and Hanslick were largely responsible for stamping out vibrato in the winds in the later nineteenth century in Austria, Wagner and von Bülow in Germany proper. But it has survived in the countries already noted, and in certain schools of American horn-playing, particularly that headed by John Barrows, who is a pupil of the late Arkady Yegudkin, principal horn with the Czar's private orchestra from 1911 until 1917. A revealing commentary on the appropriateness of the natural vibrato as an ex- pressive embellishment may be seen in the fact that the late Gottfried von Freiberg, solo horn of the Vienna Philharmonic until his death in 1962, vehemently denounced the vibrato: yet there were moments, notably in the slow movement of Richard Strauss's Second Concerto, where his own playing was enhanced by the most eloquent, though utterly unconscious, vibrato. Nor did he ever discourage the present writer, his pupil, from its use.

[1] The acoustician Bernard Hague touches on both the foregoing points in his article, 'The Tonal Spectra of Wind Instruments', in *Proc. Royal Musical Association*, lxxiii (London, 1947), p. 82. 'The tonguing technique used by wind instrument players for the various kinds of phrasing corresponds approximately to the use of dental consonants in speech . . . Much experimental work still remains to be done, but the parallel be- tween articulate speech and wind instrument playing is sufficiently close to justify on physical grounds the soundness of teaching such instruments upon a vocal basis.' It is reassuring to have a modern scientist's approval of a principle which was general know- ledge to any eighteenth-century wind-player.

as much to their phenomenal right-hand dexterity as to their beauties of sound.

Yet to anyone who has actually taught the hand horn (and here the present writer speaks from first-hand experience) it is easily seen why the early teachers thought it best to say little or nothing on this vital aspect of the horn technique of their time. Not only was the art of hand-stopping very much a trade secret, but there remained the cogent factors of individual variation amongst players and instruments which conspired to set at naught even the most reasoned attempt to put the principles of right-hand technique into writing. No two instruments are alike; and there are as many hand sizes

Ex. 41. Stopped Notes. O = normal; ● = fully stopped; ∅ = fully open.

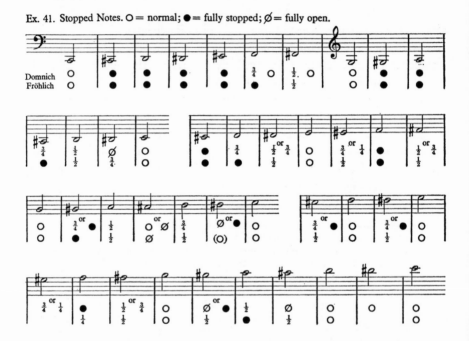

and shapes as there are horn-players. Consequently a given note which might speak clearly in a three-quarter-stopped position for the master would be noticeably sharp for the pupil with a smaller hand, in which case a fully open position would seem the proper solution; but if the pupil's horn was flat on that note, then the position would have to be altered to suit the situation, and so on. Generally speaking, therefore, no-one is in a position to dogmatize on this technique; and the only certain way to learn to stop accurately is to experiment patiently along basic principles. These are set out in Domnich's and Fröhlich's tables, which are reproduced in Ex. 41.

The disparity in the sound of the stopped and open notes is the main problem of the hand-horn, and must be moderated if a musical effect is to be had. Domnich's remarks are helpful here. 'In order to achieve this result', he writes, 'no other means has been found as yet than blowing the open notes more softly so that the stopped notes, which sound weaker, will not make too great a contrast with the open.' In other words, one must blow the open notes softly so that they will more nearly match the quality of the stopped notes, not, as one often hears, playing the stopped notes louder so that their volume will balance that of the open notes. Fröhlich warns explicitly against this latter trick on p. 16: 'Especially one must guard against blowing the stopped notes too loudly, as this produces the most unpleasant sound.' In short, a light, continuous air-stream should favour the open notes and support the stopped. The hand, says Fröhlich, should move as little as possible, and the author's experience bears out the soundness of this point. Care must be taken, of course, not to overstop; but the final word of wisdom comes from Domnich: 'For the very simple reason that one cannot prescribe the exact position of the hand in the bell, one must allow the pupil to find it on his own. One spares him much trouble by doing so.'

It has been the present writer's observation in performance that the listener's ear will naturally compensate for these unevennesses on the hand-horn just as it bridges the immediate diminuendo of every note on the pianoforte. This will happen, however, only if the player sustains with his breath the concept of a continuous melodic line. Here again a good singing technique is indispensable. Clearly the great hand-horn-players owed both their tone and their smooth stopping technique to a thorough grounding in the vocal art; and the composers of the day helped further, as we have seen, by using the stopped notes as adjuncts in phrasing and for special effects.

The hand-horn in the orchestra

Hand-stopping reached the rank-and-file orchestral horn-players relatively late in the period, becoming common only after the turn of the century, when, as we shall see, virtuoso playing *per se* was already on the decline.

Ex. 42.   Mozart: *Idomeneo.*

Isolated examples of chromatic writing for the orchestral horn are met with earlier, but are usually the result of a composer writing for a particular soloist, as for example in Ilia's aria, 'Se il Padre perdei' from *Idomeneo*, which Mozart set with a solo wind quartet accompaniment to be played by Wendling, Ramm, Punto, and Ritter (Ex. 42). Another example of this obbligato idiom occurs in the horn accompaniment to the aria 'Per pietá ben mio' from

Act II of *Così fan tutte* (Ex. 43). The majority of Mozart's orchestral horn parts, on the other hand, are clearly intended for the run-of-the-mill orchestral horn-players of the day; and considering the degree to which hand-stopping had by this stage been developed by the soloists, were remarkably conservative: so much so that when writing in distantly related keys for the

Ex. 43.   Mozart: *Così fan tutte.*

horn, as in both G minor symphonies, two pairs were called for crooked in different keys so as to utilize the greatest possible number of open notes.

One notable exception to this rule, however, appears in the earlier D major Serenade, K.131, of 1772. Stopped notes occur in all four horn parts throughout this work; but in the Adagio introduction to the Finale Mozart

Ex. 44.   Mozart: Serenade, K. 131: Adagio.

makes particularly adventurous use of chromatic notes (Ex. 44). This may be regarded as the first full-fledged solo horn quartet to appear in an orchestral context, and a direct forerunner of the quartet in the overture to von Weber's *Der Freischütz.* (See accompanying record.)

Thus when Beethoven set the horn quartet accompaniment to the High Priest's aria 'Will unser Genius' in his incidental music to *Die Ruinen von*

Ex. 45.   Beethoven: *Ruinen von Athen.*

Athen, op. 113 (1792/1812), he was by no means the first to use the chromatic horn idiom in this way (Ex. 45). By comparison the famous horn trio in the Scherzo of the 'Eroica' Symphony (1803) is less advanced in point of the actual part-writing, although it has been hailed as a turning-point in the use of the orchestral horns. The employment of three horns instead of a pair or quartet is indeed an innovation in scoring, and an effective one: but where hand-technique and musical style are concerned, the parts themselves are firmly traditional (Ex. 46). Far more progressive is the virtuoso horn trio

Ex. 46.   Beethoven: Symphony No. 3, Scherzo.

accompaniment to the aria 'Komm Hoffung' in *Fidelio* (1806). The three-horn scoring here is carried over from the 'Eroica'; but the bold chromaticism of the individual parts show a marked departure, both technically and dramatically, from Beethoven's earlier horn-writing (Ex. 47). Here is the real turning-point, as much in the technique required of the orchestral horn as in its theatrical application. The demands on the players in terms of sheer endurance and facility are formidable, and have often been more than a match for the best horns of our own day. Beethoven was evidently writing for three players of exceptional virtuosity: in all probability Michael Herbst

(1778–1883), Martin von Rupp (1748–1819) and Johann Hörmann, the three most prominent orchestral horn-players of the period at Vienna (see Chapter VIII).

Free use of the chromatic notes was now an established feature of Beethoven's vocabulary in writing for the orchestral horn. Reverting to the more traditional pair of horns in the Eighth Symphony, in keeping with its conservative orchestration, he confidently made use of the stopped notes with which he had experimented in the melodic writing of the *Fidelio* horn trio. This idiom (if we accept that the Sextet, op. 81b, for two horns and string quartet, was written under the Bonn horn-player Nikolaus Simrock's guidance) was new to Beethoven, but it was well known to his fellow composers at Vienna. The hand-horn quartet in the Larghetto from the Pianoforte Concerto, op. 89 (1827), by Johann Nepomuk Hummel (1778–1837) (Ex. 48); and the passage for six horns from the Symphony No. 5 in E flat

Ex. 49.   Krommer: Symphony No. 5.

I & II in E♭

III & IV in B♭ basso

V & VI in F

(1820) by Franz Krommer (1759–1831) (Ex. 49) clearly show that chromaticism was an integral part of the orchestral horn's ensemble style in the early nineteenth century. Chromatic solos as well are occasionally met with at this period; and the first horn melody from the first movement of the D major symphony by Krommer (1803) furnishes proof that Beethoven had been anticipated in assigning a solo line to the hand-horn (Ex. 50).

Ex. 50.   Krommer: Symphony No. 2.

I in D

In the light of this common usage, the remarkable fourth horn solo in the Adagio of the Choral Symphony (Ex. 51) appears less startling than the many writings about it would have us believe. While it is true that to set an A flat scale for a hand-horn crooked in E flat was to depart from normal practice, it must be remembered that playing scales in all keys on a given crook was by this time (1823) part of the hand-horn-player's daily drill. The solo is perfectly playable on a valveless horn (see accompanying record); and although many argue that it was written to be played by the pioneer valve-hornist E. C. Lewy on a two-valved instrument, there is no proof that Beethoven had ever come into contact with either Lewy or the valve. Quite apart from historical considerations, however, there remains the fact that Beethoven had lost his hearing by the time the valve was in its infancy: so

Ex. 51.   Beethoven: Symphony No. 9.

that there is little likelihood of his having renounced a carefully acquired technique of writing for the hand-horn in favour of an instrument which he had never heard. So far as orchestral writing for the horn is concerned, the passage in question contains fewer infractions of accepted practice than do the solo voice parts. In view of the highly chromatic style of writing for the horn at the time, and indeed of Beethoven's controlled and deliberate use of stopped notes in his other works, the writer concurs with Blandford's view that Beethoven was merely exploiting the hand-horn to its harmonic and colouristic limit.[1] In the same way as the final stages of a given period in musical style are marked by chromaticism, so the advanced chromaticism of this late hand-horn music marks the instrument's ultimate fulfilment: and at the same time both posed the need for the valve horn and prepared the way for it. Before investigating the other factors underlying the Austrian school's decline, however, let us trace briefly the other national schools of

[1] W. F. H. Blandford, 'The Fourth Horn in the Choral Symphony', in *Musical Times* (January, February, March, 1925). By far the most exhaustive and reasoned enquiry into this question, Blandford's paper bases its argument on practical knowledge of the instrument and on sound scholarship. Pending fresh information, it remains the final word on the subject.

horn-playing which sprang from the seeds sown by the Austrian and Bohemian virtuoso-teachers of the latter eighteenth century.

Some derivative national schools of horn-playing

The parent tree of the Austro-Bohemian school grew and strengthened for more than a century before sending out those first branches which were to become the national schools of the nineteenth century. German horn-makers in certain centres north of the river Main had begun to depart from the Viennese pattern by the mid-1750s. Haas and Ehe at Nürnberg, Werner at Dresden, and Haltenhof at Hanau had each by this time brought out a model which featured the more compact and penetrating tone which was later to become characteristic of the German horn. But the Austrian style of playing still held sway in the northerly principalities, and until the last decades of the century the prominent orchestral players and teachers there were Bohemians. Only in Gerber's remark of 1789 where the German preference for a more brass-like quality is first mentioned ('. . . die Schärfe, welche unsere Meister ihrem Instrumente bey voller Musik zu geben wissen, so dass man nicht mehr Hörner, sondern Posaunen zu hören glaubt': see Appendix, p. 224) do we remark a conscious break with the Austrian ideal of a soft and buoyant horn tone. With the founding of the great German families of hand-horn virtuosi, such as the Schunkes and Dornauses, the German style was firmly established by the turn of the century. (See pp. 212 and 214.) It is interesting to note, however, that in 1801 Philipp Dornaus (1769–c. 1820; principal horn to the Elector of Trier) advocated a return to Austrian instrument design and tonal principles.[1]

The throng of Bohemian virtuosi who introduced the orchestral horn to Paris in the 1750s appear to have monopolized both the concert platform and the opera pit, with few exceptions, until the first native French players began to appear in the 1770s. Jean-Joseph Rodolphe (1730–1812), who first played the hand-horn to an opera audience at Paris in 1765, was the earliest major French virtuoso, but he neither taught nor held a regular orchestral post as a horn-player. The Raoux family had begun to make concert horns of definitively French design by the 1770s, although these were based on the Austrian Orchesterhorn; and by 1781 Raoux had brought out the cor-solo. But Punto was still the principal teacher at Paris, and even his prize pupil, Le Brun, must be regarded as an exponent of the Austrian style of playing. The first senior horn professor at the Conservatoire was Frederic Duvernoy (1765–1838). His colleagues, however, were Heinrich Domnich, a Franconian, and Buch and Kenn, both 'Germans'; so that it was not until Duvernoy was succeeded by Louis François Dauprat as professor in 1817 that a con-

[1] Philipp Dornaus, 'Einige Bemerckungen zu dem zweckmässigen Gebrauch des Waldhorns', in *Allgemeine Musikalische Zeitung* (Leipzig, January 1801), p. 308.

tinuous French tradition of teaching the horn was established. The French school of hand-horn playing continued well into the third quarter of the nineteenth century, long after the valve had superseded the hand at Vienna, marking the last great era of the virtuoso hand-horn-player. It produced, however, no distinguished music for the instrument.

The Belgian school may be considered as a subsidiary of the French. Yet even today the Belgians prefer a slightly darker and softer sound than the French, a feature which points to the Bohemian virtuosi who first brought artistic horn-playing to Brussels and the Hague in the eighteenth century. The brothers Hosa came to Brussels in the 1740s; but although their influence was great, it is unlikely that they taught Spandau, who appears to have been a Saxon or Bohemian. Spandau's pupil, Othon Vandenbroek (c. 1750–c. 1810), was the leading Belgian virtuoso and teacher. In the nineties he came to Paris as a regular member of the Opera orchestra; there he published his *Methode Nouvelle et Raisonée*, which contains some early, though not particularly useful, remarks on hand-stopping.[1]

The Russian style of horn-playing today distinctly reveals certain atavisms which strongly recall its Bohemian and Austrian ancestry. Kölbel and Maresch were teaching the horn at St. Petersburg in the 1750s; and the Russian cities were host to many of the later Bohemian hand-horn virtuosi. Russian horn-players have kept the vibrato which graced the tone of the eighteenth-century soloists, and have adapted it to their own vocal concepts. The first professors at the Moscow Conservatory were Czechs, although their names have not survived; and tradition has it that the horn solo in the second movement of Tchaikovsky's Fifth Symphony was written for a Viennese horn-player named Kennesch. It is to these forebears that the Russians owe their highly individual through-the-mask singing quality, richly adorned by an unabashed vibrato.

The long-standing blood ties between the Habsburg Court and the ducal houses of Modena, Tuscany, and Milan account for the derivation of the Italian school of horn-playing from the Austrian. As early as 1756 we meet a band of horns at Florence in the retinue of Marshal Botta, head of the Austrian Regency there.[2] A Bohemian horn-player, Joseph Reichel, was a member of the Imperial ambassador's band at Genoa in the 1770s; and

---

[1] See Morley-Pegge, op. cit., p. 96.

[2] Old Marshal Botta caused his band of horns to sound fanfares from the balcony of his palace whenever news of an Austrian victory in the Seven Years War reached Florence. In a letter of 1760 Horace Mann remarks, 'You may remember, that, last year, Marshal Botta would not give leave for Masks, for fear of spoiling a victory.' Dr. Doran comments that 'It was quite a joke in Florence that Marshal Botta's French horns were never to be relied upon. They blazoned as victories what often turned out to be "victories" on the other side.' (Doran, *'Mann' and Manners at the Court of Florence, 1740–1786*, p. 68.)

Wenzel Pichl, violinist-composer to the Archduke of Milan, found two Bohemian horn duettists residing at Rome in 1775. The first Italian exponent of the Bohemian hand-horn tradition was Luigi Belloli (1770–1817), who in 1812 was appointed professor of the horn at the Milan Conservatory. He trained many fine players, and appears to have been largely responsible for the high standard of horn-playing in Italy which Rossini's horn parts reflect. Amongst Belloli's pupils were Giovanni Puzzi (1792–1876), later to win renown as a soloist in England; and some of the first valve-horn-players in Italy. Though the Italian sound today is somewhat oily to our ear, it bears distinct traces of its Austrian ancestry.

While there has not been an unbroken tradition of Bohemian horn-players in England since the second quarter of the nineteenth century, their influence nevertheless contributed to that distinctive style of which the Brain family were the last true exponents. We have already noted that the first horn-players to come to these shores in the days of Handel and Pepusch were Bohemians; and that certain of the greatest hand-horn virtuosi, including Spandau and Punto, were much appreciated here.

A definitive impress on English horn-playing was made by the famous brothers Petrides, who played at the Italian Opera in London from 1802 until their retirement in 1825 or 1826. The Petrides were succeeded by the Leander brothers, presumably Bohemians as well, but these latter players appear to have been less active as teachers. By adopting the French instrument of the Raoux model which Puzzi had made popular here, the Petrides appear to have been the first to establish the tone quality for which the best British players have since been noted: a marriage, in effect, between the breadth of the Germanic tone and the clarity of the French.[1] It is to be regretted that the adoption of the wide-bore German double horn in recent years has brought about the decline of this distinctive and beautiful quality.

The decline of the Austro-Bohemian school: musical and political causes

The fact that the hand-horn had reached its full technical and musical fruition by the opening decades of the nineteenth century was not the sole cause of the Austrian school's demise. Artistic horn-playing, it will be

---

[1] This adoption of the French instrument by German players in this country was to recur in the nineteenth century as well. When Franz Paersch and Friedrich Borsdorf arrived here in 1882 and 1879 respectively, each changed to a Raoux horn. They and their descendants, both genetic and musical, have greatly influenced horn-playing in England down to the present day. The Paersch line continued through his son Otto until his retirement in 1953. Of the two, Borsdorf was to leave the deeper impress; for his style was carried forward not only through his sons, but by a wide circle of distinguished pupils. Amongst the latter were Alfred and Aubrey Brain, in whose son Dennis the style found its greatest exponent. Aubrey Brain trained many fine players, of whom Alan Civil and Neill Saunders are well known today. Borsdorf's son Francis, who changed his name to Bradley, is still active as a player and teacher.

remembered, had its first flowering in a climate of patronage and prosperity. Later in the eighteenth century, when political events conspired to undermine the stability and affluence upon which that patronage depended, it was withdrawn, leaving the creative arts to decline or to continue as best they could on their own momentum. Instrumental music in general was fortunate in having by this time won enough popular support to carry it over the crucial period: but for horn-playing this default in personal benefaction was to bring about the end of a chapter in its history.

Just as the Jesuits, Benedictines, and Cistercians had given the art of music a particular impetus after the Counter-Reformation, so music languished when the Church began to be harassed under Maria Theresia and Joseph II. If Bohemia was the 'conservatory of Europe', then the colleges, seminaries, and monasteries of the great religious orders were its teaching-rooms. It has been shown how the leading horn-players during the first century of the valveless horn's ascent received their training almost without exception in the religious houses. During the third quarter of the century, however, a reversal set in. As early as 1765 Joseph II as Archduke had embarked on his relentless policy of reducing the Church; and with the Empress Maria Theresia's sanction began to close the monastic and religious institutions, and to confiscate their lands and properties. With his accession to the Imperial throne in 1780 this despoliation was intensified. In 1782 came the final blow: the contemplative monasteries were abolished and their inmates driven out of the country. Joseph had removed the greatest enemy to his programme of paternal despotism; but he had also deprived the arts of a vital lifeline, both intellectual and material.

A few of the monastery schools tried to keep going, but the effect of the dissolution was devastating. The teachers had gone or were leaving; and so the pupils were left to their own resources, or to seek their tutelage from the musical laity. Even the reduction of the court orchestras, enforced by the heavy taxes levied on the nobility to finance the wars of the period, could not have had such an effect upon the musical arts as the banishment of the teaching orders. Indeed, so depressed was the general situation in Bohemia that Burney remarked, '. . . these children learn so ill in these schools as to be ever afterwards incorrigible . . . these people seldom have any ambition to excel in music, as they have no opportunities of mending their condition by it.'[1] In the Prague section of the *Jahrbuch der Tonkunst von Wien und Prag* for 1796 we read further signs of the times:

Since the dissolution of the old church music Bohemia and her capital appear to have fewer lovers and patrons of music than formerly. In the country music-schools the salaries of the rectors and head-masters have been reduced,

---

[1] Burney, *Present State*, ii, p. 23.

and the majority of the monasteries dissolved. This change is to be regarded as the direct cause for the decline of the art of music in a country where it once so greatly flourished.

Thus it is not surprising that the last great Bohemian horn-players belonged to that generation which had completed its schooling before the final dissolution of the monasteries.

Added to this loss of ecclesiastical patronage was the growing danger of war. Few nobles could now afford to keep their house orchestras: as Napoleon's threat to the Holy Roman Empire grew, the economic situation worsened, and music as a whole suffered proportionately. According to the author of the article on 'Herrschaftliche Hauskapellen und Harmonien' in the Viennese section of the *Jahrbuch* mentioned above, music in the Imperial capital was nearly extinct:

In former days it was very much the custom for our great princely houses to maintain their own orchestras, in which the greatest geniuses often received their training (an example of this is our great Haydn). To the detriment of the art this admirable custom has been lost, whether due to a chilling of the love for music, or a lack of taste, or domesticity, or from other causes; in short, one orchestra after the other broke up, so that apart from that of Prince Schwarzenberg virtually none exist now.

'Instrumental music is virtually half extinguished', the Viennese writer remarks in his section on church music; and states that although each parish church has an orchestra, it is only heard on feast days. One wonders what he might say to the present musical situation, where an orchestral mass is to be heard only in the Augustinerkirche or the Hofkapelle with any regularity, and only rarely in the Cathedral!

As the eighteenth century drew to a close many of the great names of horn-playing appeared in the necrologies. Palsa had died in 1792, Thürrschmidt in 1797; Punto's death in 1803 marked for many the end of an era, just as did Dennis Brain's in 1957; and in 1804, the year when Franz II assumed the title of Austrian Emperor as a counter-move to Napoleon's threats, Joseph Matiegka, the last major horn teacher of the eighteenth century, died at Prague.

Franz's assumption of the new Austrian crown was in principle a renunciation of the title of Holy Roman Emperor. He confirmed this in fact when in 1806 he formally laid down the crown of the Holy Roman Empire, which the Habsburgs had worn since 1283. Most of the remaining orchestras in the smaller courts were now entirely dismissed, and the age of intense musical and artistic cultivation in smaller centres was ended. The concert-rooms, theatres, and cloisters which had been the vibrant backdrop to one of the most musical of all eras now stood silent, the musicians who had filled them searching for work. It was now for centralization and state subvention to prop up the vast musical edifice which noble and churchly patronage had built. The eighteenth century was over.

The ensuing period of readjustment was for the hand-horn a time of the final working-out described above. It is not without significance that the first experiments on the valve date from these years, however, and that they appear to have first been applied to the horn. It is the author's conjecture that these innovations represent an effort on the part of the instrument-makers to recover the trade which formerly had come from the courts by appealing to the newly established national armies with brass instruments which the average bandsman could play.

At Vienna and Prague the Hoftheater and Nationaltheater retained their full orchestral forces during the time of economic crisis, and soon other theatres began to reopen. In 1810 the Prague Tonkünstler-Gesellschaft set up the Prague Conservatory, which soon boasted a flourishing horn class under Paul Schebka, Matiegka's former second. Two years later the Gesellschaft der Musikfreunde at Vienna opened its Conservatory with one of the last great hand-horn teachers, Michael Herbst, on its staff. Schebka died in 1826, Herbst in 1833; and with the passing of these last major hand-horn teachers, the curtain of our narrative falls after a century and a half on what was clearly one of the most vigorous and fertile playing traditions known to any instrument.

VIII

REGISTER OF PLAYERS

Part Two

Third and Fourth Generations
1750–1830

Generation III: Working period c. 1750–1800

GLÖCKNER, *Franz Joseph*, 1734–c. 1800, was a pupil of the brothers Czermak (q.v.) at Dresden and in the course of his career carried the Austrian
style of playing to Poland. The account of his life given by Dlabacž (ii, 469)
is an interesting record of the opportunities which lay open at this period to
musicians of humble origin.

Glöckner, Franz Joseph, born in 1734 at Grünwald in Bohemia. . . . His father
sent him to study with the brothers Czermak, fellow countrymen who were
horn-players at the Dresden Court. When a finished player he was engaged by a
count or prelate in the German Empire, if not the Elector of Cologne.[1] After
Czermak's death Glöckner was called to the Saxon Court as principal horn;
and as the King was often in Poland, Glöckner made an advantageous and
happy marriage in Warsaw, where he owned a fine palace in 1794.[2]

SIEBER, *Johann Georg*, 1734–1815, 'professor and editor of music, was born
in Franconia. In 1765 he was received in the orchestra of the royal academy
of music as first horn. He was celebrated for his editions of the classical
instrumental works of all Europe.'[3] Sieber shares with Nikolaus Simrock
(q.v.) the distinction of having founded a successful publishing house after
first making his name as a horn-player. Of his actual playing little has been
written. He came to Paris about 1755, with that influx of Bohemians and
Germans who established orchestral horn-playing there in mid-century.

SCHEBKA (*Schepka*), *Paul*, 1737–post 1823, was a leading second-horn
virtuoso during the latter half of the century in Prague. For many years he

---

[1] It was. See *Musikalische Korrespondenz* (Speier), 12 April 1770.
[2] See also von Riegger, op. cit., xii, 231–2.
[3] *Dictionary of Musicians* (London, 1824), p. 435.

and Matiegka (q.v.) played in the opera orchestra there, as well as in the foremost church ensembles and private bands of the nobility. In 1810 Schebka was appointed professor of horn by the newly founded Verein der Beförderung der Tonkunst, which in 1819 became the Prague Conservatory. He held this appointment until he was succeeded by Joseph Kail (q.v.) in 1823. The *Jahrbuch der Tonkunst* (p. 131) reports that amongst the most prominent artists in Prague in 1796, 'Schepka displays great artistry and perfection on the horn.' Meusel[1] praises him as a 'Virtuose auf dem Waldhorn zu Prag'. This was in 1808, when Schepka was 71—a ripe age indeed for a horn-player. A detailed account of Schebka's many honours is given by Dlabacž.[2] (See also *Satzungen der Verein zur Beförderung der Tonkunst in Prag*, Prague, 1810; and J. Branberger, *Das Konservatorium für Musik in Prag*, Prague, 1911.)

FRANZ, *Carl*, 1738–1802, was an early exponent of hand-technique whose virtuosity influenced both Haydn and Franz Danzi. Though primarily a second horn, he was one of the first players to cover both registers with equal facility; and thus may be considered to be a forerunner of the horn technique of our own day. He was born in Silesia, in Langen-Bielau, near the Bohemian border. From his ninth year until the age of 18, he was a pupil of his uncle, a horn-player in the service of Count Zerotin at Falkenberg (Silesia). He then appears to have gone to Prague for two years, presumably to complete his studies with Joseph Matiegka, the leading teacher of the day. At the age of 20 he entered the service of the Prince Bishop von Eck at the Jesuit monastery of Olmütz (Bohemia). Here, says Dlabacž,[3] 'he brought his playing to such perfection that he knew few equals in producing pure semitones with his hand, in sheer facility, or in his command of both high and low registers (his range embraced five C's [!]).' In 1763 he went to Vienna, where he was engaged by Prince Nicolaus von Esterhazy as second horn to Thaddäus Steinmüller. His salary commenced on 9 April of that year, and was somewhat higher than that of his colleagues, as it amounted to 300 Gulden, free lodgings, and 'Naturalien'—an allowance of beer, wine, grain, and firewood. At Eisenstadt Franz immediately applied himself to learning the baryton, a five-stringed bowed instrument upon which the Prince himself was an able performer. Within a short time Franz had achieved a reputation as a baryton virtuoso comparable to that which he enjoyed as a horn-player. The numerous baryton duos which Haydn wrote between 1765 and 1775 were composed for Nicolaus and the Silesian prodigy. During Franz's fourteen years with the Esterhazy orchestra Haydn wrote a number of second-horn parts for Franz which attest to his exceptional virtuosity in the low register (see Ex. 22). The well-known concerto for second horn (1767)

---

[1] *Künstler-Lexicon*, ii, 265.   [2] Op. cit., iii, 35.   [3] i, 424.

shows an ability to leap from one register to the other which would be a credit to any player today.

In 1777 Franz left the Esterhazy orchestra to take up an appointment in the service of Prince Cardinal Batthyany at Pressburg. He appears in Forkel's list for the year 1783 together with Ignaz Boeck (q.v.). In 1784 the Emperor Joseph II, in pursuing his policy of impoverishing the Church, forced the Cardinal to dissolve his orchestra. Franz spent the following two years as a free-lance virtuoso in Vienna, where, as Pohl[1] says, 'within two years [he] had appeared as the soloist in twelve concerts with great applause.'

In the spring of 1786 the Silesian virtuoso set out on a tour of Germany, which was so successful that in 1787 he was engaged as *Cammermusicus* at the Munich Court under Franz Danzi. The lovely second movement of the Sonata Concertante for horn and pianoforte which Danzi composed in 1802, the year of Franz's death, is a fitting last memorial to his fine cantabile style (see accompanying record). (See Meusel, op. cit., i, 251; A. Hoffmann, *Die Tonkünstler Schlesiens*, Breslau, 1830; Forkel, Almanach, 1783, p. 10; Carse, op. cit., p. 67; and A. Hoboken, *Joseph Haydn*, Mainz, 1957, p. 587.)

BÄR or Beer, Bernard, c. 1740–90. Brother of the famous clarinet virtuoso, and, according to Dlabacž,[2] a 'sound horn-player'.

RAAB, Bernard, was a tutti horn-player at Wallerstein. In 1763 he left the service of Count Kraft Ernst, who in a letter of 16 March stated that 'We have been completely satisfied with him, and gladly would have kept him in our service.'

KOHL and *KRAUS* were regular members of the Imperial Court opera orchestra at Vienna from 1763 until Kraus's death in 1779. Kraus is listed alone in the *Staats- und Stands-calendar* until 1781, when he evidently left to seek his fortune at Paris. Gerber[3] mentions that Kohl published six quartets there for horn, violin, viola, and cello in 1784, but does not give the publisher.

KNECHTEL, two brothers, were horn-players in the Strahow monastery orchestra at Prague until 1764, when Dlabacž[4] says they left on a concert tour. Nothing more was heard of them. One appears to have played the trumpet as well.

MOLLER and *KELLNER, Edward*, were 'consigned to the tuition of PONTO, the famous horn-blower', according to the *Quarterly Musical Magazine* for 1818. This was in 1774, when George III assembled about him a private band of picked musicians. Though they were obviously German-speaking, these two horn-players share the distinction of being Punto's only pupils in England of whom record remains.

[1] Op. cit., i, 267.   [2] *Lexicon*, I, p. 66.   [3] *Lexicon*, 1790, i, p. 746.   [4] ii, 76.

STAMITZ, or Staimetz, Franz, may well be identical with the Parisian horn-player of that name (see p. 118). Stamitz appears in the Imperial Court archives at Vienna[1] as having played in the orchestra for various Court balls from 1773 to 1775. His fee on these occasions was four gulden.

HAENSEL, Franz, was a second horn in the Viennese Court orchestra in the 1770s; and played as Stamitz's second at various Court balls.[2]

RUDOLPH, or Rudolff, Johann Anton, 1742–c. 1810, principal horn with the Thurn und Taxis orchestra at Regensburg from about 1780 onwards, was born at Bürschau in Bohemia in 1742, and not, as Morley-Pegge[3] states, at Vienna in 1770. He is frequently confused with the French virtuoso Jean-Joseph Rodolphe (see p. 124). To judge from the first-horn parts of the symphonies which Schacht and Pokorny wrote during Rudolph's tenure of the first-horn desk, he had an exceptional command of the high register, and great flexibility. Nor was this remarkable agility his only strength, for Dlabacž[4] calls him 'a horn-player whose great fame is owing to his sweet tone and delightful style'. The horn parts of a Pokorny symphony in the Thurn und Taxis archives bear the autographs of the four players: Rudolf, Fritsche, Stumm, and Weiss: a practice still common amongst horn-players today, and often a means of keeping track of one's colleagues.

KÖRBER, Ignaz, was a product of the Bohemian tradition of horn-playing at Mainz, where he was born in 1744.[5] In the eighties he went to Paris, where his virtuosity was said to rival even that of Punto. In 1785 he accepted a post as chamber-musician to the Court at Gotha; and there set up a music shop. He composed many concerti and solo pieces for the horn. Schubart[6] said that 'His compositions are not disciplined, but are written in the spirit of the instrument'. None of his works are known to survive.

WIESBACH, Franz, Punto's fellow pupil under Matiegka at Prague, and Hampl and Haudek at Dresden, was a leading virtuoso of his day, although he seems less well known to posterity. Like Punto, he was a bondsman of Count Johann Thun, who sent him first to Mannheim to study with Schindelarž, and thence to Dresden, where he perfected his high register under Haudek. Together with Punto he returned to his lord at Prague; and being evidently of a less ambitious temperament than Punto, was content to serve as principal horn in Thun's house orchestra for fifteen years until the increasing sharpness of his teeth continually caused them to bite into his lips, when he had to lay down the horn for good.

---

[1] I HMK Varia.   [2] I HMK Varia, 1773–5.   [3] *French Horn,* p. 154.
[4] *Lexicon,* ii, 603.   [5] Bernsdorf, *Lexicon,* ii, 641.
[6] *Ideen zu einer Ästhetik der Tonkunst* (Stuttgart, 1785/1825), p. 239.

Dlabacž, who heard Wiesbach play on countless occasions, remarked that he had a natural embouchure; and his observations on Wiesbach's tone and technique are worth quoting from the *Lexicon*:[1]

Speed of execution and security in the high register were virtually part of this great artist. His tone was pure and flowing like that of a flute, and he carried the most difficult passages with admirable ease, never altering his facial expression in the slightest.

Unfortunately no music known to have been written for Weisbach has survived.

STICH, Johann Wenzel, known to posterity by his assumed name, Giovanni Punto, is discussed fully in Chapter VII, pp. 168 ff. A complete record of his life and deeds will be found there; but for good measure it is worth quoting here a little-known anecdote concerning Punto's second English tour from Michael Kelly's *Reminiscences of the King's Theatre and Theatre Royal Drury Lane*.[2] Turning to Kelly's recollections of 1787, we read that Punto had been engaged for Madame Mara's concerts at the Pantheon for that season, and played concertos to enliven the oratorios at Drury Lane, also under the management of Madame Mara.

I went one oratorio night into the green room to speak to Mrs. Crouch (writes the intrepid Kelly), but the only persons in the room were Madame Mara and Monsieur Ponte, first horn player to the King of Prussia, and a very fine performer; he was an intimate friend of Madame Mara, and engaged to play a concerto at the oratorio that night. He said to Madame Mara in German, 'My dear friend, my lips are so parched with fear, that I am sure I shall not make a sound in the instrument; I would give the world for a little water or beer to moisten my lips.'
Madame Mara replied in German, 'There is nobody here to send; and yet if I knew where to get something for you to drink, I would go myself.'
During their dialogue, I was standing at the fireside; and addressing Madame Mara in German, I said, 'Madame, I should be sorry for you to have that trouble, and I sit lazy by; I will, with great pleasure, go and get Monsieur Ponte some Porter.' I instantly dispatched a messenger for a foaming pot; and as soon as it arrived, I presented it to the thirsty musician, in the nick of time, for he was called on to play his concerto just at this moment. Madame Mara desired me to accept her best acknowledgements, and invited me to call at her house in Pall Mall the next day, at two o'clock.

It is a revealing commentary on human nature that the greatest horn-player of the time should also be vulnerable to an attack of nerves.

[1] ii, p. 209.　　[2] London, 1826, i, pp. 318 ff.

LEUTGEB, Ignaz (also spelt Leitgeb from the Salzburg and Viennese manner of pronouncing it), is of all the great eighteenth-century Austrian and Bohemian horn-players the best known to the modern public. His fame comes down chiefly through the agency of record-sleeve musicologists, who use the pranks which Mozart constantly played on his horn-playing friend to make of him a clownish dolt. Certainly the jocular exhortations with which Mozart interlarded the horn part of the Concerto, K.412, and the trick of writing the solo part of K.417 in alternating red, green, blue, and black ink, are enough to give rise to this notion, as are the innumerable practical jokes played on poor Leutgeb which Mozart's letters record. But next to nothing is known of Leutgeb's career and accomplishments, apart from the *Mercure de France* reviews and the chronicle of his extraordinary gifts as a horn-player which Mozart's solo pieces for him comprise.[1] While the writer does not disagree with Morley-Pegge's supposition that Leutgeb was one of 'Nature's gentlemen', it seems nevertheless obvious that anyone who could charm a Concert Spirituel audience with a concerto of his own composition as well as with his consummate mastery of the horn was no fool.

HÖRMANN, Johannes (also Herrmann, Hermann, Hörrmann), 1748–1816, was one of the most prominent orchestral hand-horn-players of the later Classical period in Vienna. He most probably took part in the first performance of Beethoven's *Fidelio* in the Theater an der Wien in 1806.[2] He was second horn in the Vienna Hofcapelle from 1796, first with Martin Rupp until he was pensioned in 1806 (see below); and then with Willibald Lotter from 1808 until Hörmann's death in 1816.

A letter to the Emperor in Salieri's hand dated 10 April 1796 states that the Imperial Capellmeister regarded Hörmann as the best horn-player he had heard in Vienna. This letter followed on Hörmann's application for the post of second horn in the Court orchestra. An audition was duly held; and the votes of the principal players who formed the audition committee, preserved in the State Archives,[3] show that they shared Salieri's opinion—all except Rupp, the principal horn. He avoided offending his colleagues Hradetzky and Eisen, who also auditioned for the job, by declaring himself content with whatever decision Salieri might reach. The names themselves are of considerable interest:

Meiner Meinung ist für Herman. Drobney.
Meiner Meinung ist für Herrmann. Georg Triebensee.
Ich bin Zufridn was mir die allerhögste Stelle gibt. Rupp.
Her Mann. Wendt.
Ich Gurvenka in der Meinung für den Hermann.
Meine Meinung ist für Hermann. Stadler.

[1] These sources are examined in detail in Chapter VII, pp. 163 ff.
[2] See Chapter VII, p. 186.   [3] 3 HMK Akten 1796–99.

Thus Hörmann was notified on 25 June 1796 of his appointment as 'K.K. Kammerwaldhornist' by the Obersthofmeister: 'His Majesty has awarded the post of horn-player in the Chamber Ensemble made vacant by the death of Jacob Eisen, to Johann Hörmann, who has qualified with distinction over the other competitors.'

RUPP, *Martin*, 1748–1819, was first horn in the Vienna Hofcapelle from 1782 until his retirement in 1806.[1] He served in the Esterhazy orchestra at Eisenstadt while on leave in 1783,[2] and to all evidence took part in the first performance of *Fidelio* in 1806. He was granted a patent of nobility in 1795, and died in 1819.

BRADACŽ, *c.* 1750–182(?), was according to Dlabacž[3] one of Matiegka's best pupils. He was a Bohemian; and after his studies went to Vienna, where he was engaged as principal horn to Prince Schwarzenberg's orchestra in 1800.

KUCŽERA, *Jacob*, 1749–1813, was born in Bohemia, but went to Salzburg early in life to take up the post of second horn in the Archbishop's orchestra, presumably replacing Leutgeb about 1770. Pillwein[4] calls him 'an outstanding second-horn-player'. Kučzera died at the age of 64 of a kidney ailment. Would that this much were known about the life of his predecessor.

WINTER, *c.* 1750–*post* 1798, was a Bohemian trumpeter-horn-player in the service of Count Buquois at Prague during the second half of the century.[5]

SPANDAU or *Spandauer*, principal horn in the Electoral orchestra at the Hague, who appears to have first introduced hand-stopping to London audiences, is discussed in Chapter VII, pp. 167 ff.

BERNARDON, a Bohemian, carried the Baroque tradition of doubling on the clarino trumpet and first horn forward into the second half of the century. He was principal clarinist-horn-player to Count Morizin at Prague until his death about 1800.[6]

CŽERWENKA, father and son, were members of the royal orchestra at Berlin about 1790, evidently as the second pair to Le Brun and Thürrschmidt.[7]

NAGEL, *Josef*, *c.* 1750–1802, was engaged at Wallerstein in about 1780 as principal horn, together with Franz Zwierzina (see below) as second. A fine

---

[1] HMK Varia.   [2] Carse, p. 67.   [3] i, p. 197.
[4] *Lexicon Salzburger Künstler*, 1798, p. 74.   [5] Dlabacž, iii, p. 383.
[6] Dlabacž, i, p. 143.   [7] Dlabacž, i, p. 311.

high-horn player, he was a fitting replacement for Johann Nisle; and many of Rosetti's double horn concertos which bear the inscription 'Fait pour Messrs. Nagel et Zwierzina' attest to his great skill in the upper register. On 2 February 1780 the two Bohemians wrote to Prince Kraft Ernst's agent that 'we are completely satisfied and never again wish to ask for more'.[1] Nagel died on 16 June 1802, leaving a widow, five children, and the usual debts which appear to have plagued court musicians. Dlabacž[2] and von Riegger[3] both mention him with some praise. (See also Schiedermaier, 'Die Blütezeit der Oettingen-Wallersteinischen Hofkapelle', in *SIMG*, ix, 1, Leipzig, 1902.)

MACKOWECŽKY, c. 1750–*post* 1806, a Bohemian by birth, was a pupil of Punto at Paris, later attracting some notice as a travelling virtuoso. In 1783 he turned up for a time as second horn in the Esterhazy band,[4] and in 1786 went on to Berlin, where he secured an appointment at the Prussian Court. Breitkopf published several of his compositions from 1802 to 1806, including a Duo for horn and viola. (See Dlabacž, ii, p. 249; Gerber, 1792, p. 851; von Riegger, xii, p. 256; Gassner, p. 577; and the *Dictionary of Musicians*, 1824, p. 100.)

REICHEL, Joseph, helped to spread the Bohemian style to Italy in the hand-horn period. Born at Soborten, he studied theology at Prague. He was then in 1788 appointed principal horn, at the age of 38, to the Imperial ambassador's band at Genoa, where he passed the rest of his life. He died about 1820. (See Dlabacž, ii, p. 549.)

REICHELT, Samuel, 1754–*post* 1796, went to Kallais in Poland with nineteen other Bohemian musicians from the Augustine monastery at Leipa in 1770. He became principal horn and leader of the orchestra at the Church of St. Augustine there, where he apparently remained until his death. (Dlabacž, ii, p. 549.)

STEINMÜLLER, Johann, Joseph and *Wenzel*, were the virtuoso sons of old Thaddäus Steinmüller, the principal horn at Esterhazy under Haydn. They were born at Eisenstadt from about 1750 onwards, although a search through the house archives there produced no exact birth-dates for them. Joseph, the middle brother, bore Haydn's Christian name; and the composer and his wife were godparents to all three. The Steinmüllers were much appreciated as duettists and triple-concerto soloists at Hamburg and the principal German towns in the nineties. (See Pohl, i, p. 266; Gerber, 1792, ii, p. 572; Gerber, 1813, iv, p. 265; Dlabacž, iii, p. 205; and Gassner, p. 800.)

[1] Arch. Wall.   [2] ii, p. 365.   [3] xii, p. 262.   [4] Carse, p. 67.

ZAHRADNICŽEK, Joseph Franz, born in Čzerbenitz and schooled at the Jesuit college in Dobržich, was by training a doubler on the horn and clarino. He was appointed third horn in the Vienna Court orchestra in 1787, a position he held until after 1820. (See Dlabacž, iii, p. 430; von Riegger, xii, p. 297; and the HMK Varia 1787.)

ZWIERZINA, Franz, 1750–1825, has already come to our attention as second horn in the Wallerstein orchestra under Anton Rosetti. The arrangements for the repair and purchase of instruments for the Court were entrusted to him; and his signature, together with some curiously-spelt commentaries in German, a language he never mastered, accompanies all these bills and receipts. To judge from the solo parts of Rosetti's double concertos and the second-horn parts of his symphonies, Zwierzina was a player of formidable attainments. His silhouette, clearly displaying the effects of the generous measure of beer which was part of his salary, can be seen in Plate VIII, together with that of his fellow Bohemian and desk-partner, Josef Nagel.

ANGERHOLTZER, Franz, appears as supernumerary third horn in the Vienna Hofcapelle in 1773–4. He was also a violinist.[1]

PATATSCHNY, obviously a Bohemian, was Angerholtzer's partner on fourth horn at Vienna in the 1770s.[2]

STADLMANN, Michael, was engaged as sixth horn in the Vienna Court orchestra in 1773.[3] The chief duty of these supernumerary horn-players was to play at Court balls.

SKRIŽUWANEK, Anton, was likewise an alternate third horn in the Vienna Hofcapelle from 1775 until 1799. He may be identical with the Syryyneck who played in Paris about 1750 (see p. 114).

KIRCHSTÄTTER was yet another Court-ball horn-player attached to the Hofcapelle from 1775 onwards.

WALTHER was remarked as a horn-player in the band of the Duke of Württemberg at Ludwigsburg by Burney in 1772–5: 'and Walther on the French Horn, with Jomelli to compose'.[4] Two Bohemian virtuosi were mentioned by the violinist-composer Wenzel Pichl as enjoying great popularity in Rome in about 1775. 'The Romans called them the Famous Bohemians,' says Dlabacž.[5]

THÜRRSCHMIDT, Carl, 1753–97, is discussed both as a player and mechanical innovator in Chapter VII, pp. 174 ff.

[1] 1 HMK Varia, 1753–99.   [2] 1 HMK Varia for 1773–4.   [3] 1 HMK Varia.
[4] *Present State,* i, p. 38.   [5] iii, p. 319.

PALSA, Johann, 1754–92, Thürrschmidt's principal and one of the leading duettists of the age, is dealt with in detail in Chapter VII, p. 176.

BOECK or Böck, Anton, 1754–*post* 1815; and *Ignaz*, 1758–*post* 1815, the famous Viennese duettists, are discussed in Chapter VII, pp. 177 ff.

No better impression of their playing could be had than that given in a review by the Berlin critic for *Cramer's Magazin*, whose remarks on a concert which the Boecks gave there in 1787 are reproduced here in translation.[1]

On the 20th of December the Brothers Boeck from Prince Batthyani's orchestra performed here. These virtuosi had conquered the difficulties which normally hinder this most expressive instrument to a very great degree. They played with true intonation, had an excellent tone, and produced by means of skilful muting with a Sordin which they inserted into the bell, an echo which was most deceptive and surprising in its effect, making those who had gossiped during their first concerto stop talking suddenly and pay attention. When the theme was repeated it made the sound so soft that one believed it to be coming from a distance of several hundred paces.[2]

Apart from this they played several charming little pieces, French chansonettes arranged for the horn; and several concertos of their own composition for which Rosetti had written the orchestral accompaniment. In the first of these was an Adagio of great beauty which they played in a most song-like manner, with double-notes and chords in certain places. Their range of notes, which they commanded with great precision, was very wide. They deserve to be numbered among the few artists who play this seldom well-played instrument to perfection. From here they will return to Vienna, and then travel to London.

But to all evidence their plans to visit London never materialized.

SIMROCK, Nicolaus, 1755–18(??), horn-player and publisher, was principal horn from 1773 in the Court band at Cologne, and from about 1778 at Bonn, where Beethoven met him when a viola-player in the orchestra. The conquest of the Rhineland by Napoleon in 1790 forced the Electoral Court at Bonn to disband; and it was in that year that Simrock laid aside the horn to found the prominent music publishing house which still bears his name.

It has often been wrongly assumed that Beethoven learnt his horn-writing from Punto. In point of fact the composer's first meeting with the great Bohemian horn-player was in 1799, on the occasion of Punto's first visit to Vienna. Beethoven's knowledge of the horn was founded on points he picked up from Simrock in the Bonn days; and it is no coincidence that all the chamber pieces which feature prominent horn parts, e.g. the Rondino for eight winds, the Piano Quintet, and the Sextet for two horns and strings, are

[1] p. 1400.   [2] See accompanying record.

early works. When in 1810 Beethoven finally sent in the finished version of the Sextet to Simrock for publishing, he remarked, 'the pupil has given his master many a hard nut to crack'.[1] (See also Meusel, *Künstlerlexicon*, Lemgo, 1808, ii, p. 359; and Gassner, op. cit., p. 781.)

GEHRING, Johann Michael, 1755–1833, horn-player, singer, and pupil in composition under Abbé Vogler, had a career which to the twentieth-century reader seems remarkable, but which was fairly typical of gifted musicians of the eighteenth. Meusel's account of Gehring's life is worth quoting here.[2]

His father sent him to Ebrach Monastery (Rhein Palatinate) in 1765 to study singing, reading, and writing; but singing and playing the violin interested him the most. After four years he went to study at Würzburg, where his fine voice won for him the friendship of the Abbe Vogler, who taught him music theory. With this the desire to study now left him. He then went back to his old father, a gamekeeper, to lend him a hand and to learn hunting. He thought that the ability to play the horn would be a useful adjunct; began to practise diligently without a teacher; and in fourteen days produced a hunting-piece. His father died; but Gehring, on account of his extreme youth, did not succeed to his post. He went to seek his fortune at Dresden, where Baron von Bender took him into his service and sent Gehring to study music with Hummel. During the War of the Bavarian Succession the Baron removed to Vienna, taking Gehring with him. There his dexterity on the horn soon became so well known, that the Archduke Maximilian sent for him one day and desired him to play several horn concertos at sight. From that hour onward he was attached to the court music, and was soon appointed horn-player in the Italian Opera orchestra. In 1780 Prince Graschalkowitsch established an orchestra and made Gehring a member. In 1785 he undertook a two-year tour through Germany and Switzerland and was greatly admired wherever he played.

Here we have yet another proof of the close connection between horn-playing and the hunt. (See also Gerber, 1813; and Choron, *Dictionnaire*, Paris, 1811, i, p. 264.)

EISEN, Jacob, 1756–96, was Hörmann's predecessor as second horn in the Vienna Hofcapelle, a post which he held from 1787 until his death in 1796 at the age of 40. Lichtenstern[3] remarks that 'Rup and Eisen are outstanding masters on the horn'. (See also von Köchel, *Die Kaiserliche Hofkapelle in Wien*, Vienna, 1869, pp. 91 and 95.)

HRDLIČZKA, four brothers, left their native Bohemia in 1779 for St. Petersburg, where they enjoyed both a comfortable livelihood and an

---

[1] Thayer, *Life of Beethoven* (London, 1921), i, p. 24.   [2] *Künstlerlexicon*, i, p. 281.
[3] *Beschreibung des Erzherzogthums Oestreich unter der Ens* (Vienna, 1791), p. 93.

excellent reputation in the private band of Prince Potemkin. (See Dlabacž, i, p. 669.)

HUBAČEK was a famous Bohemian horn-player at Vienna who, upon hearing the young Carl Dittersdorf, introduced him to the Prince of Sachsen-Hildburghausen. (See *Die Musik in Geschichte und Gegenwart*, iii, p. 587.)

LANG, Franz, was second horn in the Mannheim orchestra from 1763 until well after the cream of the band had removed to Munich with the rest of the Court in 1778. Mozart befriended him on his visit to Mannheim in 1778; and he appears in Forkel's list of the band for 1782. He and his brother Martin, born in 1755 and some two years younger, lived in the 'Branger' Strasse. (See Fried. Walter, *Geschichte der Musik und des Theaters am Kurpfälzischen Hofe*, Leipzig, 1898, pp. 225–6 and 369.)

ECK, Georg, was third in the Mannheim theatre orchestra in 1782. (Carse, op. cit., p. 58.)

SCHÖN was a chamber-musician to the King of France who in 1782 took up a post as first horn to the Prince of Hesse-Darmstadt. He was regarded as a great virtuoso, and composed some operas. (See Meusel, op. cit., ii, Pl. 306; and Gerber (1792), iv, pp. 283 and 443.)

DIMMLER, Franz Anton, 1756–1815, played fourth horn in the Mannheim ensemble in the 1780s, having been engaged in 1767. He composed some music for strings and horn.[1] (See also Forkel's *Almanach* for 1782, p. 126; and Walter, op. cit., p. 369.)

One *WENZEL*, probably a Christian name, was second in Berlin in 1782. (See Forkel; and Carse, op. cit., p. 54.)

ŽELENKA deputized for Carl Thürrschmidt at Berlin from 1793 until 1819, when he returned to his native Prague to take on a post in the orchestra of the recently formed Conservatory. A Joseph Želenka is mentioned in Redl's *Addressenbuch* for 1823 (p. 97) as living at No. 55, Kaiserstrasse: a significant address, as the *Erste Produktivgenossenschaft* set up there in 1901 to build their famous Vienna horns; but the two Želenkas may not be identical, as the name is common enough in those parts. (See Dlabacž, iii, pp. 437–8; and J. Branberger, *Das Conservatorium für Musik in Prag*, Prague, 1911, pp. 273 ff.)

JESSER in 1784 possessed a fine restaurant called the 'Vorgebirge zur guten Hoffnung' at Prague, where he charmed his guests by the beauty of his horn tone and his formidable technique. (Dlabacž, ii, p. 23.)

---

[1] Listed in *DTB* XVI, p. xiv.

HANISCH was a prominent horn-player in Prague, but left in 1784 to seek his fortune in Germany. (Dlabacž, i, 558.)

HERR, Johann Georg, a native of Gotha, was a pupil of Körber (see above) at Paris in the early seventies. In 1784 he scored a brilliant success at Hamburg; and was thereafter much appreciated as a soloist both in Germany and in France. (Choron, i, p. 328.)

HORŽEGGSSI, who in 1786 was principal horn in Count Kinsky's regimental band at Prague, attracted notice by his performances with the leading church and theatre orchestras as well. (Dlabacž, i, p. 668.) Whether he was the Horžizky whom Marpurg mentions as first horn at Berlin in 1754 (*Beyträge*) is not certain; but see Carse, p. 52.

HAMMER, Ignaz, and his two sons, Johann and Joseph (see below), served together in the Emperor of Russia's private band at St. Petersburg from about 1788 until 1791, when the father retired and went back to his native Bohemian town of Niederlichtwald, where Dlabacž tells us he owned a 'first-rate inn'.[1] The two sons, both pupils of Punto, remained in Russia, where they were applauded as duettists. (See also von Riegger, xii, p. 236; and J. Schaller, *Topographie des Königreich Böhmens*, Prague, 1785, iv, p. 244.)

BAUER, father and son, were both doublers on the horn and clarino as late as 1788, when Dlabacž[2] finds the one at Würzburg, the other at Richstadt.

KHÜNEL, Johann, combined his offices as a lay brother and chaplain at Böhmisch Kamnitz with playing the horn. (von Riegger, xii, p. 245.)

KUNTE, after many years of service in the band of Count Buquois at Prague, retired to the country to become a schoolmaster and edit his many concertos for the horn. (Dlabacž, ii, p. 158.)

BACHMANN, Reinert's second at Sondershausen, impressed Gerber with his facility in using the right hand as early as 1750. (See Appendix, section III.)

DOMNICH, Heinrich, son of the Hungarian-born horn-player Friederich Domnich, was born at Würzburg, according to both Gassner[3] and Gerber[4] in 1760. He was the second and most famous of three brothers: Jacob, born in 1758, who in about 1790 emigrated to Philadelphia in the American colony of Pennsylvania and appears to have taught and played extensively there; and Arnold, 1764–1827, principal horn at the Sachsen-Meiningen Court.

---

[1] i, p. 553.   [2] i, p. 97.   [3] p. 242.   [4] 1813, p. 915.

Heinrich, like his brothers, was taught the horn by his father, whose pride he was; and when only 12, according to Meusel,[1] delighted the Court by playing concertos with a fullness of tone which would have done credit to a grown man. At the age of 18 he entered the service of the Count von Elz at Mainz; but when this nobleman subjected him to the indignity of livery service, the young Heinrich betook himself in 1783 to Paris, where he found a friend and patron in Punto. He studied for two years with the great Bohemian; and in 1785 made his appearance in a December Concert Spirituel as second to Le Brun in a double concerto.[2] In 1787 Domnich joined the Opéra orchestra as Le Brun's second; and in 1795 was appointed professor at the Conservatoire, a position he held until 1817.

Domnich's importance rests on his abilities as a teacher rather than as a solo performer. His excellent *Methode de Premier et de Second Cor*, quoted at length in Chapter VII, was the first definitive tutor for the horn. Fétis mentions that Domnich wrote three horn concertos; two *sinfonie concertante* for two horns; and two collections of songs. None of these pieces survive, however. (See Morley-Pegge, p. 159; Gassner, p. 242; the anonymous *Dictionary of Musicians* (1824), p. 213; and E. von Siebold's article, 'Domnich' in *Der Fränkische Chronik*, Würzburg, 1807, p. 534.)

POKORNY, Beate, was evidently a daughter of the Regensburg Capellmeister Franz Xavier Pokorny (1728–94), although both Meusel[3] and Dlabacž[4] tell us that she was born in Bohemia. She was the first female hornplayer of any note, having distinguished herself in a concerto by Punto at a Concert Spirituel in 1780. (See also the *Dictionary of Musicians*, p. 299; and von Riegger, xii, p. 271.)

POLACK attracted favourable notice in 1796 in a concert which he gave at Prague after returning from a successful two-year stay at St. Petersburg. His strength, says Gerber,[5] lay 'especially in a pleasant, singing legato, and in a good piano'. Dlabacž[6] mentions his 'full-toned low register, and great facility'.

PRINSTER, Anton and *Michael*, joined the Esterhazy orchestra under Haydn in the early 1790s. Haydn's extraordinary Divertimento a tre of 1767 passed to the elder Prinster, who after the composer's death sent the autograph 'which our late blessed Haydn-Papa wrote for my predecessor [Thaddäus Steinmüller]', to the Precentor of the Cathedral at Raab, Silberknoll. (Pohl, iii, p. 105; and 285 ff.)

SCHWARZ left the service of Count Thun (the son of Punto's persecutor) at

---

[1] *Künstlerlexicon*, i, p. 198.   [2] *Mercure de France*, December 1785, p. 427.
[3] ii, p. 143.   [4] ii, p. 485.   [5] 1792, p. 167.   [6] ii, p. 488.

Prague to become principal horn to the Prince Bishop of Passau in 1790.[1] His second there was Wenzel Heller.

BEYERLEIN, principal horn at Rudolstadt in the eighties and nineties, was remarked by the *Musikalische Realzeitung* for 12 May 1790 to blow the horn 'very round and full-toned; and played a double concerto recently with his son a child of 6 years . . .' Of this gifted child no further information has come to light.

PORTMANN is mentioned by several contemporary writers as an important teacher of the horn and writer of a horn tutor; but where he worked has not emerged. Wagner (see below) was his pupil.

LOTTER, Willibald, or *Lother,* 1762–1844, was engaged as alternate first horn in the Vienna Hofcapelle on 1 January 1808. He no doubt replaced Martin von Rupp, who had died in 1806. We read[2] that 'Messrs. Lotter und Hörmann, both of the Court orchestra, play the horn with special distinction'.[3]

KUNISCH, Gottfried, 1764–*post* 1808, was in the latter year principal horn at the Brunswick Court, which had engaged horn-players in its opera band as early as 1710.[4] He was born in Silesia; and described by Meusel as 'an especially fine horn-player'.

HAUSER, a Swabian, distinguished himself as Polack's second when touring Italy in the 1790s. Gassner[5] praises his full low register and great facility. (See also Gerber, 1792, ii, p. 167.)

BAUMER, two brothers born in the sixties at Ansbach, were members of the King of Prussia's private band in the later years of the century. (Meusel, i, p. 47.)

FALTA, a Bohemian, took Simrock's place as principal horn when the Cologne orchestra was reorganized in 1793. (Dlabacž, i, 375.)

HELLER, Wenzel, typified in his education the scholarly bent which one finds in many of the Bohemian horn-players from Smeykal onwards. Falta, born in Kačžow, took his *Humaniora* at the Jesuit seminary in Budweis. He then read philosophy at the University in Prague, and at the same time

[1] Dlabacž, iii, p. 78.
[2] In the *Vaterländische Blätter für den Österreichischen Kaiserstaate* (1808), vii, p. 54.
[3] See also Köchel, p. 95.   [4] Meusel, i, p. 536.   [5] i, p. 606.

acquired a considerable technique on the horn. Lured by the gold rouble, he went for a time to St. Petersburg, which by this time must have brimmed with horn-players. In 1793 he returned to Prague; and in 1796 joined the orchestra of the Prince Bishop at Passau as second to Schwarz. (Dlabač, i, p. 607.)

BRANDEL was Simrock's second at Bonn in the seventies and eighties, having left his post at the Prague opera to enter the Elector's service. His wife remained behind in Prague, where Dlabač spoke to her in 1793.

KOLLER, according to Dlabač, was 'a famous horn-player at Prague in the 18th century'.[1]

VITHE, Franz, or possibly Witte, a Bohemian, was a prominent free-lance horn-player in Vienna, where Dlabač[2] heard his fine playing in 1795. (See also Gassner, p. 442.)

WAGNER, Carl, 1772–1829, 'a celebrated perf. on the horn, belonging to the chapel royal at Darmstadt in 1795, was also cons. a good vocal & instrl. composer. He was a pupil of Portmann, after whose death he publ. a new edition of his master's method for the horn'.[3] Neither Portmann's method nor Wagner's edition of it has as yet come to light.

HEROLD, Anton, a Silesian, was Vithe's second in a travelling band of Bohemian virtuosi which had great success at Vienna. This ensemble, which impressed Dlabač during his stay there in the summer of 1795, was made up of two clarinets, two horns and three(!) bassoons. (Dlabač, i, p. 616.)

HABOTEUS, Joseph, principal horn and chef to Count Kinsky at Prague, distinguished himself in a recital with the violinist Wranitzky there in 1797. The critic on the Prager Neue Zeitung[4] praised his fluent technique, remarking that he pleased 'especially in an Andante'. Haboteus was a great favourite in the drawing-rooms of the musical nobility and academics at Prague. (Dlabač, i, p. 538.)

SCHUBERT, Joseph, is listed by the Jahrbuch der Tonkunst as principal horn at the Marinelli Theatre in Vienna in 1796, together with his second, Joseph Hollreder. Was this the horn-playing uncle of Franz Schubert?

---

[1] ii, p. 103.   [2] iii, p. 301.
[3] Dictionary of Musicians (1824), p. 521. See also R. Profeta, Storia . . . degli Strumenti Musicale (Florence, 1942), p. 569.
[4] No. 3, 11 January 1797, Anhang, pp. 33–4.

LISSNER played both the horn and clarino in the orchestra of the National-theater at Prague. (Dlabacž, ii, p. 210; and *Jahrbuch der Tonkunst von Wien und Prag*, 1796, p. 151.)

MATUŠKA, Johann, c. 1725–*post* 1796, may well have gone to Mannheim with Schindelarž, for Marpurg[1] finds 'Johann Matuska aus Böhmen' playing fourth horn there as early as 1756. Matuška appears to have been lured away from the Mannheim band by the Duke of Württemberg, for Dlabacž[2] finds him at Stuttgart in 1796.

MATAUSCH, not to be confused with Matuška, was an alternate second horn at the Prague opera in 1796. (*Jahrbuch der Tonkunst*, p. 126; and Dlabacž, ii, p. 373.)

HABERZETTEL was at one point principal horn in the Emperor's band at St. Petersburg; but after 1798 his whereabouts were unknown, at least to Dlabacž (i, p. 537).

VANDENBROEK, Othon, was a Belgian pupil of Spandau, and a noted virtuoso. (See Chapter VII, p. 190; and the *Dictionary of Musicians*, p. 500.)

FRANK, a Bohemian, was Haberzettel's second at St. Petersburg; but like most second horns, stayed on while a succession of first-horn players came and went. (Dlabacž, i, p. 423.)

WALA, a 'highly accomplished' horn-player, was a house-virtuoso in the service of Count Pachta and later Count Sanal at Prague during the latter two decades of the century. (Dlabacž, iii, p. 319.)

MATIEGKA, Joseph, jun., 1767–93, son of the famous second-generation Prague horn-player of that name, was, according to Gassner, the equal of his father, and one of his best pupils. He was outlived by the elder Matiegka. (See Gassner, p. 593; and Dlabacž, iii, p. 276.)

ZALUŽAN, Wenzel, 1767–1832, studied the horn and clarino under Matiegka senior, and was a prominent performer on both instruments in the service of Count Pachta, at the Strahow monastery under Dlabacž, and at the Landesständisches Theater. In 1810 he was appointed as the first senior professor of the high horn at the newly founded Conservatory, a post which he still held as late as 1823. (See Dlabacž, iii, p. 430; and Ziegler's *Adressenbuch* for 1823, p. 202.)

[1] *Beyträge*, ii, p. 567.   [2] ii, p. 280.

MIKSCH, Georg?, 1767–1813, was Haudek's successor in the Dresden Court orchestra in 1796. The younger brother of the famous singing-teacher Johannes Miksch, he had arrived at Dresden from his native Bohemia in his brother's arms at the age of 5, and had received a thorough grounding in singing from that age. When after the auditions the Capellmeister, Schuster, recommended the young Miksch, the Elector asked his reasons for putting him forward. 'Miksch sings on the horn!' said Schuster. 'Then he gets the job,' Friedrich August replied. This anecdote is wrongly ascribed to Hampl's engagement at Dresden by Eichborn.[1] It stems from Heinrich Mannstein's *Denkwürdigkeiten der Churfürstlichen Hofmusik zu Dresden* (Leipzig, 1863), p. 6. See also pp. 7 and 45.

DORNAUS, three brothers, were important soloists who were active in the band of the Elector of Trier at Coblenz from the nineties onward. The eldest and most famous, Philipp, was born in 1769. At the age of 8 he amazed the Trier Court by performing Punto's concertos; and at 14 travelled in company with his younger brother, Ludwig, to Paris, where in 1783 they appeared together with Madame Mara at a Concert Spirituel. Ludwig played for a time at Bentheim, where his father and uncle had been members of the orchestra as early as 1766;[2] but the year 1790 found the three brothers at Coblenz, where their playing was much admired.

In 1800 Philipp set out on an extended tour of northern Germany which met with great success. The *Allgemeine Musikalische Zeitung*[3] praised the 'security, purity, and solidity' which the elder Dornaus's playing displayed at a Leipzig concert; and added that his 'accomplished performance [of a] really effective Echo gave much pleasure here'. Philipp's article, 'Über den zweckmässigen Gebrauch des Waldhorns', which appeared in the same paper,[4] contains much worthwhile information on hand-horn technique, and criticizes the direction which the German style of playing had already taken away from the sounder principles of the Austrian school. (See also Gerber, 1813, i, p. 924; and the *Dictionary of Musicians*, p. 214.)

STEINER and *TROBNER* both appear as free-lance horn-players in the *Wiener Auskunftsbuch* for 1803 (pp. 179, 180).

GUGEL, or *Gugl*, *Joseph*, c. 1770–18(??); and *Heinrich*, c. 1780–*post* 1839, enjoyed a reputation as Germany's finest duettists from 1796 until about 1816, when they went to St. Petersburg.[5] Their father, a poor assistant Capellmeister to the Duke of Württemberg, sent them as children to Vienna for a musical education, and then thrust them upon the world as child prodigies.

---

[1] *Die Dämpfung beim Horn* (Leipzig, 1897), p. 15.
[2] Musikalische Korrespondenz, Speyer, 24 November 1766.
[3] 10 February 1802, p. 332.   [4] January 1801, p. 308.   [5] Bernsdorf, ii, 266–7.

Their diligence soon raised them to the rank of major virtuosi, however; and in 1816 they were appointed chamber-musicians to the Emperor of Russia, replacing Haberzettl and Frank.

In 1824 Heinrich's excellent set of twenty-four études, twelve each in the major and minor keys, were published by Schott. Covering every aspect of technical facility, they show the hand-horn in its ultimate stage of development. Heinrich also wrote a set of 'Douze Duos', published about the same time. The Gugls made highly effective use of Thürrschmidt's chromatic mute, which Meusel[1] wrongly credits to their invention. Heinrich had two sons who were also horn-players in the St. Petersburg orchestra in the late 1830s (Gassner, p. 385; see also *Dictionary of Musicians*, p. 308).

HUTZLER, Johann Sigismund, 1772–1808, was born at Nürnberg. From his eighth year his ambition was to master the horn as a soloist. In this he succeeded; but having achieved the final goal of his life, the post of principal horn at Cassel, in 1807, he died the following summer. (See Meusel, i, p. 429; and Gassner, p. 442.)

HRADETZKY, Friederich, 1772–1846, came as a boy from Bohemia to Vienna, where he soon found a post at the opera; and in 1816 was appointed K. K. Kammermusikus. He was considered one of the finest of the Viennese virtuosi, ranking with Hörmann and Herbst. (See *Vaterländische Blätter*, 1808, vii, p. 54; Ziegler's *Adressenbuch* for 1823, p. 65; Gassner, p. 443; Bernsdorf, ii, p. 454; and Köchel, *Hofmusikkapelle*, p. 95. Hradetzky was a low-horn-player.)

AHL, two brothers, were virtuosi at the municipal theatre in Mannheim during the early years of the nineteenth century. (See *Journal der Luxus und der Moden*, Weimar, 1807, pp. 439–41; and Meusel, i, p. 14.)

BLIESENER was a horn-player at the Prussian Court who in 1801 published a set of three Quatuors Concertants at Berlin. (Meusel, i, p. 98.)

ERHARD, a Nürnberg virtuoso, attracted some notice at Paris in the nineties. (Meusel, i, p. 215.)

Generation IV: Working Period, c. 1795–1830

NISLE, Christian David, 1774–18(??), and *Johann Friederich*, 1778–18(??), were both born at Wallerstein, where their father, Johann senior, 1737–88, had been principal horn from 1750 until about 1780. Both the brothers showed considerable talent on the horn at an early age, and later were

[1] i, p. 323.

appreciated as duettists. The younger Nisle was accomplished both as a fortepianist and composer as well. His charming Duos, Op. VI, for horn and piano (1805), preserved in the Oettingen-Wallerstein library at Harburg, are useful as recital pieces. (See Meusel, ii, p. 93; Gerber, 1813, iii, p. 591; the *Dictionary of Musicians*, p. 231; and Gassner, p. 656.)

PETRIDES, *Joseph*, 1755–*post* 1824, and *Peter*, 1755–*post* 1824, were both born at Prague; and after a colourful and quixotic career far too long to relate here (including kissing publicly the feet of Pius VI, being attacked by dangerous and putrid fevers, and surviving shipwreck), landed in London in 1804. Their fame as virtuoso-duettists quickly spread, and they commanded admiration as the principal horn-players in England until their retirement in 1825. Their great influence on horn-playing in this country is dealt with in Chapter VII, p. 191. Ella's *Musical Sketches Abroad and at Home*[1] gives the following colourful description of the Petrides:

In 1822 the French horns in the band of Her Majesty's Theatre were played by the above two venerable Bohemians. In dress and appearance they resembled each other—both wearing pants fitted tight down to the ankles, a brown wig, an oddly-shaped hat, and large green spectacles. When accused, at rehearsals, of playing a wrong note, each would answer 'was mein bruder'; and until the copyist discovered that the parts were wrong, and neither of the brothers was at fault, they would snarl and utter unkind expressions toward each other, with a menacing look. At other times they were the most united of brothers.

(See also the *Dictionary of Musicians*, p. 283, for a complete and diverting account of their adventures; Kelly's *Reminiscences of the Theatre Royal, Drury Lane*, London, 1826, i, p. 26; and Lysons, *History . . . of the Three Choirs*, Gloucester, 1812, pp. 250, 254, and 259.)

SEEBACH, *Andreas*, 1777–18(??), was born near Erfurt; studied in Ronneburg; became principal horn in the theatre at Magdeburg in 1796, and ended up as Court virtuoso at Gotha. (Meusel, ii, p. 347; and Gassner, 442.)

SCHUNKE was the name of a family of six horn-players, all of international reputation, who hailed from Schkortleben near Weissenfels in Thuringia. Gottfried, born in 1777, was the first to give the family name its European rank; but it was in 1809 when he and his younger brother Michael, born about 1780, were engaged as Court horn-players at Cassel, and scored a series of triumphs as duettists there. In 1815 the two eldest brothers were given a life appointment in the newly organized Royal orchestra at Stuttgart (Württemberg, we must remember, had only been a kingdom since 1806),

[1] London, 1878, p. 337.

where Michael died in 1821. Andreas, the second brother, born in 1778, became solo horn-player in the Royal band at Berlin in 1812, succeeding Le Brun after an interval, until his retirement in 1833. Andreas was noted for the beauty of his tone. Christoph, Gottfried's first son, born in 1796, carried the family name to Stockholm, where he became principal horn to the Swedish Royal Court. Ernst, Gottfried's younger son, born at Cassel in 1812, shared the first-horn desk with his father at Stuttgart from 1828 onwards. Carl, a son and pupil of Andreas, was born at Berlin in 1811; and was considered one of the outstanding young virtuosi of the early nineteenth century hand-horn. The Schunkes were in fact the last great dynasty of hand-horn-players. (See Dlabacž, iii, p. 74; the *Musical Magazine and Review* for April 1823, p. 409; and Gassner, p. 765.)

HERBST, Michael, 1778–1833, was the last great teacher and virtuoso of the orchestral hand-horn. At first he played in the house orchestra of the Freiherr von Braun, Beethoven's friend and patron; and in 1806 was engaged as principal horn at the Theater an der Wien, where he took part in the first performance of *Fidelio*, undoubtedly as first in the virtuoso trio obbligato to the aria, 'Komm, Hoffnung'. In 1812 he was appointed as the first professor of the horn at the Vienna Conservatory, a post which he held until his death. His greatest contribution was as a teacher, and he commanded the love and respect of all his pupils. Herbst left a number of studies and the manuscript of a complete hand-horn tutor to the Gesellschaft der Musikfreunde; but repeated searches on the writer's part have failed to unearth either. (See the *Vaterländische Blätter*, 1808, vii, p. 54; Redl, 1823, p. 88; Gassner, p. 428; Bernsdorf, ii, p. 383; and Eitner, *Quellen-Lexicon*, Leipzig, 1901, p. 110.)

PINI was a dilettante at Parma who in 1822 equipped his horn with eight keys which enabled him to play the thirteen notes of the chromatic scale. News of the valve had evidently not yet penetrated south of the Dolomites. (See Fröhlich in Ersch and Gruber's *Allgemeine Encyclopädie*, Leipzig, 1834, p. 9; and P. Lichtenthal, *Dizionario e Bibliografia della Musica*, Milan, 1826, i, p. 211.)

FUCHS, Benedikt, was Michael Herbst's deputy first horn at the *Theater an der Wien*. (Ziegler, *Adressenbuch von Tonkünstlern*, Vienna, 1823, p. 88.)

KOHAUT, Franz, a horn-playing descendant of the late seventeenth-century Viennese lutanist Carl von Kohaut, also experimented with keys and holes to give the horn a chromatic scale. In 1819 he obtained a sinecure as Capellmeister to a rich landowner near Moscow which allowed him time to appear as a soloist both there and in the Russian capital, St. Petersburg, with great success. (Gassner, p. 500.)

HAASE, August, 1792–185(?), was appointed principal horn at Dresden in 1813 following the death of his fellow Bohemian, Miksch. In 1823 he set out on a highly successful duettist-tour with his younger brother Ludwig 1799–186(?). (See Gassner, p. 392; and Bernsdorf, ii, p. 288.)

PUZZI, Giovanni, 1792–1876, was a pupil, to all evidence, of the great late eighteenth-century Milanese virtuoso, Luigi Belloli, 1770–1817 (see p. 191). After a year or so at Paris in the season of 1815–16, Puzzi set off for London, where he was to become the leading soloist of his day, exerting an influence on horn-playing here equal to that of the Petrides. Nothing need be added to the notes in Morley-Pegge, pp. 163 ff., except to point out that a Sonata Concertante, written for Puzzi by Cipriani Potter and now preserved in the British Museum, reveals the Italian as a dazzling exponent of the chromatic late hand-horn technique. The difficulty of the horn part is enough to baffle the modern valve-horn-player; and one must agree with the *Musical Magazine and Review*[1] that 'PUZZI is a very extraordinary man'. (See also the *Dictionary of Musicians*, p. 326; and W. T. Parke, *Musical Memoirs*, London, 1830, ii, for 1822.)

KAIL, or *Kayl, Joseph*, a pioneer valve-horn-player and the first professor of the valve horn at Prague, figures in the present study in that he made his early reputation as a hand-horn-player, and was considered one of the best of his day. Born at Gottesgab in Bohemia in 1795, he was a pupil of Zalužan on the horn and clarino at the Prague Conservatory. In 1819 he was engaged as principal horn at the Royal theatre at Pest (Hungary), and in 1822 shared the first-horn desk at the Imperial opera in Vienna with Herbst, at the same time working with Uhlmann and the Kerners on the development of the valve. In 1825 he returned to Prague as principal horn with the Landesständisches Theater, and in that year was made professor of the chromatic horn and trumpet at the Conservatory, then under the direction of Dionys Weber, who wrote extensively for the valve horn. (See Gassner, 471; and J. Branberger, *Das Konservatorium für Musik in Prag*, Prague, 1911, pp. 273 ff.)

JANATKA, Johann, 1800–*post* 1832, was one of the last major players of the Austro-Bohemian school to receive his training on the hand-horn. A fellow pupil at the Prague Conservatory with Kail under Zalužan, he was called to Vienna in 1822 to a post at the Imperial opera. In 1828 he succeeded Herbst as principal horn at the Theater an der Wien; but in 1832 returned to Prague to take up the professorship at the Conservatory and the principal-horn post at the Ständestheater which Zalužan's death left vacant. Janatka was famous for his fine singing tone, and for his great gifts as a teacher. Unlike Kail, he taught the valve horn. (See Bernsdorf, ii, p. 483; and Branberger, loc. cit.)

[1] iii, 1821, p. 279.

IX

CONCLUSION: THE NATURAL HORN TODAY

WHEN Count Sporck died in 1738, some fifty-eight years after introducing the horn to the German-speaking world, he was very probably aware that he had helped by his patronage to found a tradition of artistic horn-playing. Indeed, within his lifetime the horn had been developed to a high degree of mechanical and tonal perfection by the Viennese maker Leichnambschneider; it had produced a number of gifted players who had encouraged the leading composers of the Austrian and German Baroque to write for their instrument; equipped with a respectable repertory, it had established itself as an orchestral instrument; and it was becoming more appreciated in a solo capacity on the concert platform. That Bach and Hasse had written for his favoured instrument must have been a great source of satisfaction to Sporck; but little could he know of the glories which were to come. Still less could he have suspected that the tradition which he had started would continue to flourish at Vienna and Prague two hundred and thirty years after his death.

One would like to think that he would be pleased if he could hear some of our modern performances of the music of his day on the instruments which would have been familiar to him. But surely Sporck would be puzzled to find that in otherwise authentic performances of the music he knew, his beloved horn in its original form was missing. It is indeed surprising that, in spite of the widespread revival of the other instruments of the Baroque and Classical orchestra, the horn has received little attention. It is to that end that this study is offered.

From the evidence afforded by the instruments, the music, and the writings about the many fine players of the school of horn-playing which Sporck founded, it is eminently possible to reconstruct the playing style of the eighteenth-century horn-players in both periods. We now know which mouthpiece Bach's horn-players used, and what instruments; and both are readily reproduced. Nor is the hand-technique which Leutgeb and Punto used to play the music Mozart wrote for them any longer a mystery; and their embouchure, it now emerges, was like our own.

The early horn obviously has no place in performances where modern instruments and massed forces are used: it lacks the volume necessary to sustain its part in these situations. But where historically authentic per-formances and smaller ensembles are concerned, a return to the horn of the Baroque and Classical periods would benefit many.

The player's task would be made easier if he could play these earlier horn parts on the instruments for which they were written. Technically and musically, the eighteenth-century instrument is more suitable, as has been shown. For the student of the modern horn this would confer a twofold advantage. In playing on the natural horn, even if only as an exercise, he would be forced by its very limitations to develop a healthy basic technique. It is not often recognized that many recent mechanical improvements, such as shortening the tube length and adding to the number of valves, are in effect ways round the inherent difficulties of the instrument. Tone-quality and intonation suffer accordingly, and the pupil easily develops lax playing habits. An acquaintance with the natural horn is a distinct help in develop-ing an accurate ear. But of course its greatest value lies in the fact that it provides an authentic ideal of horn tone upon which the student can model his own sound to advantage. Armed with this experience, he is well equipped to counter the aesthetic limitations of the B flat or F alto horn, should his later professional circumstances require him to take it up.

Audiences too would gain increased pleasure from again hearing that soft, clear sound which our forebears enjoyed. The twentieth-century ear, sated with the richness of the Romantic orchestral colours which it has inherited, responds above all to clarity, sweetness, and definition in instrumental sound. The eighteenth-century horn offers these qualities in full measure. In the writer's experience, the public show a keen awareness of the differ-ences between the modern horn and that of the eighteenth century in its proper musical setting.

In these various ways, therefore, a revival of the early horn, supported by an appreciation of its values on the part of players, students, listeners, and ultimately (one hopes) conductors and composers, would effectively keep the horn's most desirable aesthetic qualities fresh in our ear, and so prevent them from vanishing entirely into the mechanized degeneration which encroaches upon them daily.

APPENDIX

Gerber's Article on the Horn, 1789

So frequently is reference made to the article on the horn in Ernst Ludwig Gerber's *Historisches-Biographisches Lexicon der Tonkünstler* (Leipzig, 1792), both in the present work and in other writings on the eighteenth-century horn, and so great is its value as a key source, that it is reproduced here complete. Although the article was entitled 'Spörken', it contains a wide variety of information not only concerning the founder-patron of horn-playing but relating to the development of the instrument and its playing technique as well. Most of Gerber's information seems to have come to him through his friend and associate Carl Thürrschmidt, the horn virtuoso discussed in Chapter VII. The article contains some perplexing vaguenesses, however, which are probably owing to Gerber's lack of a first-hand technical and historical knowledge of the instrument; yet despite these inconsistencies it presents an unusually clear picture of the horn at a time when hand-horn-playing had reached its zenith. Mention of Clagget's invention as having fallen in the previous year establishes the date of Gerber's article as 1789; it was not published, however, until 1792.[1]

For convenience of reference, Gerber's text has been divided into sections and paragraphs (or their equivalent—the sentence was to remain the prime unit of German literary thought until well after Goethe's death).

I A SPORCK, Franz Anton, Count, of the Lower Saxonian branch of the Spörcken, seat and estates in Bohemia. He was one of those rare musical amateurs who not only amuse themselves with music, but take the greatest pleasure in its improvement and growth as an art. We have received only sparse information, unfortunately, concerning his actual connection with music during his lifetime. But even this is worth setting out here both for the honour of his memory and as an example for other wealthy musical dilettantes to emulate. He first became a patron of music when, as Mattheson reports,[2] he gave to this art two first-class masters whom he sent to Rome to study at his own expense: the famous organist at Lissa [Johann Heinrich Krause] and the Breslau organist, Franz Tiburtius Winkler.

---

[1] Clagget's device for combining two horns pitched a semitone apart in order to produce a chromatic scale is fully described in Morley-Pegge, op. cit., p. 27.

[2] *Grundlage einer Ehrenpforte* (Hamburg, 1740), p. 43.

B   He was furthermore the indirect creator of an instrument to whose general usefulness and widespread employment wherever music is found even the Violin itself must yield. An instrument which in the drawing-room moves soft Beauty's heart with its melancholy flute-tones; and in the forest and on the mountain-top awakes the raw and brutal Hunter to his wild pleasure. An instrument, which in the hands of the master in the concert-room, so captures the admiration of the connoisseur, and at other times spurs the Warrior to the bloody battle with its piercing tone. What could this be but the Horn, which we hear daily in field and forest, in church and concert-room?

C   The occasion for Count Sporck to make this gift [to music] arose on a trip in 1680 to Paris, where the horn had been invented a few years earlier.[1] Sporck, as a patron, friend, and passionate protector of the arts with the broadest of vision and understanding in these matters—as can be seen from his biography in the Lives of the Learned in Bohemia and Moravia[2]—took such delight in this instrument that he straightaway had two of his Bohemian

[1] Most eighteenth-century writers shared the belief that the invention of the cor-de-chasse occurred in the decade before Sporck's providential arrival at Versailles. The cor-de-chasse proper actually had its beginnings in the helical horns of the late six-teenth century, in France. For a description of the horn's early evolution the reader is referred to the Introduction. It is appropriate here to draw attention to a passage by one of the more reliable nineteenth-century writers, Josef Schantl. Schantl, for many years principal horn of the Imperial Opera at Vienna and professor at the Academy, brought out his *Die Österreiche Jagdmusik* in collaboration with the historian Carl Zellner in 1886. The following excerpt is taken from page 7:

> The magnificent Gobelin tapestries now in the Louvre, drawn by Lucas de Leyde, depict the hunt at the time of Francis I of France (1494–1547). Huntsmen are shown wearing a small horn on a long, broad baldrick. This horn, instead of being circular in form, was constructed in the shape of a pentagon or hexagon, with sharp corners. Not until the reign of Charles IX (1550–74) were these corners rounded off. In the engravings of this period, especially those illustrating the book of the royal hunt (whose author was Charles himself, also a good horn-blower), we see hunters with horns having a hoop so large that it encircled the body of the huntsman; these were generally worn over the left shoulder and rested on the right hip. These great singly-wound horns were called 'cors-de-chasse', as distinguished from the small half-moon-shaped horn to which the name 'huchet' or Hift-horn (oliphant) was given. Under Louis XIII (1601–43) the horn was not substantially changed; nor did hunting-music make any noteworthy progress, save that the signals became more varied as a result of the improved singly-wound horn.
>
> The hunting-music which ultimately enjoyed such fame was first developed during the reign of Louis XIV (1638–1715). As the horn's tubing had now been substantially lengthened and wound two and a half times upon itself, the instrument's response was freer and its compass greater: so that about this time fanfares began to be written for it. The considerable diameter of the horn's hoop was dictated by the headgear of the period.

[2] F. Pelzel, *Abbildungen der Böhmischen und Mährischen Gelehrten und Künstler* (Prague, 1773), ii.

servants taught in the art of playing it.[1] Upon his return to Bohemia these two men soon became the fathers of horn-playing there. And since that time who can measure the progress of the Bohemians on this instrument? For such is their skill that even Paris herself when she wants good horn-players, has been obliged for years now to fetch them from Bohemia.[2]

C1 To this love of the horn on the part of the Bohemians, and Sporck in particular, the Hunting Order of St. Hubert, which has as its heraldic symbol a golden horn, is indebted for its founding.[3] This worthy man died in the year 1738. May his memory be sacred to the Muses!

II I trust that I am not entering upon superfluous labours when I trace, so far as my knowledge of this instrument goes, the path which people have followed in improving it from time to time. In its infancy the horn appears to have been used solely as a hunting instrument. It is possible that occasionally a pair of more accomplished horn-players were placed at the far end of a garden to enliven the party with their music. But its tone at this time was much too raw for the music-room.[4]

B The first attempt to combine the horn with other instruments was evidently made in military music.[5] One may be convinced that this venture

[1] Röllig and Sweda, q.v.

[2] A commentary on the supremacy of the Bohemian school of horn-playing at a date when the French and Germans were beginning to produce good native players.

[3] The founding of the Order of St. Hubert by Sporck in 1723 has been discussed on p. 17, note 2.

[4] See Chapter II, pp. 36–38.

[5] The first recorded use of horns with oboes and bassoons was in the music of the hunt, and it is in scenes evocative of hunting and the out-of-doors that ensembles of horns and oboes are met with in opera and ballet in the early 1700s. It appears that horns were not adopted by military bands in Gerber's part of Germany until 1725 or thereabouts. The description of the royal military manoeuvres at Mühlberg in 1730 affords one of the first mentions of the horn's use in military music.

In Vienna the horn's association with military bands begins somewhat earlier than in Saxony and Prussia, and reputedly dates back to the beginning of the eighteenth century. Records for this early period are sparse, but to all accounts horns began to be included in the immensely popular Turkish bands shortly after the turn of the century. These Turkish bands, as well as the normal military ensembles, formed an integral part of the musical backdrop of everyday life in Vienna until the mid-nineteenth century, when they were supplanted by the larger all-brass bands.

The *Jahrbuch der Tonkunst für Wien und Prag* (Prague, 1796), p. 7 *et passim*, gives an accurate description of the instrumentation of both types of band, and affords an interesting glimpse into an era when instrumental serenades formed a regular part of an evening's walk round the parks. The *Jahrbuch* speaks of the late afternoon concerts 'given daily on the Bastei [a broad bastion on the city wall] near the lemonade-kiosk by the regimental bands. ...The military music', the article continues, 'consists either of the ordinary field bands or the Turkish bands. A field band or *Harmonie* is made up of two horns, two bassoons, and two oboes; these instruments are found in the Turkish band, as well as two clarinets, a trumpet, a triangle, a piccolo, a very large [bass] drum, a side

was successful merely by hearing the marches which the various regiments now play every day. Presumably the regimental musicians made increasing use of this instrument in their serenades. This then gave them the opportunity to observe its good effect when used in combination with stringed instruments indoors. Now one sought to use it for the theatre; but at first it was only rarely employed in opera, perhaps in the overture or in festive choruses.

C   To all evidence this stage had been reached by about 1730. The horn was still hindered in practice, however, by its limited number of notes; and even these were only available in the key of E flat major. Attempts were made to get round this difficulty by means of terminal crooks and tuning-shanks, and by making separate horns for the keys of G and B flat alto, thereby gaining the scales of D, E flat, F, G, and B flat. But these improvements brought with them new problems of tuning, intonation, and embouchure, the latter resulting from the changes in the actual instrument's position according to the different length of each crook.[1]

D   As a remedy for these vexing faults an artisan at Hanau devised the so-called Inventions-horn. This discovery was reported in Cramer's Magazine by the author of that excellent treatise, *Concerning Music for Amateurs of the*

drum, and a pair of cymbals. A field band is heard when the palace guard changes. Turkish bands are heard in front of the barracks of a summer evening in fair weather; and at times with the main watch.'
    Gerber's dating of the horn's appearance in military music in about 1730 is correct, then, if we except the Turkish bands of the Viennese; and each of the regimental bands which abounded throughout Germany in Gerber's own day had its pair of horns. But the balance of his historical remarks, as he admits, is founded on conjecture.

[1] Gerber has described here the Orchesterhorn which the Leichnambschneiders developed in Vienna in the first decade of the century (see Chapter II). Recent research confirms his list of crooks at this early stage. Crooks are never dated; but by association with the instruments for which they were made, it would appear that crooks in A and A flat alto, and those in C and B flat basso were not known before *c.* 1757. This evidence, though external, may help to resolve the B-flat-alto-versus-basso controversy.
    Far too much has been made of the difficulties arising from the difference in mouth-pipe length amongst the various terminal crooks. In practice this means that for each key the distance between the mouthpiece and the body of the horn is altered. The left hand adjusts instantly to these minor variations, however. The Germans were disturbed by this inconsistency, and this dissatisfaction led to the development of the Inventions-horn, which had its crooks in the body of the instrument. The Viennese, on the other hand, have kept to the terminal crook until the present day. The Inventionshorn model was brought out by Geier in Vienna about 1776, but its popularity there was short-lived. Geier's horns of this type were prized in Germany, according to Forkel (*Musikalischer Almanach für Deutschland*, Leipzig 1782, p. 205). The author once asked Anton Ciƶek, the patriarch of the present-day Viennese horn-makers, to comment on the failure of the Inventionshorn to gain a foothold in Austria. 'Die Deutschen,' he replied, 'sind allezeit bei ihrer schweren Präzisionsmechanik g'blieben.' (The Germans have always stood by their heavy precision machinery.)

Flute, whose name I unfortunately cannot recall for my readers.[1] Within the main circle of the Inventions-horn were two short sockets into which were fitted two little tubes; these being led into the circle to describe various curves according to the length of the inserted crook. At each change of key a different crook was now pushed into these sockets: with the result that they soon wore, allowing the crook to wobble and leak.[2]

E   This weakness was corrected at Vienna about 1780, as the author mentioned before reports, not only by lengthening the sockets to five inches, but by leading them out of the plane of the main circle at an angle. In this way the crook could be moved beyond the periphery of the circle even while the horn was being played; and the pitch could be lowered considerably. A further refinement was that one of these sockets was made into a tenon, the corresponding socket now being fixed on the crook: so that one leg of the crook fitted into the socket in the horn, and the other leg now fitted over the tenon in the horn; the two being spaced at a distance of four inches.

F   I am convinced, however, that this improvement occurred thirty years earlier, and that its origin is scarcely Viennese.[3] Particularly as Herr Reinert[4] of Ludwigslust brought a pair of these horns with him to this Court as early as 1757; and they had crooks for the keys B flat, C, D, E flat, E, F, G, A, and B flat alto. He had had them made by Werner[5] in Dresden in 1755. Our Prince bought them from Herr Reinert when he left his service, for eighty

[1] The artisan at Hanau was Johann Georg Haltenhof, who worked there from the 1770s until 1815 or later. (A pair of his *Inventionshörner* with fixed mouthpipes bearing this later date are in the Prince of Öttingen-Wallerstein's collection at Schloss Harburg in Bavaria. See also Morley-Pegge, Plate IV.) The article which Gerber mentions was not to be found in Cramer's *Magazin der Musik* (Hamburg, 1750–1810), a complete set of which was examined in the University Library at Vienna.

[2] For a detailed discussion of the Inventionshorn's nomenclature and development, with illustrations, see the present writer's article, 'Some Historical Notes on the Horn in Austria and Germany' in *Galpin Society Journal* XVI (London, 1963).

[3] Gerber corrects this assumption later in his article on Thürrschmidt. See p. 174.

[4] Karl Reinert, 1730–c. 1800, principal horn in the orchestra of the Duke of Mecklenburg. Reinert supplied Gerber with much information about the horn. See Chapter IV, p. 124.

[5] Johann Werner, a mid-eighteenth-century maker of great reputation. He executed Hampl's design for the Inventionshorn, the first model appearing about 1750. Reinert had a pair of these horns made for him by Werner in 1755, which he brought with him to Sondershausen two years later. Prince Günther Friederich von Schwarzburg-Sondershausen bought these instruments for his orchestra when Reinert left to join the band at Ludwigslust. These horns formed the basis for Gerber's biographical note (*Lexicon,* 1792, ii, p. 798) on Werner:

Werner, Johann, an instrument-maker at Neustadt near Dresden about the middle of this century, was an outstanding master in the manufacture of brass instruments, such as horns, trumpets, etc. In the instrument-room at this court (Sondershausen) is a pair of Inventions-horns for several keys made by him, remarkable for their beauty and purity of tone. They are dated 1755.

Thalers, and gave them to the court orchestra. And it is evident from their excellence of workmanship and purity of intonation *that they are not the first attempt at horns of this model* on Werner's part.

G　These are the genuine Inventions-horns, which because of their convenience have been adopted in all the great orchestras. At the moment so-called Inventions-horns for all the keys are being sold at Leipzig. The true amateur must beware of them, however: for with them the pitch is changed by means of the old-fashioned coiled crooks which fit into the mouthpipe, wherefore they are not only out of tune in themselves and with other instruments, but have all the old bedevilments. In addition to the ease with which orchestral players, equipped with good Inventions-horns, can now change key in the space of a few bars' rest, must be mentioned the brilliance which our professors elicit from these instruments in full tutti passages, so that one has the impression of hearing trombones rather than horns.[1]

H　All of these improvements have been devised specifically for the betterment of those horns which accompany in the orchestra. For solo playing and duets the virtuoso uses only the simple horn without crooks.[2]

I　About the year 1760 an artist at Petersburg named Kölbel sought to give his horn a chromatic scale for solo work and to make its tone softer by means of keys like those on the bassoon, and by a lid on the bell.[3] Another man in

---

[1] This preference for 'sharpness' (*cuivrée*) in forte passages marks an essential difference between the Austrian and German styles of playing. The Viennese and Prague horns of this period retain their soft quality through the forte range without a hint of 'brassing' until the extreme fortissimo level is reached. Even today the German style of horn-playing is marked by a distinct edge on the tone which is veiled by inserting the hand quite far into the bell. The Viennese tone is softer in basic quality, and the bell is left comparatively free. The German style was beginning to emerge in the 1780s. Gerber's remark is one of the first indications that the Germans were breaking away from the Austrian concept to establish their own national style.

[2] This information comes as a surprise. At face-value Gerber's statement indicates that all soloists at the time used the simple severally wound orchestral Jagdhorn with fixed mouthpiece, 'without any crooks'. But we know that Thürrschmidt, Palsa, and Punto used the cor-solo with its insert crooks after 1781, when Raoux brought out the first model of Thürrschmidt's design in Paris (see Chapter IV infra Thürrschmidt, Carl); and that the terminally crooked horn was the standard instrument of the Bohemian and Austrian virtuosi until the end of the hand-horn period. It is quite true that nothing surpasses a well-made Jagdhorn-type Waldhorn for accuracy of intonation and security of delivery: but for a travelling virtuoso to carry a complete set of these horns about with him would have posed serious problems of transport. The soloists Gerber would have heard at Sondershausen were probably of a minor order, with one or two stock pieces in their travelling repertoire. (The nearest court of any size was Erfurt, some forty miles to the south.) Otherwise his comment can only be taken as an idealized generalization. What is probably meant, though, is Raoux's cor-solo (see note 4 on p. 225).

[3] Kölbel's remarkable *Amorschall* is discussed on p. 108.

the same city, Maresch, bound together two horns tuned a minor third apart, which enabled tones to be played on one or the other as the melody required.[1] Since no further use has been made of this contrivance, however, and since our present-day masters of this instrument are able to deliver more than is ever demanded of it without the aid of these artifices, further mention of the subject here would be superfluous.

Rather Mr. Clagget's invention at London last year is much more worthy of our attention, it seems. He has bound two horns together as well, but enables them to be played by one person through the device of a common mouthpiece. According to the player's wish the air-stream can be directed into one horn or the other by a valve in this mouthpiece as the various notes particular to each are required. When the two horns are pitched in the keys of, say, D and E flat, the player can produce immediately the notes E flat, E, F, F sharp, A flat, A, B flat, B natural, C, and C sharp without the slightest effort.[2]

J   Still more remarkable, evidently, is the new kind of mute which the Viennese brothers Boeck used on their tour in 1783. This device makes the tone sound as though it were coming from a distance of a hundred paces. According to Herr Cramer's description it is a hollow brass cone covered with leather, which fits into the bell of the horn.[3]

K   The Parisian artisans appear nowadays to be the most advanced in the manufacture of simple horns for concerto work. They are made there for one hundred Carolines even in silver, like the superb pair owned by Messrs. Palsa and Thürrschmidt in Berlin.[4] The art of refining the tone on the solo horn has reached the greatest heights today. When a pair of virtuosi mount the platform, one seems not to hear the sound of brass instruments, but a flute accompanied by a gamba.[5]

[1] In this idea Maresch anticipated Clagget by about twenty years. See p. 101.
[2] A full description of Clagget's 'Cromatic Trumpet and French Horn' is given in Morley-Pegge, *The French Horn*, pp. 26 f.
[3] The non-transposing mute appears to have been a by-product of Hampl's experiments with hand-stopping. The Brothers Boeck, Carl Thürrschmidt, and Palsa all used mutes from about 1775 onwards. It is hoped that this knowledge will dispel the uncertainty surrounding the 'con Sordino' marking in the Finale of Beethoven's Symphony No. 6. See Chapter IV under 'Hampl', 'Thürrschmidt', and 'Boeck'.
[4] The instrument referred to here is the cor-solo which Carl Thürrschmidt designed in collaboration with the distinguished Parisian maker Raoux. This model featured a fixed mouthpipe and insert crooks which fitted into sockets in the centre of the body of the horn. See Morley-Pegge, *The French Horn*, pp. 22, 23, 158; and for details of the development of the cor-solo, see the author's article in *Galpin Society Journal*, xvi, p. 36. See also Chapter IV under 'Thürrschmidt'.
[5] This is an interesting comment on the difference in tone quality between first and second horn, and on the softness of both.

III   Not yet content with these refinements, players sought further to fill in the gaps which occur in the natural scale of this instrument. This was especially the province of the second-horn-players, who already knew how to form the entire great bass octave with the hand about the year 1750: a feat which I have often watched the gifted Bachmann perform, who was Herr Reinert's second before his death.[1] Nowadays even the first-horn-players use this hand technique, which enables them to produce all the major and minor scales possible on one and the same horn. With the second-horn-players this sleight-of-hand has reached the point that whoever hears Herr Thürrschmidt play a concerto and watches his hand in the bell of the horn, must doubt whether the movements of a pianist's hand could be more lively.[2] Thus through patronage and devotion we have seen this instrument in the space of a hundred years brought to a degree of perfection which leaves nothing more to be desired.[3]

[1] Nothing further of Bachmann is known beyond the fact that he was Reinert's second at Sondershausen.

[2] *Heftig* must here be taken to mean quick. Any vigorous or excessive motion of the right hand in the bell merely displaces the instrument.

[3] The period at which Gerber was writing was truly the heyday of the great hand-horn virtuosi. Punto was in his prime; and Leitgeb, the Steinmüllers, Thürrschmidt, Palsa, Spandau, and the brothers Boeck, to name a few, were applauded all over Europe. One wonders what Gerber's reaction would be to the technical feats demanded of the orchestral horn-player today.

GLOSSARY OF TERMS

Collar: Any ring, in effect a short length of tubing, which overlaps the join between two sections of tubing. Its inside diameter is just large enough to allow a sliding fit over the tubing to be joined; final bonding is effected by sweat-soldering. Collars are often the subject for turned ornament, and are useful for purposes of comparison. Similarities in decoration on collars have enabled instruments to be identified, and in some cases have helped historians establish connections between master and pupil.

Cor à l'anglaise: This was the French name for a cross between the Inventions-horn and the early Waldhorn with master-and-coupler crooks which was adopted in England in the 1760s. It retained the central tuning-slide of the Inventionshorn, but rejected its fixed mouthpipe, keeping instead to the earliest form of crook whereby several loops of tubing are joined together for the lower keys. The cor à l'anglaise appeared about 1780.

Cor-de-chasse: Literally, horn of the hunt. From the late seventeenth century until the middle of the eighteenth the French used this term as well as 'trompe-de-chasse' to mean the large open-hooped hunting-horn. Like the Parforcejagdhorn, which was modelled on its lines, the cor-de-chasse had a three-foot hoop, an eight-inch bell and a fixed mouthpiece. Its conical bore was smaller throughout than that of the Jagdhorn, and the expansion of the bore was less rapid. The tone of the cor-de-chasse was more trumpet-like than that of the Jagdhorn. Until about 1750, when the horn was reintro-duced into France in its orchestral form, the terms trompe-de-chasse and cor-de-chasse were synonymous. I have used the latter to avoid any confusion with the trumpet. But after the middle of the century the designation cor-de-chasse usually meant the orchestral horn, whereas trompe-de-chasse denoted the hunting instrument. All of these early terms were used at random, and resist every effort of the twentieth-century historian to impose some kind of order upon them.

Cor d'orchestre: The French name for the Orchesterhorn. Makers at Paris began to produce a smaller-bore version of the Viennese model in the early 1780s. A separate terminal crook was used for each key, and a tuning-slide was fitted.

Corno da Caccia: In Italian eighteenth-century usage the orchestral horn or Waldhorn. The mounted hunt was virtually unknown in Italy, and for this reason the Italians first encountered the horn in its orchestral form. We must except the isolated example of the 'Corni' in Cavalli's opera Le Nozze di Teti e di Peleo of 1639. If this work saw an Italian performance the horns were doubtless of the French cor à plusiers tours type: conical in bore, some eight to twelve feet in length, and wound spirally with the coils touching.

The most plausible illustration of this horn can be seen in Marin Mersenne's *Harmonie Universelle* (Paris, 1637), V, p. 245. There is no record of Corno da Caccia being used to mean an octave-transposing Jagdhorn, whatever that may be.

Corpus: The body of the horn exclusive of the mouthpipe and bell: the central coils.

Cor-solo: A model intended exclusively for the soloist. Brought out by Raoux in the spring of 1781, it was in effect a highly refined version of the Inventionshorn. The cor-solo incorporated a fixed mouthpipe and insert crooks which were supplied in D, E flat, E, F, and G only: the keys of the solo concerti of the period. The taper of the bore was adjusted to these lower crooks without any need to compromise with the higher orchestral pitches. The crooks themselves were conical except for their sliding tenons, with the result that the cylindrical tubing, which detracted from tone quality, was kept to a minimum. The cors-solo which Raoux made for Thürrschmidt, Palsa, Punto, and Le Brun represent some of the most sophisticated products of the horn-maker's art. Surviving examples are unsurpassed for tone quality and superior playing characteristics. Many were of silver with bells elaborately decorated in gold floral or geometric figures on coloured metallic lacquer grounds.

Garland: A band of metal some two inches wide and fitted flush to the outside of the bell rim. Its purpose was both to strengthen the bell structurally and to damp out any frequencies germane to the bell itself which might conflict with frequencies being played.

Insert crook: A length of tubing coiled into a U shape or circle according to the length and pitch desired, with its legs extended in parallel to form tenons. This device was then fitted into the sockets in the centre of the circle described by the corpus, and could be moved for tuning. See Inventionshorn.

Inventionshorn: Literally, a horn with innovations or improvements. In substance this was a rationalized orchestral horn with crooks which fitted into the body rather than attaching to the end of the mouthpipe (see below). In its final form it had a fixed mouthpipe, and the crooks could be moved for tuning. The Inventionshorn is described more fully on page 127. It was developed by Joseph Hampl in conjunction with the maker Werner in about 1755.

Jagdhorn: Literally, a hunting-horn. The term is used for the purposes of this study to distinguish between the instrument used for the chase and that employed in the orchestra. There are two types, the smaller sixteenth-century horn in G, A or B♭ alto having a single coil of six to eight inches in diameter and a bell of four to six inches in diameter at the rim; this was the instrument of the standing, or non-mounted hunt. The second type, sometimes called the *Dampierre-horn* because of its association with the Marquis de Dampierre, who wrote harmonic hunting fanfares for its French counterpart, is the one dealt with here. It is distinguished by a large, open-hooped body measuring as much as three feet across in some of the earlier examples, and a bell some seven to nine inches in diameter. A fixed mouthpipe is common to both types. The latter instrument, because it was used exclusively for the mounted hunt, was often called the Parforcejagdhorn from its association with the *chasse à parforce*. Until the middle of the eighteenth century the term Jagdhorn was used indiscriminately to mean either the large hunting-horn or the smaller-bodied Waldhorn which was developed from it. Modern usage of the word Jagdhorn has been further confused by the music encyclopedia *Die Musik in Geschichte und Gegenwart*, which has translated all terms referring to the horn into Jagdhorn without regard to period, country, or context.

Master and coupler: A system of dividing a set of terminal crooks into a series of connecting or coupler links of cylindrical tubing. When these were all joined together, the lowest pitch was obtainable; lengths were subtracted to produce higher pitches. Usually these sets had two 'master' crooks, one longer and one shorter, whose tubing was conical. The system was a cheap expedient for providing orchestral players with a complete range of pitches. Soloists kept to the fully formed crooks, which were tonally superior, owing to the fact that their tubing was conical and continuous with the bore of the horn itself. Undoubtedly of Viennese origin, the master and coupler system none the less found its longest and most widespread acceptance in this country. See Plate XIV(b).

Mouthpipe: The first branch of tubing leading from the mouthpiece to the body of the horn. In the case of horns fitted with tuning-slides or insert crooks, the mouthpipe ends at the first socket. On terminal crooks the mouthpipe is roughly that length of tubing which leads from the mouthpiece and describes the first loop. In both cases the bore expands throughout the length of the mouthpipe.

Mouthpipe inlet: The first half-inch or so of the mouthpipe, having a contracting taper corresponding to that of the mouthpiece shank, which it receives.

Neck: The portion of the horn's tubing, some six inches in length, which expands into the throat.

Orchesterhorn: A Viennese adaptation of the Inventionshorn having terminal crooks and retaining the U-shaped tuning-slide. Because of the cylindrical tubing which was necessary to accommodate the length of the tuning-slide, the tone of this model was inferior to that of the standard terminally crooked Waldhorn. Yet the slide made it easy to tune, and so became the favourite of the orchestral player. The Orchesterhorn appears to have emerged between about 1760 and 1770.

Stay: A brace with a foot on each end soldered into place between two adjacent parts of the instrument to strengthen them. Stays are either turned out as posts or hammered out of sheet stock.

Tenon and socket: There are two varieties. The earlier is the conical sort used on terminal crooks. The tenon is a short section of tubing having a slight taper, which is soldered with an overlapping fit to the far end of the crook. The socket, similarly soldered to the end of the tubing at the top of the first coil, on the corpus, receives the tenon in a corresponding taper. The second and later type of tenon and socket is found on insert crooks and tuning-slides. This arrangement consists simply of two cylindrical pieces of tubing four to six inches long, one of which is a close sliding fit inside the other. The smaller of the two is the tenon; it is soldered to the crook or slide, forming in effect the leg of the U. The larger is, of course, the socket which is attached at the far end to the inward-turning branch of the corpus. Here the inside diameter of the tenon is the same as that of the slide or crook, to which it is fixed by a soldered collar-joint.

Terminal crook: A loop of conical tubing (Dr. Burney called it a 'wreath') which is inserted into the corresponding socket on the main tubing of the corpus to change the horn's fundamental pitch. Crooks of higher pitch are short and singly wound, describing a loop of some three to four inches in diameter; crooks for the lower pitches are proportionately longer, and wound twice or thrice into a circle varying from five inches across to some ten inches in diameter in the case of the C or B flat basso crooks. The distinguishing feature of the terminal crook is that it is fitted at the end of the tubing at the top of the circle near the point at which the player's hand grasps the horn.

Throat: That section of the bell where the expansion describes an outward parabolic curve. The throat is crucial in the matter of tone colour.

Tuning-shank or bit: A short conical piece of tubing, usually provided with 'ears' or knobs at its wider end to aid its removal, which could be had in sets of six varying lengths for tuning. The shank was inserted into the socket on the body of the horn and received the crook in turn.

Waldhorn: Literally, forest horn. The term is in a sense an abstraction in that it applies to an orchestral horn which recalls the forest by connotation. Rightly or wrongly, I have expanded it to mean the Germanic type of horn as opposed to the French. Specifically it means the two forms of concert horn which were developed from the Jagdhorn. The first of these, also the first in chronological order, is the orchestral horn with terminal crooks. Here the coils of the body have been reduced to a circle of some twelve to fifteen inches in diameter, often wound twice upon itself. The bell remained much the same in shape and size as that of the Jagdhorn. This design, originated in 1703 by Michael Leichnambschneider in Vienna, arose in response to a need for a more convenient horn for indoor use. The fundamental pitch of this instrument could be changed as required by interchangeable crooks of different lengths; this system conferred the additional advantage of doing away with the complete set of horns, one for each pitch, with which each player had to be equipped. One instrument now served for all keys. The second type, sometimes called an orchestral Jagdhorn (a contradiction in terms), is simply the Jagdhorn wound twice or thrice upon itself to make a smaller body for orchestral purposes. This model was a cheaper version of the terminally crooked horn described above. The main difference between the two was that the latter had a fixed mouthpipe.

BIBLIOGRAPHY

Abert, Hermann, *Niccolo Jommelli als Opernkomponist*, Halle, 1908.

Almanach Historique du Théâtre, Paris, c. 1770.

Altenburg, Johann Ernst, *Versuch einer Anleitung zur heroisch-musikalischen Trompeter- und Pauker-kunst*, Halle, 1795.

Ancelet, *Observations sur la Musique, les Musiciens et les Instruments*, Amsterdam, 1757.

Apollo's Cabinet: or the Muses Delight . . . with twelve duettos for the French Horns, composed by Mr. Charles and instructions for the voice, violin, harpsichord or spinet, German-flute, common-flute, hautboy, French horn, bassoon and bass-violin, Liverpool, 1757.

Baines, Anthony, *Catalogue of Musical Instruments in the Victoria and Albert Museum*, ii, London, 1968.

Barbour, Murray, 'Franz Krommer and his Writing for Brass' in *Brass Quarterly*, Vol. 2, No. 1, Durham, N.H., 1957.

Bartholinus, Caspar, *De Tibiis Veterum*, Amsterdam, 1679.

Benedikt, Heinrich, *Franz Anton Graf von Sporck, 1662–1738: Zur kultur d. Barockzeit in Böhmen*, Vienna, 1923.

Bernsdorf, Edward, *Neues Universal-Lexicon der Tonkunst*, Dresden, 1856.

Bessaroboff, Nicholas, *Ancient European Musical Instruments*, Boston, 1941.

Blaikley, D. J., 'On Brass Wind Instruments as Resonators' in *The Philosophical Magazine*, vi, London, 1898.

Blandford, W. H. F., 'The Fourth Horn in the Choral Symphony' in *Musical Times*, London, January, February, March 1925.

Blandford, W. H. F., 'The French Horn in England' in *Musical Times*, August 1922.

Branberger, Dr. Johann, *Das Konservatorium für Musik in Prag*, Prague, 1911.

Brenet, Michel, *Les concerts en France sous l'ancien régime*, Paris, 1900.

Bresler, Ferd. Ludw. von, 'Sporck' in *Allgemeines Historisches Lexicon*, Leipzig, 1722.

Buchmayr, J. W., *Böhmische Oden und Fabeln*, Prague, 1798.

Budapester Staatsarchiv, Acta Musicalia, 1676–1800, fol. 45: 1762.

Bunge, Rudolph, 'Johann Sebastian Bachs Kapelle zu Cöthen und deren nachgelassene Instrumenten' in *Bach-Jahrbuch*, Leipzig, 1905.

Burney, Charles, *The Present State of Music in Germany*, London, 1775.

Carse, Adam, *The Orchestra in the Eighteenth Century*, Cambridge, 1940.

Chambers, E., *Cyclopedia or an Universal Dictionary of Arts & Science*, London, 1779.

Al. Choron et F. Fayolle, *Dictionnaire Historique des Musiciens*, Paris, 1811.

Cramers Magazin der Musik, xi–xii, Hamburg, 1785.

Cucuel, G., *La Pouplinière et la Musique de chambre au XVIIIe siècle*, Paris, 1911.

Cucuel, George, *Études sur un Orchestre au XVIIIe siècle*, Paris, 1913.

The Daily Advertiser, London, 1747: No. 5290.

Dampierre, Marc Antoine Marquis de, *Tons de Chasse et Fanfares à une et deux Trompes*. See under Serre' de Rieux.

Dart, Thurston, 'Bach's Fiauti d'Echo' in *Music and Letters*, xli, 1960.

De Jeze, ed., *Etat (ou Tableau) de Paris*, Paris, 1757–65.

Dent, Edward, *Alessandro Scarlatti*, London, 1905.

Deutsch, Otto Erich, *Handel. A documentary biography*, London, 1955.

Dictionary of Musicians, London, 1824.

Diderot, Denis, & D'Alembert, *Encyclopédie, ou Dictionnaire Raisonné des Sciences des Arts et des Metiers*, Tom. IV, 1754; Tom. IX, 1765.

Dlabacž, Gottfried Johann, *Abhandlung der Schicksalen der Künste in Böhmen*, Prague, 1797.

Dlabacž, Gottfried Johann, *Allgemeines-Historisches Künstlerlexicon für Böhmen*, Prague, 1815.

Dlabacž, Johann Gottfried, 'Versuch eines Verzeichnisses der vorzüglichen Tonkünstler in oder aus Böhmen' in von Riegger, J. A., *Materialen zur Alten und Neuen Statistik von Böhmen*, xii, Prague, 1794.

Döbel, Heinrich Wilhelm, *Jäger-Practica, oder der Wohlgeübte und Erfahrener Jäger*, Leipzig, 1746.

Domnich, Heinrich, *Méthode de Premier et de Second Cor*, Mainz, 1808.

Doppelmayr, Johann Gabriel, *Historische Nachricht von den Nürnbergischen Mathematicîs und Künstlern*, Nürnberg, 1730.

Dornaus, Philipp, 'Einige Bemerckungen über den zweckmässigen Gebrauch des Waldhorns' in *Allgemeiner Musikalischer Zeitung*, Leipzig, January 1801.

Das fröhliche Dressden, als daselbst zu Ehren Sr. königl. Maestät in Preussen & c. und Dero Cron-Printzen kgl. Hoheit, bey Deroselben hohen Anwesenheit, täglich Lustbarkeit angestellt, und vergnügliche vollbracht worden, Daselbst gedruckt, 1728.

Dresdnischer Hof- und Staats-Calendar auf das Jahr 1715.

Dressdnisches Diarium Auf den Monat September, 1719 vorstellend den den Prächtigen Einzug in Dressden, der . . . Fürstin Marien Josephen, vermählter kön. Poln. u. Churfürstl. Sachs Prinzessin, geborner Erz-Herzogin zu Oesterreich, sowohl auch die von Ihro k. Maj. in Polen und Churfürstl. Durchl. zu Sachsen. Deroselben, zu höchsten Vergnügen angestellte Festivitaeten.

The Dublin Mercury, Nos. 13 and 28, Dublin, 1742.

Du Fouilloux, Jacques, *La Vénerie*, Poitiers, 1561.

Eichborn, Hermann, *Die Dämpfung beim Horn oder Die musikalische Natur des Horns*, Leipzig, 1897.

Eichborn, Hermann, 'Die Einführung des Horns in die Kunstmusik' in *Monatshefte für Musikgeschichte*, Leipzig, 1889.

Eichborn, Hermann, *Über das Oktavierungsprincip bei Blechinstrumenten, insbesondere bei Waldhörnern*, Leipzig, 1889.

Eisel, *Musicus Autodidactus 1*, Erfurt, 1738.

Engel, Carl, *A Descriptive Catalogue of the Musical Instruments in the South Kensington Museum*, London, 1874.

État actuel de la musique de la Chambre du Roi et des trois Spectacles de Paris, Paris, 1758–80.

Faulkner, George (ed.), *Faulkner's Dublin Journal*, Dublin, 1728–1825.

Fantini, Girolamo da Spoleti, *Modo Imparare a Sonare di Tromba*, Frankfurt, 1638.

Fétis, F. J., *Biographie Universelle des Musiciens*, Paris, 1868.

Fitzpatrick, H. A., 'Some Historical Notes on the Horn in Austria and Germany' in *Galpin Society Journal*, xvi, London, 1964.

v. Fleming, Hanns Friederich, *Der Vollkommene Teutsche Jäger*, Leipzig, 1719.

Forkel, Johann Nicolaus, *Allgemeine Geschichte der Musik*, Leipzig, 1788.

Forkel, J. N., *Musikalisches Almanach für Deutschland auf das Jahr 1782*, Leipzig, 1782.

Fritsch, *Allgemeines Historisches Lexicon*, iv, Leipzig, 1722.

Fröhlich, Joseph, *Vollständige Theoretisch-Pracktische Musikschule*, Bonn, 1810–11.

Fröhlich, Joseph, *Hornschule / nach den Grundsätzen der besten über dieses Instrument bereits / erschienenen Schriften*, Bonn, 1811.

Fröhlich, Joseph, 'Horn' in Ersch und Gruben, Allgemeine Encyclopädie der Wissenschaften und Künste, Leipzig, 1834.

Fürstenau, Moritz, *Geschichte der Musik und des Theaters am Hofe zu Dresden*, Dresden and Leipzig, 1861/2.

Funke, Ph., & Lippold, G. H. C., *Neustes Natur- und Kunstlexicon*, Vienna, 1825.

Furetière, Antoine, *Dictionnaire Universel . . . des Sciences et des Arts*, 1727.

Galpin, Francis W., *Old English Instruments of Music*, London, 1910.

Gassner, Ferd. Simon, *Universal Lexicon der Tonkunst*, Stuttgart, 1847.

The General Advertiser, London, 1744: No. 2945: 23. iv. 1744.

Gerber, Ernst Ludwig, *Historisches-Biographisches Lexicon der Tonkünstler*, Leipzig, 1792.

Gerber, Ernst Ludwig, *Neues Historisch-Biographisches Lexicon der Tonkünstler*, Leipzig, 1813.

Gerbert, Martin, *De cantu et Musica Sacra a prima Ecclesiae aetateusque ad Praeseus Tempus*, Prague, 1774.

Ambts-Qiettung Bey den Löblich-Exempten Stüfft und Closter Göttweig, 1709.

Goldschmidt, Hugo, 'Das Orchester der Italienischen Oper im 17. Jahrhundert' in *Sammelbände der Internationalen Musikgesellschaft*, II, Leipzig, 1901–2.

Gottron, Adam, *Tausend Jahre Mainzer Musikgeschichte*, Mainz, 1960.

Gregory, Robin, *The Horn*, London, 2nd ed. 1969

Gregory, Robin, 'The Horn in Beethoven's Symphonies' in *Music and Letters*, October 1952.

Günther, Johann Christian, *Das Ebenbild der Wahrheit und Gerechtigkeit, Vorgestellt in einem kurtzen Entwurff des Lebens, seiner Excellenz Herrn Frantz Antonii Grafen von Sporck*, Vienna, 1721.

Hague, Bernard, 'The Tonal Spectra of Wind Instruments', *Proc. Royal Musical Association*, LXXIII, London, 1947.

Hampl/Punto, *Seule et vraie Méthode pour apprendre facilement les Elémens des Premier et Second Cor aux jeunes Elèves*, Paris, 1792–8.

Gottfried Benjamin Hanckens, Kgl. pohln. und churfurstl. sächs G. A. Secretarii. Weltliche Gedichte, nebst des berühmten Poeten . . . Neukirchs . . . Satyren, I, Dresden and Leipzig, 1727.

Hasse, Karl, 'Die Instrumentation J. S. Bachs' in *Bach-Jahrbuch* 26, Leipzig, 1929.

Haupt, Helga, *Wiener Instrumentenbau um 1800*, Dissertation, Vienna, 1952.

Haupt, Helga, 'Wiener Instrumentenbauer 1791–1815' in *Studien zur Musikwissenschaft*, Bd. 24, Vienna, 1960.

Hinrichs, J. C., *Entstehung Fortgang und jetzige Beschaffenheit der russischen Jagdmusik*, St. Petersburg, 1796.

Hoffmann, A. C. J. A., *Die Tonkünstler Schlesiens*, Breslau, 1830.

Holme, Randle, *Academy of Armory*, Chester, 1688.

Holmes, Edward, *A Ramble among the Musicians of Germany*, London, 1828.

Hore, J. P., *History of the Royal Buckhounds*, Part I, London, 1893.

Jahrbuch d. Tonkunst von Wien und Prag, 1796.

Kade, Otto, *Die Musikalien-Sammlung des Grossherzoglichen Meckelnburg-Schweriner Fürsten-hauses aus den letzten zwei Jahrhunderten*, Schwerin, 1893.

Karstädt, Georg, *Die Extraordinairen Abendmusiken Dietrich Buxtehudes*, Lübeck, 1962.

Karstädt, Georg, 'Das Textbuch zum "Templum Honoris" von Buxtehude' in *Die Musikforschung* X, Kassel, 1961.

Kelly, Michael, *Reminiscences of the King's Theatre, and Theatre Royal Drury Lane*, London, 1826.

King, Hyatt, 'Haydn's Trio for Horn, Violin and Cello' in *Musical Times*, December 1945.

Kingdon Ward, Martha, 'The Horn in Mozart' in *Music and Letters*, October 1958.

Kircher, Athanasius, *Musurgia Universalis sive Ars Magna consoni et dissoni*, Rome, 1650.

Kleefeld, Wilhelm, 'Das Orchester der Hamburger Oper, 1678–1738' in *SIMG* I, 2, Leipzig, 1900.

Kling, Henri, 'Le Cor de Chasse' in *Revista Musicale Italiana* XVIII, Torino, 1911.

Kling, Henri, 'Giovanni Punto, célèbre Corniste' in *Bulletin Française de la Société International de Musique*, Paris, 1908.

Köchel, Ludwig Ritter von, *Die Kaiserliche Hof-Musikkapelle in Wien 1573–1847*, Vienna, 1869.

Kunitz, Hans, *Horn*, Leipzig, 1957.

Langwill, Lyndesay, *An Index of Musical Wind-Instrument Makers*, Edinburgh, 1962.

Landon, H. C. Robbins, *The Symphonies of Joseph Haydn*, London, 1955.

Lichtenthal, Pietro, *Dizionario e Bibliografia della Musica*, Milan, 1826.

Lysons, Daniel, *History of the Origin and Progress of the Meeting of the Three Choirs of Gloucester, Worcester and Hereford*, Gloucester, 1812.

Mahillon, Victor Charles, *Catalogue Descriptif et Analytique du Musée Instrumental du Conservatoire Royal de Bruxelles*, Vol. II, Gand, 1909.

Mahillon, Victor Charles, *Le Cor, son Histoire, sa Théorie, sa Construction*, Brussels, 1907.

Mahillon, Victor Charles, *Experimental Studies on the Resonance of Conical, Trunco-Conical and Cylindrical Air-Columns*, London, n.d.; *c.* 1911.

Majer, Joseph Fried. Bernhard Caspar, *Neu-eroffneter Theoretisch- und Praktischer Music-Saal*, Nürnberg, 1741.

Marpurg, F. W., *Historisch-Kritische Beyträge zur Aufnahme der Musik*, Berlin, 1754–7.

Mattheson, J. G., *Critica Musica*, Hamburg, 1722.

Mattheson, J. G., *Das Forschende Orchestre*, Hamburg, 1721.

Mattheson, J. G., *Der Musicalische Patriot*, Hamburg, 1728.

Mattheson, J. G., *Das Neu-Eröffnete Orchester*, Hamburg, 1713.

Mattheson, J. G., *Der vollkommene Capellmeister*, Hamburg, 1739.

Mattheson, J. G., *Grundlage einer Ehrenpforte*, Hamburg, 1740.

Menke, Werner, *Die Geschichte der Bach- und Händel-Trompete*, Leipzig, 1934. Translated by Gerald Abraham, London, 1934.

Mennicke, Carl, *Hasse und die Brüder Graun als Symphoniker*, Leipzig, 1906.

Mercure de France, Paris, 1750–78.

Mersenne, M., *Harmonie Universelle*, II, Traité des Instrum., V, 245, Paris, 1637.

Mersenne, M., *Harmonicorum libri XII*, Paris, 1635.

Meusel, Johann Georg, *Teutsches Künstlerlexicon*, Lemgo, 1808.

Montague, Lady Mary Wortley, *Letters of the Right Honourable Lady M——y W——y M——e*: Vol. I, London, 1763.

Montfaucon, Dom Bernard de, *L'Antiquité Expliquée, et illustré en Figures*, Paris, 1724.

Mooser, Robert Aloys, *Annales de la Musique et des Musiciens en Russie au XVIIIe Siècle*, III, Geneva, 1951.

Morley-Pegge, R., *The French Horn*, London, 1960.

The Universal Director or, the Nobleman and Gentleman's TRUE GUIDE to the Masters and Professors of the Liberal and Polite Arts and Sciences by Mr. Mortimer, London, 1763.

Musikalische Korrespondenz, Speyer, 1770–88.

Musikalische Realzeitung, Speyer, 1788–91.

The Quarterly Musical Magazine and Review, London, 1818.

Ausführliche Nachrichten über Böhmen, vom Verfasser der Nachrichten über Polen, Salzburg, 1794.

Nettl, Bruno, 'Das Musikalieninventar des Zisterzienstiftes Osseg in Böhmen' in *Zeitschr. für Musikwissenschaft,* 6, iv, Leipzig, 1920.

Neuer Teutscher Merkur, ed. C. M. Wieland, Weimar and Leipzig, 1790.

Archiv des Pfarramt Oberroth bei Memmingen, Taufbuch der Pfarrkirche, Osterberg, 1670–1700.

Österreichisches Staatsarchiv, Archiv des Obersthofmeisteramts, 1720–1830: Hofmusikkapelle Varia, 1753–1850; Stallbücher, 1742–80.

Fürstliche Öttingen-Wallersteinsche Bibliothek: Hofcassa Rechnungen, 1750–1801; Pfarramt Wallerstein, 1753–1801.

Parke, W. T., *Musical Memoirs, 1784–1830,* London, 1830.

Paul, Ernst, 'Musikalisches in der Jagd: Die Jagd in der Musik' in *Wild und Weidwerk der Welt,* Vienna, 1955.

Paul, Ernst, *Die Entwicklung des Hornes vom Natur- zum Ventil-instrument,* Dissertation, Vienna, 1932.

Pelzel, Franz Martin, *Abbildungen der Böhmischen und Mährischen Gelehrten und Künstler,* Prague, 1773.

Piersig, Fritz, *Die Einführung des Hornes in die Kunstmusik und seine Verwendung bis zum Tode Joh. Seb. Bachs,* Halle, 1927.

Pohl, C. F., *Joseph Haydn,* Leipzig, 1878.

Praetorius, Michael, *De Organographica: Syntagma Musicum II. Theil: Theatrum Instrumentorum,* Wölfenbüttel, 1619.

Prochaska, Faustinus, *De Saecularibus/Liberalium/Artium/in Bohemia et Moravia Fatis Commentarius,* Prague, 1784.

Rasmussen, Mary, 'The Manuscript Kat. Wenster Litt. 1/1–17 b: A Contribution to the History of the Baroque Horn Concerto' in *Brass Quarterly,* V, No. 4, Durham, N.H., 1962.

Rees, Abraham, *The Cyclopedia or Universal Dictionary of Arts, Sciences, and Literature in Thirty-Nine Volumes,* London, 1819.

Fürstliche Thurn und Taxische Hofbibliothek zu Regensburg: Musikalien-archiv, 1760–1825.

Richter, P. E., 'Eine 2-ventilige Trompete aus d. J. 1806' in *Zeitschrift für Instrumentenbau,* Jg. 30, Leipzig, 1909–10.

Ridinger, Johann Elias, *Der Fürsten Jagd-Lust oder der Edlen Jagtbarkeit,* Augsburg, 1729.

v. Riegger, Joseph Anton Stephan, *Materialen zur alten und neuen Statistik von Böhmen,* VII Heft, Leipzig and Prague, 1788.

Rousseau, Jean-Jacques, Lettre à Grimm sur l'opéra Italien (1750), repr. in: Jansen, Albert, *Jean-Jacques Rousseau als Musiker,* Berlin, 1884.

van der Roxas, Ferdinand, *Leben eines herrl. Bildes wahrer . . . Frömmigkeit, welches Gott . . . in F. A. Riechsgrafen von Sporck als einen Spiegel reiner Gottes-furcht . . . aufgerichtet hat,* Amsterdam, 1715.

Rühlmann, Julius, 'Das Waldhorn' in *Neue Zeitschrift für Musik,* Berlin, 1870.

Sachs, Curt, 'Die Litui in Bachs Motette "O Jesu Christ" ' in *Bach-Jahrbuch*, Leipzig, 1921.

Schantl, Josef, and Zellner, Carl, *Die Österreichische Jagdmusik Musikalischer Theil*, Vienna, 1886.

Schering, Adolf, 'Zur Gottfried Reiches Leben und Kunst' in *Bach-Jahrbuch*, 1918.

Schiedermair, Ludwig, 'Die Blütezeit der Oettingen-Wallersteinschen Hofkapelle' in *SIMG* ix, 1, Leipzig, 1902.

Schlosser, Julius, *Die Sammlung Alter Musikinstrumente*, Vienna, 1920.

Schmidt, Günther, *Die Musik am Hofe der Markgrafen von Brandenburg-Ansbach*, Cassel, 1956.

Schmidt, Gustav Friederich, *Die frühdeutsche Oper und die Musikdramatische Kunst Georg Caspar Schürmanns*, Regensburg, 1933.

Schneider, Wilhelm, *Historisch-Technische Beschreibung der musikalischen Instrumenten*, Leipzig, 1834.

Schubart, C. F. W., *Ideen zu einer Ästhetik der Tonkunst* (c. 1785), Stuttgart, 1825/27.

Schweikert, Karl, 'Die Musikpflege am Hofe der Kurfürsten von Mainz im 17. und 18. Jahrhundert' in *Beiträge zur Geschichte der Stadt Mainz*, Bd. II, Leipzig, 1921.

Serre' de Rieux, Jean de, *Les Dons des Enfants de Latone* (Paris, 1734).

Sittard, Ludwig, *Zur Geschichte der Musik und des Theaters am Württembergischen Hofe*, Stuttgart, 1891.

Smithers, Don, 'The Trumpets of J. W. Haas', in *Galpin Society Journal*, xviii, London, 1965.

Sporck, Franz Anton Reichsgraf von, *Sämmtliche Korrespondenz und Akten des Herrn Reichs-Grafen Frantz Antonii von Sporck*, Prague, c. 1703–38.

Kais- und Königl. wie auch Erz-Herzoglicher und dero Residenz-Stadt Wien. Staats- und Stands Calender, auf das Jahr 1712–1740, Vienna.

Stählin, Jakob, *Notice sur la Musique en Russie: Notice sur le Premier Opéra Russe en 1755*, Leipzig and Riga, 1770.

Starzer, Albert (ed.), *Quellen zur Geschichte der Stadt Wien*, I. Abt. VI. Band. Auszüge aus d. Ehematrikeln v. St. Stephan, Vienna, 1908.

Steffen, Gerhard, *Johann Hugo von Wilderer (1670–1724) Kapellmeister am kurpfälzischen Hofe zu Düsseldorf u. Mannheim*, Cologne, 1960.

Talbot, James, The Talbot Manuscript, 1689–1701.

Tans'ur, William, *The Elements of Musick Display'd*, London, 1772.

Taut, Kurt, *Beiträge zur Geschichte d. Jagdmusik*, Leipzig, 1927.

Terry, Charles Sanford, *Bach's Orchestra*, London, 1932.

Vegetius, *De Re Militarii* (Basle, 1532).

Virdung, Sebastian, *Musica getutscht u. ausgezogen*, Basle, 1511.

Walter, Friederich, *Geschichte der Musik und des Theaters am kurpfälzischen Hofe*, Leipzig, 1898.

Walther, Joh. Gottfried, *Musikalisches Lexicon*, Leipzig, 1732.

Ward, Ned, *The London Spy*, vi, London, 1699.

Weigel, Christoff, *Abbildung der Gemein-Nützlichen Haupt-Stände von denen Regenten bis auf alle künstler und Handwerker*, Regensburg, 1698.

Weigel, Johann Christoph, *Musicalisches Theatrum*, Nürnberg, *c.* 1720.

Werner, Arno, *Städtische und fürstliche Musikpflege in Weissenfels bis zum Ende des 18. Jhdt.*, Leipzig, 1911.

Werner, Arno, 'Die thüringer Musikfamilie Altenburg' in *SIMG* VII, 1, 1905.

Archive der Stadt Wien: Bürgereidbuch, 1750–91, 1792–1835.

  Hauptregistratur-Departementbücher, 1791–1815.

  Steuerbücher, unbehaustes Katastrum, 1791–1818.

  Abhandlungs-Sperrverzeichnisse, 1798–1850.

  Testamente, 1791–1850.

  Totenprotokolle, 1791–1860.

  Magistratische Verlassenschaft.

  Verlassenschaft Schotten.

Gemeinnütziges Schema der kaiserl.-königl. Haupt- und Residenzstadt Wien, Vienna, 1779.

Wiennerisches Diarium, Vienna, 1703–50.

Wörthmüller, Willi, 'Die Nürnberger Trompeten- und Posaunenmacher des 17. und 18. Jahrhundert' in *Mitteilung des Vereins für Geschichte der Stadt Nürnberg*, Vols. 45 and 46, 1954 and 1955.

Allgemeine Musikalische Zeitung, Leipzig, October 1798–September 1802.

Prager Neue Zeitung, Nr. 3, Prague, 1797.

Wiener Zeitung, October 1791.

Zedler, Joh. Heinrich, *Universal-Lexicon*, Leipzig, 1732–50.

Ziegler, Anton, *Adressenbuch von Tonkünstlern, Dilettanten, Hof-kammer-Theater- und Kirchenmusikern*, Vienna, 1823.

The following works refer specifically to brass-making:

Agricola, Georgius, *De re metallica libri* XII, Basle, 1556.

Hamilton, Henry, *The English Brass and Copper Industries to 1800*, London, 1926.

Paracelsus, *Of the Nature of Things, in Nine Books*, London, 1650.

Sachs, Hans, *Eygentliche Beschreibung aller Stände . . . mit Kunstreichen Figuren*, Frankfurt, 1568.

INDEX OF MUSIC

Rosetti, Anton, Concertos for high horn (1775) (1772), 120; Concerto for low horn (1779), 174

Scarlatti, Alessandro, *Telemaco* (1718), 70; *Tigrane* (1715), 64, 65
Schacht, Theodor von, Symphony in D (1779), 118
Schmelzer, Ballet (1680), 8
Schürrmann, Georg Caspar, Cantata, 'Komm, O Tröster' (1717), 57, 95; Opera *Clelia* (1730), 57, 95

Stamitz, Johann, Symphony in G, 112
Stricker, Gottfried, *Alexander und Roxane* (1708), 22

Tchaikovsky, P. I., Symphony No. 5, 190
Telemann, G. Ph., *Musique de Table* (1733), 71
Thürrschmidt, C., Duet, 175

Weber, C. M. von, *Der Freischütz*, 12, 60, 184

INDEX OF NAMES

GENERAL INDEX